TALK DOWN

TALK DOWN

BRIAN LECOMBER

COWARD, McCANN & GEOGHEGAN, INC.
NEW YORK

First American Edition 1978

Copyright © 1978 by Brian Lecomber

Library of Congress Cataloging in Publication Data

Lecomber, Brian.
  Talk down.

  I. Title.
PZ4.L4538Tal 1978 [PR6062.E34] 823′.9′14 78-5794
ISBN 0-698-10937-6

Printed in the United States of America

Author's Note

To the best of my knowledge the events in this book have not actually happened. Several similar incidents have occurred, in which the people concerned have usually lost their lives, but as far as I am aware none of them have been exactly parallel to the situation I have used here. It *could* happen, however, at any time; and if the circumstances should be as I have set them out, then I believe the outcome would also be very much the same. Indeed, so real is the danger of an occurrence of this nature that both the Federal Aviation Administration in America and the Civil Aviation Authority in Britain have for some years been actively encouraging the introduction of abbreviated "get you down safely" flying courses for regular passengers in single-pilot light aircraft. The response, alas, has been almost non-existent.

B.L.

This book is dedicated to the following:

A. J. Cheshire; F. Indyk; M. J. Stapp; R. D. Campbell; P. Payne; D. Campbell; L. Rackham; B. Beadle; I. Mackie; B. Tempest; W. Bohike Jr; R. Brown; T. Tucker; E. Serrano; R. Kaufman; M. Fernandez; G. Burrowes; P. Meeson; R. Goode; I. Senior; I. Dalzeil; C. Rollings; W. May; R. Davidson; J. Ryan; A. Pecnik; P. Falk; J. Steel; R. Neal; C. Taylor; R. Taylor; V. Deadman; L. Burt; H. Hannah; P. Cox; M. Pleet; J. Jobber; M. Grandis; A. Peters; R. Sharp; D. Baker; J. Hawkin; E. Hill; M. Kemp; J. Chalmers; L. Sinden; D. Turner; A. Peters; B. Turner; A. Dowsett; C. J. Chabot; C. Chabot; C. Levine; L. Sattin; A. Preston; D. Read; S. Ramment; T. Hewlett; J. Webber; R. Owen; A. Baker; P. A. Wraight; D. Ward; B. Keogh; V. Gibbs; R. Saunders; J. Harthill; G. Dunn; P. Haines; R. Moore; R. MacFarlane; P. Smith; N. Stevens; T. Thomson; P. Vaughan; M. Dolman; J. Bundy; T. Green; M. Rice; G. Hilliard; P. Zdanowski; M. Eastwood; N. Holmes; B. Beattie; P. Roberts; K. Mason; I. Foinette; C. Spurrier; A. Herm; G. Chittenden; A. France; R. Green; P. Hember; R. Mayo; N. Mathias; D. Cresswell; P. Tory; P. Hunt; P. Fraser; R. Martin; G. Martin; A. Black; B. McCurdy; J. Cadenhead; V. Cheeseman; M. Gibbs; R. Mattin; A. Leverton; J. Kernot; J. Palmer; D. Page; J. Busby; P. Shepher; J. Mitchell; R. Percy; R. Grace; B. Edmundson; J. Glanville; T. Peckham; R. Henley; S. Bennett; J. Poyser; C. Eastwood; P. Farara; C. Widdows; B. Kahler; L. Bardoo; P. Lewis; R. Morris; T. P. Tubbs; J. Baldwin; D. Graham; H. Levine; A. Ackerman; G. Greaux; E. Edwards; D. Thomas; T. Reid; C. Maynard; A. Picciotti; P. Larvo; J. Meikle; R. Williams; G. Coyne; W. James; J. Watt; J. Baldwin; N. Henwood; M. Grimes; C. Bryan; B. Joseph; K. Denson; P. Balwin; J. Clabburn; P. Preece; B. Beck; R. Rothstein; M. Argent; E. Curtis; J. Beaulieu; H. Hoff; G. Ricker; M. James; G. Spillane; Y. Vanderboch; P. Jackson; P. Boyes; U. Heidenreich; R. Farara; C. Burleigh; T. Micheau; J. Morgan; R. Bryan; V. Michael; A. Davies; S. Olsen; P. Price; G. Kreps; A. Breeze; B. Martin; E. Broadbent; C. Taylor; T. Williams; S. Norton; T. Barnes; H. Hakam; J. Topley; H. Jukkema; C. William; T. Goldspink; T. Finney; J. Henry; P. Ailles; M. Richardson; R. Erkman; K. Craig; J. Strider; K. Howes; N. L. Whyte; P. Ray; V. Fleming; M. Jackson; K. Craig; P. Chadderton; F. Kleinsorgan; T. Wharton; P. Springer; G. Gomes; J. Byerley; S. Rowley; C. Butler; P. Laverack; T. Giordano; B. Masterson; C. Carver; Harrison; B. Lander; M. Fuller; B. Weaver; J. Hooks; G. Matthew; C. Cockburn; L. Borne; C. Appadoo; B. Gonsalves; G. Maine; R. DeShazo; B. Hall; A. Child; S. Goldspink; T. Butler; M. Cleary; M. Gill; R. Margrave; B. Chadeayne; L. DeSoto; H.

Mackinley; M. Heczey; T. Brunner; R. Nicholson; D. David; J. Bright; B. Weaver; K. Powellson; P. Goldspink; H. Van Beever; I. Presser; R. Scott-Hughes; A. Linton; J. Burnett; S. Laundy; J. Walter; G. Bandano; T. Kazanjian; B. Horsley; E. Volker; F. Pickup; K. Kaye; J. Winter; E. Nanton; P. Courtland; B. Fentum; H. Smit; D. Cook; N. Peacock; H. Hultberg; K. King; W. Handley; J. Smith; J. Marcik; M. Faber; C. Nielsen; C. Lashlee; D. Parry; R. Cummer; V. Saunders; R. Tomlinson; M. Barlow; H. Hector; L. Manning; V. Smith; P. White; T. Nichols; S. Beale; V. Reynolds; J. Farrell; D. Byrne; G. Grimwood; C. Denby; J. Eccott; M. Smith; G. Waldron; T. O'Connell; T. Clinch; Y. Speck; A. Whiter; C. Bowles; P. Bouvier; A. Attwood; V. Smith; P. Lee; B. Jennings; F. Pearce; B. Shrapnell; T. Baker; K. Grundon; H. Ober; R. Ansell; C. Thompson; G. Hodge; T. Carter; W. Keddie; J. Harris; T. Isted; R. Brown; C. Cubitt; B. Duckling; J. Dryer; J. Moore; D. Susman; D. Winter; S. Upton; J. Ager; A. Powell; H. Middleton; M. Duncan; J. Seibert; B. Speck; M. Chivers; N. Dunford; H. Illingsworth; R. Tye; T. Dorman; R. Jupp; M. Ower; R. Goto; H. Patel; T. Collison; M. Webber; A. Eammons; R. Burrows; M. Basson; J. Myers; V. Myers; A. Marks; R. Harris; W. Goode; A. Start; R. Mills; E. Jenvey; B. Cooper; R. Head; N. Mayes; M. Goode; D. Ellis; G. Thaw; R. Gardner; J. Hemsley; V. Tate; K. Pointing; L. Evans; B. Foster; G. McGrath; I. Merrick; M. Field; B. Neech; V. Ash; P. Hutchins; R. Hinchcliffe; P. Wenman; G. Hutchinson; N. Brendish; R. Saunders; K. Lewis; J. Bond; J. Pearson; G. Cruse; R. Brown; W. Stenson; J. Childs; D. Burd; N. Radford; J. Acraman; S. Carrel; B. Paul; J. Gore; I. Haddon; D. Horton; P. Cooper; I. Henry; P. Henry; G. Purcell; J. Alldridge; T. Grey; G. Bedggood; J. Hall; M. Evans; J. Nelson; G. Templeton.

In memory of thousands of hours instructing in many
different cockpits and many different skies.—B. L.

TALK DOWN

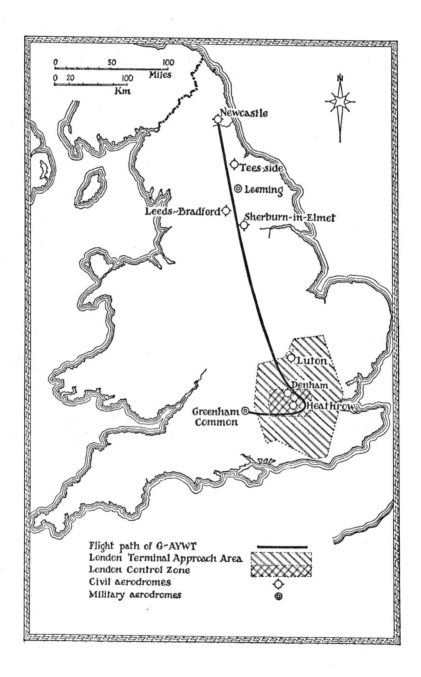

0   50   100
Miles
0   20   100
Km

N

Newcastle

Tees-side
Leeming

Leeds-Bradford   Sherburn-in-Elmet

Luton
Denham
Heathrow
Greenham
Common

Flight path of G-AYWT
London Terminal Approach Area
London Control Zone
Civil aerodromes
Military aerodromes

1

1240–1340

AT FORTY MINUTES past noon on a bright January day, the coldest place in the world is the open cockpit of a Stampe SV4B biplane.

It had been cold before, on the ground. Breath had puffed like smoke in the crystal air, and heavy boots had squeaked on frost as they'd pulled the red and yellow Stampe out of the hangar. But that had been nothing; nothing but a gentle foretaste of what was to come.

At two thousand feet, it was really cold.

The blaring gale of the slipstream was a solid force of coldness, invading the cockpit with a million icy knives. Keith Kerr could feel his nose, his cheeks, and the narrow exposed strip of forehead between goggles and leather helmet going tingling numb in the rawness of it.

Beneath the fabric wings the East Riding of Yorkshire was a vast patchwork of browny-frosty fields, bright and new-looking in the dewy glare of the winter sun. Here and there tendrils of morning mist still lingered, while the sun bounced occasional flashes of light off windows in the scattered villages. Above the land, the sky was cold and clear and enormously blue; one of those rare winter days when an airman's world aloft is pure brilliance, the visibility brittle-sharp and unlimited. On such a day a young man in an old biplane might believe that he can see forever.

Kerr felt the familiar happy-frightened fluttering in his

stomach. He leaned his head back and sang, shouting into the freezing blast of the airflow.

> "*Bye, bye, Miss American Pie,*
> *Drove my Chevvy to the levee*
> *But the levee was dry-y . . ."*

The Stampe growled up into the blue dome, filling the sky with the harsh flat blatter of its Gipsy Major engine.

Two thousand two hundred feet.

Kerr lowered the long nose to just below the horizon and eased back the throttle. The red aluminium cover over the empty front cockpit drummed slightly in resonance as the bellow of the engine flattened back to the snarl of max continuous cruise.

Reaching round the cramped cockpit, he went through his chores. The hollow feeling in his stomach deepened as he yanked all seven strap-tails one by one, trussing himself so tightly into the seat that it was difficult to take a deep breath. He double-checked that the brakes were fully off – leaving a few notches of wheel-brake engaged can restrict the rudder movement in a Stampe – and then pushed the red mixture lever into lean cut-off. The engine died abruptly, windmilled for a few seconds, then picked up its steady blaring again as his numbed fingers pushed the blue handle labelled INVERTED SYSTEM.

Now he was ready.

He wheeled the biplane into a steep left turn, helmeted head twisting this way and that as he searched the sky for other aircraft. There'd been nothing about during the spiralling climb, but a careful pilot doesn't put his trust in a minute-old look-out. Other aeroplanes can materialise out of thin air in seconds, especially when there's no haze to provide a back-drop.

The sky was empty.

Kerr rolled out of the turn on a westerly heading, craned his neck to look over the side of the cockpit, and watched the grass runways of Sherburn-in-Elmet airfield sliding back towards the leading edge of the left lower wing. He was aware of his attention narrowing down, the way it always did at the start. The night, the letter in his pocket, the clutter of everyday life, all forgotten, everything normal blanked out, even the cold. The strong-featured face and the pale blue eyes behind the goggles were very still, lost in total concentration. His arms were the wings, his fingertips the ailerons and elevators.

The far boundary of the airfield disappeared under the wing. He opened the throttle fully and pushed the nose down hard, nearly to the vertical.

The solid blast of engine and airflow wound up rapidly in the dive, thundering and tightening. The frosty sunlit ground and the hangars expanded in the frame of the centre section struts, filling the world. The blue eyes flicked steadily from ground to instruments and back to ground again, while his brain clicked over calmly in the maelstrom of wind, noise and cold. The shifting factors of increasing airspeed, diminishing height, wind-drift, engine revs and position over the runway all slotted into place and were juggled according to their changing importance. Speed and altimeter *so* . . . throttle back halfway to keeps the revs at 2,400 . . . runway squarely over the nose . . .

1,200 feet and 140 knots.

He pulled the stick back smoothly, checked for a moment in level flight, then pulled back again.

The Stampe reared up. The long scarlet engine cowling clubbed through the horizon and on up into the blue. The helmeted head glanced left, noted a distant wood as a landmark, and then twisted right to watch the angle between the bottom wing tip and the horizon. As the wing reached the vertical he checked forward and held it, keeping the biplane pointing straight up into the endless sky.

The wind noise began to sink down the scale as the airspeed unwound.

Kerr counted "One thousand and one", then slammed the stick over to the right.

The Stampe pivoted in a vertical half roll. Kerr ignored

the weightless twisting sensation and concentrated on the wing tip, hands and feet making continual tiny corrections to maintain the exact vertical. The shadows of struts and wires flickered across his face as the wing traversed round the horizon. The howl of the airflow waned, the engine labouring...

The distant wood slid out from under the right wing tip.

Kerr snapped the stick central to stop the roll, held the biplane balanced straight up for the space of a further two heartbeats, and then kicked on full right rudder.

For an instant, nothing happened. The Stampe seemed to hang motionless in the sky, suspended by the flat snarl of the engine. The needle of the airspeed indicator sagged tiredly below 40 knots...

Then, quite slowly, the red and yellow wings pivoted round in a perfect stall turn.

Hanging vertically downwards, the wind-roar swelling again around him, Kerr found time to grin. The fluttering in his belly had subsided to a small hard knot of concentration. It was being a good day...

He half-rolled downwards, then pulled out of the dive. For a brief two seconds of level flight he bellowed *"Bye, bye, Miss American Pie"* into the slipstream. Then his face went still again as he pulled up for an avalanche.

*   *   *

Fifty miles to the north of Sherburn-in-Elmet, Tony Paynton blew chalk dust off his hands and stood with his back to the blackboard, facing his student.

"So much for the forces in the spin, Jules," he said. "In a minute we'll deal with the practical aspects. But first, do you have any questions?"

Jules Martin swallowed. Forty-one next week, learning to fly in a last-ditch attempt to recapture a youth he'd never really had, there were times when he secretly doubted that he would ever make a pilot. The prospect of the spinning exercise had been worrying him for the past month, but up

14

to now a prolonged patch of bad weather had put the detail off.

Today, the weather was perfect. The January sun streamed in through the windows of the Cleveland Flying Club, and the sky over Tees-side Airport was gin-clear and cold electric blue. He looked at the spidery diagrams on the blackboard and felt slightly sick deep in his belly.

He said, "No. That's clear."

"Fine." Paynton rocked on the balls of his feet, pinching the bridge of his nose as he lined up the familar instructor's patter. "So now let's consider the way it actually works. The Chipmunk's a lovely aeroplane, but it can be a bit reluctant to come out of a spin after four or five turns. So we have to be sure of getting the recovery action dead right; then there's no problem. That means first, power off. Then full opposite rudder, pause, and control column forwards. If necessary *fully* forwards, even if we have to push with both hands. So power off, full opposite rudder, and stick forwards. Is that quite clear?"

Martin swallowed again and said, "Yes."

"Right. Good." Paynton regarded him dubiously, knowing perfectly well that nine-tenths of the briefing hadn't gone in. "So now let's nip out and have a go at that, then. You go and pre-flight the aeroplane, and I'll come out when I see the engine running. Okay?"

Martin nodded and scraped his chair back. Paynton backed over to the radiator and watched him as he walked out into the cold sunshine.

*   *   *

One of the plugs had packed up.

Kerr taxied the Stampe slowly onto the tarmac and stopped in front of the hangar. He tested the magnetos again, feeling through his bones the flat uneven blatting as the engine ran on three cylinders on the left bank. Then he twisted the ignition switch to Off and opened the throttle wide. The propeller whipped to a stop, bouncing between two com-

15

pressions. He wriggled around in the cockpit, pulling off his helmet and draping it over the Perspex windscreen, then clambered slowly out on to the catwalk on the right lower wing and from there down to the ground.

The apron was quiet and momentarily deserted; everyone was either in the clubhouse or up in the air. He pulled off his gloves, his movements awkward with the cold and the bulk of his clothing, and then walked to the tailplane and pushed the Stampe round and back into the hangar. Behind it, in shadow, the usual interlocking gaggle of Cherokees and Cessnas looked shabby and uninteresting; mere aerial motor cars with the romance of flight long designed out of them on the altar of dull efficiency.

He grinned, an action which made his face take on a look of surprising mischief, then ran his fingers through his wiry fair hair and started fishing in his pockets for cigarettes. Cessnas and Cherokees were his livelihood – for the moment, at any rate – but on a golden day like this you could keep them: they were insensitive hunks of ironmongery, and an insult to a flying man's art. On a day like this, happiness was a morning off and a pre-war aerobatic biplane. Even if that biplane had just burned out a plug on the left hand bank.

He lit a Gold Leaf, cupping his hands round the match and afterwards blowing it out with a jet of smoke before dropping it into the frost and putting his foot on it. Then he squeezed past the Stampe's tail to get to a row of lockers up against the hangar wall. He opened the clanging metal door of the one marked STAMPE SV4B G-AXSN, rooted around until he found four new plugs in their polythene wrappers, then collected up a canvas bag of tools and made his way back to the biplane's nose.

The aluminium engine cowlings were ice cold under his fingers. He opened them up, and started pulling out the steel rods securing the cooling duct on the left side of the engine. As he worked he whistled through his teeth, the sound echoing round the corrugated walls of the hangar.

The thought occurred to him, *This is where I came in.*

He blew on his hands for a moment, remembering back

16

fifteen years. A very young and eager Keith Kerr then, on a small grass airfield not unlike this one. Serving fuel, polishing wings – and changing plugs – in exchange for precious, carefully hoarded minutes of flying time. And then the day when an instructor walked away from a clattering Tiger Moth and left that same young man to the jittery elation of his first solo . . .

He lifted the two halves of the cooling duct away and put them down carefully on the hangar floor. Then he took a last drag on his cigarette, trod on it, and knelt down and rumpled through the tools in the bag, looking for the plug spanner.

That day in the Tiger Moth seemed a very long time ago, now. A long time and a lot of distance.

He started unscrewing the first plug, thinking about other days on other areodromes.

His first full-time flying job had been instructing, which is the way it usually is for an impecunious young man seeking to make a living in the sky. The apparent paradox of low-time pilots beginning their careers by teaching others to fly is explained by the hard commercial facts. Big-time aviation concerns are disinclined to trust their expensive equipment to newly-qualified barbarians, whilst the world's flying schools, who are usually operating the simplest of aircraft on the permanent ragged edge of bankruptcy, are notoriously willing to employ anyone with wings who walks slowly past the door; the only important requirement is that the applicant be prepared to fly incredibly long hours for a wage which would insult a builder's labourer.

Kerr had worked for a Sussex flying school for a year, and then been offered another instructing job in Kenya.

He could remember those mornings all right.

It was up at five a.m. then, pre-flighting the Cessnas in the muggy light of dawn so as to get started before the heat of the day wound up. Then the four-hour mid-day break, sprawling in a cane chair and boiling in your own perspiration and never quite managing to doze. And listening to old Piet van den Hoyt, the enormously fat flying school owner-cum-chief-instructor, as he sweated out gin and told you over and over again to quit instructing and get into the airlines.

He disengaged the spanner and unscrewed the first plug through its last few threads by hand. High above, so high as to be completely silent, a jet was drawing a sharp white contrail across the icy blue sky. His airman's instinct made him look up, and he took a step towards the open front of the hangar to get a better view. Bundled up with pyjama trousers under his jeans and several layers of sweaters under his Barbour motor-cycle jacket, he resembled nothing so much as a short blocky teddy bear come out to defy the cold. Deep crows-feet wrinkled the corners of his eyes as he stared up at the sky, the way another man might survey his own home from afar. Unconsciously, one hand came up and rubbed a short jagged scar alongside his left eye.

Maybe I should have listened to Vandy, he thought. Maybe if I had, I'd be in that cockpit by now . . .

But at that time, ten years ago, he hadn't wanted to be in any jet cockpit. At twenty-two years old, with his parents long divorced, there had seemed to be plenty of time for a chunky young man with a commanding manner and a smooth touch with an aeroplane: years ahead in which to see something of the world before settling down in England and picking up the threads. The ultimate destiny probably would have to be an airline, of course; but there was no need to rush into it. Everyone knew that airline flying was a boring bus driver's job, best suited to pilots approaching middle age . . .

Kerr fingered the scar again, then turned back to the engine.

The years had passed quickly in some places, more slowly in others. Sometimes counted by Christmasses and birthdays but more often, in the way of his kind, by logbooks filled, aircraft flown, and experiences lived. Instructing and crop-spraying in Australia; Pipers, Austers, AgWagons, and a total of 3,000 hours. Chartering and instructing in Canada: Cessnas and Pipers again, plus Beavers, Aztecs and an ancient Republic Seabee; the time up to 4,000 hours and the number of forced landings up to five. Dusting and instructing in

Florida, Agcats and Stearmans and most light twins. At some-where around the 5,000 hour mark a brief but disastrous marriage. Then instructing at Isla Grande in Puerto Rico . . .

And then the island of St. Lucia. The Caribbean paradise. Sun-bleached wood, coconuts and bananas, and a half-tame mongoose who broke and ate eggs in a tiny oven-like opera-tions room. Up at four a.m. in the trilling velvet darkness, filling the spray-hoppers of the Thrush Commanders in the yellow pools of the hangar lighting, and then sitting around, oily and sweating, while you waited to go banana-spraying in the calm heat of first light. And then the morning when the last thing you could remember was the Pratt & Whitney coughing as you pulled up out of a valley at the end of a spray-run . . .

Kerr unscrewed the last of the four plugs, rummaged through the toolbag until he came up with a pair of tinsnips, and started decapitating the tough polythene tubes contain-ing the new set. The scar near his eye was itching again, the way it did when it was getting ready to eject yet another tiny fragment of splintered Perspex.

Still, at least the leg was all right this winter. When he'd first come back to England thirteen months before, the left knee had practically locked solid every time the weather went damp.

England had needed some adjusting to, this time round. Quite apart from the stiff leg.

Now, most of his old flying friends were married. Some were with the airlines, some had quit professional aviation altogether, and all of them seemed more concerned with children and mortgages than they were with looping speeds and stalling angles. When he went into the homes of the few who invited him, he was awkward and out of place; a vivid stocky stranger with an indefinable accent and the weathering of faraway winds in his face.

The airlines had felt the same way about him.

To the corporation minds who hire line pilots he was an anachronism, a barnstorming albatross who had forgotten to move with the times. A good flier, perhaps; but the same logbooks which prosaically revealed his skill with many aeroplanes in many lands also indicated him as a dangerous individualist. More single-engine time than multi ... no line experience ... no turbine time ... rides a powerful motor bike instead of driving a Ford or a Volvo ... to the corporation mind, such qualifications are not likely to make a good Company man.

After six weeks of idleness he'd gone back to instructing, because there'd been nothing else available.

The four new plugs were finger tight in their threads now. Kerr paused to light another cigarette, rubbed his hands together vigorously in a futile attempt to restore feeling to his numbed fingers, then picked up the spanner again.

The Leeds Aero Club had been delighted to get him, of course. British flying schools normally think in terms of low-paid, low-time aspirants who are using instructing purely as a stepping-stone to higher things; any 6,000 hour pilot who is still prepared to teach is a rare catch indeed. And Kerr, after more than a decade of tutoring all manner of peoples, was an excellent Chief Flying Instructor. He ran the school with growling bantam-rooster aplomb, and if one or two of his fellow instructors suspected that his happy knack for teaching the apparently unteachable was founded in a deep inner streak of sensitivity, they were careful not to say so in his presence.

For his own part he quite enjoyed the job – apart from heartily disliking the current owner of the Aero Club, who fortunately rarely bothered to turn up there – but as the months went by he'd found himself increasingly conscious of its lack of future. As an anodyne he'd turned back to an old love; aerobatics. During his working days he flew sober Cessnas and Cherokees out of the strictly-controlled environs of Leeds-Bradford Airport, and in his spare time he rode his motor bike twenty miles to Sherburn's small grass field and practised vertical rolls and inverted spins in the Stampe. As an exercise, the hobby had proved successful: he had won the Esso Tiger Trophy three months previously, stood a good chance in the Intermediate level of the forthcoming

Icicle Aerobatic Contest, and already had a dozen air-show bookings confirmed for the summer season ahead. But aerobatics cannot fill all the gaps in a life, however much a person may be lost to flying. Against his will he'd found himself being sucked into the conventions of modern Britain, secretly yearning for the roots he'd once despised. A house of his own, a steady girl, a car as well as his beloved Norton, a career instead of a job . . .

And now, suddenly, it was happening. Just like that.

He tightened the last plug, clipped on its high tension lead, and picked up the first section of the cooling duct. The movement rustled the letter in his back pocket. He knew the wording by heart, so that he could almost see the typed lines. *British Island Airways are pleased to offer you the position . . . report at Gatwick Airport for the commencement of conversion training on the Dart Herald aircraft at 0900 hours on Monday February 16th . . .*

It felt good. He finished fitting the cooling duct, blew a jet of smoke at the engine, then collected up the tools and carried the bag back to the locker. British Island wasn't quite Pan Am and the Herald wasn't exactly a 747, but it was an honest-to-God airline job, with the prospect of a Captaincy within two or three years if he kept his nose clean and didn't become pugnacious with the wrong people. It might feel a bit odd being a co-pilot – he begged the line's pardon, *first officer* – after so many years of freedom and command, but he could handle that. Why, one or two of the captains might even be old students of his . . .

It felt very good. He whistled loudly as he banged the door of the locker.

And then there was the other thing, too.

He walked slowly to the hangar doorway and just stood there for a moment, a lone figure looking out over the airfield.

Last night had surprised him considerably. Had surprised them both, probably. The letter had come yesterday morning, he'd suggested a drink in the evening because by that time he'd been bursting with it and had to tell someone – and things had just sort of gone on from there. And after knowing her for five months and never an inkling . . .

He rubbed his scar again and smiled into the raw sunshine, his face taking on an unusually tender expression in place of the usual mischievous grin. A small voice of caution, well-developed since his short-lived marriage, warned that last night could have been meaningless, a passing thing to be enjoyed for a moment and then forgotten. But it hadn't felt like that, somehow. There'd been a sort of . . . kindness about it. As if both of them had come in from the cold and found something warm and happy and totally worthwhile.

Like . . . coming home, he thought. Like coming home when you didn't even know you had a home.

After a minute he spat his cigarette into the frost, turned his back on the sun, and went to check the Stampe's oil and close up its cowlings.

2

1350–1423

THE AIRPORT OF Woolsington, Newcastle, looked much the same as any other British provincial airport on a January weekend. The wide concrete apron held a sprinkling of BAC 111s and HS 748s of Dan Air and British Caledonian, the long low terminal building contained the usual smattering of aimless-looking passengers and staff, and a quarter of a mile from the terminal – again as usual on provincial airports – the Tyne Flying Club was housed in a dingy wooden hut sandwiched between two hangars.

Roy Bazzard and Ann Moore arrived there at ten minutes to two in the afternoon: the same moment that Tony Paynton and Jules Martin were lifting off the runway forty miles away at Tees-side, and Keith Kerr was closing the hangar doors on the Stampe at Sherburn-in-Elmet.

Ann, who had never been in a flying club before, found the place mildly un-nerving.

The inside of the hut was dusty and well worn. There was a small counter in one corner behind which sat the club operations-manager-cum-receptionist, king of aircraft bookings and flight sheets and all the other paperwork of a six-aeroplane flying school. Alongside the counter was a large noticeboard covered with NOTAMs, TAFs, a few humorous pictures from the Roger Bacon column in *Flight*, and a number of terse little typewritten memos signed by the Chief Flying Instructor. The rest of the walls were plastered with pictures of aeroplanes, diagrams of Piper cockpits and electrical systems, and a series of cartoon posters advising pilots to Fly With Prudence. The whole building had the air of lived-in neglect which comes from a lot of people passing through but nobody ever stopping, and the drinks machine required tenpence plus an educated thump from Bazzard's fist before it condescended to gurgle out two mud-coloured coffees into plastic cups.

Ann perched on the edge of a tired leather chair and sipped her coffee. She was conscious of being watched by four young men who were lounging against the counter, and uncomfortably aware that the collection of suitcases and coats on the floor beside her must look awfully like a couple going away for a dirty weekend.

Roy went to the counter and came back with a Passenger Membership form for her to sign. The wording covered half a sheet of foolscap and included the sentence, "*No claim shall arise out of any accident involving club members or club aircraft.*" She read it through twice, trying to ignore the small flutter of tension in her stomach, then filled it in and scribbled her name at the bottom.

"There you are." Her voice was a shade over-casual as she tried to hide her nervousness. "I've signed away all my rights."

"Splendid." Bazzard was six-foot-one, with an easy smile. "You didn't even notice the cheque underneath it, either."

Ann smiled back, grateful for the small humour. "Oh yes, I did. I signed it 'R. Bazzard' and kept it. I'll fill the rest in later."

At the other end of the room, a young man with red hair and a serious face appeared at a door marked CFI. He looked directly at Ann for several seconds, then moved his eyes to Bazzard and said abruptly, "I'd like a word with you, please." Bazzard got up immediately and went in like a lamb, reminding Ann somehow of a sixth-former summoned to a headmaster's office. He came out again a few minutes later looking slightly sheepish.

"That's Barry Turner, the CFI," he told Ann quietly as he sat down again.

"What's a CFI?"

"The Chief Flying Instructor."

"Oh. What did he want you for?"

"Er, well . . ." Bazzard rubbed the back of his neck, looking rueful. "He gave me a bit of a rocket, actually, for booking the aircraft for the whole weekend and then not turning up until this time to take it. I didn't know what time we'd be leaving when I made the booking, you see."

"Why should he object to that, though? I mean, if you've hired the plane for the weekend, what's it got to do with him when you take it?"

"Well, we're using the Arrow. It's the only one on the school, and people often want check-rides in it at the week-ends. So if they'd known we weren't coming till now they might've got another hour or so's utilisation on it. He's a bit of a pedantic sod, old Barry, but he's right really. I should have let them know."

"Oh." Ann bent to her coffee. She wasn't sure she'd followed the quietly-spoken explanation, but she didn't want to embarrass him by asking any more questions. Inwardly she was amazed at the way Roy, normally very self-assured and confident, had meekly accepted his rocket from the young man with the red hair, who looked at least five years his junior. Being totally ignorant of the aviation world she had no way of knowing how the pecking order in any aero club revolves entirely around flying seniority, with no regard at all for any of the normal social scales: still less did she have any idea of the autocratic power wielded over the paying customers by the average Chief Instructor.

For the next ten minutes she sat leafing through an old copy of *Flying* – which she found almost totally incomprehensible – while Roy busied himself with maps, clipboard, and his little plastic navigation computer. As a nursing sister in a large hospital, she was accustomed to the rigmaroles surrounding the use of precision machinery. But nonetheless, the preparations and paraphernalia of flight seemed to be incredibly complicated, and somehow increased her nervousness. After a while she got up and went into the Ladies, where she renewed her lipstick unnecessarily.

25

Looking at her face in the mirror, she found herself searching for the tell-tale signs of strain which had been there for the last few weeks. It was an attractive face in a general sort of way, with blue eyes and bushy neck-length blonde hair – but still the signs were there, when you knew where to look. The corners of that rather wide mouth, for instance; they were pressed together again, the way they seemed to be much too much of the time these days. It made you look prim and disapproving; the beginning of that intangible aura of severity which you used to notice in other nursing sisters. Too many long hours in the casualty ward, perhaps, with not enough relaxation in between. Too much efficiency, too much being ultra-cool and serious . . .

She smiled tentatively, watching the effect. It created a minor transformation, widening the eyes, making the mouth warm and friendly, and giving the slightly tipped-up nose a cheeky air. The sternness and tension were gone, which, she told herself, was the way it should be for a healthy twenty-five-year-old girl at the beginning of a long weekend off. Even if you *were* a bit nervous about your first flight in a light plane . . .

She went back to applying the lipstick, resolving to smile more often over the next three days. Forget the Royal Infirmary and its pressure-cooker workload, stop worrying about going in the plane, and most of all, stop worrying about Roy.

Roy . . .

She caught herself frowning into the mirror, and tossed her head. It was ridiculous, worrying about whether you were in love with someone after you'd only known them three weeks. Quite ridiculous. Going to stay with his parents for a weekend – even flying down to his parents – didn't mean a thing: nothing except that you enjoyed each other's company and wanted to go walking and horse-riding in Buckinghamshire, and into London in the evenings. And if it should end up in bed before you've got it all neatly thought out and diagnosed – well, maybe that's just what you need. Maybe that's exactly what you need before you get a shade *too* well-balanced, a little too much the super-organised senior nurse . . .

She found she was blushing, embarrassed by the sudden strength of her own feelings. She waited until the colour had subsided, smiled again briefly at the mirror, then dropped the lipstick into her handbag and went back into the club-house.

*   *   *

Bazzard had made a mistake.

The track he needed to fly from Newcastle to the aero-drome of Denham, just above London, was almost due south. The wind was from the west, which meant from his right – and yet the heading he'd just calculated on his Airtour computer gave him a drift-correction angle to the left, which was quite patently rubbish. The error was puerile and im-mediately recognisable – he'd put the wind-dot below the grommet on the wind-vector scale instead of above it – but his tidy accountant's mind was irritated that he should have made it at all. The flight computer – little more than a circular slide-rule – was, after all, childishly simple compared with the calculators and computers he used every day; he couldn't remember ever making an idiot mistake like that with it before.

He massaged the back of his neck, which was aching along with his shoulders. In spite of the prospect of the long week-end with Ann, he was feeling stale and waspish: he'd woken up this morning with all the symptoms of a hangover although he'd had nothing to drink last night, and his neck was wincingly stiff with the same apparent lack of cause. He'd put the malady down to overwork – at thirty-six years old he was the junior partner in an old Newcastle firm of accoun-tants, pushing hard to establish his footing – and told himself that he'd feel better as the morning went on. But he hadn't felt better; the undeserved hangover had persisted, and beneath his outward cheerfulness he still felt sluggish and used-up.

He rubbed his eyes with his knuckles, wondering for a

moment whether he really ought to fly today. He was basically a cautious man, still mildly nervous of the air after ninety-two hours of piloting, and he was very aware that his one-year-old Private Pilot's Licence was a flimsy guarantee against the occasional infantile mistake when the workload was high in a cockpit.

But then there was Ann. He'd told Ann that if the weather was good they'd fly down to Denham instead of driving, and she'd seemed to like the idea. And the weather, apart from a warm front forecast for well after their arrival, indisputedly *was* good . . .

He shrugged his shoulders, then jabbed his Chinagraph pencil down on the correct spot on the wind-scale and re-calculated his heading: it came to 185 degrees magnetic.

A few seconds later Ann walked back into the room, and he looked up smiling.

*   *   *

They walked out to the aeroplane at a quarter past two.

Outside the clubhouse the sunshine was cold and brittle, with regular-shaped patches of frost still blanketing the tarmac in the shadows of the hangars. The line of parked aircraft were all sleek and modern-looking except for one, right on the end: a tiny, chunky biplane, garishly painted in an improbable colour scheme of chocolate and yellow. Ann blinked at it as they walked by.

"Is that one of the flying school planes, Roy?"

Bazzard glanced round. "No, not that one, love. That's a thing called a Pitts Special. Specialist aerobatic job. Some wealthy playboy type owns it and lets Barry Turner use it for displays and competitions. I expect Barry's got it out to do a bit of practising." He glanced up at the brilliant blue sky, streaked now with wisps of high cirrus. "Nice day for it, too, if you like turning yourself upside down."

She said, "Can you do that, Roy? Stunts and things?"

Bazzard grinned and put on a deep voice. "Madam, I'd like to tell you that I'm the greatest aerobatic pilot that

28

ever lived." He resumed his normal tone. "I'd *like* to tell you that, but unfortunately it isn't true. I can just about do a loop, but anything else makes me go a delicate shade of green. And that thing'd be a bit too much for me, anyway. That's what the Americans call one hot little ship." He walked on a few paces, then gestured towards a sober blue and white Cherokee Arrow parked next but one to the biplane. "This is more my line. Nice airborne motor car, easy to fly, enough nav equipment for a small airliner, and room for the prettiest nurse in Newcastle to sit beside me. *Regardez votre chariot*, Madam!"

Close to, the plane was bigger than Ann had expected. The white platforms of the wings were wide and thick, and she couldn't see over the body at all except at the back end near the tail. She stood shivering in the January breeze while Roy walked all round it, moving the control surfaces and kneeling to see the undersides. When he'd finished his inspection he announced, "Everything seems to be glued on," and then stepped up on to the black-painted walkway on the starboard wing root and opened the cockpit door. Ann handed up the suitcases, the coats, and his black plastic flight bag, and he leaned in and stowed them behind the front seats.

Then the pain hit him.

It came very suddenly, like a red-hot skewer behind his eyes. Vision blurred. For a few seconds it seemed as if his head was about to burst. The agony was indescribable. He wanted to cry out but couldn't ...

And then it was gone.

Bazzard blinked in astonishment. He was still leaning awkwardly into the cockpit, one hand supporting himself on the door frame. For a moment he wasn't even certain there'd been any pain at all. But there had been something, surely? He moved a little, and felt a renewed twinge across his stiff neck and shoulders. Ah! That was it: must be. He must have put pressure on a nerve or something while he was reaching in with the second case. Stiff shoulders at thirty-six, for Christ's sake! He'd have to get more exercise ...

Folding himself into the cockpit, he twisted round and

29

called to Ann to come up. Ann hadn't noticed the little step sticking out of the fuselage behind and below the starboard flap, so she clambered awkwardly on to the walkway straight from the ground. Bazzard shifted over to the left hand seat as her legs arrived in the doorway.

"Sorry I couldn't help you in, love. But I sit on the left, so I have to get in first since they only put one door on these crates. Chivalry seems to be dead in the Piper Aircraft Corporation."

Ann smiled, a little whitely, and lowered herself into the right hand front seat beside him. The line of parked aircraft was right outside the clubhouse, and the performance with the luggage must have looked even more like the two of them off on a dirty weekend. She was glad she'd decided to wear jeans and a thick-knit white sweater; the thought of giving the red-haired Chief Instructor a leg show getting into the plane with a skirt on did not appeal.

When she was in the seat Bazzard stretched across her and swung the door to, then reached up and twisted the top clip above her head to the Locked position. As he brought his arm down he rested it lightly across her shoulders and leaned over and kissed her quickly on the cheek.

"Don't, Roy."

"Oh. Sorry." He withdrew his arm.

"Hey, don't get huffed. It's just that there's people watching. In the clubhouse."

"Ah." Bazzard brightened. "Not to worry. I'll wait until we're in the air."

"No, you jolly well won't. You'll be busy flying the plane, or the passengers are going to start complaining."

"Aha." Bazzard waved a hand, ignoring the twinge across his shoulders. "That's all you know, Madam. This little buggy caters for that. Once at altitude, the gallant aviator sticks it on autopilot and then has both hands free for nefarious pursuits such as chasing young ladies around the cockpit."

Ann immediately burst out laughing, which surprised him considerably. After a moment she gasped, "Has it really, Roy? Got an autopilot?"

"Sure it has. Right here –" he touched a pair of buttons on the bottom left hand corner of the panel " – two axis wing-leveller and heading-hold, if you're interested. What's so funny?"

"Oh . . ." Ann subsided into giggles. "It's just that Shirley – my flatmate – was talking about autopilots this morning, before you came. She said your plane was bound to have one, and that I'd have to fight for my honour all the way to – where is it? – Denham."

"Oh, she did, did she?" Bazzard assumed an exaggerated hungry leer. "In that case, Madam, I shall consider it an omen. Prepare to fight for thy honour unto the French coast and beyond, if need be!"

Ann's eyes rounded. "Oh sir! No, sir . . ."

". . . three bags full, sir!"

Still chuckling, Bazzard showed Ann how to slide her seat forward and strap herself in; then he turned his attention to the chores which have to be performed before starting an aeroplane's engine. While his hands moved across the controls, Ann took her first good look around the cabin. The quality of the trim and decor surprised her. She'd vaguely imagined that a small plane cockpit would be coldly functional, like the fighter cockpits you saw on films; the notion that a company the size of Piper Aircraft Corporation would maintain an Interior Design Department with the object of making their cabins as soothing as possible to a non-flyer was one which had never occurred to her. The whole inside was tastefully finished in various shades of blue, matching the blue engine cowling and the flashes down the fuselage sides. The neatly-fitting carpets were blue, the seats were blue leather and broadcloth, the sidewall trim was blue, and the cabin headlining was clean and white. The over-all impression was like being in an expensive, if slightly antiseptic, motor car; even the two half-wheel control yokes, one in front of Roy and a duplicate in front of her own seat, were vaguely reminiscent of a car.

Forward of the wheels, however, the similarity ended. The curved blue nose of the aeroplane was far higher than any

31

car bonnet, so high that she had to crane her neck to see over it. And the matt-black instrument panel most definitely *was* functional. It seemed to be covered with literally hundreds of dials and switches and levers and radios, all jostling for space and all completely incomprehensible. Ann blinked at the array in bewilderment, vainly trying to find a single familiar gauge or control. She'd had a vague sort of idea there'd be a speedometer and a thing for telling you how high you were, but this lot was completely fantastic.

"How on earth do you know what all these things are for, Roy?"

Bazzard, halfway through the pre-start checks, paused with his hand on the mixture control. That question was familiar to any pilot.

"Oh, it's not as bad as it looks. You're never using everything at once, for one thing. Most of the time you're just keeping track of the basic flight instruments – speed, altitude, heading and so on, over here – and then glancing down occasionally to the engine instruments, this lot, to make sure the clockwork hasn't fallen out. Then the rest are mainly radio navigation aids, which you only use when you need them. Once you've got everything divided into sections in your mind, it's not difficult at all. Nothing like as complicated as those damn great X-ray machines you've got at your hospital."

Ann shook her head. "Not that *I've* got. I'm hopeless with mechanical things; they wouldn't let me within fifty yards of an X-ray unit. They save my kind of job for people who can't handle anything more complicated than a bedpan." She paused, groping for something intelligent to say, then added, "So how fast will we be going, Roy?"

"Once we've finished climbing we'll cruise at about 155 m.p.h. We'll get to Denham in an hour and a half."

Impressed, Ann said, "Is that fast for a small plane?"

"Yeah. For a single engine job, anyway. This thing's a Piper Cheokee Arrow. Two hundred horsepower engine, fuel injection, constant speed prop, and retractable undercarriage. That's about as sophisticated as you can get with a single."

"Retractable undercarriage? You mean the wheels go up?"

"Yep." Bazzard was continuing with the checks. Mixture – rich; throttle – quarter inch open; prop – fully fine; boost pump . . .

"What happens if they don't come down again?"

Bazzard grinned. "Ah. Well. In that case we'd land on our belly and go skating along the ground amid much embarrassment. But don't worry about it, love. For one thing they always *do* come down, for another this particular kite's got an automatic device which puts them down for you if you forget, and for yet another the fuselage is designed to take a belly landing without much damage anyway. I'm going to start the engine now, okay?"

Ann nodded. Bazzard twisted the key. The propeller churned over tinnily on the starter, then vanished into sudden invisibility as the engine burst into life. The Arrow nodded on its nosewheel, and then the noise was settling to a steady rushing rumble as Bazzard throttled back to 1,000 r.p.m. Ann watched his hands and eyes moving round the cockpit, checking mysterious gauges and switching unknown switches. She felt out of her element and slightly silly, cloddish in her total ignorance of what he was doing. The purposeful growl and the gently thrumming vibration made her stomach feel hollow. For an illogical moment she caught herself hoping that he'd find something slightly wrong; just wrong enough so they'd have to stop the plane and get out and go down by car . . .

A voice from somewhere in the cockpit bellowed suddenly: "CALEDONIAN ONE-SEVEN-FOUR CLEAR TAXI RUN-WAY TWO-FIFE . . ." Ann jumped, and Bazzard's hand whipped up to the number one radio to turn the volume down.

"Sorry about that, love. You never know if you've got it too loud until somebody talks. It's easier to tell if you're wearing headsets, but all ours are in the training aircraft today, so we're stuck with the hand-mike and the cabin speaker. Pity, that; headsets are quieter in the air."

Ann nodded, not understanding a word. "That was the radio, was it" She had to raise her voice over the thrustle of the engine. "The one you talk to the people on the ground with?"

"Eh? Oh – yes." Bazzard glanced at her, noticing the slight paling of colour and the set face. Her obvious nervousness surprised him: she was normally so calm and collected. Have to keep an eye on that . . .

He picked up the microphone from its hook on the throttle quadrant and showed it to her.

"This is what you talk into," he said. "In a moment I'm going to press this button here and ask the tower for taxi clearance. You're not allowed to move until they clear you, you see."

Ann nodded again. Bazzard winked at her, brought the microphone up so that the top of it touched his upper lip, and pressed the button.

"Newcastle, good morning: this is Golf Alpha Yankee Whisky Tango, pre-flight check and request taxi."

The speaker over their heads replied immediately, talking fast. "Whisky Tango fives, clear taxi runway two fife, QNH one-zero-one-four, QFE one-zero-zero-fife, wind two-three-zero at one-two."

To Ann, it sounded like almost total garble. She looked at Roy, wondering how on earth anyone could understand the high speed metallic voice. But Roy was sitting calm and confident, making notes on his clipboard. After a moment he lifted the microphone again and replied.

"Whisky Tango fives also, runway two-five, QNH one-zero-one-four." The speaker click-clicked in return.

Bazzard turned his head. "Sounds impossible the first time you hear it, doesn't it? Everyone thinks they'll never understand a word, then suddenly you get it." He winked again, then added: "I'm going to start taxiing now, all right?"

Ann smiled nervously. The rumble of the engine seemed to be shivering in her stomach.

Bazzard reached down and released the parking brake, added a little more power, and the Arrow started to move. He checked the toe-brakes, then screwed his head round to make sure the taxiway was clear. The movement shot a bolt of pain through his neck, making him wince.

"Here, Ann, do you know anything that's good for neck-ache?"

The girl was looking out of the windscreen, straining upwards against her straps to see over the nose. She'd had no idea that aerodromes were so big: the expanse of the taxiway looked wide enough for a whole motorway . . .

"Oy, Madam! I be talking to you!"

"Sorry, Roy." She glanced across at him. "What did you say?"

"I asked Madam if Madam knows anything good for neck-ache."

"Why, have you got one?"

"Yes, just a bit." Bazzard yawed the Arrow gently right and left as he taxied, checking the movement of the turn needle and the compasses. "Shoulders and neck. In the muscles, it feels like."

Ann was immediately sympathetic. In the alien world of the small cockpit, a muscular pain was something she could understand.

"Is it bad?"

"Only hurts when I laugh, love. But I think I'd better put something on it, if there's anything that does any good."

"Well, most of the stuff you get's only a counter-irritant, but I do know one or two things that aren't bad. They smell a bit horsey, I'm afraid, but they do work. I'll get some at a chemist's when we get there, and rub it in for you. How long have you had it?"

"I haven't, yet."

"The stiff neck, Romeo."

"Oh, ah. The stiff neck. Woke up with it this morning. Must be gettting old, y'know."

"Dreadful, isn't it?"

"Sure is." He glanced at her. "Not too old to appreciate having my neck rubbed by you, though."

"Thank you, kind sir."

Bazzard waved a hand. "The pleasure," he said, "is mine. I hope."

Ann smiled, relaxing.

At the end of the taxiway Bazzard turned the Arrow into wind, ran up the engine, and checked the propeller and magnetos. Ann sat still, awed by the deep roar of the Lycoming, and watched his hands moving around the controls.

With the engine-run completed, Bazzard throttled back and started on the pre-take-off checks. Ann watched him again as he ran round fuel, flaps, and all the rest, touching each control or dial in turn as he came to them in the mnemonic checklist which Turner insisted on. The last item was "controls full and free", and Bazzard wound the half-wheel from lock to lock and back and forth, looking out at ailerons and elevators to check their movement. Ann watched the duplicated control yoke in front of her own seat moving in unison.

"Is this dual controls, Roy?"

Bazzard nodded. "Yep. You're sitting where the instructor sits when you're learning to fly. Everything I've got you've got on your side as well, except the toe-brakes. You can have a go at flying it when we're in the air, if you like."

"Er, no thanks. I'd rather you did it, this time."

Bazzard grinned again. "Me and the autopilot, love, me and the autopilot. I've got better things to do once we're under way."

Ann laughed, nervousness abated for the moment.

The Arrow pulled out on to the runway and growled into the air at 1423 Greenwich Mean Time.

3

1423–1430

TONY PAYNTON WAS frozen. The harsh brilliance of the January sun gave an illusion of warmth, but that was all it was: an illusion. He tugged at the fur collar of his flying jacket for the twentieth time in a futile attempt to shut out the twin draughts that whistle in under the rear edges of all Chipmunk cockpit canopies, then gave it up and went back to staring moodily forwards.

The view ahead was less than inspiring, as were several other aspects of his tiny world aloft. Compared with the soggy unresponsiveness of modern Cessnas and Pipers, the de Havilland Chipmunk is a delightful aeroplane to fly, but at the same time it is undeniably lacking in certain creature comforts. For one thing it is completely unsilenced, which means that the flat blare of the Gipsy Major engine dins into your bones during a heavy day of instructing: for another, it has a glasshouse canopy and is totally unheated, which causes the occupants to bake in the summer and freeze in the winter. And on top of it all the seating is in tandem; in effect two entirely separate single-seat cockpits, each with its own set of controls, one behind the other under a single long canopy. This is an advantage for certain exercises, such as solo aerobatics, but a considerable nuisance during basic training. The student sits in the front seat, where he can see what's happening, while the instructor cranes around in the back, where the draughts are, and hopes that he will see enough of what's happening to prevent actual disaster. The

37

Perspex side windows of the rear cockpit are bulged outwards to aid him in this craning, but even so the total effect is one of peculiar detachment and isolation; a Chipmunk instructor is uncomfortably aware that his pupil could turn green in the face or fly straight at another aircraft without him knowing a thing about it.

At this moment, with Chipmunk G-BCYL climbing through 6,500 feet, Paynton's forward vista consisted of the back of Jules Martin's head, the inverted U-shapes of the canopy framework, and then nothing but the wide brilliant sky and a vague brown line above the wings which was the distant horizon.

He pinched the bridge of his nose, and watched the altimeter as the aircraft levelled out clumsily from the climb. He waited for a half minute, thinking idly about the misfire in his MGB, while Martin settled down to level flight. Then he raised his left hand and tapped the boom-microphone attached to his headset closer to his lips.

"Jules." His voice was calm and stolid with its Midlands accent. "Jules, that last one was better, except you still didn't get the stick far enough forward. Also, you kept your full opposite rudder on for a bit after the spin had stopped. So watch out for those two points, okay?"

A hesitant nod from the silhouette in front. A timid "Yes", in Paynton's earphones, metallic over the intercom.

"Okay then, Jules. So now we'll do another one, to the left this time, and we'll hold it in a bit longer. Don't recover till I tell you. Got that?"

The shoulders under the head hunched slightly, as if their owner was trying to scrunch down still further in the seat he was already firmly strapped into. Jules Martin was feeling apprehensive and a little airsick; the only thing he'd really taken in from what Paynton had said were the ominous words *"hold it in a bit longer"*. He swallowed hard and tried to quell the hollow vacuum in his stomach by keeping his eyes in the cockpit, on the matter-of-fact instruments and the scratched black surface of the panel. It didn't help very much. The all-pervading roar of the engine seemed to boom through his body, turning his bones to jelly and numbing his brain. He was very conscious that he was sitting on a few thin sheets of aluminium 7,000 feet up in the sky.

The headphones spoke again. "You got that, Jules?"

Martin mumbled, "Yes. Okay."

"Right then, me old mate. So go . . ." the voice in Martin's ears suddenly dissolved into a clashing crackle, which itself subsided in a couple of seconds and became a new voice, speaking slowly in a North-Country accent.

". . . Charlie India's estimatin' Tees-side in, eh, abowt five minutes," it said. "Requestin' roonway in use an' . . . er . . . Quebec Fox Echo. Eh, ah . . . over."

Paynton, who'd stopped talking when the new voice cut in, stayed silent while he waited for the Approach Controller at Tees-side Airport to reply to the pilot of Charlie India and get the radio conversation over with. It was a bloody nuisance having the air-to-ground radio and the front-to-rear cockpit intercom all going through the same box of tricks; for the hundredth time he wished there was some way of utilising the old RAF-style mute-switch, so that the instructor could cut out external transmissions while he was nattering on the intercom. If he'd had the radio in his own cockpit he could have achieved the same result by flipping the selector round to a quieter frequency for a couple of minutes; but the radio box was in the front, and by the time he'd talked Jules into changing frequencies the interruption would probably be all over anyway.

The headphones said distantly, "Aircraft calling Tees-side Approach, you are strength three; say again your full call sign."

"Eh, . . . er . . ." The North-Country voice hesitated, uncertain. "Er, Tees-side, Charlie India . . . um . . . say again please. Over."

Paynton raised his eyes to heaven.

"Aircraft calling Tees-side, you are unreadable; try Tower on 119.8. I say again, switch to Tees-side Tower, 119.8."

"Eh . . . Tees-side Approach; this is Golf Charlie India. What was that . . . I mean, er, say again . . ."

Paynton muttered, "Oh *fucking* hell!" under his breath, then spoke loudly into the intercom, drowning out the other voice.

"Switch over a frequency or two, Jules."

Martin said, "What? Er – say again?"

The radio said, "... calling Tees-side, switch to ..."

Paynton bellowed, *"Change the bleeding frequency, Jules! This dumb bugger'll be yapping away all day on this one!"*

"Oh. Ye – roger." Martin leaned forward to reach the radio, stretching against his straps. The headphones said, "Charlie India, understand one-one ..." and then went quiet as he twisted the frequency knob from 118.85 MHz to 116.85. He didn't know it was 116.85, and he didn't care: he was just glad that all the talking was over. Or at least, half-glad, anyway. Getting rid of the distraction meant that he was going to have to spin the aeroplane, which he didn't want to do – but on the other hand, the sooner it was over with the sooner they could get down from this dizzy height and land, which was all he was really interested in now. He sat back, feeling hot and prickly in his hands and face and hollower than ever in his belly.

"Okay then, Jules." Paynton's voice was back to normal, any irritation in it lost in the black box of the intercom and the steady blare of the engine. "Let's do a clearing turn, and then go into our spin."

Martin nodded miserably and edged the stick to the left. The horizon canted over and slid sideways across the engine cowling as the Chipmunk lurched into a turn.

"Getting tense, Jules. Just relax, eh?"

Martin found he was pressing his feet hard on the rudder pedals, so that his knees were quivering. He tried to slacken his muscles, and was partially successful.

The Chipmunk snarled on, turning gently.

"Okay Jules; that'll do for the look-out. Now let's see you spin it."

Martin rolled out of the turn with slightly crossed controls. He held the Chipmunk level for a moment, then took a deep breath and closed the throttle. The racket of the engine subsided immediately to a gently shuddering ruffle, making his stomach crawl under the tightened-down harness. He was horribly aware of the endless nothing beneath the wings and the tiny unmoving earth so far below.

Paynton's voice came metallically into his ears, loud in the unnatural quietness.

"Come on, me old mate; get that nose up. She'll go on gliding for ever like this."

Martin nodded. His feet were trembling on the rudder again. He pulled the stick back a little, staring rigidly ahead over the matt-black engine cowling so that he wouldn't see the frightening nose-high attitude in its entirety. The hiss of the airflow wound down ominously as the speed dribbled away. The Chipmunk seemed to be reared up, hanging in the sky . . .

In the back cockpit, Paynton moved his feet and his right hand so that they rested lightly on rudder pedals and stick. His left hand went unconsciously to the throttle.

"Nose higher now, then full back stick and left rudder when she goes."

The airframe shuddered as the airflow over the wings started to break up at the beginning of the stall. Martin jerked backwards on the stick, kicked out with his left foot, and shut his eyes.

The Chipmunk stalled, then spun.

It was quite violent, as spin entries go. To Paynton, muscles instinctively braced against his straps, the pictureframe of Martin's head under the canopy-struts whipped round a vicious half snap-roll which put the earth fleetingly above him before the nose plunged down. Then the cockpit was pointing straight at the ground and rotating, winding round faster and faster. The sound of the airflow rose from a whistle to an eerie shriek, and something clattered in the luggage locker behind his head. He ignored it and waited dispassionately, counting the turns. At somewhere beyond five the details of the ground blurred, merging into a greeny-brown spinning disc in front of the nose. The huge sense of twisting and accelerating went on, endless . . .

He muttered, "One thousand and one," then bawled, "RECOVER, JULES!"

41

Martin opened his eyes. For a second he could only stare, utterly horrified, at the appalling catharine-wheel over the nose. Then, moving with the treacly slowness of nightmare, he felt himself pushing on right rudder and following it by shoving the stick forwards.

The spin continued.

Jesus! God! It wasn't coming out!

"PUSH *HARD*, JULES! *ALL* THE WAY FORWARD!"

Martin pushed with all his strength, straining on the edge of panic. Nothing seemed to happen; just the stick pushing back at him and the gut-wrenching twisting and the wild howl of the airflow . . .

For a few seconds, the spin got faster.

Then it stopped.

It stopped with slamming abruptness, the way all spins do if they're ever going to stop at all. The fields far below were instantly stationary, and swelling slowly in front of the nose. The wind-noise was increasing and Martin, horribly giddy, was dimly aware that he was hard against his straps, trying to float up out of his seat. There was something he ought to be doing but the thought was paralysed, much too slow in coming . . .

"Pull OUT, Jules!"

He hauled the stick back. Much too hard. The nose reared up in front of him and the giant hand of G-force punched him hard into his seat. The Chipmunk struggled to come out of its past-the-vertical dive, buffeted sharply in the beginning of a high-speed stall . . .

"I'VE GOT HER, JULES!"

Martin let go of the controls.

Instantly, order returned. The buffeting stopped as Paynton relaxed some of the back-pressure, and the lurching sideways skid that Martin hadn't even noticed ceased as the instructor centralised the rudder. Martin watched helplessly, pressed into his seat, as the engine cowling rose smoothly up through the horizon and on, further and further until it was pointing at the cirrus-streaked sky at an incredible angle. The air-speed dribbled back round the dial. As it passed ninety knots,

Paynton eased the throttle open and started lowering the nose. At sixty, the Chipmunk was in level flight with full power on, having soared up from 3,000 feet to nearly 4,000 in the zoom.

Paynton started talking, his voice clattering over the intercom. Martin sat in silence, not taking it in. His brain was whirling and he was feeling ill. The only thought he had was that he wanted very much to be back on the ground.

*   *   *

At the same moment, fifty miles away, Cherokee Arrow G-AYWT was passing through 1,000 feet. With the wheels and flaps up, Bazzard reduced power to the en-route climb setting and then glanced across at the girl for the first time since take-off. Her face was pale and set and she was staring fixedly at the blue sky beyond the pitched-up nose, as if she were frightened of looking anywhere else.

Raising his voice over the muffled roar of the engine he said, "You all right, love?"

"Yes." She sounded strained. "Yes, fine."

He watched her anxiously for several seconds. "You sure, now? If you really don't like it, just say. We can always go back and drive down instead."

"Oh, no. I'm all right." Ann swallowed. "It's just a bit ... strange at first, that's all. It's not like a big plane at all, is it?"

Bazzard nodded, his eyes sliding back to the instruments and the business of flying. "That's true," he said. "This is real flying, something like this. Those big jets are like riding on the Underground."

"Hmmmm."

The Arrow droned on up the sky, passing 2,000 feet three minutes after take-off. The left wing dipped below the horizon as Bazzard eased into a gentle climbing turn on to course. He looked at Ann again, and waved a hand at the left side window.

"We picked a lovely day for it. You can see the whole of Newcastle. Look."

Ann twisted her head. The city was spread out far below, vast and clean and toy-like in the brittle winter sunshine. Outside the window, the wing tip marched slowly backwards across the miniature landscape as the aircraft turned. It felt as if they were just hanging in space, suspended on nothing at a dizzy height and not moving forwards at all. She swallowed again, and forced herself to keep looking out.

Bazzard said, "Look, you can see right the way from Gosforth to Jarrow. You're lucky today; all you usually see of the dump this time of the year's a blanket of industrial crud."

Ann licked her lips, then said, "Why's that?"

"The smoke and vapour from all the factories." Bazzard rolled the Arrow out of its turn on a heading of 185 degrees magnetic, and maintained the climb. The low winter sun glared in through the right hand side of the windscreen. "All the muck gets into the air and forms a great big smoggy bubble over the place. Most big cities are like it most of the time. You don't know what pollution is until you see it from the air."

Ann nodded, and turned her head again. Shading her eyes from the sun, she looked at the ground ahead of the wing on her own side. She felt a fraction better now they weren't banked over any more, although her stomach still fluttered at the height. She was amazed at the way the plane didn't seem to be moving; she had to look directly down in front of the wing before she could be sure that the ground was sliding backwards at all.

"How fast are we going, Roy?"

"A hundred miles an hour at the moment. I'm climbing up to four thousand to get over the top of all the military zones down south, particularly Leeming; they give you a right old run-around if you get into their airspace. We'll go a lot faster when we've finished climbing."

"A hundred! It doesn't feel as if we're moving at all."

Bazzard smiled. "It always feels like that. It's because of the height. The only time you get any impression of speed's when you're flying very low." He chuckled. "Or when you're learning to fly and you get lost, of course. Then the scenery

44

scoots past, all right. Instant acceleration to about Mach Two."

Ann smiled weakly and looked round again, trying to ignore the nervousness in her stomach. The sprawl of Tyneside was obvious enough – but which part was which, she hadn't the faintest idea. If she hadn't known it was Newcastle it could have been anywhere from Manchester to Marrakesh. Of the airport, which had seemed so enormous on the ground, there was no sign whatsoever.

"How on earth *do* you know where you are, Roy? I mean, everything looks so . . . different, up here."

Bazzard grinned. "Everyone finds that at first, love. After a bit you get the knack of map-reading, though – " he tapped a finger on the colourful topographic air map on his knees " – and then later on you learn how to use the nav aids, as well. That makes it dead easy." He glanced at the altimeter and added, "I'm going to level out from the climb, now. When we're level you'll be able to see something out of the front."

Ann's right hand gripped the armrest on the door beside her seat. Bazzard eased the nose down gently from the climbing attitude, then sat making small adjustments to the trim wheel and listening to the changing engine note as the speed built up. After a moment he reached out and tapped the glass face of the VOR.

"This here's the VHF omni-directional rangefinder," he said. "Worth its weight in gold for navigating. When the needle's in the middle, where it is now, it means we're tracking outbound along a southerly radio beam from the beacon back at Newcastle. If we wander off it, the needle'll point in the direction we have to turn to get back to it. Dead clever, these Chinese."

Ann blinked at the rows of dials, not understanding a word he'd said and feeling foolish because of it. After a moment she just nodded again, meaninglessly.

The airspeed crept up to 150 m.p.h. Bazzard eased the throttle back until the manifold pressure stood at 24 in Hg., then made a tiny adjustment to the propeller pitch to settle the revs at exactly 2,400. Then he lowered the nose a fraction further below the horizon, and watched the altimeter as the hands slid down 200 feet to precisely 4,000. He checked the descent there, and carefully trimmed both elevator and rudder for straight and level flight.

The speed settled at 155 m.p.h.

Experiencing the small superior glow that every pilot feels when he's successfully put his aircraft "on the step", he set about going round the cockpit doing all the little after-climb chores which ought to be dealt with before switching in the autopilot and taking it easy. Mixture – leaned off for the cruise; boost pump – on for a moment for the switch from left tank to right, then off again; directional gyro – re-set to magnetic compass and autopilot heading-bug adjusted; radio – correct frequency selected for the last call to Newcastle, then ready to change to Tees-side Approach for a listening watch until he was past their aerodrome and getting near to RAF Leeming.

All okay.

He moved the heater levers to about half of full cabin heat, reached up and twisted the two sun visors, and then looked at Ann again. His neck twinged as he turned his head.

"Better now we've finished climbing, love?"

Ann smiled at him. She was still pale, but not so tense as she had been. She'd found that if you looked out forwards, at the distant horizon which was just visible over the nose, you weren't quite so aware of the ghastly void below. It seemed to be mainly the visual impact of looking *down* which made you feel all hollow inside; the sight of the white slab of the wing, remote but at the same time sort of attached to you, bobbing around in space with nothing underneath it except the ground all that way below . . .

She shivered slightly, then said, "I'm fine. Just beginning to get used to it."

Bazzard studied her for a moment. She looked as if she'd be all right after all. He grinned suddenly and said, "Roger, Miss Moore. *Et maintenant*, Madam, I weel now sweetch in ze fiendishly cunning autopilot. *Regardez, s'il vous plait!*"

He pressed the two white buttons on the bottom left hand side of the panel, and let go of the control yoke with a

46

flourish. The tenor of the Arrow's flight immediately underwent the subtle change which comes over all light aeroplanes when they go on to automatic stabilisation: a sort of mechanically-rigid feeling that you can't quite put your finger on but is nonetheless distinctly different from a human hand on the controls. The aircraft made a tiny course correction, two or three degrees, then droned on steadily. Ann watched the two unattended control wheels, momentarily fascinated. Their miniscule corrective movements as the wing-leveller operated were too small for her to see.

Bazzard said: "*Voilà*, Madam. *Et* further *maintenant*, now ees ze time for ze in-flight *passional!*" He reached out and squeezed her knee playfully, then picked up her left hand out of her lap and held it.

"You will obsairve," he said, waving his free hand, "zat Biggles ees about to leap on you and tear off all your cloze!" He glanced down. "An' especially, I may say, zose sexy tight jeans!"

"Oh, sir! No, sir . . ."

They both laughed. The Arrow snored on placidly, the sunshine warm in the cockpit. After a minute by the instrument panel clock, Bazzard disengaged his hand and picked the microphone off its hook.

"Got to call Newcastle to say goodbye."

Ann nodded.

He raised the mike to his lips and pressed the button. "Newcastle, Whisky Tango; leaving your area to the south, flight level four-zero, switching to Tees-side Approach."

The speaker clicked and replied, "Roger, Whisky Tango; good day, sir." This time Ann heard the "good day", but the rest was still a meaningless cackle.

Bazzard clicked the transmit button twice in acknowledgment, then put the microphone down in his lap while he reached up to change the radio frequency. It was on Newcastle Approach,126.35, and it had to be switched to Tees-side on 118.85. He started by twisting the decimal knob from .35 to .85 . . .

And then passed out.

It happened in an instant of time, so quickly that he him-

47

self was hardly aware of it. There was a split-second bolt of blinding pain in the back of his head, as if he'd been clubbed, and then consciousness blinked out. His body slumped forward against the diagonal shoulder strap. His head stayed up, rigidly square on his shoulders.

It was several seconds before Ann realised that anything had happened at all. She heard Roy make a small grunting noise, and turned to look at him. He was sitting more or less upright, with his eyes closed.

She said, "Pig. Say pardon when you burp."

Bazzard didn't say anything.

Ann stared at him for a long moment, the smile fading off her face. Even then she didn't realise the calamity. Her first thought, like someone who goes back to their parked car and finds it missing, was that she'd got it wrong or that she was the victim of some cruel joke. Conscious of a strong feeling of disappointment – she hadn't thought Roy was the sort to play vicious jokes – she said icily and distinctly, "You rotten sod. That isn't even a tiny bit funny."

Bazzard didn't move.

Suddenly furious and frightened, Ann twisted in her seat, took as big a swing as she could in the confines of the cockpit, and slapped him twice round the face with all her strength.

Bazzard toppled back, shoulders resting half against the seat-back and half against the side of the cockpit. His head stayed upright, eyes still closed.

The Arrow flew on. The burring rumble of the engine seemed to fill the cabin.

Realisation trickled through.

Ann's eyes dilated. Her face changed from anger to terror, colour draining away, as she stared at Roy's body. A knuckle came up to her mouth. The implications hit her one by one; slowly, then in a rush. After a long moment she swung wildly round in her seat, staring at the far reaches of the empty horizon, panic welling up in her throat.

Then, because she'd seen Roy using it, she snatched the microphone from his lap and pressed it against her mouth.

She screamed.

48

4

Jules Martin belched loudly, the sound of it lost under the blare of the Chipmunk's engine. He wiped a hand over his face, fumbled with the boom-mike, then said abruptly, "D'you mind if we go back, Tony?"

In the rear cockpit, Paynton was instantly sympathetic. Like most flying instructors, he'd made his own acquaintance with airsickness on more than one occasion.

"Certainly, Jules. Soon as you like. You have control. Turn to a heading of – er – zero-two-zero, and we'll be home in ten minutes. We're not far away from Tees-side."

Martin nodded. The Chipmunk made little uneasy lurching movements as he took over again. The motion was far more sickening than the smooth flow of Paynton's flying, but the first thing an instructor always does if a student feels ill is to make him fly the aeroplane; it gives him something else to do apart from sit there waiting to puke.

Paynton said, "Do you want the canopy open, Jules? We can have it back to the first notch since we're just going to fly steadily now."

Martin swallowed and mumbled, "No . . . er, yes. P-please." The hollow feeling in his guts had become a nasty churning sensation. His face was burning while his feet were freezing; the blattering of the engine seemed to be gripping him round the throat so that he couldn't breathe properly.

Paynton reached up and forward, twisted a yellow handle on the inside of the canopy roof, and hauled backwards.

49

Slowly – since the airflow curls round a Chipmunk canopy and tends to hold it shut – the whole Perspex glasshouse over the two cockpits slid backwards, creating a gap between itself and the fixed windscreen. The noise of the airflow deepened immediately to a booming open roar, and the cockpit became colder than ever. Paynton shivered, and stopped hauling when the canopy was three inches open.

"That better, me old mate?"

"Uh...er...yes. Yes." Martin was past thinking about whether it was better or not. Cowed by the naked blast of the gale and the thunder of the engine, he just wanted to get down. He blinked at the rolling fieldscape below, coldly drab in the winter sun, and wondered blearily where they were and how far it was to the airfield.

Paynton lolled in the back, slackening his shoulder straps and pulling at his collar again. Instinctively his eyes swept round the sky, looking for other aircraft. There was nothing there; nothing but freezing bright blue, streaked with occasional fifty-mile brush-strokes of sparse high cirrus. He watched the cirrus, and thought about his car again. Spitting and hesitation under acceleration ought to be carburation – but it wasn't, because he'd already had the twin SUs apart and checked them. So maybe plugs ... ?

In the front, Martin belched again. The taste of vomit welled up in his throat. His stomach seemed to be moving, bubbling ...

"C'n you take her please, Tony?"

Paynton stopped thinking about spark plugs and took the controls.

"Okay, I've got it. Not feeling so good, Jules?"

The head in front of him waggled miserably, then scrunched down as Martin bent forward and fumbled in the map pocket for a sick-bag. Paynton leaned left and then right, looking down. A railway line was sliding under the left wing, the town of Darlington was about five miles ahead and slightly to the left, and a river – the River Tees – meandered through the fields directly underneath them, 4,000 feet below. That made the aerodrome spang under the nose and about four miles away . . .

"Nearly home now, Jules. Just two or three minutes. Will you switch the radio back to 118.85, please?"

Martin's stomach heaved, pushing bile into his throat. He spat into his sick-bag, waiting in the dreadful limbo when you know you're going to spew but your insides haven't quite finished gathering themselves up.

Paynton reduced power to 1,600 r.p.m. and tilted the nose down. The Chipmunk started to lose height. He tapped the boom-mike closer to his lips and said loudly, "Hey, Jules! Change that frequency back to 118.85, will you?"

Martin stretched forward and reached for the radio. His hand was shaking. He got hold of the wrong knob first, the decimal one, and twisted it from .85 to .00. Three clicks brought it back to .85. He shifted his fingers to the left knob, the main frequency selector, and turned it quickly and clumsily. Too far. The little white figures in the frequency window flicked from 116.85 right through to 129.85. As they went, there was a momentary screeching in Martin's headphones. He winced and turned the knob back again quickly. 118.85 came up obediently, and he sat back with a grunt of relief.

"Tha's it," he said, slurring. "118.85."

Paynton was frowning. That split-second screech had been an odd sort of sound, somehow unlike carrier-wave or the usual sort of interference. It wasn't the time to start mucking around with the radio – not with Jules about to bring his guts up – but all the same, it *had* sounded strange . . .

"Hey, Jules," he said suddenly. "Just flip back to that frequency you hit a moment ago, will you?"

Martin groaned. He could feel sweat on his hot face, and his stomach seemed to be splashing up into his chest. It was going to be any second now . . .

"Jules!" Paynton's voice was spaced-out and clear, with a hard edge to it. "Will you run back over those frequencies, please?"

Slowly, Martin leaned forward again and twisted the knob. The movement made his head swim. The frequency figures

51

clicked round to 119.85, 120.85, and on.

At 126.85 the noise came back, piercingly loud. For a few seconds it sounded like nothing but feedback screech – and then, suddenly, it resolved into a woman's voice, screaming and almost incoherent.

"Jesus GOD ... please ANSWER! He's DEAD! Somebody ... anybody ... HELP me ... !"

* * *

Martin vomited.

Some of it went in the sick-bag, but most of it spattered into his lap and up the sleeve of his windcheater as he pushed the headset mike away from his mouth just in time. The spasms squeezed through his whole body, filling his head with a huge dull roaring and leaving him clawing for breath in between the retching.

Paynton didn't even notice. For endless seconds he just sat, frozen with shock, while the blood-curdling shrieking in his earphones went on and on without break or pause. The raw panic in the woman's voice seemed to paralyse his brain and turn his muscles to water. Dimly in the background he knew he ought to be doing something, but he couldn't think what.

"God, oh GOD! Won't someone ANSWER! PLEASE help me ..."

Paynton snapped back to life in a rush.

Reaching up to the yellow handle, he slammed the canopy shut. The hollow roar of the gale ceased abruptly, and the cockpit was suddenly filled with the acrid tang of Martin's puke. Paynton ignored it, forcing himself to think. After a moment he opened the throttle to full power, pulled the nose up towards the cold blue sky, and bent the Chipmunk into a gentle climbing turn. As constructive ideas went it wasn't much, but it was something: the first essential was not to lose the screaming transmission, and more altitude meant more radio range.

The Chipmunk blared upwards in a slow spiral. The voice

went on, babbling and crying in non-stop hysteria. Paynton re-trimmed for the climb and wondered what to do next.

The problem was horrible in its simplicity. From the distorted words he could pick out among the screams and sobs it was fairly obvious that the woman was alone in an aeroplane somewhere with the pilot passed out or dead, but on the face of it there seemed to be nothing, absolutely nothing, that he could do about it. For the moment, at least, he couldn't even talk back to her. An aircraft radio is so designed that it cannot transmit and receive simultaneously; pressing the transmit button automatically cuts out the receiver. So until she stopped screaming and let go of her transmit switch, she'd had it: Paynton couldn't get through even if he yelled his lungs out.

Not that it would make any difference one way or the other, he thought. Because whatever happened, the woman was going to die within the next few minutes.

The reason for this was as basic as the radio problem: it was simply that no aeroplane, left to its own devices, will continue to fly straight and level for very long. The oft-quoted term "she flies hands off" is, as every airman knows, completely untrue. What actually happens if a pilot takes his hands and feet off the controls is that after a short while the aircraft will adopt a banked attitude, one way or the other, and this bank will cause a turn. The turn itself will then create further bank in a self-perpetuating process, until the machine ends up in a steeply-banked, steeply-descending spiral dive. How long this takes to happen depends on the individual aeroplane and the smoothness of the air at the time, but even on the calmest day and with a perfectly trimmed aircraft, you would expect a spiral dive to develop within five minutes of letting go of everything: on a rough day, the first wing-drop would start the chain reaction almost immediately. The phenomenon is not a problem to a pilot, since preventing a spiral dive while you're flying is as instinctive as steering a straight line in a car – but the chances of a non-pilot, someone who didn't have the faintest idea about flying, stumbling on the correct recovery action from a spiral

53

before the aircraft hit the ground were so small they just didn't exist.

And the one thing that was clear about the voice in Paynton's earphones was that this woman didn't have the faintest idea about flying.

So he waited for her to die.

The Chipmunk snarled on, winding slowly round and up towards the wispy cirrus, steady and sure in his hands. The canopy-struts dappled moving shadows across his face. Passing 5,000 feet Martin vomited again, shaking his head from side to side in his helplessness.

The voice went on, pleading now, the words blurring into wild sobbing.

Paynton was sweating in the freezing cockpit. Large beads of perspiration rolled down the sides of his face and sponged into the earpieces of his headset. Listening to the woman crying was somehow like an intrusion; nobody had the right to listen to another human being panicking through the last seconds of their life before they went in. He wanted to yell at Jules to switch frequencies again, so he wouldn't have to hear the final terrible screams and the aching silence that would follow . . .

He kept his mouth shut. For some reason it didn't seem right to let the woman die alone, either. He pinched the bridge of his nose and waited, desperately trying to think of something he could try.

Maybe she was on autopilot.

The thought came with sudden clarity, halting his racing brain in its tracks. Cursing himself for not thinking of it before, he examined the possibility. It could well be right, at that: he'd been listening to her now for – what would it be? – say, four minutes. There must have been a time-lag before that, and yet here she was, still in the air. Nor was there anything in her sobbing which suggested any change in her flight regime. *And* it was reasonable to suppose that any pilot who thought he might be going to pass out would switch in the autopilot if he had one . . .

Christ.

He drew in a deep breath, finding he was shaking with tension. She certainly *could* be on some kind of autopilot. And that made a difference. In that case something might be done. He ought to switch back to Tees-side, get out a Mayday call . . .

The crying in his headphones suddenly stopped.

5

TERROR, COMPLETE AND undiluted terror, is a violent physical force. The nearest parallel in mechanical terms is of a supercharger suddenly cutting in on a cruising engine : the mental reaction to fear triggers the injection of adrenalin into the bloodstream, galvanising both mind and body to superhuman efforts. If these efforts can be channelled into action to tackle or escape from the cause of the fear, well and good; but if they cannot, if the reaction has to be contained because there *is* no escape, then terror feeds on itself and multiplies, pushing the brain towards unreasoning panic.

For Ann Moore, suddenly alone in the Arrow's softly roaring cockpit with its thousand alien controls, the only outlet for terror was the microphone; the primeval need of a person in deep fright to communicate with another human being.

When nobody answered, panic grew like a spreading fire.

How long she screamed and sobbed she had no way of knowing: it was actually about five minutes, but to her it could have been five seconds or five hours. In between screaming she slapped Bazzard's face hysterically; slapped again and again, struggling against her seat belt, stinging hands leaving faint marks of blotchy red on the growing pallor of his face. She pinched the lobes of his ears with her nails and shouted, half at him and half into the microphone, imploring him to wake up.

Bazzard sat unheeding. Eyes closed, head stiffly upright.

The Arrow droned on smoothly, the autopilot holding it rock-steady in the calm winter sky.

In the end, Ann crumpled up. Crying wildly, she buried her face in her clenched fists, trying to shut out the sight of the cockpit and the terrifying emptiness all around. No one was listening, no one was going to do anything . . .

The microphone slipped down, clunking softly on to the carpeted floor.

Immediately, the speaker in the cabin roof crackled and broke into slow, deliberate speech.

*   *   *

"AIRCRAFT IN TROUBLE. DO NOT DO ANYTHING, AND DO *NOT* ATTEMPT TO REPLY TO ME YET. I REPEAT, DO *NOT* ATTEMPT TO REPLY TO ME YET."

The voice caught Ann totally unprepared. She jerked in her seat, shock making her shriek in new fright.

Then she screamed and laughed all at once, unable to stop herself.

Her hands went to her ears to shut out the horrible sound of her own hysteria; for a long moment she heard nothing but a garble of noise. Then, slowly, the screaming began to subside. Her hands slid down to her mouth, fingers curling into fists again. Her eyes, pupils dilated with fear, stared ahead over the nose at the distant horizon and the glaring winter sun. A small part of her brain seemed to be weirdly detached, watching herself shivering all over, watching the way the tears streamed down her face. You've got to pull yourself together, she thought desperately. You're a nurse; you're supposed to be cool, sensible, reasoning . . .

The voice started speaking over the radio again. She took a long, ragged breath. She *must* get hold of herself. *Must* listen and take it in . . .

"Aircraft in trouble, I say again." The words were clearly pronounced, matter-of-fact. "Do *not* attempt to reply to me until I tell you. Up to now you have been holding your micro-phone button down all the time. When you do that, you cannot hear me talking to you. Now in a moment, but not until I tell you, I want you to speak to me again. But this time, just press the microphone button, say 'yes', and then release it again. I say again: press the transmit button, say 'yes' *and then release it again,* so that I can talk some more. If you understand that, say 'yes' now; if you do not, then do not say anything, and I will explain it again."

For God's sake, where was the microphone?

Ann looked wildly round the cockpit, panting. The forest of dials and switches and levers seemed to mock at her helplessness, hiding the black matchbox-sized cube amongst them. She made a small mewing sound of terror, which was swallowed up by the steady dirge of the engine. If she didn't find it the voice would go away. She'd had it just now; it'd been hooked under the bulge where the coloured levers were . . .

Then she saw the curly black lead it was connected to. Her eyes followed it down to the floor – and there it was. Just under the front of the seat.

The only thing was, she couldn't reach it. The lap-and-diagonal seat belt prevented her leaning far enough forwards.

Sobbing, she fumbled desperately with the harness buckle. It was like a car safety belt clip. In normal times she would have undone it without a thought, but now, nothing she did would persuade it to release. The moment seemed to stretch on into eternity. She was going to be too late, the man would go away . . .

Then a grain of reason returned. She grabbed the lead, hanging from the throttle pedestal, and pulled it up like someone paying in a rope. A second later she had the microphone in her hands. She snatched it up to her lips and squeezed the button with all her strength.

"Yes. *Yes!*" It came out in a muted, terrified croak. She swallowed and screamed "*YES!*" as loudly as she could.

It was several seconds before she remembered to let the button go.

". . . that, I'll say it again. Tell me calmly and clearly what has happened, without speaking for too long, and remember to release the microphone button when you stop talking. Tell me now."

Ann took a deep breath, feeling her whole body shuddering. She *must* calm down. However crazy, however incredible it was to be talking to a disembodied voice speaking in the cockpit out of thin air, she *had* to calm down. Had to be sensible, had to answer . . .

"I'm . . . in a plane. Roy's – the pilot's – passed out." The words sounded hollow and strange; disconnected, as if somebody else a long way away was saying them. She gripped the microphone tighter and tried again. "I'm in a plane with my . . . my boy friend – " the words 'boy friend' sounded silly, somehow " – and he's p-passed out. He passed out suddenly, and I can't make him wake up. I don't . . . don't know . . ."

She heard the disconnected voice rising towards panic, and stopped herself. It was another long moment before she took her thumb off the transmit button.

This time, the man seemed to have been waiting for her.

"All right, miss. Just relax, and we'll get this sorted out. Now first of all, do you happen to know if the aeroplane's flying on autopilot? I say again; do you know if it is flying on autopilot?"

For a moment, Ann blinked – and then the fear came welling up in her throat with renewed force as the implication sank in. What the man meant was that if the plane *wasn't* on autopilot it could fall out of control at any moment: go tumbling down and down, unstoppable, taking both of them with it . . .

She stared round the sky, heart pounding. The vast blue void and the distant horizon were dead steady. The little room she was trapped in seemed completely motionless, roaring quietly as it hung in space, not going anywhere or doing anything.

And it *was* on autopilot.

The memory came suddenly. Of course it was. There'd been all that talk about it. Roy had switched it on, she'd watched the steering wheels, and then they'd held hands.

Of course it was.

She felt the trickle of new tears on her face. Bending her head down, she screwed the palm of her left hand into each eye in turn, pressing hard enough to hurt. She *had* to stop being stupid ...

"Come on now, miss." There was a trace of urgency in the voice this time. "Tell me if you know whether your aeroplane's on autopilot, please. I need to know that now."

Ann raised the microphone and said hoarsely, "Yes." She cleared her throat. "Yes, it is. He put it on before ... before it happened."

"Ah. Good." Paynton's relief was lost over the miles in the distant hiss of the Chipmunk's transmitter. "That gives us plenty of time, then. So first of all I want you to sit back and relax, get a grip on yourself, and just listen. Tell me when you're ready to listen. Take you're time about it: I'll still be here."

The voice was unruffled and masterful: Paynton was a good instructor. After a moment Ann squeezed her eyes shut and leaned back, gripping the sides of her seat, trying to still her fluttering muscles. Just pretend it's a hospital emergency, she thought lightheadedly; calm down and think sensibly, as if it were a normal hospital emergency. Or pretend that it isn't really happening at all, that it's just a nightmare. Anything – only you *must* get a grip on yourself ...

The Arrow flew on. The sunshine glaring into the cockpit was warm on her face.

After a time, she opened her eyes. The sight of the bright endless sky outside the windows made her stomach cringe again. She stared at the radio panel directly in front of her, and raised the microphone. It quivered in her hand.

"I'm ... all right, now."

"That's good." The slow disembodied voice seemed to fill the cabin. It had a matter-of-fact Midlands accent, which was somehow steadying. "Now, my name's Tony Paynton. I'm a flying instructor, and I'm in the air at the moment over Tees-side. I'm going to help you, and I want to start off by asking you some questions. Okay?"

The speaker went silent. Ann pressed the microphone

button and said, "Yes."

"Fine. Well, first of all you'd better tell me your name; I can't just call you 'oy, you', or you'll guess how bad my manners are. And when you speak, keep your microphone about half an inch away from your mouth; I think you might be holding it a bit too close at the moment, which distorts the words. So tell me your name now."

Ann moved the microphone slightly and said, "Moore. Ann Moore."

"Good, that's better. You're coming over clear as a bell now, Ann. So first off, let's just make sure I've got everything straight. You're in an aeroplane, on autopilot, and the pilot has passed out. He's unconscious. I don't want any details yet, but is that right?"

Ann looked at Bazzard's still figure beside her. His face was deathly white and immobile, lips slightly parted. Under his brown tweed jacket his shirt-front moved in slow, irregular jerks as he breathed. She had a sudden feeling of unreality. This *couldn't* be happening: all she had to do was go back five or ten minutes in time, to when everything was all right. Cancel it out, start again . . .

She wrenched her eyes back to the radios, feeling herself trembling. It *was* happening. Had happened. She *must* concentrate, *must* think only about answering the questions . . .

She swallowed stickily, and pressed the microphone switch.

"Yes. Yes . . . that's right."

"Okay. I see." The voice paused for a moment, then went on. "All right, then. Now the next thing is, have you been talking to anyone else at all? Or was I the first person to answer you?"

"You were . . ." Ann swallowed again. "You were the only one."

"Right. And next, have you tried to wake your pilot at all? Slapping his face, or anything like that?"

"Yes. I did slap his face." Ann felt more tears starting down her cheeks. She wiped at them with her left hand.

"I see. And I suppose it didn't achieve anything?"

"No." A sob welled up in her throat in spite of herself.

61

"N-nothing. No r-reaction." She released the transmit button.

"All right, Ann. Don't worry about it." In spite of the radio static the voice was somehow soothing, reassuring. "Forget that for the moment; we'll come back to it later on when we've got a doctor lined up on the ground. Now, I've got one or two questions about the aeroplane you're in and where you are. Okay?"

Ann took a deep, shuddering breath. "Yes. Go on."

"Right. First, do you know what kind of aeroplane it is?"

She bit her bottom lip, trying to think. Roy *had* said what it was. When they'd first got in, before they'd started moving on the ground . . .

But it was gone. She couldn't remember it.

"I don't know. He – Roy – said, but I don't remember." She heard her voice rising again, and tried to control it. "It . . . um . . . the wheels go up and down, I remember that, if that's any help . . ." She squeezed her eyes shut, fighting the tears that were starting in earnest again. "I don't know . . . I . . . mean . . . I've never been in a small plane before . . ." She tailed off, hopelessly.

"Aye, I'd rather got that impression." The voice was deliberately droll and unconcerned, reminding Ann suddenly and ridiculously of the Senior Medical Registrar at the hospital. "It doesn't matter, though, because we can easily find that out from somewhere else. What you *can* tell me though, I expect, is the pilot's name."

"Bazzard." Ann rubbed her eyes with the knuckles of her left hand. "R-Roy Bazzard."

"Would that be B-A-double-Z-A-R-D?"

"Yes."

"Fine. And now, would you tell me where you took off from, and where you're going to?"

"We went from Newcastle. We were going to . . . er, Denham. Near London."

"Newcastle to Denham. Good. Do you have any idea what time you took off from Newcastle? How long ago it was?"

Ann pushed her fingers into her hair, trying to cast her mind back. She hadn't noticed the time before they left, and like most nurses she didn't wear a wrist watch. The take-off seemed like hours ago now, although logic said that it couldn't really be anything like that long. After all, they'd only just finished climbing up when it ... when it happened.

She cleared her throat and said into the microphone: "I don't know. It was ... um ... after lunchtime. About ... about half an hour ago, or less, I suppose. I d-don't know."

"All right, not to worry. Now can you tell me where the sun is in relation to you? I'll say that again: where the sun is, in relation to you? It may sound silly, but it'll tell me which way you're heading, you see."

The sun ... ?

Reluctantly, she raised her eyes to the windscreen. The huge emptiness of the sky and the vast distance of the horizon brought on a new rush of fear, like sudden cold water in her stomach. She looked back in at the instrument panel again, feeling herself shivering all over.

"It's to the r-right. Ahead and a bit to the right."

"Good. And now, lastly, it'll help if you can tell me whether your aeroplane has one engine or two. In other words whether it's got two propellers, one on each wing, or just one on the nose, in front of you. Do you happen to have noticed that, Ann?"

"Um ... yes. J-just one, on the nose. Roy said it was s-single engine."

"Ah, that's fine. You've done very well, Ann." The voice hesitated, then carried on. "Now, I'm going to have to leave you for a moment while I talk to the people on the ground. I'll be back to you in a minute or two, so just sit tight and don't touch anything. Okay?"

Ann nodded, shutting her eyes again. The idea of touching anything in the cockpit filled her with horror. She didn't even dare look out of the windows ...

"Okay, Ann?"

She lifted the microphone and said dully, "Yes. Okay."

"Good. All right then, I'll leave you now, and be with you again in a minute. You just relax."

Ann nodded for the second time. With the voice gone, the

steady burr of the engine seemed to close in, pressing on her ears. She suddenly felt terribly alone. She clenched her teeth to stop them chattering, and gripped the microphone tightly in her right hand, as if it were something infinitely precious.

The Arrow roared on, serene and steady.

*   *   *

"Jules!"

In the front seat of the Chipmunk, Martin didn't respond. He'd stopped listening to the voices in his earphones some time ago; they'd just become part of the background to an interminable sick nightmare.

"Jules! Come on! Switch the radio to 118.85!"

This time, the sound of his own name penetrated. He coughed, swallowed on the acid taste of bile, and pulled the headset-mike down to his mouth.

"Uh . . . wha'?"

"SWITCH THE FUCKING FREQUENCY TO 118.85, FOR CHRIST'S SAKE!"

"Oh." Martin belched, then leaned forward laboriously and twisted the main frequency knob. He didn't know what Paynton was doing, and felt too ill to care. He was sick and feeling sicker, worsened by the reek of his own vomit in the cockpit, his body swept by alternate waves of hot and cold. All he wanted was to get to his feet on the good earth and never, never get into an aeroplane ever again.

Paynton, on the other hand, was just cold. Cold and worried and beginning to feel the need to urinate. Holding the Chipmunk in its blaring upwards spiral, he tried to assemble the important factors logically in his mind before he started talking to Tees-side Approach. Pilot's name . . . point of departure . . . single with retractable gear heading more or less south according to the sun-position . . . on autopilot . . .

He fumbled with his 1:500,000 air map for a moment, holding it awkwardly in frozen fingers. Then he screwed his head from side to side, searching the empty sky. There was no sign of anything, which was about what he'd expected:

an aircraft out of Newcastle half an hour ago and heading south at, say, 150 m.p.h. should be *somewhere* in this area – but *somewhere* covered an awful lot of sky. And even if by some freak of chance he did see it, there was nothing he could do about it; whatever the runway was, if it had a retractable undercarriage and an autopilot it was certainly something a damn sight faster than any Chipmunk.

And then there was the other problem, too.

Fuel.

Because he'd wanted the Chipmunk light for Martin's spinning exercise, Paynton had taken off fifty-five minutes ago with considerably less than full tanks. Now, the port fuel gauge read just under two gallons while the starboard one indicated between 0 and two – and even that wouldn't be accurate, since Chipmunk gauges are somewhat optimistic when the aircraft is climbing. The more likely figure was a total of two gallons or a fraction more in both tanks. And a Chipmunk burns six gallons of 100 octane an hour.

Paynton pinched the bridge of his nose. After a moment, he pulled the throttle back from fully open to two-thirds open, and leaned off the mixture. The flat thunder of the engine muted slightly, and the rate-of-climb sank from 500 feet a minute to 200. He frowned at the instrument panel, pursing his lips. Then he pressed the transmit button on top of his control stick.

"Mayday, Mayday, Mayday," he said calmly. "Tees-side from Golf-Bravo-Charlie-Yankee-Lima, d'you read?"

The radio crackled, hesitated, and then replied.

6

Two and a half miles north of Heathrow Airport, in a road called Porters Way, West Drayton, is a large concrete and glass building constructed on the graceless lines of most modern industrial architecture. At first glance it looks like any one of a thousand office blocks in and around the City of London: the only obvious departures from the normal are the police guardhouse on the gate and the soaring tower of radar dishes alongside. There is nothing else to indicate that the staff of this ugly block are the guardians of most of the airspace over England.

The building is known as the London Air Traffic Control Centre – abbreviated to LATCC and usually referred to as "Latsie" by everyone concerned in aviation – and the use of the word "London" in the title is misleading, considering the range of the Centre's operations. For here, under one roof, practically every inch of the country's Airways network is monitored and controlled minute by minute, twenty-four hours a day. Radar pictures and radio links are "piped in" from fifty or sixty ground stations all over the country, and over a hundred licensed Air Traffic Controllers are on duty at all times. Thus an aircraft flying on, for example, Airway Amber One between Prestwick and Manchester will be talking to a controller sitting in the LATCC building at West Drayton. This system means that as an airway's flight progresses through different radar areas, the aeroplane is "handed off" through a number of controllers sitting within yards of

66

each other instead of hundreds of miles apart. The only time a pilot will speak to a controller who is actually *at* the place he is calling is when he is in contact with local facilities such as an airport Approach Tower or sub-centre or a Military Air Traffic Zone.

LATCC's responsibilities, moreover, do not end with en-route Airways' control.

Two corridors away from the main Centre Control Room with its eighty-odd radar screens is another, much smaller room; dim-lit, cluttered with sophisticated equipment, and frequently fuggy with cigarette smoke in spite of the air conditioning. This room is known throughout aviation circles simply as "D and D".

D and D stands for Distress and Diversion, and the correct name for this room is the Emergency Cell.

The rôle of D and D is as the title suggests: to provide and co-ordinate action in the event of an airborne emergency. The service is run by the RAF (as opposed to most of the rest of the Centre, which is operated by the Civil Aviation Authority) but its function is by no means restricted to military aircraft alone. Any aeroplane in any kind of trouble in the skies of England may be assisted by D and D – and at times this assistance can be mighty, since the drawing-room sized Emergency Cell has at its immediate call every facility of every aerodrome, military or civil, throughout the land. The four-man watch – two officer-controllers and two NCO assistants – probably have more practical power than any other individuals in the entire Air Traffic Control Service.

On this Saturday afternoon, it looked as though that power might come in useful.

The call from the Chief Controller at Tees-side Airport was taken by Flight Lieutenant John Peterson, the number-one D and D controller on duty. As the Yorkshire voice talked in his headphones, Peterson made brief notes in his log: time and nature of emergency. Elsewhere in the LATCC building tape recorders were turning, automatically recording every word of the conversation for dusty posterity.

When the man had finished, Peterson sat silent for a

67

moment. A tall, wiry, nervous-energy type, his natural impulse in any emergency was to jump straight in and *do* something. But his years of military flying, before this present ground-borne tour of duty, had taught him to rein himself in: taught him that whenever there was even a little time to spare in an aircraft incident, it was invariably worth using that time to think things over before you acted. And that was especially so when the emergency was an oddball, like this one; out of the usual run of engine failures, weather diversions, and low-time private fliers who were just plain lost.

He frowned at the foot-round radar screen on the console in front of him for nearly half a minute, nibbling unconsciously at a fingernail while he examined the problem. At the end of that time, he swung round suddenly in his chair.

"Corporal!"

His corporal assistant was returning from the gents. He said calmly, "Sir?"

"Listen." Peterson spat out a small rind of fingernail. "We've got a civilian instructor in a Chipmunk orbiting over Teesside, who's picked up a transmission from a woman on 126.85. This woman says she's in an aeroplane with the pilot passed out or died or something. She doesn't know anything about the kite except that it's a single engine retract, on autopilot, heading more or less into the sun, and it took off from Newcastle bound for Denham about half an hour ago. The Chipmunk pilot's talking to her again now, and he's going to call Tees-side back in five minutes."

The corporal said quietly, "Jesus!"

"Right. Jesus. Now one thing I want to know is, what ground stations have 126.85? See if you can find that out bloody quick, will you?"

The corporal said, "Sir" again, and crossed the floor in three paces to the shelves of reference books at the back of the room.

Peterson started on another fingernail. Finding out who had the 126.85 frequency was important – ground radio installations cannot switch frequencies like aircraft receivers, which meant that his only chance of talking to the woman directly was if some station within her range already had the frequency – but it wasn't by any means the only important factor. Far more urgent than that, for example, was the two-fold problem of locating the runaway aircraft and getting a doctor organised to advise on bringing the pilot round. That was the first priority.

He leaned forward, flicked a switch to connect his headset with the Mediator telephone, and dialled the code for Woolsington control tower, Newcastle. The Mediator lines are a private telephone network between air traffic controllers: they are not subject to the normal vagaries of the Subscriber Trunk Dialling system, and they have the further advantage of linking you directly to the person you want without passing through the thrombosis of destination switchboards and extensions. Five seconds after he'd finished dialling, Peterson heard the telephone picked up at the other end. A northern accent said briefly, "Newcastle, Woolsington; go ahead."

"D and D, Drayton here." Peterson visualised the Newcastle controller snapping to sudden alertness: like most men engaged in the emergency services he still got a tiny, almost guilty, kick out of people's reactions to his title. "We have an emergency on an aircraft outbound from you for Denham, took off from Newcastle probably about half an hour ago. Pilot's name Bazzard; Bravo-Alpha-Zulu-Zulu-Alpha-Romeo-Delta. That's all we know about it at the moment, so I want aircraft type, callsign, the owner or operator's name and phone numbers, anything else you can give me. The pilot seems to have passed out, and there's a woman on board screaming for help."

"Christ!" The voice in Peterson's ears sounded shaken. "Stand by, D and D. I'll check."

Peterson said, "Thanks," and then waited, tapping his pencil against his teeth. He heard distant sounds of the receiver being put down and the controller shouting into an extension for someone to look in the booking-out book, the legally-required log which is kept at all British control towers to record details of every landing-away flight.

The man was back in under a minute.

"Got it, Drayton. Bazzard's flying a Piper Cherokee Arrow, Golf Alpha Yankee Whisky Tango, VFR to Denham. He took off at – " a short pause " – 1423 hours."

Peterson wrote fast on his notepad, then said, "Roger. D'you know who owns the aircraft?"

"I think it's one of the Tyne Flyin' Club's planes. They're on Newcastle 72876. Would you like me to call 'em?"

"No, I'll do it. You sure it's theirs?"

"Ninety per cent. I'll check it out and call you back if it isn't."

"Thanks. Now, do you have 126.85 up there at all? Or if you haven't, do you know anyone else who has? Apparently that's what the woman's transmitting on."

"Negative. Nearest we've got's our Approach, 126.35. Next nearest'd probably be one of Tees-side's, I should think. They've got some .85s, at any rate: their Approach's 118.85, an' they've got – er – Radar on 128.85."

"Okay. Much obliged." Peterson started reaching for the Mediator switch, then stopped with his hand in mid-air. "One last thing: d'you happen to know what an Arrow cruises at?"

"Er ... 'bout 130 knots, I think. 130 or 140."

"Right. Thanks again. Just call me back if that owner's anyone else."

"Roger. Good luck with it."

Peterson acknowledged, broke the connection, and glanced at the clock on the wall. The time was 1441, which meant that Cherokee Arrow G-AYWT had now been airborne for just about eighteen minutes. Less than the woman had said, but that was hardly surprising: it probably felt like eighteen years to her. He chewed the end of his pencil for a moment, calculating. Knock off a bit for time-to-climb, and reckon on an average of 115 knots: so 115 knots for eighteen minutes ...

Call it thirty-five miles. Between thirty-five and forty.

He reached forward and gripped the butt of a swivelling

device like a miniature machine-gun mounted on the top edge of his radar console. Squeezing the trigger produced a small cross of light on a sheet of milky-white glass which occupied most of one wall ten feet in front of him. Painted on the glass was a simple outline map of England, showing nothing but the shape of the coastline, the position of various aerodromes, and a few major control zones, towns, and radar stations. Flexing his wrist, he traversed the light-cross along and up to Newcastle. Then, slowly, he brought it down again, almost due south, for a distance equating to roughly forty miles.

The cross ended up almost abeam the small bight of the Tees estuary, about fifteen miles north of the RAF Master Airfield of Leeming, in the North Riding of Yorkshire.

Well, that was a start, anyway.

Peterson leaned back, chewing his pencil again. If he was right, if the runaway *was* somewhere around there, then the news was both good and bad. The good part was that the Arrow should already be painting a trace at least on Leeming's radar screens, and quite possibly Tees-side's as well . . .

And the bad part was that that in itself might not be much help.

The reason for this was that the whole of the North Yorkshire/Durham area consists entirely of uncontrolled airspace, particularly above 3,000 feet, and aeroplanes flying in uncontrolled airspace, as opposed to within Control Zones of Airways, are not obliged to be in radio contact with any ground authority at all. So, whilst they may be showing up on one or more radar pictures – since Britain is just about totally blanketed by various radars of one form or another – they remain under the heading of "unknown" traffic because they are not identified: they are merely blips on a screen, with no callsigns, no intentions, and no meaning. On a fine day like this the radar at a station such as Leeming, with a large coverage of uncontrolled airspace, might well be picking up anything between three and thirty such unidentified traces at any given time. And Arrow Whisky Tango could be any one of them.

The known speed and approximate heading would be a help, of course – or at least, it would be if the runaway stayed on its present heading, which was by no means guaranteed without knowing what sort of autopilot it had and how it had been set up – but even so, positive identification could only be achieved by a process of elimination and finally an interception by another aircraft, all of which was very obviously going to take time. And even *that* assumed that the bloody thing was high enough to be accurately tracked by radar in the first place . . .

Still worrying a fingernail, Peterson reached out to the console with his free hand. He groped around for several seconds before he remembered that the packet of Marlboro and the lighter weren't there any more: his wife was making him give up smoking. He grunted in frustration, and dug for the tube of Polo mints in his trouser pocket. He was going to look like a fucking Polo soon . . .

He popped one in his mouth, crunched it up, and thought briefly about what they were going to do when they *had* found Whisky Tango. If the pilot was dead or otherwise unrevivable, there would obviously have to be some sort of attempt made to talk the woman through flying and landing the aeroplane. And that raised the question of how the hell to do it.

As a pilot himself, on a ground-duty tour now after five years on Argosys with Transport Command, he had no illusions about the chances of successfully talking down a non-pilot from the ground. That idea was strictly for comic books and film producers, who carefully avoided any close contact with the actual problems. In real life, it simply couldn't be done. If the person in the aircraft knew enough to circle over you so you could sit underneath and watch the results of your instructions it *might* just work – but if she was flying in a straight line a couple of hundred miles away then there wouldn't be a chance in hell, period. Telling her to pull back a little on the stick might produce a two-degree nose up pitch-change or it might send her screaming up into a loop, and sitting in front of your radar screen you'd have no way of knowing which. So that seemed to leave an interception by another aircraft as just about the only possibility: get the talk-down pilot sitting in formation with her where he could follow her progress second by second.

Peterson filed that thought away to be tackled as the next priority. The first thing was still to get the search under way and a doctor available, and time was passing. He swallowed the last grains of peppermint and looked up expectantly as the corporal reappeared at his elbow.

"I can't find anyone with 126.85, sir." The man sounded apologetic, as if he felt personally responsible. "It seems to be a spare frequency, unless some company's got it privately."

Peterson said, "Fuck it!" very softly. Then he looked down at his pad, where he'd written *New 126.35* and *Tee 118.85 & 128.85*. The notations were ringed with swirls and curlicues, where he'd doodled unconsciously while the Newcastle controller had been talking.

"You know what could have happened," he said slowly. His finger tapped on the scrawled page. "Our pilot could've been switching from Newcastle to Tees-side when he went out. He'd have been on 126.35, so if he'd switched the decimals first, and then passed out, he'd have ended up on his 126.85. See what I mean?"

The corporal sucked his teeth, looking doubtful. "He'd have to have passed out bloody quick for that to've happened, sir."

"That's true." Peterson shrugged. "But on the other hand, why else would he be on 126.85? I can't see him deliberately switching to just about the only unused frequency in the bloody book just for the sole purpose of making it impossible for us to talk to him, can you?"

The corporal said stolidly, "No, sir."

"No. Still..." Peterson brought the flat of his hand down on the pad and sat forward abruptly in his chair. "No use thinking about the why of it: if no one can get her to change frequencies it means we're stuck with relaying through other aircraft, and that's that. So now then: I want you to get me the Tyne Flying Club, Newcastle 72876. Get the Chief

73

Instructor – full priority, haul him down out of the air if necessary – and hold him until I can speak to him. Right?"

"Sir. Newcastle 72876."

"Right. Then after that, find out the availability of any service aircraft with VHF radio at Lee – er, no, not Leeming, I'll talk to them – at Dishforth, Linton, Church Fenton, Scampton and Cranwell. Then get Leeds-Bradford Approach on the Mediator."

"Yes, sir." The corporal looked slightly stunned. He finished noting things down, snatched a headset over his ears, and reached for the telephone switches.

Peterson glanced down at the small panel of buttons on his console which control the direct ground-link to all RAF Master Aerodromes. His finger hovered for a second and then stabbed the one marked LMG, for Leeming.

*   *   *

The Approach Control Room at RAF Leeming, thirty-five miles north of Leeds, is a quiet place on a Saturday afternoon. With British service flying cut back to a minimum over the weekends – presumably on the tacit understanding that no one will attack the nation on a Saturday or Sunday – the controllers have little to do except keep a general eye on civil aircraft in the vicinity and issue occasional Military Air Traffic Zone clearances to aeroplanes en route below 3,000 feet. If the weather is poor they may have some mildly busy moments helping the odd lost pilot to find himself again; but when the visibility outside is good, the two men in the dim-lit radar room can become mightily bored indeed.

Flight Lieutenants John Myers and Mark Trowbridge, manning the Approach and Director screens respectively, were holding ennui at bay on this afternoon by an inexpert discussion on the finer points of house mortgages. It was a subject which interested them both: Trowbridge because he'd bought his first house ten years ago, before the boom, and could therefore show off his cleverness, and Myers because he'd been married five weeks and was currently wondering

74

how the hell any man could ever afford to buy any house, especially when his wife was four months pregnant.

"What you want," Trowbridge was saying, "is an endowment mortgage. That way you start paying off the capital immediately – or anyway, that's what it amounts to – so when you get your next posting and have to sell the place, you get something back. An ordinary mortgage you spend the first ten or fifteen years paying off practically nothing but interest, and nothing to show for it."

Myers nodded. He had his chair tipped back on the point of balance, with his legs up nearly to his chest and his feet on the edge of his control desk. While he spoke he kept half an eye on his radar screen, noting amost subconsciously the various traces within the sweep. There was quite a lot about this afternoon: the unexpected fine weather had brought out all the weekend birdmen.

"Yes, that's all very fine." He scratched an ear to promote thought. "But don't you only get tax relief on the *interest* part of the payments, not on the bit that's paying back capital? Surely that effectively means you're paying out more per month for a good many years?"

Trowbridge made an impatient gesture. "Oh no, you're not. An endowment's actually an insurance policy, remember, and that's claim . . ."

The red telephone on Myers desk rang.

Myers whipped his feet down. His chair crashed on to all four legs as he grabbed the receiver. He said crisply, "Leeming Approach Controller."

The voice on the other end said, "D and D Drayton, number-one controller," although it didn't need to. The red telephone was a direct ground-link to Distress and Diversion and nowhere else. Every RAF Master Station in the country has a similar red phone, and when it rings it means *move*.

Myers said, "Go ahead." He looked round his control desk, then snapped his fingers urgently. Trowbridge handed him a ballpoint pen.

The voice on the telephone started speaking rapidly. "We have a civilian light aircraft in your vicinity with the pilot dead or passed out, and a woman on board who can't fly. She's talking to the pilot of a Chipmunk overhead Tees-side Airport. This Chipmunk will be handed off to you from Tees-side in about three minutes, and he's requesting a doctor on hand to relay advice. Can you get your MO on the spot?"

Myers snapped, "Stand by," and turned to Trowbridge. "Get the MO up here double quick: there's an aircraft coming on with the pilot passed out."

Trowbridge grabbed for the internal telephone.

Myers said, "Okay Drayton, that's in hand. Is this aeroplane in my area?"

"Affirmative. Or at least, we think it is. It's a Piper Cherokee Arrow, Golf Alpha Yankee Whisky Tango, off Newcastle at 1423 for Denham. According to the woman it's on autopilot, and by her sun position it sounds as if it's on course, more or less southerly. It's cruising at around 130–140 knots, so it ought to be ten or fifteen miles north of you at this time. The woman's transmitting on 126.85, which is an unused civil frequency, so you won't be able to get a DF on her unless the Chipmunk pilot can get her to switch. But we've got to find her somehow, so in the meantime start trying to sort her out on radar. Okay?"

Myers said, "Christ!" His initial reaction was the same as Peterson's had been two minutes before: that sorting out one unidentified blip from all the others was going to be next to impossible. His radar screen was sweeping a thirty-mile radius and could be extended to fifty miles, but unless an aircraft was actually inside the Leeming Military Air Traffic Zone, a small hatbox of controlled airspace with a radius of five miles round the aerodrome and extending up to 3,000 feet, it had no reason to contact him at all. At the moment he had eight or ten traces on his screen, civilian aircraft en route or on training flights, but only one, a Piper Apache from Norwich on its way north to Carlisle, was in radio contact. The rest could be anything: he hadn't even been watching which ones were on steady courses and which ones were turning frequently, which usually indicated a training or pleasure flight.

76

The voice in the receiver said, "I know, but we've got to try. Flight Information'll be switching their known traffic in the area to you for ident, and we'll be calling the light aircraft fields to get their pilots to contact you as well. You should be able to eliminate most of them, anyway. Call me back when you've got anything, and also when you've spoken to the Chipmunk. Okay?"

Myers said, "Roger." He put the phone down as it went dead, clapped his headset on, and reached for a Chinagraph pencil to start tracing the echoes on his screen.

7

1440–1450

WHILE PAYNTON WAS setting the wheels in motion with his Mayday call to Tees-side, Ann Moore was making Bazzard as comfortable as she could.

The realisation that up to now she'd practically ignored him came to her suddenly, penetrating through her fear like a shock of cold water. Here she was, a senior nursing sister, sitting beside someone who had passed out and not doing a thing about it. It was incredible. For all she knew Roy might be dying for want of some tiny, trifling attention.

Moving slowly, her mind seeming to trudge along in a daze, she set to work. Twisting in her seat, trying to avoid looking out of the window, she pulled his tie loose and un-buttoned his shirt collar. It made no visible difference; he just went on breathing slowly and erratically, each breath pumping his chest and rasping through his slightly parted lips, soundless under the burr of the engine. She fumbled with his seat belt, her fingers shaking and clumsy, until she got it undone. Then she unfastened the top of his trousers and pulled the fly-zip down a few inches, to relieve the pres-sure on his abdomen. The thought of how he might have reacted to that had he been awake didn't even occur to her; she just did it automatically, her brain numbed. After that she tugged and struggled with the buckle end of his lap-strap until the adjuster suddenly slackened off, then re-connected the belt and pulled the limp body forwards until it rested against the diagonal shoulder strap as well as the side of the cockpit. The bent-forward position would constrict his diaphragm a little, but that couldn't be helped: with his neck rigid as it was, it was the only way of getting his head far enough forward to ensure that he wouldn't choke on his tongue.

After that she sat back, trying to think what to do next. Her mind seemed to be a great woolly blank, every thought disjointed and sort of spaced out, as if she were watching some other person on a slow-motion film. That was the effect of shock, of course. The brain recoiling, refusing to operate at its normal level ...

She squeezed her eyes shut and pressed her fists hard into her thighs. The roar of the engine had receded from her consciousness, the way steady continual sounds usually do, so that the cockpit seemed warm and quiet around her, smelling faintly of plastic and aluminium. There must be *something* else she ought to be doing ...

Examine him. That was it. Examine him, and then make sure he was warm enough.

She opened her eyes, and picked up his right hand. It was a large hand, very masculine and capable-looking, which somehow made its unconscious flaccidness all the more frightening. His skin was cool under her fingers as she felt for the pulse on the inside of the wrist. The beat was thin and erratic and seemed slow. She put a hand back in his lap after half a minute, and reached up to his face. The sight of the vast blue emptiness outside the window behind his head made her stomach go suddenly hollow again. She swallowed hard, and forced herself to concentrate on raising his eyelids, first one and then the other. The eyeballs were rolled upwards, but the bottoms of the pupils were still visible. Both were dilated.

That ought to add up to something, she thought vaguely. Neck muscles in spasm, pupil dilation, irregular pulse and respiration ...

She brought her arm down, and her elbow knocked the left hand control yoke. The Arrow dipped its right wing

79

twenty degrees, then recovered with a stiff little yank like a car running back on to a level road.

Ann jerked back in her seat, making a small animal noise of terror in her throat. The plane was tipping, going over and down . . .

Nothing happened. The cockpit wriggled for a moment and then settled, a tiny sunlit cell hanging rock-steady in the middle of nothing.

She found she was crying again, the tears running down her cheeks and tasting salt in the corners of her mouth. She gripped her face in her shaking hands and tried to stop it. Think about something else, she told herself desperately. Think about . . . Roy's symptoms. Concentrate on them, as if he'd just been admitted into hospital.

Sudden collapse; neck in spasm; irregular pulse and respiration . . .

The words squirrelled round her mind, repeating themselves in a mocking rhythm. Somewhere, dimly, they seemed to ring a bell, as if she'd heard them before. She tried to catch them, to wrench the meaning out of them, but they wouldn't stand still. It was like being drunk or only half awake; you knew that what you wanted was there but it kept sliding away, vanishing into a fog, leaving you fumbling blindly behind it.

Sudden collapse; neck in spasm; irregular pulse and respiration . . .

It was no good. She couldn't remember. She shook her head and whispered hopelessly, "Please be all right, Roy. *Please* be all right . . ."

After a long moment she brought her hands down from her face and took a deep breath. Then, taking great care not to touch the control wheels again, she twisted round as far as her seat belt would allow and reached back to where her thigh-length white coat was lying on the left rear seat. She pulled it over to the front, opened it out, and draped it over Roy's shoulders like a cloak, pushing it down behind his back and struggling awkwardly to get it tucked around his left shoulder. It wouldn't make much difference, but it might help a bit. Body temperature was very important . . .

Paynton's voice came over the speaker with startling suddenness.

"Hello there, Ann. You still with us?"

She gasped with shock, then fumbled in her lap and snatched the microphone up to her mouth.

"Yes." She cleared her throat. "Yes."

"Say agai – er, what was that? Say it again, please?"

Ann said loudly, "I said yes. Yes."

"Oh. Good. Just keep speaking up, like you did then, okay? Keep your voice nice and loud and clear."

"All right."

"Fine." There was a moment's pause, and then the voice came back. "Now, I want you to tell me about – er, Roy, isn't it? So that I can pass it on to a doctor in a minute. I'll ask questions, and you answer as many of them as you can. Are you ready to do that?"

Ann glanced nervously at Bazzard. The stillness of him suddenly frightened her more than ever, making her stomach sink and her face hot and tingling. She swallowed several times.

"Y-yes," she said. "Yes. I'm ready."

*   *   *

At 8,000 feet, still climbing in a slow spiral, Paynton was frozen to the marrow. His hands and feet were almost totally numb, the twin draughts coming in under the canopy-rim were turning his ears to ice-chips under his headset, and he was shivering constantly. Flying alternately with one hand and then the other, he was attempting to thaw out his frozen fingers by pushing them under his crutch. The exercise wasn't a great success; the warmth of his body refused to percolate through his thin leather gloves to any noticeable extent, and furthermore the movement kept reminding him how badly he wanted to urinate. The snarl of the Gipsy engine seemed to vibrate right through his body, aggravating the sharp physical pain of restraining his bladder.

But he wasn't thinking about the cold, or even the desire to piss. As the Chipmunk's nose slowly traversed the winter horizon, his entire concentration was focused on two things. The first was the urgent need to ask the girl in the runaway aeroplane the right questions and take in her answers . . .

And the second was the fact that her radio signal strength was fading.

It was the first thing he'd noticed when he came back to her after talking to Tees-side; her voice was markedly fainter than it had been five minutes before. He could just about make out what she was saying at the moment, but if she continued to fade at this rate she was going to become totally unreadable within a very short time.

He pinched his nose, then pressed the transmit button on top of his control stick again and spoke slowly and loudly, keeping the anxiety out of his voice.

"Let's start off with any advance symptoms, Ann. So tell me if there was anything wrong with Roy at all before he passed out; if he was complaining of anything."

The girl's voice came back blurred and distorted. "He had . . . uscular pains this morning . . . his neck and shoulders . . . thing apart from that."

Paynton thought, *It's the fucking distance, of course*. She must have been just about abeam Tees-side when he first heard her – and now she was flying away from him, down south, which was lengthening the radio range. The obvious answer was to quit making small circles over Tees-side and turn south himself, to follow her. He wouldn't catch her up – the best he could sustain, even in a gentle dive, would be about 120 knots, while any *single* engine retractable would be batting along at 140 or more – but at least he'd be slowing down the rate of separation, which would keep her in radio contact for as long as possible.

The only thing was, you don't normally turn your back on a known airfield when you only have fifteen or twenty minutes' fuel left. Or you don't if you're a pilot who wishes to both reach old age and to remain fully employed, anyway.

Paynton wavered, undecided. His teeth chattered in the

freezing cockpit. After a moment he thumbed the transmit button again.

"Okay Ann, I've got that; you're doing fine. Now, can you tell me just *how* he passed out? How sudden it was, whether he said anything, whether he moved his hands to any part of his body, that sort of thing. Okay?"

"... didn't see him ... pass out ... heard him grunt ... then unconscious. It ... ve ... sudden."

Straining his ears, Paynton caught most of it. He waited a few seconds to make sure she'd really finished speaking, then pressed the button again.

"I just want to make sure of this, Ann: did you say he passed out very suddenly?"

"Yes ..." The voice in his headphones was almost indecipherable. "He ... as if ... been hit."

Paynton's frustration broke. He shouted, "Oh, FUCK it!" and abruptly slammed the stick to the left and pulled back. The Chipmunk rolled instantly into a steep turn, distant earth and sky twisting nearly to the vertical and the hazy line of the horizon streaming rapidly past the nose.

Martin's head jerked with shock under the wigwam of the canopy-struts. His hands jumped to the combing over the front instrument panel and hung on, petrified.

Paynton held the turn, his arms heavy with the G-force, until the engine cowling passed through the blazing glare of the sun. Then he rolled the Chipmunk violently upright, tilted the nose down into a shallow dive, and pushed the throttle fully open. The lazy snarl of the engine swelled to the blare of full power, and the airspeed wound up rapidly. He dropped his left hand to the trim wheel and spun it half a turn forwards, and then shouted into the intercom.

"Jules! Turn the radio volume up full, and re-set the squelch."

There was no response. The back of Martin's head remained unmoving, hunched tightly down into his shoulders. Craning, Paynton could see his knuckles, whitely gripping the front combing.

"JULES! TURN THE BLEEDING RADIO UP FULL

AND RE-SET THE BLEEDING SQUELCH, WILL YOU?"

After a long moment, the head bent slowly forwards. The left hand reluctantly let go of the combing and dropped down out of sight. A few seconds later the carrier-wave hiss in Paynton's headset abruptly increased, broke into a steam-pipe rush of receiver noise for a moment, and then backed off again as Martin turned back the squelch knob.

"Thanks, Jules. Sorry about all this, but we won't be at it much longer."

Martin gave no sign of hearing. Sick and terrified, he'd succumbed to the pressure in his bladder during the shock of the unexpected steep turn. Now, he stared down at the slowly-spreading warm wet patch in his trousers in horrified disbelief.

Paynton eased back the throttle a little as the airspeed crept past 110 knots, and adjusted the nose position so that the needle of the vertical speed indicator settled on exactly 300 feet a minute down. Then he pressed the transmit button again.

"Hello, Ann. Sorry about going off for a moment there. Now, can I just confirm that you said Roy passed out very suddenly, with no warning signs? Speak up nice and clearly."

This time the girl's voice was louder, although more distorted than before. Paynton had been expecting that; most aircraft receivers produce a lot of "mush" when the volume is turned right up. He only hoped that his dive to the south would keep him in radio range for long enough to achieve something useful. It would be ironic if he threw away his chances of getting back to Tees-side and still lost radio contact . . .

"It . . . very sudden. He grunted . . . then . . . unconscious."

Paynton frowned, thought for a moment, then said clearly, "Okay, I've got that. Now you said you slapped him, Ann. So can you confirm that that produced no response at all? He didn't move, or groan, or anything?"

"No. No r . . . sponse."

"Oh. Hmmm." Paynton filed the information in his mind, and tried to think what to ask next. Even as he thought about it, part of his brain was worrying about his own destiny. If he kept up this dive for another five minutes he was going to have to forget about going back to Tees-side. So maybe he'd best admit it to himself right now; think in terms of lobbing into RAF Leeming or RAF Dishforth, fifteen and twenty-five miles to the south respectively. They might not like him pitching up out of the blue, but . . .

He shook his head, cleared his throat soundlessly against the background roar of the dive, and thumbed the button again.

"What about now, Ann? Is he still ali – I mean, what is his breathing like, now? Is it slow and deep, or what?"

There was a pause, filled with the light rushing sound of the Chipmunk's receiver. Then the girl's voice came back, hesitant and faint.

"No . . . irregular . . . depth and timing. Pulse is al . . . irregular. His neck . . . scles . . . in spasm. Pupils are . . . dilated."

Paynton blinked, startled by the phraseology. After a moment, on impulse, he said, "Are – er – are you in medicine at all, Ann?"

"Par-pardon?"

He spoke louder and slower in the howl of the steady dive. "I said, are you in medicine, by any chance? You seem to know what you're talking about."

"I'm . . . nurse. A n . . . ing sister."

"Oh." Paynton hesitated, glaring sightlessly at the altimeter. The hands were winding down through the seven thousands. "Well, er, could you repeat those things for me again, please? Say them again, nice and slow and clearly?"

The voice came back almost instantly, a little louder. The radio distortion wowed and hissed like someone a long way away using a loud-hailer.

"Resp . . . ation and pulse are irregu . . . Neck is . . . spasm, rigid. Collapse was very sudden."

Paynton squeezed his eyes shut for a moment, concentrating. Then he said, "Respiration and pulse irregular. Neck in spasm. And the collapse was sudden. Is that right?"

". . . es."

"Okay. I've got that, then. Do you – ah – have any idea what it might be, yourself, that I could pass on? I mean, er – " his voice trailed off as he realised he was getting in too deep. He released the transmit button.

There were a few seconds silence. Paynton finicked with the trim wheel and looked out at the sun glaring on the wings, belatedly wondering if he might have said the wrong thing. If the pilot wasn't going to recover it might not be a good idea if she realised it all of a sudden . . .

Then the girl came back, slower and fainter than ever.

"I can't . . . can't seem . . . think . . . properly. Just don't . . . c-can't . . . emember. It's . . . it . . . like . . . oh, *God!*" Her voice rose suddenly, almost to a scream. "Oh *God . . .*"

Paynton heard the carrier-wave noise cease as the mike switch in the other aircraft was released. He yelled "*Bollocks!*" at the top of his voice, furious with himself. Then he took a fast breath, pressed his own transmit button, and spoke calmly and soothingly.

"Well, don't worry about it any more, Ann. I'm sure I've got enough now to pass on to a doctor and get some help. So you just relax for a bit and don't worry about it. Okay?"

For a long moment, there was nothing but the frying-pan sizzle of the radio. He pressed his left earphone hard against the side of his head with a frozen hand, and clenched his teeth to stop them chattering. His right thumb hovered over the stick-button, hesitating, while he tried to think of something else to say.

Then the voice came again, slow and wavering with terror, catching on the words.

"Oh, God . . . he . . . I think . . . he's had a s-subarachnoid haemorrhage."

8

SQUADRON LEADER DR. JOHN OSCOTT arrived in the Leeming Approach Room at fourteen minutes to three. Large and florid and puffing, wearing an old tweed jacket and muddy Wellington boots, he looked more like a country gamekeeper than the Senior Medical Officer of a major RAF station. Trowbridge's telephone call had caught him in his garden on the married quarters estate, and he'd come straight away. He swept into the dim-lit radar room in a gust of cold air, then stood there breathing diminishing plumes of condensation while he waited for someone to speak to him.

One of the controllers turned his head, nodded, held up one finger, and then went back to his screen. The other took no notice of him at all. Oscott waited quietly, rubbing his muddy hands on his jacket. He'd only been in the control room once before, but the subtle tension of emergency was recognisable anywhere.

Trowbridge and Myers were busy on the radio, trying to eliminate as many radar echoes as possible as quickly as possible. Myers had his Approach radar cranked out to its maximum fifty-mile range, while Trowbridge looked after the inner twenty-mile circle on the Director screen. The Flight Information Service was obviously hard at it, too; aircraft after aircraft was coming on to the Leeming frequency for identification and instructions. Myers was busy with his Chinagraph, following the tracks of ten aircraft traces on his screen and occasionally marking one off with a callsign after it had been positively identified. He was speaking into his boom-mike almost non-stop.

"Golf Echo Papa, turn to zero-niner-zero for radar identification."

"Echo Papa, roger, zero-niner-zero . . ."

"India Oscar, Leeming, I have you identified four miles east of Sutton Bank on a south-westerly heading, confirm . . . ?"

"Affirmative for India Oscar."

"Roger. Break, break . . . Golf Whisky Delta, Leeming?"

"Whisky Delta, go ahead."

"Whisky Delta, we have an emergency here: would you intercept an aircraft for me for identification?"

"Certainly, sir."

"Thank you, Whisky Delta; turn left heading two-four-zero and stand by for further steers. Target is two o'clock to you heading right to left, range six miles."

"Whisky Delta to two-four-zero, negative contact this time."

"Roger. Break, break . . . November four-zero Tango, say your heading . . ."

It was another two minutes before the call they were waiting for came through.

"Mayday, Leeming; Golf Bravo Charlie Yankee Lima."

The other traffic shut up instantly; a Mayday call has priority over everything. Myers turned his volume up – Yankee Lima sounded distant and faint, with a lot of carrier-wave – and then replied, "Yankee Lima, Leeming has you strength three. Go ahead."

"Roger, Leeming." Paynton's voice was a little louder. "Yankee Lima has been handed to you from Tees-side. Confirm you have my details, and do you have a doctor there?"

Myers said, "Affirmative, Yankee Lima; we know about you, and we have the doctor. But stand by for that, I have some information for you."

"Go."

"Roger. D and D says your target aircraft – " Myers used the service term unconsciously " – is a Piper Cherokee Arrow, Golf Alpha Yankee Whisky Tango. Confirm you're still in radio contact with it?"

"Ah – not sure about that, Leeming. I've just been speaking to her now, but she was getting very faint to me so I may not be able to get her again. I'm descending on a southerly heading at 110 knots, now about eight miles south of Tees-side passing four-five, and I think she's ahead of me, to the south, and going faster than me. I'll try and get her again if there's a simple query, but anything more than that's out."

Myers glared briefly at his radar screen. Four of the blips on it were holding approximately southerly headings. One – a Cessna 172 – was identified, and another one, coming in from the top of the screen, was probably Yankee Lima. The remaining pair were a little way below Leeming, flying approximately parallel to each other and about six miles apart.

Myers pressed his transmit switch and said, "Understood, Yankee Lima: could you get her to change frequency for DF?"

"Negative, Leeming, not possible. She doesn't know anything about anything and she's pretty upset at the moment; if she starts trying to switch we'll probably lose her altogether."

Myers hesitated, wondering for a few seconds if he ought to press the matter. As things were the search for the runaway was very much a hit-and-miss affair, whereas if the girl could be persuaded to change to a Homer frequency – one used for Radio Direction Finding – she could probably be located in a moment the next time she transmitted. Then he realised that not only was the Chipmunk pilot probably right – the girl would be fiddling with a panel of at least four radios of various kinds, and the danger of her cutting herself off for good would be very real indeed – but he was also in no position to even think about questioning the instructor's judgment: in an emergency in the air the decision of an aircraft captain is over-riding and final.

He said quickly, "Roger, Yankee Lima; stand by to talk to the doctor."

"Okay." The voice buzzed with static. "Put him on."

Myers swung round to Oscott, who was still waiting

patiently. Slipping the left earphone of his headset back from his ear, he spoke fast.

"We've got a civvy kite on autopilot with the pilot passed out, sir. There's a girl in it who can't fly, and we want to know if it's possible to bring the pilot round. We can't talk to the girl, but I'm in contact with another pilot who's been on to her. Would you speak to him and see what you can make of the medical side?"

Oscott nodded and stepped forward. Standing by the orderly technical clutter of the radar consoles he looked more like an out-of-place gamekeeper than ever. Trowbridge reached across and handed him a plugged-in headset. Oscott pulled it over his head, leaving muddy fingermarks on the earpieces. Myers said, "Press this button here when you want to speak; the callsign of the man you're talking to is Yankee Lima."

Oscott nodded again, cleared his throat, and pressed the button.

"Yankee Lima, Squadron Leader Oscott here." When he spoke, the gamekeeper image receded: his voice was deep solid BBC, just the right sort of voice for comforting the sick. "I'm the Leeming MO. What can you tell me about this man who's passed out?"

"Ah, roger." In his racketing cockpit ten miles away Paynton hesitated, on unfamiliar ground and not wanting to miss anything out. "The girl in the aircraft's a nursing sister. First, she says the pilot was complaining of pains in his neck this morning. Muscular pains, she said. Then when he passed out, it was very sudden. He just grunted and went out. Now she says his breathing is irregular and so is his pulse. His neck's in ... in spasm, and his eyes are dilated. She's tried slapping him round the face, but nothing happened. She says she thinks it's a – ah – suberanoid haemorrhage. I think that was it."

Oscott's face went blank. Myers, watching him, was suddenly reminded of another doctor a year before, telling him his mother had just died. His face had looked like that.

Oscott said, "Would that word be *subarachnoid* haemorrhage?" He pronounced "subarachnoid" slowly and carefully, stretching the syllables.

"Er – say again?"

"I said, would the girl have said *sub-ar-ach-noid* haemorrhage?"

There was a pause. Then, "Yeah, that's it. Subarachnoid." The unaccustomed word came over blurred with carrier-wave, but readable.

"All right, Yankee Lima; that's a very lucid report. Just wait a moment now, please." Oscott released the transmit switch and stared unseeingly at the radar console, thinking. The fingers of one hand drummed soundlessly on the top of the control table. Myers fidgeted, watching him, knowing that he had to have thinking time but still, illogically, resenting the delay.

After half a minute, Oscott seemed to come to some sort of conclusion. He pressed the transmit switch again and said, "Yankee Lima?"

"Go ahead."

"Yankee Lima, I think you must proceed on the assumption that the girl is probably right. That means you must not expect the pilot to recover sufficiently to fly the aircraft. Over."

There was a few seconds silence. Then the tinny voice said, "*I* won't be proceeding at all, in that case. But you say there is *no* chance of the pilot recovering, confirm? Nothing at all the girl can do to bring him round?"

Oscott frowned, hesitated, and then said distinctly, "That is correct, Yankee Lima. On the data you have given me, it sounds very much like a subarachnoid haemorrhage, or possibly a cerebral haemorrhage. In either case, there is no reasonable chance of recovery for a minimum of twelve hours or so, and probably a lot longer. There is nothing the girl can do apart from keeping him warm and making sure his breathing is not restricted. Over."

"Roger; understood. Can I have the controller now, please?"

Myers, who was listening on his own headset, nodded briefly to Oscott and then pressed the transmit switch.

"Leeming controller here, Yankee Lima."

"Roger. Ah – you heard what the doctor said?"

"Affirmative."

"Roger." The voice paused for a moment, then came back. Even through the poor transmission it sounded weary. "Look, there doesn't seem to be anything more I can do, now. I'm low on fuel and I need to land at your field, and there doesn't seem any point in starting another conversation with the girl if I have to break it off after a couple of minutes. I've already told her to expect someone else to be taking over from me. I'd – er – advise an instructor in another aircraft to formate on her, try and talk her down. And pretty quick, because I had to leave her in a bit of a state, what with her radio fading. D'you get all that?"

Myers said, "Roger, Yankee Lima. That's understood, and thanks for all you've done. Do you want a steer for Leeming?"

"Be appreciated."

"Okay; stand by." Myers glanced across at Trowbridge and raised his eyebrows. Trowbridge nodded, said quickly, "I've got him," and reached for his transmit switch.

Myers leaned back, slipped his headphones down around his neck, and looked up at Oscott.

"Is that what I should tell D and D, sir? That this pilot probably isn't going to recover?"

Oscot pulled off his headset and put it on the table. He made a gesture between a headshake and a shrug.

"Well, obviously I can't be sure, or anywhere near it. You can't make a diagnosis without seeing the patient. But as a completely off-the-cuff opinion then I'd have to say yes; I don't think you should expect a recovery in time to be any use. The symptoms as described are right for a subarachnoid, and a nursing sister would probably know one when she saw one anyway."

Myers nodded. "All right, sir. Er – can you just give me some idea what a subarachnoid haemorrhage *is*, please? D and D might want to know."

"Ah. Yes. D and D." Oscott rubbed the side of his nose with a large forefinger, leaving a muddy mark on his face.

"Well, briefly, it means an artery bursting within the subarachnoid cavity. That's the small cavity between the brain and the skull. Blood pumps out of the leak and increases the intra-cranial pressure, so that the brain gets – ah – squeezed, if you follow me. That squeezing restricts the blood supply into the brain itself, which causes unconsciousness and possible brain damage. It's not an uncommon thing in men of thirty-five to forty. It's largely due to a congenital deficiency in one of the artery coatings. The patient sometimes gets a stiff neck beforehand, rather like a muscular pain, and then when the artery bursts properly they go out like a light, with no other warning. The best indication that it's happened is that the neck muscles go into spasm at the same time; the neck's as rigid as a board in spite of the person being completely unconscious."

"I see, sir." Myers finished scribbling notes and looked up. "So if that's what's happened, then there's no chance at all of bringing him round long enough to land the aircraft?"

"Oh, no." Oscott was quite definite. "If it *is* a subarachnoid, then there's no chance whatsoever. It's a very serious condition, you understand. If this man isn't wheeled into a neurosurgical centre very soon, he quite probably isn't going to come round at all. He may very well be dead already."

Myers swallowed. After a moment he said "Jesus," very softly. Then he reached for the red telephone.

*   *   *

While Paynton was talking to Squadron Leader Oscott, the chain reactions to the emergency were spreading out from the Distress and Diversion Cell like ripples on a pond, widening and gathering momentum as they went. Radar controllers at Leed-Bradford Airport, Manchester and Northern Radar at RAF Lindholme were notified and told to begin eliminating as many unidentified echoes as possible on their screens. At the same time, telephones rang at five RAF aerodromes and urgent questions were asked about aircraft availability. The answers to these questions were mostly less than helpful;

on this Saturday afternoon the only service machines in the air in the whole of Yorkshire and Lincolnshire were a handful of Bulldog trainers – which with a level flight maximum of 120 knots had no more chance of staying with a Cherokee Arrow than Paynton's Chipmunk had had – and one Hercules on an Army co-operation parachute-dropping exercise over a disused airfield in East Riding.

Also at the same time, working on the pyramid system of communication, a total of seventeen police stations were alerted to the possibility of an air crash within their parishes. They in turn notified fire and ambulance services to stand by. Five light aircraft fields were called with the request that their off-the-circuit traffic should report to Leeming by radio, and similar instructions were given to six individual aircraft on the Flight Information Service frequency en route over Yorkshire. Altogether, within fifteen minutes of Paynton's first Mayday call, more than 300 people had become either directly or indirectly involved in the fate of Arrow Whisky Tango.

Three of these people – one in a provincial fire station and the other two on small airfields – picked up telephones and dialled numbers which began 01-353.

The *Sunday Express*, the *Sunday Mirror*, and the *People* swung into action.

*   *   *

The telephone rang in the Tyne Flying Club at fourteen minutes to three.

The call was taken by Peter Castlefield, the receptionist/ manager. As he picked up the receiver, Barry Turner, the red-haired CFI, came into the clubroom and headed for the tea machine. He was running late, and was peevish because of it: he'd just come in from an irritating hour of circuits with a less-than-bright dock foreman, he had two more lessons to fly before the end of the day, and *that*, since there was only one and a half hours of daylight left, meant that there wouldn't be time for the aerobatics practice he'd planned to have in the Pitts Special. He dropped a fivepence piece into the machine, thumbed the button marked Black Coffee with Sugar, and reflected gloomily that it was always the bloody way on a fine winter's day. You started off with only two or three students booked, hauled the Pitts out because there was *bound* to be time to sneak a practice session in between the lessons – and then everybody and his bloody dog promptly turned up wanting to go flying, so that before you knew it you were booked up solidly right through to dusk while the Pitts just sat there on the tarmac looking at you.

Well, this was the last time. From now on he was going to start doing what Tony Bianchi and Phil Meeson and Keith Kerr and the rest of them did: get to the aerodrome just after daybreak, get into the air before anybody else arrived, and then turn the bloody radio off and stay up there for an hour whether anybody else liked it or not. Let someone else push the school aircraft out and open the club up; it wouldn't hurt them a day or two a week. And he'd better get a move on with it, too. The Icicle Aerobatic Contest was only a few weeks away, and he hadn't even practised the known sequence yet. If he didn't get weaving he was going to get trounced by Keith Kerr in that Stampe again, the way he had been in the Esso Trophy. And *that* was embarrassing because Keith was an old buddy and didn't ought to be pushing a pre-war Stampe around better than Barry Turner could aerobat a nice new Pitts. Hell, there wasn't much point in *having* the loan of a Pitts if you couldn't out-fly a bloody Stampe . . .

Peter Castlefield called across the room, "Barry; phone for you. Bloke wants to speak to the CFI."

Turner thumped the tea machine with the heel of his hand. The dispenser belched internally and spat out his fivepence through the Rejected Coins slot. He muttered under his breath, then said aloud, "See if you can deal with it, Pete. Or ask them to hang on a mo'."

Castlefield spoke into the phone again. After a few seconds his expression changed to sudden surprise. He covered the mouthpiece with one hand and said urgently, "Barry! It's Distress and Diversion. They say it's important."

Turner brushed through the clump of people standing around the reception desk, grabbed the receiver, and snapped, "Chief Flying Instructor." Behind him the tea machine gurgled, failed to produce the requisite plastic cup, and widdled black coffee brainlessly into its own runway.

A neutral male voice said, "Distress and Diversion Cell West Drayton, here. The number-one controller wants to speak to you. Hold the line please."

Turner said, "Roger," and waited. Flight Lieutenant Peterson came on the line after thirty seconds.

"D and D number-one controller here. Am I speaking to the Chief Instructor?"

"Yes. Barry Turner."

"Right, sir." The voice was brisk. "Does your club operate a Piper Cherokee Arrow aircraft, Golf Alpha Yankee Whisky Tango?"

Turner said, "Yes," feeling his face going stiff.

"And can you confirm that this aircraft took off from your aerodrome about twenty-five minutes ago for Denham, pilot's name Bazzard?"

"Yes, affirmative. Why? Has something happened to it?"

"I'm afraid so, sir. It appears that the pilot's been taken ill in the air, and passed out. We have the pilot of another aircraft in radio contact with a woman on board, and we're trying to locate your machine on radar."

Peterson paused to let the news sink in. Turner stared sightlessly at the club noticeboard, tingling with shock. After a moment he said, "Shit!" softly and emphatically.

Peterson said dryly, "Quite so. Now, I've got some questions for you, please, which I need to have the answers to as quickly as possible. Firstly, can you confirm that the aircraft has dual controls, and also some form of autopilot?"

Turner seemed to shake himself. "Yes. Full dual except for the toe-brakes, and standard Piper wing-leveller and heading-hold. It's on auto, is it?"

"We think so. The woman says it is, and it would've fallen out of the sky by now if it wasn't, anyway. Now; do you know this woman in the aircraft at all?"

"Negative. All I can tell you is she's about twenty-five and

96

blonde. She looked like Bazzard's girl friend. If you want to come back to that in a minute I'll have her membership form dug out and give you what I can on her." Turner spun round and snapped at Castlefield, "Get me the membership form for Roy Bazzard's passenger, double quick." Then he spoke into the phone again. "Go on."

"Right, thank you. Next, can you confirm the aircraft's cruising speed's about 150 m.p.h., and do you know what its fuel state is?"

"Cruising's nearer 160, true air speed. Stand by on the fuel." Castlefield handed him a sheet of printed paper; Ann Moore's Associate Membership form. Turner took it and said to him, "Check the fuel book and the flight sheets on Whisky Tango, pronto. I want to know how much fuel it had when Roy took off." Then, into the receiver, "I've got the girl's details now. Ready to copy?"

"Go ahead."

"Right. The name's Ann Moore. Miss. Address is Wallsend Road, Jesmond, Newcastle. Telephone Newcastle 74853. Occupation, nursing sister, Newcastle Royal Infirmary. Newcastle 56000."

"Five-six-zero-zero-zero, was that?"

"Affirmative. That's the hospital number."

"Okay, got it. You don't know if she has any flying experience, sir?"

"No idea. Hang on a mo'." Turner swung round on the room at large and said loudly, "Anyone know anything about Roy Bazzard's bird? Whether she's done any flying or not?"

Everyone looked blank. After a few seconds Bill Holmes, the deputy CFI, said in his broad Yorkshire accent, "That the bit of crumpet was here a bit back? The one with the serious-looking mush an' the lovely bum?"

"Yeah. Come on, don't piss about – d'you *know* anything?"

Holmes shrugged. "I'd say she didn't know owt; I saw her lookin' at the Pitts like it were a brontosaurus."

Turner glared for a second, then pivoted back to the phone. "We don't think she's done anything, but we really don't know. Her passenger form's newly dated so I doubt if she's been up here before, anyway."

Castlefield shoved a flight sheet under his nose and said quietly, "Fuel." Turner said into the receiver, "Hang on a minute, I'm getting the fuel figures," and looked at him enquiringly. Castlefield said, "Bill filled it up yesterday lunchtime: after that it just did thirty minutes in the afternoon."

Turner frowned for a few seconds, calculating, then spoke into the phone again. "It should have at least three and a half hours' fuel on board. Maybe a bit longer if Bazzard leaned it off, but call it three and a half hours for certain."

Peterson replied, "Three and a half hours. Roger. Okay then, sir. That's all for the moment, but I'd be obliged if you'd stay by the telephone until we've got the aircraft down, in case we need anything else."

Turner ran a hand through his red hair, thinking fast. After a few seconds he said, "Okay, sure. But just how *are* you going to get it down? Try to bring the pilot round, talk the girl through flying it, or what?"

"I'm not sure yet, sir. We haven't even got the aircraft located yet. I've got a doctor at Leeming who should be talking to the relaying pilot now, though, so we ought to be getting some idea soon of the chances of the pilot recovering. If that isn't possible, of course, it will have to be some sort of talk-down, as you say."

"Yeah, right." Turner pulled his left ear. "Well – er – what d'you have in mind for that, if it comes to it? You're not thinking of doing it from the ground, are you?"

For the first time, Peterson hesitated. In his small room 280 miles away he was in a considerable hurry, but he also realised that in Turner he was talking to a pilot who probably had as much if not more over-all experience than himself, and was furthermore in current instructional practice on the particular aircraft involved. Peterson himself hadn't been in the air at all for five months, hadn't flown anything smaller than a twin engine turbo-prop for several years, and had never even sat in a Cherokee Arrow.

He said quickly, "No sir, I don't think it'd be possible from the ground. Whoever does it'll have to be in sight of the aircraft, so he can see how the girl responds. Once we've got it located I'm thinking of getting something else in the air to sit behind her and talk to her from there. If you can add anything to that, though, I'm listening."

Turner stared blankly out of the window at the winter sunshine for a moment. Then he said, "No, you're right. That's about the only thing you can do. But you say you don't know where the bloody thing is, yet?"

"That's right. It's transmitting on an unused frequency for some reason, so we can't use any direction-finding equipment on it. All we know is that it took off from you at 1423, and its present heading's just to the left of the sun. So we're working on the assumption that it's more or less on a straight line from Newcastle to Denham, and that it's between forty-five and fifty-five miles out from your end. If we're right about that we ought to find it before too long."

Turner nodded to himself. "That sounds reasonable. If it's on autopilot it ought to be going in a straight line." He pondered for a few seconds, then added, "Who're you going to get up when you do find it? I'd go myself, but I certainly haven't got anything here that'll catch an Arrow with a half hour start."

Peterson said, "I'm checking service aircraft availability now. We should be able to get something up somewhere near your machine's extended track-line. Maybe an instructor from Cranwell."

Turner frowned. "I shouldn't have thought an RAF kite'd be any good. You won't catch an Arrow with a Bulldog, so it'd either have to be something big or something stupid like a Jet Provost. And then you'll have a pilot who doesn't know what an Arrow's cockpit's like or what its speeds are or anything. I'd've thought you'd have been better off with a civvy instructor who knows the aircraft and'll probably be flying something similar himself."

Peterson started to say "Yes, bu..." and then went silent for a moment. He'd had the emergency on his hands for just ten minutes now, and in the rush to get the radar search and everything else organised he hadn't been able to give much thought to the possible talk-down aircraft at all. Being a serviceman his immediate reaction had been to think in terms of service machinery, and that was as far as he'd got. Now, he brought himself up short: this instructor had a good point. The RAF had fast aircraft and it had slow aircraft – but it *didn't* have a single engined piston-powered retractable with a 160 m.p.h. cruise. Nor did it have any pilots who were used to flying that sort of American light aircraft, let alone any who would be intimately acquainted with the Arrow's particular cockpit layout. So maybe he *should* think in terms of a civilian instructor . . .

"You could be right about that, sir," he said slowly. "I'll get someone on to checking round a few flying clubs. Can you think of anywhere in particular that might help, off the cuff?"

Turner flustered for a moment, caught off balance by the question. "Not . . . um . . . not offhand." He realised that time was wasting. "I'll think about it and call you back if anything occurs to me, shall I?"

"Right, sir. It's West Drayton 44077. Thanks."

"Christ, it's me to thank *you*, man." Turner pushed the fingers of his right hand through his hair. "That's one of my pilots up there."

Peterson said, "Okay, sir. We'll try and get him down." He broke the connection.

Turner put the phone down and stood staring at it, oblivious to the silence that had fallen in the clubhouse. The news of Bazzard's emergency had shaken him considerably. Like all good Chief Instructors, he felt a deep-seated responsibility for every pilot, experienced or beginner, who flew the aeroplanes belonging to what he regarded as *his* school. If someone who had learnt to fly in *his* school bent an undercarriage, got seriously lost, or violated someone's airspace, he could never escape the feeling that it was *his* fault; that the person concerned had entrusted him personally to pass on sufficient of his skills and judgment to enable them to fly safely, and that somewhere down the line he'd failed, broken that trust, either through negligence or inadequate discipline or some other reason. Now, he felt that way about Bazzard. What had happened could never be construed as a reflection on him, but that wasn't the point; it had no more relevance than the fact that he didn't particularly like the man, and considered him too self-assured and precise ever to be a really good pilot. The point was simply that Bazzard was one of *his* pilots; and that, logical or not, was enough to make the emergency *his* responsibility. His instinctive reaction was to jump into the first aeroplane he could find, chase after the Arrow, do the talk-down himself . . .

Except, of course, that it wouldn't work. To stern-chase something doing 160 m.p.h. with a half hour start would need an aircraft capable of at least 250 knots to make the slighest sense at all, and apart from the Dan Air BAC 111s there wasn't anything on the airport anywhere near that fast.

He ran his hand through his hair again, leaving spikes of scarlet sticking up. If Bazzard was fifty or fifty-five miles away going south . . .

He suddenly said "Shit!" very loudly, and strode over to the air map of England that was pasted on the wall beside the tea machine. He gripped the fifty-five-mile mark on the distance-tape which hung from a drawing pin in the Newcastle Airport symbol, and swung it over an arc to the south. His thumbnail passed over Thirsk and just below RAF Leeming: the arc was about thirty miles north of the yellow butterfly-shaped blob which was the twin cities of Leeds and Bradford.

He said "*Shit!*" again, and spun round abruptly to the reception desk. "Pete! Get me the Leeds Aero Club on the blower, quick. I want the CFI if he's there, guy called Keith Kerr. Then get D and D back; West Drayton 44077."

Castlefield grabbed for the phone with one hand and the club contacts book with the other. Running a finger down the page of Ls, he said without looking up, "Is that your mate? The aerobatic bloke?"

"Yeah. He's also one of the best instructors in the business, *and* he's got an Arrow down there. He's the one to catch this bloody aeroplane for us."

9

AT 1446, WHILE the call from Distress and Diversion was being put through to Barry Turner, Keith Kerr was doing 100 m.p.h. on the A6120 between Sherburn-in-Elmet and Leeds-Bradford Airport.

Winding the twistgrip hard open against the stop, he blared the Norton past a gaggle of slow-moving Saturday motorists, cut in, and laid the bike over into a long, sweeping right hand bend. The tearing snarl of the vertical twin hitting 6,000 r.p.m. was lost to him in the thunder of the airflow past his crash helmet. The force of the wind pulled his cheeks back into a death's-head grin and rammed freezing air into his throat as he breathed.

He rounded the bend in the classic fashion: starting near the verge, out to the white line at the apex, then drifting back in towards the verge again on the exit. As the road straightened he pulled the Norton upright and snatched a quick glance back over his shoulder. The bend behind was empty; the procession of family cars hadn't got there yet.

No sign of any flashing blue lights.

Kerr held the throttle open, tucked his elbows in, and scrunched down over the tank. The speedo needle wavered over the 105 mark, and went on crawling up. The gaunt winter hedgerows on each side were a tumbling greeny-brown blur as the road unwound in front of him. He grinned into the gale, elated. *That should have lost the buggers: let's see 'em catch me now in their bloody great Granada...*

It had started ten minutes before, as he'd accelerated out of the village of West Garforth on the A63. He was riding the way he usually did, fast but confident, obeying the posted speed limits – more or less – but ignoring the footling 60 m.p.h. blanket. He'd wound it up past the last straggling houses, enjoying the solid power and the arrogant snarl of the exhaust – and ten seconds later he'd zipped past a police Granada parked in a farm entrance. He'd been doing seventy in third at the time, much too late to slow down, and he'd only seen the car for a split-second. But in that split-second he'd also caught a glimpse of a blue uniform whirling round and starting to move, galvanised by the rapid blast of his passage.

That was enough. He dug his knees into the tank and opened up harder still, riding as fast as he could, zapping past the few cars on the road in a solid blare of sound. The cops might not be following at all, of course, but if they were, they were going to have to sprout wings to get anywhere near him before he nipped off into the airport . . .

Kerr's ideas of the rights and wrongs of speeding were simple black and white, born of his natural inclination to rebellion and nurtured by his years in countries less cloistered than England. Blanket limits were some inane politicians' whim, not to be taken seriously, and if the cops couldn't catch you to pace you, you were in the clear.

It didn't occur to him that the police in the Leeds area might be getting to know a certain distinctive black-and-chrome Norton 650SS rather well by now.

Still grinning, he sat upright at the end of the straight, squeezed the brakes for a moment, then wound the throttle open again as he laid the Norton into a left-hander. The bike chopped mildly over some ripples and then settled into the bend, stabilised by acceleration. By now, with the lead he must have built up, he wasn't really worried whether the police were chasing him or not: he was just going fast because he liked going fast. The grin widened and he started singing, bellowing into the freezing blast of the airflow.

"Bye, bye, Miss American Pie,
Drove my Chevvy to the levee
But the levee was dry-y . . ."

When he reached the airport, there was still no sign of the police car. He swung into the rear entrance in the western perimeter fence at twenty, flicked over to the right with his foot scraping the ground, and headed up a narrow concrete roadway. The Norton reached and exceeded the airport speed limit in a single sharp bark of acceleration in second, and then he was braking again and swinging into the small car park alongside the low straggling buildings that house the Leeds Aero Club.

Home and dry.

He pulled in beside an ageing grey Mini, listened to the flat lumpy batting of the Norton's tickover for a moment, then switched off the ignition and turned off the fuel as the engine died. His face tinged with returning feeling. He pulled his goggles down, hauled off his crash helmet, and concentrated briefly on the distant sounds of traffic passing by on the road outside.

No pim-pam-pim-pam of police sirens.

He swung himself off the Norton and pulled it back on to its centre-stand. Then he picked up his helmet and strolled towards the clubhouse, whistling as he went. His breath plumed whitely in the brittle winter sunshine, a visible punctuation to "American Pie".

Inside, the place was the usual weekend between-lessons crowd of milling instructors and students. The two forty-five details had just landed and the three o'clocks – again as usual – were going to be a couple of minutes late getting off. Kerr shouldered his way through the door marked "Instructors Only", dumped helmet, gloves and goggles under the table in the instructors' rest room, and paused to light a cigarette. He blew smoke at a Letraset notice pinned to the wall which said HELP FIGHT MALNUTRITION – INVITE A FLYING INSTRUCTOR TO DINNER, then walked through another door into the area behind the bookings counter, unzipping his Barbour jacket as he went. The counter was being managed by an attractive black-haired girl in blue jeans and a red floppy-necked sweater, who was currently dealing with half a dozen students who all wanted to sign in, pay, and book their next lessons at once.

Kerr watched her for a moment, his blue eyes softening, then said quietly, "How goes it, Maggie?" His voice was deep and carrying, the more arresting for its unconscious trace of trans-Atlantic accent.

Maggie looked round and saw him for the first time. She blushed, flustering in momentary confusion, and then shyly returned his brief conspiratorial smile.

"Fine thanks. Very well." She was unable to keep a small illogical note of relief out of her voice as she added, "How did the aerobatics go?"

Kerr grinned wickedly for a second, then said deadpan, "Good. The rolling manoeuvres went especially well." Maggie blushed again, made as if to speak – and then suddenly seemed to remember something. She flicked an apprehensive glance over his left shoulder, and bent her head quickly back to the bill she was writing out.

A grating Yorkshire voice behind Kerr said, "What sort o' bloody time d'you call this, then?"

Kerr's smile faded. He took a slow, deliberate drag on his cigarette, and then turned his head. He hadn't noticed that Edward Tomms was there, and the realisation didn't please him.

Tomms had purchased the Leeds Aero Club from its previous owners seven months before, and he and the Chief Instructor, two completely opposing types of men, had disliked each other practically on sight. Tomms had had a brief career as a bomber pilot in the Second War, but hadn't flown an aeroplane at all in the last thirty years. About to go into semi-retirement from the haulage business he'd built up over that time, he'd acquired the flying school solely as an investment, and his only interest was the financial return. He paid badly, expected his staff to work long hours – which they did, since the instructors were only too well aware that things wouldn't be much different anywhere else – and quibbled constantly at the cost of maintaining the aircraft and what he referred to as Kerr's "namby-pamby" reasons for grounding machines with technical faults. Kerr's occasional comparisons between the operation of the Leeds Aero Club and their competitors on the airport, the better-run Yorkshire Aeroplane Club, only served to drive him into a fury. The antipathy between the two of them had deepened over the months until it was ready to erupt into an open row at any time. Kerr was well aware of the fact, and up to now had avoided a showdown with uncharacteristic patience.

Today, however, things were different. The letter crinkling in his back pocket made all the difference in the world. *British Island Airways are pleased to offer you the position...*

He blew a slow jet of smoke and said, "I'd call it sort of just before three, chum. Unless my watch is vastly out, of course."

Tomms heaved himself up out of the chair he'd been sitting on. He was shortish, fifty-nine years old, and his expensive dark overcoat didn't hide the fact that he was getting tubby. He had a mop of short-cut iron grey hair on top of a bullet head, and wore a pair of thick-lensed spectacles which exaggerated his aggressively staring eyes. When viewed from straight ahead the pupils frequently became two dark pools of irritation, seeming to fill the whole of the lenses.

"Eh!" He confronted Kerr at a range of three feet. "Eh – just before bloody three! An' you were supposed to be here a bloody hour ago."

"Very true." Kerr ground his Gold Leaf into an ashtray on the counter, and then grinned suddenly and savagely into his employer's face. "Except that according to my contract, chum, *you* don't tell me when I take my time off anyway. For your information, should you be interested, I checked in just before lunch and found that my first booking was three o'clock. So I figured that what with the extra half day I worked Thursday when Ian Mackenzie was ill, plus the fact that I'm night flying until eight tonight, which I don't get paid anything extra for, this was a good time to give myself an extra half hour off instead of twiddling my thumbs doing nothing in here. Okay?"

Tomms blinked, momentarily taken aback. Then his temper, never far under the surface, boiled over.

"No, it's *not* bloody okay! You get flyin' pay if you fly extra hours, an' I don't pay people to saunter in this time o' the afternoon just 'cos they bloody feel like it! An' furthermore – " his hot eyes flicked down to Kerr's motor cycle boots and back up again " – I don't pay my bloody instructors to turn up lookin' like ton-up boys an' wearin' roll-neck sweaters, neither. Ain't you got a shirt an' tie, lad?"

Kerr's blue eyes narrowed. On the other side of the counter, several students watched with interest.

The phone rang and Maggie answered it, keeping her eyes on the two men.

Kerr slipped his hands into his back pockets and rocked gently on the balls of his feet, club-like arms akimbo. After a moment he said slowly, "I'm doing an aerobatic detail in the Pup in a few minutes time, chum. And the Pup, as you may or may not know, has had its heater U/S for a month. So, not wishing to freeze my balls off, I'm wearing boots and a jacket and a sweater for it. See?"

Tomms stabbed a blunt finger at his face. "Nay lad, *you* bloody see! You can wear what you fuckin' like in th' planes – but when you coom in 'ere I want you in a shirt an' tie, or you'll be bloody *out*! Got it?"

Quite slowly, Kerr reached up and pushed Tomms's hand away. Then he said deliberately, "Right, chum. If that's the way you want it, then this is your lucky day. Because I *am* out. Quit. I'm giving you a month's notice as of right now, or you can fire me and give me a month's money. Either way, I'd like to give you an unsolicited testimonial. I want you to know that you're a sonofabitch; the worst niggling bastard I ever worked for, bar none. Period."

Tomms's eyes seemed to go almost black behind the thick glasses. His face mottled with rage and his breath came in short, sharp pants. Twenty years in a tough business had taught him to count three before letting himself go, and he

107

counted three now. Then he took a deep breath . . .

Maggie, holding the telephone receiver, said suddenly into the electric silence, "Keith! Someone called Barry Turner. He says it's urgent."

Kerr ignored her. So did Tomms. His head was thrust forward, face suffused with fury. He said heavily, "Right then, young man. *I'm* giving *you* bloody notice, an' you'll work out the whole month. I won't have any man . . ."

Maggie wailed, "Keith! He says it's an aircraft emergency!"

Kerr spun round, took two steps across the room, and snatched the receiver. Tomms started forward angrily, but the instructor had his back to him as he started speaking.

"Kerr here. What's the problem?"

"Keith – Barry Turner. Listen, I've got to be quick. We've got a real bastard here: one of our guy's has taken off in our Arrow to go down to Denham, and bloody passed out in the air. He's left the kite on autopilot with his bird in it, and she's screaming for help on the radio."

Kerr said, "Jesus Christ!" The receiver jiggled against his left ear as his fingers unconsciously rubbed the scar near his eye. He'd known Barry Turner for years – they'd been on an instructors' course together once, and been bumping into each other in the small worlds of training and aerobatics ever since – and it didn't occur to him to ask time-wasting questions. If there was nothing to be done, Barry wouldn't have called him. It took less than twenty seconds to absorb the problem and its implications.

"Where is it?"

Behind him, Tomms said angrily, "Eh, I'm bloody talkin' to you . . ." Kerr ignored him.

Turner said, "Nobody knows yet. He got off from here at 1423, so if he's on a straight line for Denham he ought to be about fifteen or twenty miles north-east of you by now. Distress and Diversion are looking for him on radar. Can you get into the air and try and talk the girl down for me if it comes to that, Keith? I haven't got anything here that'll catch the bloody thing."

Kerr thought for perhaps ten seconds, juggling and calculating. Then he snapped, "Right. The only thing I've got that's fast enough's our own Arrow, so I'd better get moving. You stand by the phone and I'll get someone to call you and relay to me; I'll want a lot more gen once I'm in the air."

"Roger, will do. Thanks, Keith."

"S'okay. Talk to you later." Keith crashed the phone down and whirled round, the problems of the emergency racing through his mind. Uppermost was the vital, overwhelming need for speed. If he was going to do any good he'd have to formate on the other Arrow, practically fly it from his own cockpit – and in order to do *that*, the first requirement was to catch the bastard. That ought to be possible providing he got into the air for an interception while the runaway was still heading towards him, but once it had passed abeam Leeds-Bradford and was flying away, he'd be stuck with chasing it. And with two Arrows of similar performance it could take him half an hour to close a gap of even five miles. So what he had to do was get off the ground *now*, immediately, then head south to stay in front of her and start worrying about vectors later . . .

Tomms said, "Eh! Look! What the bloody 'ell's goin' on . . . ?"

Kerr stepped round him and snapped, "Maggie! Call Distress and Diversion, West Drayton 44077. Tell them I'm getting up in Romeo X-ray to try and catch their runaway from Newcastle. They know all about it. Tell them to get on to Approach here – I'll be talking to them first and I'll want information and vectors. Okay?"

The girl flustered. 'What *is* it, Keith? What's going on?"

Kerr was scanning rapidly down the board behind the counter where the aircraft keys were hung, looking for the one labelled G-BCRX. "Haven't got time to explain, love – just *do* it. Tell D and D to call Leeds Approach."

Maggie caught the urgency in his voice and reached for the phone, wide-eyed. Kerr located the keys to Cherokee Arrow Romeo X-ray and snatched them off their hook. He spun round towards the door . . .

And found Edward Tomms standing solidly in his way.

"Where the bloody 'ell d'you think you're goin'? You don't talk to me like that an' then go gallivantin' off in one of my planes wi'out a word of explanation! You're supposed to be working'…"

Kerr snarled, "Get out of it, you stupid bastard!" and made to push past. Tomms grabbed his jacket, livid with fury. Kerr pulled against his grip for an instant, boots scuffling on the lino as he nearly lost his balance, then suddenly swung back. His right fist came up from near his waist and crashed on to Tomms's nose. The older man let go and staggered back, blood spurting, hands coming up. Kerr rocked on his feet and punched him again, hard in the stomach. Tomms reeled, collided heavily with the wall, and then slid down on to his knees, like a man praying.

The whole thing had taken three seconds.

The clubhouse went dead still, suspended in shock. For perhaps another three seconds there was total silence, broken only by a deep retching groan from Tomms as he fought to suck air into his winded lungs.

Kerr stepped round him and ran.

Banging the clubhouse door open, he pounded across the perimeter road and up to the short taxiway that led to the light aircraft hangar. The club machines were standing in a line on the edge of the concrete apron: four Cessna 150s, a Cherokee 180, a Beagle Pup, and then the Arrow. Kerr cut across the grass, making straight for the Arrow, and arrived at it panting and coughing with exertion. He jumped on to the walkway on the starbord wing, fumbled with the doorlock for a few seconds, then flung the door open and plumped into the right hand seat with a loud grunt. No time for pre-flight inspections on this one: in one continuous flurry of movement he slammed the door, twisted the top catch, and slid the seat forward. Then his hands were darting round the controls. Fuel – on, left tank: mixture – rich; master – on; boost pump – on; primer – three strokes…

Ten seconds after the door had closed, the propeller jerked over with the characteristic tinny grinding noise of a Lycoming starter. The blades chunked over four or five compressions, then disappeared as the engine blared into life. Kerr immediately reached down, released the park-brake, and shoved up the power to a purposeful roar. As the Arrow started to move, his hands and eyes ran automatically through the after-start routines. Radio and beacon – on; oil pressure – coming up; oil temperature – on the zero; fuel pressure – in the green; tank contents – between a quarter and a half on each side . . .

He said, *"Bugger it!"* aloud.

A third of a tank a side meant a maximum endurance of an hour and a half even if he leaned off the mixture heavily and left nothing in reserve. For a few seconds he thought about stopping to re-fuel and accepting the fact of a stern-chase afterwards, and then realised suddenly that it wasn't going to matter anyway.

In an hour and a half's time it was going to be dark.

The radio – the number one set only; the number two had been out for servicing for the past week – warmed up with a small fizzing noise. Kerr grabbed one of the two headsets resting on top of the instrument panel, pulled it over his ears, and thumbed the transmit button on the control yoke as he swung the Arrow on to the taxiway out of the apron, rolling fast.

"Leeds, Mayday traffic Golf Bravo Charlie Romeo X-ray, at the Aero Club. I am attempting to intercept an aircraft heading down from the north with the pilot incapacitated. Request taxi and immediate take-off runway one-zero."

The tower came back instantly, which surprised him: he'd expected a pause for consternation.

"Roger, Mayday Romeo-X, cleared taxi. Leeds Approach is working on this emergency at the moment. Confirm you intend to intercept in order to talk the woman down if necessary?"

Kerr said briefly, "Affirmative."

"Roger. Runway in use is two-eight, but take one-zero at your discretion. QNH one-zero-one-two, QFE nine-eight-niner, wind two-four-zero at twelve knots. Squawk standby."

"QNH one-zero-one-two, squawking standby, and I'll take

one-zero." The easterly runway meant a downwind take-off, but in a lightly loaded Arrow with 3,600 feet of concrete to play with he was prepared to accept that: the threshold of one-zero was less than two hundred yards from the light aircraft hangar, whereas using the reciprocal, two-eight, meant a three or four-minute taxi across the aerodrome. He pushed the throttle open a bit more and bowled down the taxiway at thirty m.p.h., checking magnetos and exercising the constant-speed propeller as he went. In the background of his attention he heard the tower ordering a British Airways Viscount on final approach to overshoot and break right immediately. The Viscount acknowledged calmly, with no trace of annoyance in the voice; in the air emergency traffic takes priority over all, and that's that. Kerr, running quickly through the pre-take-off checks as he rolled down towards the runway, grinned briefly to himself at the random notion that at this moment he had precedence over everything up to and including a Concorde. God bless the British Air Traffic Control Service with all their overstaffing and inefficiencies . . .

Engine husking, scuttling fast on its three ungainly legs, the Arrow taxied past the airport's western entrance. Kerr didn't notice the police Granada nosing in from the road outside; he was too busy in the cockpit.

He swung on to the runway at exactly one minute past three, and opened the throttle.

10

NOT MANY YEARS ago, when light aviation was still a playful puppy gambolling at the heels of more serious airborne enterprise, a single-engined private or club aeroplane was a comparatively simple piece of machinery. It would have the basic flight controls, an unsophisticated and unsilenced engine, perhaps five or six instruments on the panel – and that was that. A very few might be blessed with one rudimentary communications radio, but this was a luxury which rarely functioned without fault and was in any case regarded with considerable suspicion by the majority of private pilots.

Nowadays, things are different.

A modern four-seat single like a Cherokee Arrow is not designed as a fair-weather fun machine: it is intended to be, and is, a feasible means of high-speed transport, capable of operating anywhere in the world in practically any kind of weather short of hurricanes or severe in-flight icing conditions. It is sometimes criticised by helmet-and-goggles pilots as being sloppy on the controls, over-stable, and too easy to fly, and so it is, by the standards of aerobatic machines like Chipmunks or Stampes. But it is made this way for a purpose; and part of this purpose is to reduce the workload of the actual flying to a minimum, and so leave the pilot free to apply himself to different challenges which are outside the scope of the more agile aeroplanes. A machine like an Arrow frequently has weather-beating systems and equipment equal to those carried by many a multi-engined trans-

113

port: there are fifteen major flight and engine controls – not counting those which are doubled up for the purpose of the dual control facility – up to seven radios for various purposes, between twenty-five and fifty ancillary knobs and switches depending on the particular avionics fitted, and then a total of twenty-four or twenty-five instruments to keep track of flight attitude, navigation, and engine performance. The average private pilot flying in his spare time can expect to take two or three years, and spend two or three thousand pounds on training, before he can fully utilise the potential of such a machine.

At this moment, merely in order to fly straight and level, the Tyne Flying Club's Arrow had four electric motors running, three gyroscopes spinning at speeds between 12,000 and 18,000 r.p.m. and two electronic mini-computers actuating the wing-leveller and heading-hold. Bazzard, a hundred-hour neophyte in the art, had had to set nine separate controls just so before switching in the autopilot, and twenty-one dials were now providing a continuous flow of information concerning various aspects of the Arrow's performance and progress.

To Ann Moore, who had no way of understanding that in a less sophisticated aeroplane she and Bazzard would already have been dead for ten or fifteen minutes, the machinery was nothing but a low steady hum pervading her prison cell in the sky. With the voice over the radio gone, the huge emptiness outside the flimsy windows seemed to press in on her with a physical weight, producing a peculiar effect of claustrophobia in the tiny plastic room in the middle of nothing. The cockpit temperature was too hot for comfort, which was also weird in the midst of the cold winter blue. Her stomach ached as if an iron fist was gripping her insides.

She clutched the microphone in her lap, and tried to think about flying the plane.

No one had told her she would have to do it. Paynton had merely said before he left her for the last time that "Someone else will be talking to you next". But nonetheless, she knew. People who suffer a spontaneous subarachnoid haemorrhage do not regain consciousness within an hour or two; they slip into a deep coma which commonly lasts a minimum of twelve hours even under intensive care in a neurosurgical unit. So, quite simply, there was no other alternative: she was going to have to fly the plane.

She tried to think about it, and failed. The snoring hum of the machinery seemed to fill her body, dinning softly into her bones.

The realisation that Roy *had* had a subarachnoid had been both instantaneous and appalling. In the moment of saying the words to the unseen instructor she'd appreciated with sudden clarity that she'd actually known it for several minutes, but the defence mechanisms of her mind had prevented her from accepting it. Then, after she'd pronounced her own sentence, the terror had come back again, re-doubled in force. Her body had shaken uncontrollably and her stomach had tightened, squeezing the acid taste of panic into her throat again. Paynton's voice had pattered on out of the speaker, but the only thing she'd taken in had been the words, *"Someone else will be talking to you next"*. The rest was nothing but a jabber of sound, intended to be soothing but grating on her fear by its very matter-of-factness.

Then the voice had gone, and she was alone again.

For what had felt like a long time, she could do nothing but fight her terror. It seemed to lap and recede in waves, dimming for a moment in apparent exhaustion and then welling up again in a fresh swamp of hot and cold, tingling through her body. She'd wanted to give way to it and scream and scream, but for some reason it seemed vitally important to hang on, keep control. She clenched her teeth, tightened every muscle in her body in an attempt to still the shivering. She forced herself to think about the hospital: about what you do when you have a subara – no – a cardiac arrest case. List everything you do: call cardiac arrest team; check respiratory passages clear; initiate external cardiac massage ...

Eventually, lacking action to fuel it, panic had burned itself out and died down to a steady background throb of fear, like the echo of a pain. And in its wake had come the peculiar lassitude which attaches to drawn-out terror, where the brain refuses to concentrate on any one thing for more than a few moments.

She yawned, and wiped her face with the sleeve of her sweater, leaving lipstick traces on the white wool. Her tears had run down under her chin and dampened the roll-neck collar, making it clammy-prickly round her throat.

She had to fly the plane.

Dully, she wondered about it. Roy had said it was dual controls. That would be the half-wheel thing in front of her. She supposed they'd tell her what to do over the radio: how to push or pull or turn it and when to do it, and which gauges to look at and what they ought to read. Unless they just abandoned her, of course: decided there was nothing anybody could do, and just forget about her. They could be doing that at this moment: shrugging helplessly, writing her off, pretending she and Roy had never existed . . .

The engine snored on, solid in the silence of the sky.

She swallowed, and blinked at the forest of dials and levers. The pain in her stomach was a slow cold ache. Probably caused by adrenalin, she thought vacantly; the gastric fluids becoming over-acidic, rather like indigestion. You took alkaline tablets for that, to absorb the acid. Absorb it or balance it, anyway. Mr. Hutchins, at her last hospital, had been the expert on that: for a consultant orthopaedic surgeon he knew a great deal about stomach medication. Maybe he drank so much he always had a stomach ache, and had to take a lot of tablets himself. She used to be able to tell when he'd had a few gins at lunch time; his breath would carry a scent of cachou sweets, and he'd keep patting her on the bottom. "Nip along and fetch this, sister" – and then pat-pat as she went. She'd always been going to slap his face for it, but never quite plucked up the courage. But they'd said he was a wonderful surgeon, whether it was a cachou afternoon or stone cold sober. It was amazing how many doctors drank too much; she'd read somewhere that medical people had a greater incidence of alcoholism than any other section of the community. Still, she wished Mr. Hutchins was here

116

now. If there was any way of bringing someone round after a subarachnoid then he'd know about it . . .

She rubbed her eyes with her knuckles, trying to halt her wandering thoughts. There wasn't any way of bringing a person round after a subarachnoid: a subarachnoid stayed in coma for a long time, and sometimes didn't recover at all. *She* knew that . . .

She turned her head and looked at Bazzard. He was still and pale, breathing raggedly in his unconsciousness. His left trouser leg fluttered gently in a small draught from a heater-vent on his side of the cockpit. For a moment, as if her mind was determined to plod off stupidly down every possible side-track, she found herself thinking in a vague way about what might happen between them in the future. Except that here, now, the familiar questions seemed ridiculous and paltry, utterly disconnected from reality. Whether you were in love, whether you should go to bed with someone – these were half-remembered conventions of some other world, incredibly distant. Even the unfaced question of whether Roy would recover or not recover, live or die, held no shock, no impact. He was just . . . there; a part of a nightmare which she couldn't bring her brain to concentrate on, couldn't get to grips with . . .

The plane. Come on, now – think about the plane. Force yourself to think.

She shook her head and ground the heels of her hands up and down her face and across her eyes. When she stopped it took a long moment for vision to clear and re-focus. She frowned at the instrument panel, and immediately yawned again. That was no good; she *must* concentrate. Must, must, *must* . . .

The nearest dial had figures round the outside, and a needle in the centre of a blue and yellow arc. A knob with the letters OBS on it stuck out of the rim. It didn't mean a thing to her. She looked at the one below it, which pictured the outline of an aeroplane pointing straight up and had more figures round the edge. That had the initials ADF on the face, and *that* didn't mean anything, either. None of them did. There

117

was one with just a blank face, blue in the top half and black in the bottom, another with an aeroplane outline that seemed somehow different from the one labelled ADF, three or four which looked like complicated car speedometers . . .

She leaned back in her seat, shivering in the burr of the engine. It was hopeless, impossible; the cockpit was a jungle of things she didn't even begin to understand. There wasn't a single familiar item to start from. She felt herself beginning to sob again and buried her face in her hands, feeling the wetness of tears between her fingers. She hadn't known it was possible to be so frightened; it just kept welling up again and again, blotting out thought, everything. There seemed to be nothing that would stop it. And in a minute they – someone – would be talking to her. Then she'd *have* to get a grip on herself, *have* to face up to it . . .

After a long moment she took a deep breath, raised her head, and looked deliberately out of the wide window.

Immediately outside was the sun-glaring white expanse of the starboard wing. It was real and yet not real; lines of rivets, small scratches in the paint around that cap thing – a part of the little complicated room she was in, yet at the same time utterly remote out there in the emptiness. Peering down close to the fuselage she could see the black non-slip walkway on top of the wing root. She'd stood on that getting in. It was less than eighteen inches from her right elbow on the other side of the Perspex, and yet it was completely untouchable, as far away as the moon. If she opened the door and stepped out on to it now she'd be snatched off and there'd be nothing underneath. She'd be falling, falling . . .

She bit her lower lip, and forced herself to look at the ground creeping under the wing leading edge.

Four thousand feet below, the North Riding of Yorkshire was a cold patchwork in the harsh winter sun. The hills were flattened, the fields an irregular mosaic. Some were brown, some were vaguely green, and most still bore a white threadbare tracery of last night's frost. Nestling in a fold in the patchwork was a tiny grey-brown village, incredibly detailed in the bright afternoon. Wisps of smoke ambled away from the toy houses, and matchbox-model cars made pinpoints of colour in the miniature streets. She'd been born and raised in a village like that, in Northamptonshire. Her mother was still there. For a moment she remembered the cold-earth smell of the winter country and the swish of the Saturday cars as they turned into the pub opposite their house.

Then the village slid under the wing, and there were just the fields. In the far distance ahead and to the right was the vague smear of a city, but apart from that the landscape seemed to be nothing but tiny fields, stretching away to the wide horizon in every direction. And above the horizon-line the sky, endless and towering and coldly blue. The sky somehow looked much ... *bigger*, from up here. A wing might cover several square miles of ground or a windscreen pillar obliterate an entire small town, but there was no such trifling with the sky. That was an overwhelming emptiness of deep varying blue, above and around and on all points: the naked yellow glare of the winter sun and the sparse high streaks of cloud only serving to emphasise the limitless expanse of nothing. The Arrow's quietly-droning cockpit, £40,000-worth of streamlining and aluminium and plastics and electronics, seemed very small and puny against the vast indifference of the sky.

Ann looked back in at her trembling hands. Two fresh tears rolled down her cheeks.

She thought about the hospital again.

*　　*　　*

Ten miles to the south, Keith Kerr was climbing up into the same sky. As Arrow Romeo X-ray snarled through 3,000 feet he finished struggling his motor cycle jacket off, tossed it into the back, and wriggled himself into a comfortable slouch in his seat. Beneath him, the sun-lit clutter of Leeds spread away in all directions; the usual noise-abatement procedure of not overflying the city was being torn to shreds in the emergency.

He'd dropped into the Arrow's right hand seat out of sheer

force of instructing habit: all small Pipers have dual controls, and since the command seat in any aeroplane is on the left the instructor becomes accustomed to flying from the right. Now, elbow on the armrest in the door, he moved the control yoke with tiny flexings of his right wrist while his left hand pulled a Gold Leaf out from the packet on the empty seat beside him. His light blue eyes, surrounded by a hundred tiny wrinkles as they narrowed against the glaring sun, casually surveyed the familiar vista of sky above and earth far below. Once every minute or so he pulled his gaze in from the distance to glance at the instruments, absorbing the information of a dozen dials in a single brief scan. The action was part reflex, part caution, and largely unnecessary, since an experienced pilot flying in clear weather has little need of the readings of gauges to keep him informed of the flight pattern of a familiar aircraft. To him the invisible air was not an emptiness but a vast fluid, real of substance and tangible to the touch. The nerve-endings of his body were attuned to the supporting flow of that fluid over wing-skin and control surfaces, so that any trifling skid or wandering of airspeed was instantly transmitted to the marrow of his being quite regardless of the tale-telling dials.

He leaned back, picked the cigarette lighter from the panel as it popped out, and blew smoke at the windscreen. The debacle with Tomms was temporarily forgotten, pushed out of his mind, as were thoughts of the previous night or contemplation of his new career. All of those things were ground matters, most of which have a way of receding in importance once an airman has returned to his chosen element.

His headphones made a small pipping noise, then clattered metallically in his ears.

"Romeo X-ray, Leeds; say your passing level?"

Kerr glanced at the altimeter as his right thumb pressed the transmit switch on the control yoke.

"Romeo-X passing three five. D'you have this runaway aircraft located yet?"

"Ah, negative, Romeo-X. We have two suspect traces eight and nine miles north of you and about ten miles apart, both moving approximately south at about 160 m.p.h. We're trying to get some identification on them."

Kerr frowned at the blue sky and muttered, "Sonofabitch!" Then he pressed the switch again and said, "So where are you putting me, then? In between them?"

"Affirmative, Romeo-X. We're positioning you in between the two extended track-lines with the intention of turning you south to stay ahead of them. What is your present heading?"

"One-three-zero."

"Roger. Turn right now to 140."

Kerr said, "One-four-zero," and made a brief climbing turn. Then he trickled smoke through his nostrils while he considered the mathematical odds against there being *two* unidentified radar echoes in more or less the right place going at the right speed in the right direction at the right time. On the face of it they must be astronomical; except, of course, that a lot of aircraft go up and down England every day, and this route was a good alternative to flying over the Pennines and all through the complex of industrial control zones to the west.

He said, "Sonofabitch!" again, and glared down at the smoothly-winding ribbon of the M62 in the sunny-frosty depths below his right wing.

Visualising the radar screens, he saw himself making the basepoint of an inverted triangle, with the two unknowns forming the other two corners to the north-east and the north-west. Either of them – or, of course, neither of them – could be the runaway, and the only way to find out which was for someone to get alongside at least one and make a visual identification. In a few minutes he himself could be circled to allow them both to catch up, and then vectored on to either one with no great difficulty, but having done that, he'd have shot his bolt: if the aircraft he intercepted turned out to be the wrong one, he'd have used up his vital ten-mile lead for nothing.

So – stalemate. Stalemate with the Leeds controller doing the only thing he could: positioning Kerr in between the two projected track-lines and then making him run on ahead until such time as the unknown aeroplanes were identified.

He rubbed the scar near his eye, wondering how the people on the ground *were* expecting to make the identifications. If they had a high-speed volunteer in the vicinity who was prepared to do some intercepting, all well and good, but if they didn't, this thing could go on indefinitely. For a few seconds he thought about calling up and asking, then decided against it; the controllers obviously had enough on their plates without getting unhelpful radio chatter from someone who didn't have any answers.

The Arrow droned on up into the blue, passing 5,000 feet. Kerr glanced at his fuel gauges, then eased the mixture lever back towards the lean position until the fuel flow meter registered just under eleven US gallons per hour; his endurance *could* still become a factor, however unlikely it seemed at the moment. The cylinder head temperature crept slowly up and finally stopped with the needle just below the red line at 260 degrees centigrade. He frowned, and tapped the glass of the dial with his finger. Cylinder head temperature gauges were a daft thing to put into a modern aeroplane; nowhere near accurate enough for optimum leaning of the fuel mixture in a Lycoming engine. He'd been asking for months for an exhaust gas temperature gauge in the Arrow instead, but Tomms had overruled him. The stupid bastard had probably had CHT gauges in his bloody Wellington and didn't see why anybody should ever need anything else . . .

Drumming the fingers of his left hand on the throttle quadrant, he went back to surveying the streaks of high cirrus beyond the invisible propeller. After a moment his lips formed an O, and he whistled "American Pie" soundlessly into the snore of the engine.

*　　　*　　　*

At that moment, forty miles to the north, Tony Paynton was waiting for his engine to stop. Level at 2,000 feet, with the Chipmunk sogging along at its best economy cruise of sixty-five knots, his eyes were flicking across constantly from his fuel gauges to the distant sun-lit criss-cross of Leeming's runways.

The runways were three miles away, almost hidden under the nose. They crawled nearer with agonising slowness.

The fuel gauges both read zero.

In spite of the cold, Paynton was aware of a hot prickle of tension in his face and the clamminess of sweat on his palms under his gloves. Every now and then he glanced down at the fields below, where he would have to attempt a dead-stick landing if the fuel ran out before he reached the aerodrome. They all looked terrifyingly small, and every one of them seemed to be bounded by hard grey lines. Those lines, he knew, were the low stone walls which are a feature of North Yorkshire farmland. His throat tightened every time he looked at them; if you hit one of those during a forced landing you were going to write off the aircraft at the very least ...

His headphones said, "Yankee Lima, Leeming; you have two miles to run, join right base for runway three-zero. No known traffic."

Paynton pressed the stick-button and replied, "Right base for three-zero." His tongue seemed large and clumsy, clacking in the dryness of his mouth. He looked at the fuel gauges again. Then he muttered to the lazily-snarling engine, "One more minute, pal. Just keep running for one more minute."

In front of him, Jules Martin's head lolled mute and miserable under the wigwam of the canopy-frame. Paynton ignored him, craning to the right and squinting into the sun as he stared at the approaching runways. Three-zero was *that* one there, parallel to his starboard wing. Tuck in close, be ready to go for the southerly runway instead if she quits before you can make it ...

A minute went by. The hangars on the north side of the aerodrome crept slowly under the wing leading edge. The engine was still running.

Paynton muttered, "Glory hallelujah!" and closed the throttle.

The roar died away to the uneasy thrustle of airborne

123

tickover. Hands and feet moving in unconscious unison he lowered the nose into the glide, re-trimmed, and then dipped the right wing into a smooth right-hand slipping turn. Bring her round on to finals *now*, flaps *now*, steepen the slip a little *now* . . .

The Chipmunk rolled its wheels on to runway three-zero at Leeming at five minutes past three. It made one stiff-legged little bounce, settled, and finished its landing roll abeam the first taxiway. Ignoring the tower's instructions to continue to the next exit, Paynton turned off the runway, taxied fifty yards, braked to a standstill, and then switched off the magnetos and opened the throttle wide to prevent the engine backfiring. The propeller slowed, swished back and forth between two compressions, and stopped.

The sudden silence in the cockpit was intense, woolly on the eardrums. Paynton pulled off his headset, which went on bleating distantly at him to say his intentions. He rubbed his eyes with his right hand, then reached up and slid the canopy all the way back. The cold January air smelt incredibly sweet after the stench of vomit in the cockpit. He unfastened his harness, stood up with one foot on the seat, and heaved himself slowly and carefully out on to the wing walkway. As he stepped gingerly down to the ground he was aware of Martin stirring weakly in the front seat, but for the moment he was too preoccupied to worry about him. From far away came the wailing of a siren as the crash-crew turned out to see why he'd stopped in the middle of the aerodrome. The hell with them, too . . .

Paynton took two stiff, careful paces, unzipped his flies with frozen fingers, and urinated with enormous relief on the rear of the fuselage.

Martin staggered out of the cockpit behind him, half-fell off the wing, and then sank down into an awkward sitting position on the taxiway, both hands flat on the cold concrete as if he needed reassurance that it was real.

"God –" he coughed and spat, head hanging feebly, " – thank Christ . . . that's . . . bloody over . . ."

Paynton leaned against the fuselage, fumbling to zip up

his trousers. For a moment he had a vision of the girl, still trapped in the Arrow's cockpit as it droned on southwards, still terrified . . .

"It's not over, Jules," he said slowly. His teeth chattered in the cold. "It's not over at all, yet."

*   *   *

The inside of the Distress and Diversion Cell at West Drayton looked exactly the same as it had fifteen minutes before: the only thing to indicate that a full-scale emergency was in progress was the presence of one more man.

The newcomer was a totally bald individual, about forty-five years old, with a narrow, quizzical face which somehow suggested that its owner was constantly on the point of saying something sarcastic. This impression was, in fact, only partially accurate: Squadron Leader Arthur Lyle, Duty Officer Commanding Distress and Diversion on this Saturday afternoon, could wax sardonic when the occasion arose but was more normally a quiet, watchful man who was well liked by his subordinates because he exercised the priceless virtue of leaving them to get on with their work unpestered, so long as that work was being adequately carried out.

At the moment he was standing behind Flight Lieutenant Peterson's chair, sucking on a well-chewed pipe but saying nothing.

After a minute or so, Peterson stopped talking into his microphone and just sat, staring blankly at the radar screen in front of him. The fingers of his right hand tapped softly on the edge of his console.

Lyle removed his pipe from his mouth and said quietly, "What's happening, John?"

Without looking round, Peterson said, "Bits of everything, sir." He counted off points by flicking up the fingers of one hand. "One; the Leeming MO says that this girl's pilot's probably had some kind of haemorrhage, so he isn't likely to come round. Two; there's a civvy instructor up from Leeds who's prepared to try and talk the girl down. He's a highly

125

recommended bloke and he's in another Arrow, which must be a good thing. And then three –" his left fist came down on the arm of his chair in exasperation, "– we just can't seem to find the bloody aeroplane."

Lyle said calmly, "How's that progressing, then? Finding it?"

"Well. Leeming've identified all their traffic travelling in straight lines except for two machines heading south, both at about 160 m.p.h. I handed control over to Leeds-Bradford a couple of minutes ago, when those two traces got about ten miles north-east of Leeds, but Leeds can't get the buggers identified either. They don't seem to have anything within practical range for an interception except this instructor in his Arrow, and they're frightened to steer him on to one of the traces in case it turns out to be the wrong one and he misses the girl because of it. I can see their point, an' all. At the moment they're planning to run him down south ahead of the unknowns until they get at least one of them identified, and they're screaming at me for something else to do an interception with."

Lyle nodded, and said, "So what've we got in the way of service machines near there?"

"*That's* the other part of the problem." Peterson stabbed an accusing finger at his notepad. "All we've got's a few Bulldogs which are too far north to do any good, and one Hercules. The Herc's out of Lyneham on a supply-dropping exercise over –" he named an ostensibly disused airfield not far from York "– and his VHF's packed up, for God's sake. Sod's Law, of course: it has to bloody well happen the one time in a thousand we want one of our blokes to talk to a civvy."

Lyle nodded again. In addition to the normal RAF ultra-high frequency radio, most service aircraft except for strike/interceptors also carry very high frequency sets for speaking to civilian controllers: it was just the sheerest bad luck that this particular Hercules happened to be a deaf-mute in the VHF band at this particular time.

He said, "The Herc's UHF's all right, is it?"

"Yes, sir. They've been talking to Lyneham." Peterson paused for a second, then added diffidently, "They've – er – got some NATO top brass on board to observe the drop, I gather."

The Officer Commanding D and D scratched his ear with the stem of his pipe.

"Well," he said dryly, "they're going to have to observe something else instead. Get on to the Herc on UHF emergency and have Leeds vector him through you to the nearest suspect trace, pronto. Tell him to make himself useful by getting up close and identifying the aircraft visually; at least he can eliminate one of the possibilities for us."

Peterson looked mildly shaken. He muttered, "Jesus, that'll please the Army." Then he took a deep breath, flicked a switch alongside his radar console to transmit on the UHF emergency frequency of 243 M.h.z., and started talking fast.

*   *   *

Two hundred miles away, over the desolate moorland of the East Riding, the huge predatory shape of an RAF Hercules rolled out of a ponderous turn at 800 feet and began its three-mile run-in to the Dropping Zone. The vast rear door of the aircraft gaped open like a wrong-way-round crocodile mouth, ready to spew out an armoured car and two light field guns to the Army unit which was ready and waiting below.

On the abandoned airfield, the Major in charge of the unit stamped his feet against the cold and watched the aircraft through his field glasses. It got steadily bigger in head-on silhouette, while the air around him vibrated with the growing dirge-like whine of the four engines. It was going to be bang on line, he thought – which was just as well, with half the NATO generals in Europe standing ten yards away from him and the other half watching from the aircraft. Now just so they made the drop at *exactly* the right moment, and the men managed to get the car and the guns unlimbered without muffing anything. If that bloody young Captain made a cock of it this time he was for the high jump good and proper...

127

Breathing out plumes of condensation in the icy sunlight, the Major concentrated on the empty air behind the aircraft's great door. Waited for the three small dots to drop out and blossom into mushroom-clumps of parachutes. Not yet, not yet ...

Nothing dropped out. Instead, with a mile or more still to run, the shape of the aircraft seemed somehow to be changing. The Major blinked and stared, unbelieving. The deep pregnant-looking fuselage appeared to be getting thinner, almost as if it were breathing in.

Then he realised what is was. It was the rear door closing. He blinked again, totally astonished. What the *bloody* hell ... ?

As the Hercules thundered in over the airfield boundary the crocodile-jaw champed finally shut. The noise of the engines wound up immediately to a shrill, deafening scream, and the seventy-ton aeroplane cranked steeply over on to its left side. While the ground shook with the din the Major lowered his binoculars and stared upwards, mouth open: the vast bulk of the aircraft seemed to be crawling, almost stationary, hanging in the air and pivoting on its wing tip directly over his head. Nothing could fly that slowly; any second now it must stall out, roll right over on its back and plunge into the trembling ground ...

The Hercules bent majestically out of its turn on a south-westerly heading, then tilted its nose up into a climb. The earth stopped quivering to the noise of the engines, and shortly after that the decibel rating dropped back to the level where the human brain is capable of rational thought.

The Major just stood and stared at the dwindling shape whining away into the cold blue sky. He was still staring at it when his radio operator came running over with a sheet of paper in his hand.

11

1508–1514

"ROMEO X-RAY, LEEDS?'

Kerr slapped the headset-mike closer to his mouth and snapped, "Romeo-X, go ahead."

"Romeo-X, you are now in between the two extended track-lines. Turn right heading 180, and continue climbing to flight level seven zero. Also, we have some information for you."

"Romeo-X to one-eight-zero, and out of six for seven. Go ahead with the information."

"Roger." The voice was flat, unemotional. "First, Distress and Diversion have detailed an RAF Hercules to investigate one of the unidentified aircraft. They are vectoring the Hercules to the eastern possibility, and expect interception very shortly. D and D suggest that we vector you on to the other possibility if the Hercules ident is negative."

Kerr whistled, the sound lost in the steady roar of the engine. If the RAF were diverting a Hercules they were taking this seriously. He stared out at the pure blue sky beyond the windscreen for a few seconds, thinking fast. The plan sounded as good as any: if the Herc drew a blank on one echo and then he did the same with the other they'd have had it anyway, so nothing would have been lost. In that case, the only possible conclusion would be that the runaway was miles away in some unguessed-at portion of the sky, or that it was too low to be picked up on radar at all. In either of those events the chances of anyone finding it

129

would be so small as to be practically non-existent.

He said, "Roger, Leeds. That sounds okay."

"Roger, Romeo-X." The voice in his ears paused for a second, then went on. "Next thing is that D and D now have a doctor's opinion on the pilot's illness. They are not expecting any recovery, and advise that you proceed on the assumption that the girl will have to land the aircraft. I say again; they are *not* expecting the pilot to recover, and advise that the girl will have to land the aircraft. D'you copy that?"

Kerr's left hand, holding a cigarette, ground to a halt halfway up to his mouth. After a long moment he pressed the transmit button and said deliberately: "Roger. Copied."

"Okay, Romeo-X; maintain 180 and stand by for further steers."

Kerr said "Roger" again. The radio double-clicked in acknowledgment, then went silent.

*   *   *

So. It was really happening.

For several seconds Kerr just stared out over the nose, blind to the empty sky and the dwindling earth far below. Up to now, his rôle in the emergency had been a nebulous thing; *if* we find the aircraft, and *if* the pilot doesn't come round, then we'd like you to be up there to try and do something. He'd appreciated the problem, recognised the possibility – but deep down, he now realised, he hadn't expected it to come to that. It was too . . . melodramatic. Like witnessing a bank robbery and chasing the getaway car; the sort of thing that only happened to other people, never to you.

Except that it *was* happening.

He said "Christ" into the engine roar. Then he took a deep drag on his cigarette, scratched his scar with his left thumbnail, and applied himself seriously for the first time to the problem of how the hell you go about teaching someone to fly and land an aircraft between ten past three and nightfall on a winter's afternoon.

On the face of it, the act of re-uniting an aeroplane with

the ground is one single exercise, flowing and straightforward. You merely line the machine up with the runway, descend, and then just before the moment of touchdown pull back to check that descent so that the landing becomes a gentle transition from one element to the other instead of an angry collision with the earth.

That is on the face of it.

Delving a little deeper, however, that seemingly simple operation breaks down into a hundred separate elements, all demanding prerequisite skills for their proper execution. For example, in order to get to the runway at all you must first be able to turn the aircraft, probably several times and certainly to within fine limits of accuracy. Turns, if correctly carried out, involve the co-ordinated use of rudder, ailerons, and elevators, which is not, initially, an easy process. As any flying instructor is only too well aware, a normal student requires a solid hour of his airborne course devoted solely to turns before he achieves anything like an adequate performance.

Kerr had an hour and a half to go before dark.

And then there was setting up the descent: for you cannot descend an aeroplane for a landing merely by pointing the nose down into a high speed power-dive. Even the crudest of landing approaches requires the pilot to begin by making an accurate power reduction, follow that with a careful adjustment of the up-and-down nose position in order to achieve the correct airspeed in the descent, and finally re-set the elevator trim. Thereafter, you may expect to have to re-correct all three of these factors several times before your angle of descent is precisely right in relation to the approaching runway threshold. This aspect of the aviator's art usually requires at least five hours of intermixed practice before the neophyte can be more or less relied upon to manage something approximating to a decent approach.

Kerr had an hour and a half to go before dark.

Then there were all the other factors. Flying straight and level; slowing down so she could put the undercarriage down; lowering the flap, if possible; making sure the mixture

131

was in full rich; locating the manifold pressure gauge and the throttle for the power changes; switching out the auto-pilot; making the all-important landing flare-out itself . . .

Kerr muttered "Christ" again. The hands of the altimeter crept round to 7,000 feet. He eased the nose down from the climb until the distant winter horizon sat three inches above the crash-pad on top of the instrument panel, then slowly brought the throttle and then the propeller-pitch back as the Arrow accelerated to its normal level-flight cruising speed.

An hour and a half.

Well, the short answer was that it simply wasn't possible: no one could teach any person to fly and land an aeroplane from scratch in ninety minutes. The only way it might be done was to forget any notion of *teaching* in the normal sense, and concentrate instead on achieving blind parrot-fashion obedience. Use the girl as an extension of himself, so that *he* flew the aircraft through her hands. The flying time would have to be devoted to just that, and not much else; getting her to carry out the bare minimum of manoeuvres using the bare minimum of controls, with the accent on immediate response to every command he gave her.

Okay. So what *was* the bare minimum of manoeuvres and controls?

Kerr sucked hard on his Gold Leaf, breathed out slowly, and frowned at the instrument panel through the swirling smoke.

The obvious place to start was pitch control; nose-up and nose-down exercises. If she couldn't do that she wouldn't be able descend or land at all. Then there'd have to be power changes to get her used to handling the throttle, culminating in a pitch, power and trim change all at the same time in order to get the aeroplane slowed up enough to put the wheels down and make an approach. Then after that there'd be turning. She could make a crude rudder-less travesty of a turn by using ailerons alone, or it might be safer to leave the autopilot heading-hold switched in and have her change direction by moving the heading-bug on the gyro compass.

132

Except that *that* would take a hell of a lot of explaining over the radio . . .

He shook his head angrily, mashed his cigarette into the armrest ashtray, and shelved the problem of turns until such time as he knew more about the girl and how she was reacting. For the moment, there were more urgent things to be considered.

One of them was the runaway's autopilot.

Initially, the best thing would be for her to leave it switched in. She'd be able to override it on the manual controls – all autopilots operate through a series of clutches which are designed to slip if the human pilot has a difference of opinion with the black box – and leaving it engaged carried the obvious advantage that the aircraft would recover itself, at least in roll and yaw, if she panicked and let go of everything. Later on – well, later on he'd have to think again : it might well be safest to leave something like the wing-leveller mode switched in all the way to the ground.

Which, of course, raised another small point. At the moment he didn't know what sort of autopilot the other Arrow had, and that meant that until he found out he was stuck with it anyway. It was probably the same Piper two-axis unit fitted in his own aircraft – but *probably* wasn't good enough : if the engagement buttons were in a different place or someone had crammed in an entirely different set-up he could make a very serious mistake.

Changing hands on the control yoke, he leaned forward against his shoulder strap and fumbled around in the map pocket down by his right leg. After a moment he came up with a stub of Chinagraph pencil. He scrawled *AUTO-P?* on the bottom front corner of the side window, frowned at the sky for a few seconds, and then added the words *FREQ?, FUEL, NAMES??* and *ILLNESS*. Then he pressed his transmit button.

*   *   *

Six miles behind Keith Kerr's Arrow, Geoffrey Carrington was suffering from an eight-cylinder hangover. Lounging in the left hand seat of Rockwell Commander G-BCOY he bleared at the rolling countryside 3,000 feet below and wished he was back at home in his £50,000 house in Harpenden. Flying back to Luton was no joy whatsoever after the way those Edinburgh types drank on a Friday night. He felt like death warmed up, and even the rare winter sunshine and the thought of the contract he'd screwed out of that man MacDonald did nothing to cheer him. He slouched in his seat, letting the two-axis autopilot do the work, and occasionally checked his position against the half-million scale air map on his knees. The radio speaker above his head was issuing pawky pop-music: he had the ADF receiver tuned to Radio Leeds, and the communications radio turned right down. He'd been outside controlled airspace for the past hour, and would stay that way until he got near Luton: he had no need to talk to anybody for at least the next fifty minutes.

Yawning, he glanced casually round the sky in a circular sweep. From the distant grey fuzz behind the right wing-tip that was Leeds, over the nose, round to the left . . .

His jaw shut with a snap and he grabbed the control yoke, shock punching through his body. Beyond the left wing, where there'd been nothing but emptiness a minute ago, the huge bulk of an RAF Hercules was sliding past not 200 feet away. It was so close it seemed to fill the whole sky; he could see the sun-lit green-brown camouflage, the red triangles on the escape hatches, even the co-pilot's face looking at him out of the right hand window of the cockpit. Heart pounding, he hauled the control wheel to the right, overriding the autopilot. The Commander sheered abruptly away and up.

By the time he looked back again the Hercules was half a mile ahead, showing its cream belly as it peeled sedately off to the left. He swung the Commander slowly back on to course, feeling his temples throbbing and a sour dry taste in his mouth. Bloody Air Force bastards playing silly buggers with a damn great thing like that . . .

*   *   *

"Romeo X-ray, Leeds, d'you read?"

The voice in Kerr's ears sounded urgent, almost jubilant. He pushed his transmit switch and said briefly, "Go."

"Romeo X-ray, the Hercules has identified the eastern possibility as a single engine Rockwell Commander aircraft, Golf Bravo Charlie Oscar Yankee. Confirm you are prepared to intercept the second aircraft?"

"Affirmative."

"Roger. Turn right heading one-niner-zero for interception with the target's extended track-line. You are about four miles ahead of the aircraft."

"Roger: one-niner-zero." Kerr banked to the right for a moment, then added, "You'll tell me when I'm on the target's extended track-line and I'll start circling then, confirm?"

"Affirmative."

"Right." Kerr picked a cigarette out of the packet, lit it, and then thought of something else. He pressed the transmit switch and said, "Leeds, Romeo-X; what's the registration of this aircraft?"

"Er – G-AYWT, sir. Golf Alpha Yankee Whisky Tango."

"Yankee Whisky Tango. Okay, thanks." Kerr craned his head round to look back over his right shoulder, searching the depths of the sky below and behind. Four miles was a long range to spot another light aircraft, but you never knew. Out of the corner of his eye he could see his own starboard tailplane, white and close at hand, bobbing gently up and down over the hazy line of the horizon. The snoring of the engine drummed through his skull as he rested his head against the cold Perspex of the side window.

After a moment the voice in his headphones came back again.

"We have the answers to your questions now, Romeo-X. Ready to copy?"

"Go."

"First, the aircraft is transmitting on 126.85. I say again, 126.85. Apparently it's an unused frequency."

Kerr raised his right eyebrow. Then he shrugged, fished for the Chinagraph, and jotted *2685* on the window. He said, "Roger; 126.85."

"That's correct, Romeo-X. Next, the fuel state. The aircraft took off at 1423 Zulu, with fuel on board for a minimum three and a half hours flying."

"Fourteen-twenty-three and three and a half hours." Kerr took two seconds to absorb the figures, then mentally crossed "fuel" off the list of the runaway Arrow's problems: he might have fuel troubles himself, but Whisky Tango was fat.

The controller's voice paused, then came back.

"Next, the autopilot. The aircraft operator says it's a standard Piper Autocontrol Three. The engagement buttons are under the left hand corner of the instrument panel on a small white plastic rectangle. The wing-leveller button is on the left, the leveller control knob in the centre, and the heading-hold button on the right The buttons are both press-to-engage, press again to disengage. There is no altitude hold. D'you copy that?"

Kerr stretched his neck to see his own autopilot panel, on the far side of the left hand control yoke. It bore the black-printed legend *Autocontrol III*, and the left hand button was labelled WNG LVLR. Exactly the same as Whisky Tango.

He said, "Roger, copied. Standard Autocontrol Three."

"Okay, Romeo-X. You are converging on the target's extended track-line now, range from you three miles. Suggest you begin a slow circle to the right now."

"Roger. Circling right." Kerr tilted the horizon twenty degrees with a small pressure of his fingers, and stared out of the side window again. After a few seconds he added, "D'you have the answers to my other questions yet?"

"Affirmative, Romeo-X; just coming to that." The controller sounded slightly piqued. "D and D say the girl is a nurse, name Ann Moore, no known flying experience. The pilot's name's Roy Bazzard. An RAF doctor has confirmed his illness

136

as a probable, er – " the voice slowed up, stumbling on the pronunciation " – sub-ar-ach-noid haemorrhage. That means a haemorrhage in the brain, apparently. According to the pilot of another aircraft who's been speaking to her, the girl is aware of this. D'you get all that okay?"

"Got it." Kerr frowned out at the emptiness below, memorising the names and the word "subarachnoid". The town of Pontefract revolved slowly under his right wing, white-flecked brown in the winter sun. His feet were cold inside his motor cycle boots. After a moment he added: "What's my range from the target now?"

"Just under two miles, Romeo-X. Confirm negative contact?"

Kerr snapped, "Negative," resisting the temptation to add *What do you think I bloody asked you for?* He stared until his eyes smarted for want of blinking, willing himself to see the tiny speck which was out there somewhere, crawling towards him. His eyes quartered the cold blue sky and the patchwork quilt of the earth, searching in vertical strips.

Nothing. The sky as clear as a bell, visibility nigh on perfect – and nothing.

The cabin-pillars and then the port wing dappled shadows across his face as the Arrow turned across the low afternoon sun. He snatched a glance at the gyro compass, found he was passing through a northerly heading, and slammed the control yoke round to the left, kicking on left rudder at the same time. The top of the instrument panel twisted swiftly upright, and then on without pause into a steep left turn. G-force pressed him into his seat as he pulled back hard on the yoke. The horizon, tilted over to eighty degrees, streamed past the curved red engine cowling for several seconds and then suddenly pivoted back to a more moderate angle as he rolled off most of the bank. He went back to staring out, this time across the empty left hand seat and over the left wing.

Still nothing.

The headphones said, "Romeo-X, your target range now one mile."

The controller's calm was maddening. Kerr snapped,

"Negative contact," and went on looking. After a few seconds he lowered the left wing further still, pushing on hard right rudder at the same time to keep the rate of turn down. The Arrow crabbed through the sky in a powered sideslip, controls heavily crossed. Without taking his eyes away from the void, he reached out his left hand and increased power.

"Romeo X-ray, target range now half a mile. Target bearing about three-five-zero from you."

Kerr felt his temples prickling. His eyes darted quickly, urgently. He *must* be able to see the bloody thing from half a mile away. Another few seconds and it'd reach him and then be flying away . . .

"Range completely closed, Romeo-X. Single radar trace."

Kerr yelled *"Shit!"* aloud, glanced at the gyro compass again, and hauled the Arrow round on its left wing tip in another steep turn. No use circling now: now he'd have to fly south again and get out to one side and . . .

Then he saw it.

It was almost directly beneath him, thousands of feet below. A small, scurrying beetle with straight white wings, inching across the brown-green earth.

He pressed the transmit button and said, "Got it! Going down for a look." His own voice sounded tense in the side-tone through his headphones.

Leeds said something in reply, but he wasn't listening. Keeping his eyes on the white beetle he twisted the control yoke round to its full left deflection and at the same time pulled the throttle all the way back. The engine popped twice and died away as the Arrow rolled through almost to the inverted. Then the shining red cowling clubbed upside down into the panorama of the landscape, stopped when it was pointing directly at the moving crucifix of the other aeroplane, and rolled raggedly right-way-up as Kerr reefed into a steep curving dive. He stared over the nose, eyes narrowed and still, completely oblivious to the fact that he'd just executed a manoeuvre supposedly outside a Cherokee Arrow's capabilities. The noise of the airflow rose to a solid thrum-

ming roar as the speed wound up. 180 m.p.h....190...
200...

The white crucifix floated up and back, becoming a model aeroplane swimming in space. Details grew rapidly obvious. Square-cut wings and tailplane; blue nose.

At a range of a quarter of a mile, Kerr was diving at nearly 220 m.p.h. He banked slightly left to come down alongside the other machine, then pressed the transmit switch and said calmly, "Romeo X-ray closing on the target aircraft now. It's certainly a Cherokee: either the fastest 180 in the world or an Arrow."

The Leeds controller suppressed his own excitement in formality. "Roger, Romeo-X; advise when you have the air-craft positively identified."

At 200 yards, Kerr began flattening out of his dive. The aeroplane ahead seemed to rise out of the depths, gathering momentum, until it suddenly popped up above the horizon. Kerr pulled back hard on his control yoke, left hand slowly opening the throttle, eyes watching the target's underbelly.

The wheels were retracted. And the only square-winged retractable in the Cherokee range was the Arrow.

Using the speed of his dive, he pulled up until his height matched the other aircraft. It moved obliquely back towards him, skating crabwise across the horizon as the gap between them closed. At a range of a hundred yards he slapped his throttle shut momentarily and banged on left rudder and right aileron. The Arrow lurched into a cumbersome sideslip, killing its overtaking speed. He straightened up abruptly, shoved the throttle open to keep in station three or four wingspans to the right and slightly behind, and stared out of the right window.

The other Arrow floated serene and steady, completely oblivious. He could read the registration letters on the side of its fuselage without even squinting.

They were G-AYWT.

12

ANN MOORE WAS looking at the dust in the cockpit. The top of the dashboard was very dusty, and motes of it danced in the small flow of air from the windscreen demister. The low winter sun, glaring in from the right, caught the specks and made them shine as they bobbed and swirled and then disappeared. It was like the dust in the tiny ward office at the hospital. You could sweep and sweep and clean and clean but as soon as the winter sun shone in, there it was again. She remembered reading something about it at school once, years and years ago. Something about the low angle of the sun changing the quality of the light and making everything show up . . .

She clenched her teeth together, and rubbed her eyes hard with her knuckles. She *must* stop rambling like this. It was quite ridiculous, wandering off thinking about things like dust. She *must* concentrate on something useful. Look at the dials again, for example. Look at the dials and try . . .

Without warning, the radio speaker over her head came to life. The voice was a new one, clear and slow and sounding incredibly close, almost as if the man was in the cockpit with her. Ann started violently and whipped her head round. The two empty back seats leered at her.

"Good afternoon, Ann. My name's Keith Kerr, and I'm going to help you. Can you hear me all right?"

She fumbled, snatched the microphone out of her lap, and said, "Yes!" It came out low-pitched and hoarse, like some-

140

body speaking through a bad cold. She cleared her throat and said it again, louder. "Yes. Yes, I can hear you."

"Great. That's fine. Now, I'm in another aeroplane, just like yours, and I'm right alongside you, on your left. If you look out of the window you'll be able to see me."

Ann's head snapped round for the second time, eyes wide with shock. For a long moment there was only the vast blue sky mockingly empty. Then she looked further back, out of the rear side window behind Bazzard's seat . . .

And there it was. Another plane, hanging in the void alongside and slightly behind. It looked incredibly close; less than fifty yards away, as if it had been parked alongside in the sky. It seemed impossible that it could have got there without her seeing it or hearing it, but she couldn't hear it, even now. It was just *there*, rising and falling gently and silently beyond the left wing tip, the sun glaring white on its body. She could even see the pilot, inside the cockpit: indistinctly, but enough to see that his face was turned towards her. He was the man who'd spoken. He was watching her, talking to her . . .

She suddenly found she was laughing and crying, all at once. Her stomach was hurting, she was giggling, and tears were rolling down her face at the same time. Someone was here! The man in the other plane might not be able to do anything but he was *here*, and for some reason that was terribly important. It meant that people were trying to help her; she wasn't abandoned, wasn't alone.

The voice said calmly, "Can you see me all right, Ann?"

Still staring at the other plane, she brought the microphone up to her mouth. It trembled violently against her top lip. She said, "Yes. Ye-yes." Her voice caught on a sob, and she released the mike button.

"Great." The man's speech was deep and unhurried, with a trace of mid-Atlantic accent. "Now first, I want to talk to you. So I'd like you to just sit back and relax. I'll be staying here all the time, so you just sit back and relax. Okay?"

Relax.

Ann found she was twisted round in her seat, straining

against the lap-and-diagonal belt. Slowly, reluctant to lose sight of the other plane, she turned to face the front again. Squeezed her eyes tight shut, and forced herself to untense her muscles. She took several slow deep breaths, feeling herself shivering all over, and tried to stop the convulsive sobs which kept welling up in her throat. This was where she *had* to pull herself together; *had* to be sensible . . .

After a long moment she opened her eyes and blinked at the radio panel, directly in front of her. Then she raised the microphone, pressed the button, and said, "Okay. I'm all right." The calmness of her own voice surprised her.

The man came back immediately.

"That's fine, Ann. You sound as if you're bearing up very well. Now, I understand you're a nurse. Is that right?"

"Yes." The question was unexpected, and she answered automatically. "I'm a nursing sister."

"Good for you. That's a job I'd never be able to do in a hundred years. Now, I gather you've got some idea of what's wrong with your pilot. Roy. Is that right?"

"Yes." The cold feeling in her stomach tightened. She shot a frightened glance at Bazzard, and then looked back at the radios again. "I think . . . he's had a subarachnoid haemorrhage."

"Well, I understand a doctor on the ground agrees with you : he thinks you could be right. So to be on the safe side, we ought to consider what we're going to do just in case Roy doesn't come round for a while. You with me?"

Ann took another deep breath, then said, "You mean flying the plane. I've got to fly the plane."

"Yes, that's right." The man's matter-of-factness surprised her. It was strangely reassuring, so that the confirmation of her fears somehow had no particular impact. "You've obviously thought it through for yourself. I'm going to be sitting here in formation with you until you're safely back on the ground, so the most sensible way to use our time is to have you work on controlling the aeroplane in case it's necessary. Okay?"

"Yes." Her throat was dry, but the trembling had died

142

down. Now it was actually happening she suddenly felt very still, nerves poised on a razor-edge of calmness.

"Okay then. Now, am I right in thinking you've never flown in anything at all before?"

"No. I mean, that's right. I've only been up in a big passenger plane, once."

"Okay, I see." The voice sounded unperturbed. "Well, at least you won't have any preconceived wrong ideas. Do you drive a car?"

"Yes." Ann stared at the radios, not looking out.

"Right. Well, the the first thing I can tell you is that what we're going to do is actually easier than driving a car. If I was going to teach you to fly properly it'd be much more complicated, but for what we need to do today, which is just to descend, turn and land, there isn't any great problem at all. The only controls we'll need to touch are the steering wheel in front of you, the throttle, and two other small items which I'll be telling you about later. Also, you won't be needing any of the instruments except one very simple gauge, which again I'll be telling you about. All the rest you can forget. You with me all right?"

Ann blinked in astonishment. This wasn't what she'd expected at all. She'd assumed all the dials and levers were important, and steeled herself for the impossible task of trying to take them all in. Her eyes darted round the cockpit, unbelieving: it seemed incredible that you *didn't* need all those things, that you could fly the plane without them. That *couldn't* be right, or what were they all there for . . . ?

She pressed the mike button and said, "You mean . . . just the wheel, alone?" She could hear the doubt in her own voice. "You don't need . . . er, anything else, at all?"

"Just about." The voice from the speaker was strong; calm and confident over the drone of the engine. "As I say, it's not as if you were learning to fly in the normal way. If I was teaching you to be a pilot properly you'd have to understand the instruments, watch your height and speed and position, all sorts of things, but since I'll be formating with you all the time, I can look after all that myself. All you'll

143

have to do is move the wheel and the throttle exactly when I tell you, plus a couple of other things which you'll only have to move once and then forget about. You follow me?"

Ann swallowed. For the first time, the idea of flying the plane suddenly seemed real and possible. If she really only had to move the wheel . . .

She raised the microphone and said, "Yes. I see."

"Okay, good." The voice hesitated for a moment, leaving just the burr of the engine, then came back. "One other thing I ought to mention is your autopilot. I believe you know that your plane's flying on autopilot at the moment?"

Ann said, "Yes," aware of her stomach going suddenly hollow again. He was going to tell her to switch the autopilot off . . .

"Well, you might like to know that what we're going to do, for the time being at any rate, is to leave the autopilot switched on. You'll be able to over-ride it with your control wheel, but it means that if you let go at any time the aeroplane'll just go back to flying straight and level on its own, like it is now. You understand that?"

"Um . . . I think so." Ann frowned at the radios, trying to make herself concentrate. "You mean it'll come back to . . . as it is now. By itself."

"That's right; you've got it. It means that if you mess anything up — not that you will — you can just let go and the aeroplane'll sort itself out. So bearing that in mind I'm going to explain now what we want to do first, and why. Okay?"

She took a deep breath and then said, "Okay."

"Fine. Well, what we'll do for a start is just raise and lower the nose a little. Just that. We need to do that because, fairly obviously, the nose must be pointed downhill a bit to descend, and then picked up again for the landing. We call that pitch control — moving the nose up and down — and I want to get it so you can raise or lower the nose when I tell you, and hold it in its new position. You with me so far?"

"Yes." The word came out hoarsely, and she cleared her throat. "Yes."

"Good. Now in a minute I'll be telling you how to raise

and lower the nose – but first, we have to have some point of reference so we can see how *much* we've raised it. For that, we use the natural horizon. So what I'd like you to do is sit normally in the seat, as if you were fly . . . er, driving, look forward over the top of the instrument panel, and tell me how far above the top of that panel the horizon is. One inch, two inches, or whatever. *I'd* tell *you*, only the actual position depends on how tall you are and how high your seat's adjusted. So I'd rather hear it from you."

Ann swallowed, and then slowly raised her eyes. The sight of the cold endless sky and the huge glare of the sun made her stomach cringe again. She clenched her fists, feeling the slipperiness of her own sweat on the plastic microphone, and made herself stare out over the nose, squinting into the hard winter brilliance.

The distant horizon-line was just visible over the imitation-leather crashpad on top of the instrument panel. She tilted her head back, craning her neck to see it better.

"It's – " she swallowed again, trying to keep her voice from trembling " – it's . . . just above the nose. About two inches above."

"Okay, great. Now then, Ann, I want you to make a very careful note in your own mind of just *exactly* where it is, so that when we come to move the nose up and down I can say to you 'raise the nose by an inch', and you'll have some reference to judge it by; you'll just raise it so that it's an inch higher against the horizon, and hold it there. Got that?"

"Ye-es."

"Okay. Now it'll probably be that at some point we'll be raising the nose actually *above* the horizon a little bit. When we do that, you'll need to look at where the horizon cuts into the panel on the right hand side. You see what I mean?"

The words "raising the nose above the horizon" produced a new flutter of nervousness. She closed her eyes for a second, letting the steady din of the engine wash through her, then opened them again and looked to the side of the panel. The crashpad, curving down to meet the bottom of the wind-screen, formed a V-shaped gap between itself and the back-ward-sloping pillar between the windscreen and the door. The distant landscape filled in the vee; she could just make out the faint blurred arc of the yellow propeller tips against the faraway fields.

"You see what I mean, Ann? If the nose is too high to see over it, then you'll have to look *alongside* the panel to see the horizon."

She said, "Yes. All right." The words sounded husky out of her dry throat.

"Okeydoke, that's super." The voice paused while Kerr tried to think of something to break the tension. After a few seconds he said, "By the way, did you know you can smoke? You can have a cigarette, if you want one."

Ann blinked. "No . . . no thanks. I don't smoke."

"How very wise of you. Did you manage to give it up, or never start?"

"Er – I never started." She was flooded with a sudden feeling of unreality. Sitting here, trapped in this sun-lit cockpit in the middle of nothing, and then talking to someone in another plane about smoking . . .

"Pity: I was hoping you'd be able to tell me how to give up, later on. Anyway, back to work. You've got that horizon position nicely memorised, have you, now?"

"Um – yes." The feeling of unreality persisted. She shut her eyes for a moment, and fought down a shudder which ran through her whole body.

"Right. Good. So now we come to just *how* we move the nose up and down. Do you see the control wheel in front of you? The thing like half a car steering wheel?"

"Yes."

"Great. Now then, don't touch it for the moment, but just listen. To raise the nose, we pull that wheel *back*; and to lower the nose we push it *forward*. You got that?"

Ann rubbed her eyes, forcing herself to pay attention. "Yes. All right."

"Good. It's the logical way to it, when you think about it. Back to pull the nose up, forward to push it down. The other thing is that you only push or pull very lightly, and over a very small distance. With me?"

"Yes."

"Okay. Now, I know this is going to sound silly, but I just want to make sure we've got it right: so what do we do with the wheel if we want to *raise* the nose?"

The cold ball in her stomach swelled up. She licked her dry lips with a dry tongue, aware of the microphone shaking in her hand. "P-pull back. We pull back."

"Right on." The voice was the same as ever, deep and steady. Like a surgeon during an operation. "Okay then, Ann. So now, that's what I'd like you to do: take hold of the control wheel and pull it back. Very gently, and not very far. Look forward over the nose as you do it, and just raise the nose an inch or so on the horizon. Then hold it there until I say. Do that in your own time."

Ann looked at the yoke. Now the moment had actually arrived, she was suddenly strangely calm. Her face was hot and her muscles were tingling—but the raw fear was draining away, leaving a kind of fatalistic acceptance. It was almost as if she were sitting outside herself, watching her body reacting of its own volition. Out of her subconscious came a sudden disconnected memory of the night when she'd first gone to bed with somebody, four years before. She'd felt the same way then: frightened and shivery beforehand, but at the last moment quite calm. The battle of conscience was over, the resolution made; now it only remained to carry out the act.

She put the microphone down in her lap, took a deep breath, then reached out and gripped the control wheel.

Nothing happened. The Arrow just rumbled on, serene and steady as ever.

She blinked in surprise. She didn't know quite *what* she'd expected when she took hold of the wheel, but she'd certainly expected something; some sort of reaction. But all there was was the hard plastic, cool against her fingers. It wasn't like a car steering wheel at all: it felt weirdly solid and insensitive, as if the plane was determined to ignore her.

The thought made her suddenly, unreasonably angry.

147

Craning her neck to see the distant horizon better over the top of the panel, she pulled slowly and firmly backwards.

Smoothly, without any hesitation, the nose canted upwards towards the brilliant blue canopy of the sky.

*   *   *

It is a peculiarity of formation flying that if the leader should make a small, unannounced pitch change into a gentle climb or descent, his wing-men are very often the last people to notice it. The reason for this apparent paradox is that the following pilots in any formation are neither watching their instruments, nor the horizon, nor anything else which might give them an immediately obvious reference to their pitch angle: the *only* thing they are watching, with eyes glued and often smarting for want of blinking, is the fuselage and wings of the lead aircraft. In this concentration, jockeying throttle and stick and rudder in an endless series of sometimes quite violent corrections in order to keep in station, the leader becomes their entire frame of reference. If he raises his nose a few degrees the wing-men will follow suit, but may never be aware of having done it: so far as they are concerned they are merely doing whatever is necessary to hold position, and the hell with everything else.

Without consciously thinking about it, Keith Kerr had closed up so that his starboard wing tip was parallel to the runaway's port tailplane and about two wingspans away. Holding there, making continual small power changes and control movements to match speed and position exactly, it was several seconds before it dawned on him that the girl *had* raised her nose. The realisation only finally clicked when he found he was having to pull back on his own control yoke more or less constantly in order to stay in formation. A lightning glance forwards through the windscreen and then in at the instruments confirmed it. His own engine cowling was just above the horizon instead of below it, the speed had sagged to 145 m.p.h., and the rate-of-climb indicator was showing 300 feet a minute Up.

148

He said, "Bollocks!" explosively, without pressing his transmit button, then twisted his control yoke slightly to the left and trod gently on the left rudder pedal. The other Arrow immediately skated ahead and sideways in the clear winter sky, moving with the peculiar crabbing illusion you always get when you pull away from another aeroplane in the air. When the gap between them had widened to a hundred yards Kerr turned a fraction right again to hold it at that. The change in perspective was instantly apparent; now he could see the runaway's slightly nose-up attitude against the distant level line of the horizon. At the same time his own task of flying became suddenly easier, since maintaining a rough station 300 feet away from another aircraft is far less demanding than holding exact formation at a tenth of that distance.

He hunched his shoulders briefly in a deliberate attempt to relax. The sun was warm on his face through the Perspex of the cockpit, and his feet were beginning to thaw out inside his motor cycle boots. He reached out and moved the Cabin Heat lever a little way back from its maximum position.

Slowly, almost imperceptibly, the other Arrow's nose drooped down. From pointing five degrees upwards in relation to the horizon-line, the shark-shape of the fuselage tilted gently forward and began to pull away, becoming a cruciform of white wings and tail as it sank into the brown-green depths below.

Keeping his eyes on it, Kerr allowed his own nose to pitch down gently to follow. His thumb hovered over the transmit button for a second and then moved away again.

What was happening was very simple, and was concerned with just one thing: workload. In the very early stages of learning to fly, when everything about the environment is utterly alien and unfamiliar, a student's mental efficiency whilst in the air shrinks to a tiny fraction of his or her normal ability on the ground. In this reduced state the very simplest of tasks can quite easily absorb a person's entire workload capacity to an extent which, in the coolness of retrospect back on the ground, they find astounding and incomprehensible. The concentration required in merely taking hold of the control yoke for the first time, for example, is such that after a short period the student frequently loses track of where he or she was supposed to be holding the nose in relation to the horizon. The aeroplane's natural tendency to restabilise itself in level flight then takes over, and the nose sags down; the machine adopts a gentle descent for a little while as it accelerates back to its original cruising speed, and then gradually picks itself up to the level flight attitude it was in before the nose was lifted. Throughout all this the nose only moves up and down very slowly and by a relatively small amount; the pitch change is so subtle that the entire cycle of events can, and very often does, take place with the student clinging white-knuckled to the control column throughout but completely failing to notice anything amiss.

The problem for the instructor lies in deciding what to do about it.

Some initiates in this situation will respond to being told to hold the nose *up*, just *there* – whilst others, more nervous, will only become flustered if their mentor attempts any such coercion while their attention is concentrated on holding the controls for the first time. In these cases the man in the right hand seat must exercise the most difficult skill in instructing; that of knowing when *not* to open his mouth. He must sit quietly for a while, letting the student gain confidence, then take over control again himself and carry out a second careful demonstration of raising and lowering the nose against the horizon and *holding* it in its new position.

That is the normal answer.

Kerr, unconsciously rubbing the fingertips of his left hand up and down the scar near his eye, reflected that the normal answer does tend to assume that the instructor is sitting in the same aircraft as his student. He also reflected that if the girl *couldn't* learn to adjust and then hold her nose position, she was in big trouble. Probably fatal trouble.

He shook his head irritably and stabbed at the cigarette lighter on the panel. In a little while he'd have no choice; he'd have to hustle, push her along, prompt her more or less non-stop against the kind of mistake she was making now. But at the moment, at this initial stage, the finely-honed instinct which experienced instructors sometimes call "gut-feel" warned him that he could easily overdo it. The girl's voice had been outwardly cool, much calmer than he'd expected, but there'd also been something in it that was brittle, stretched near to breaking-point. Gut-feel told him that urgent as the time factor was, the first vital requirement was to let her alone for a few brief moments to build up her confidence: too much pressure now and that confidence would shatter, leaving her broken and terrified and her reactions totally unpredictable.

Well, maybe that made it time he sorted out some other things. Or, better still, got someone else on to sorting them out.

Ahead and to the right, the other Arrow was slowly levelling off from its shallow descent. Kerr followed suit, allowing himself to drift down slightly lower. The streamlined profile bobbed up above the horizon and hung there, a stationary plastic model floating in the empty glare of the winter sun.

The clock on the instrument panel said 1521.

He picked the cigarette lighter out of its housing as it popped out, blew a long streamer of smoke, and then pressed the transmit button.

"Hey, you did that all right, Ann." He kept his voice light as he uttered the oldest confidence-booster in the book. "You *sure* you haven't done this before?"

There was a very long pause, ending with the unmistakable *clack* of a microphone being keyed. Then the girl's voice said in his ears, "No. N-no, I haven't." Beneath the tension there was an undertone of surprise, almost relief.

Smiling into the headset-mike – since the act of smiling comes over in the voice – Kerr said, "Well, you must be born to it, then. Nice natural touch; real gentle. How did you find it, yourself?"

Another pause. Then, "Not . . . so difficult. Er . . . heavier than I'd expected, I think."

"Yes, it is heavy. Bright of you to notice. Mr. Piper makes

151

a very easy aeroplane to fly, but he does seem to think that all pilots are built like Russian weight-lifters." Kerr paused for a second, then allowed his voice to become fractionally more brisk. "Okay, then. So what we need to do now is exactly the same again, only this time with the emphasis on *holding* the nose up after you've raised it. You let it drop down a bit last time. Raise it so the top of the instrument panel is just on the horizon-line, and then hold it there until I say. You'll have to keep pulling back on the wheel, maintaining your back-pressure, and you'll find that the trick is to keep your eyes on the horizon all the time. Every moment. You understand that okay?"

"Ye-es." The relief was gone out of the voice now, leaving only the tension. "I'll try."

"Good lass. Now while you're doing that, I'm just going to talk to the ground for a moment. I'll still be here, and I'll be back to you in two ticks. Okay?"

"Yes."

"Right. You raise that nose now, then, in your own time."

For a long moment, nothing happened. Kerr took a deep drag on his cigarette and stared through the drifting smoke, pale blue eyes fixed on the model-shape of the other Arrow. Then, very slowly, its nose lifted up. It began to climb gently, a tiny white bird crawling upwards into the vast blue dome of the heavens. Kerr raised his own nose to follow, instinctively winding his trim-wheel back a couple of inches to relieve the control pressure. He had to reduce power a shade to stop himself catching up; being one-up and carrying less fuel, his climb performance was slightly better. He gave it half a minute, then pressed his transmit button.

"That's lovely, Ann. Don't bother to reply to me, but just go on holding the nose up there, where it is now. I'll be back to you in a moment."

The Arrow climbed on steadily.

Kerr put his cigarette in the corner of his mouth, reached out to the radio panel, and flicked the frequency of the single radio to Leeds Approach on 123.75. When he spoke, the smile and the gentleness were gone from his voice; the words were snapped and urgent.

"Leeds, Mayday Romeo X-ray."

No reply.

"Mayday, Mayday: Leeds Approach from Golf Bravo Charlie Romeo X-ray."

For a moment, there was still no reply. Then a new, calm voice said in his ears, "Mayday Romeo X-ray from Dan Air zero-six-one. Leeds are replying to you, sir. Would you like me to relay?"

"Ah – affirmative, 061; I can't hear 'em. They know all about me, and I just want to know who I'm being handed off to, please."

"Roger. Stand by. D'you get that, Leeds? He wants to know who he's being handed off to." A pause, then, "Okay, copied. Romeo-X, Leeds says switch to Northern Radar, one-three-one-decimal-zero-five."

"Roger; 131.05. Thanks a lot, Dan Air."

"Any time. Good luck with your problem."

Kerr double-clicked the transmit switch, thanking a benefactor somewhere in the sky whom he'd never meet. Then he changed the frequency again.

"Northern Radar, Mayday traffic Golf Bravo Charlie Romeo X-ray."

"Romeo X-ray, this is Northern Radar." A stolid north-country voice, somehow very obviously RAF. "We have you strength five, radar identified, and we have your details."

"Roger." Kerr spoke fast, flying with small flexings of his muscles, keeping his eyes on the runaway. "What's my position, please?"

"You're about fifteen miles north-east of East Midlands airport, Romeo X-ray. The big town ahead on your right is Nottingham."

Kerr visualised the map of England, and whistled soundlessly. No wonder he hadn't been able to hear Leeds. He glanced below Whisky Tango and found the sprawl of Nottingham about five miles away up-sun, a smudgy red-grey rag flung down on the clean frosty landscape. He thumbed the transmit switch again.

153

"Roger, Northern Radar. I'm going to need some help on this: there's some things I need done. Ready to copy?"

"Go ahead, sir."

"Roger. First thing is aerodromes. We're going to be flying in a straight line for the next – ah, say half hour, forty minutes, so I need details of the biggest aerodromes within our reach before dark after that time. You with me?"

"That's understood, Romeo X-ray."

"Good, thanks. Now, I'm going to need the longest and widest available runway which has flush landing lights, no obstructions either side, and is as near into wind as we can get; she'll run off the side for sure if there's a cross-wind. Also I'd like the details of the largest available grass airfield where she can land in more or less any direction. I'll make the decision on which to go for when I know what's available."

"Roger, Romeo X-ray, understood." The voice hesitated for a moment, leaving a small hiss of carrier-wave, then added diffidently, "Ah – be advised your present track will take you into the London Control Zone in about forty minutes, sir."

Kerr frowned for a couple of seconds, and then shrugged to himself. If he had to go through Heathrow's patch he had to go through, whether they liked it or not. He pressed the switch and snapped, "Roger; I'll worry about that later. When we've decided on an aerodrome I'll be calling for radar steers when I can. I haven't got any maps here, and anyway I'll be too busy to navigate."

"Okay, Romeo X-ray. Can you maintain a listening watch on this frequency?"

"Neg . . . stand by. Stand by." Whisky Tango was sinking down, dropping gently below the horizon into the drab brown depths of the distant landscape. Kerr hesitated a moment, waiting to make sure it *was* sinking rather than he himself having pulled back for a second, then pushed his own nose down and reduced power. The runaway floated slowly up and back, swimming in space, until it was suddenly just above the horizon again. Kerr held his position, squinting into the sun as he watched the other aircraft. After a few seconds he began gradually feeding on power, and then glanced in at his instruments. The airspeed was steady at 160 m.p.h. and the rate of climb indicator read zero, neither up nor down.

Level flight.

That meant the girl had done much the same thing as before; allowed her nose to sink back down instead of holding it up. Again, she herself almost certainly wouldn't have noticed the slow change of flight attitude. It wasn't her fault: quite apart from the workload factor, earth-bound eyes are simply not accustomed to considering the immutable horizon as an errant and elusive variable. Such three-dimensional awareness is something which has to be taught.

Kerr rubbed his scar again. Then he took a fast drag on his cigarette and thumbed the transmit button.

"Northern Radar, Romeo-X; sorry about that, I had to watch something here. Say again your query?"

"Eh – " the controller flustered for a moment, then came back. "Eh, can you maintain a listening watch on this frequency, Romeo X-ray?"

"Negative." Kerr glanced at the rectangular hole in the radio panel which normally housed the number two nav/com set. "I've got the second set out in this thing, so I'll have to keep switching."

"Roger, Romeo X-ray. D'you want to come up on 121.5 each time then, sir? That'll save you bothering about hand-offs."

Kerr blinked, then thought for a few seconds. The man was dead right. If he stayed on the normal frequencies he could have the same problem he'd had with Leeds every time he passed from one radar area into another, whereas if he used 121.5, the universal aircraft emergency frequency, he could be picked up by Distress and Diversion direct or by any other major control tower in the country; 121.5 was one frequency almost everybody had.

He said, "Affirmative, sir. Thank you."

"Okay, Romeo X-ray. Squawk 7700 now."

Kerr repeated, "Seven-seven-zero-zero," and reached out to the transponder. As the figures clicked up in their little windows his face creased in a brief savage grin. A transponder is an electronic radar 'reflector' capable of painting up – or "squawking" – any four-figure code for easy identification on an air traffic controller's screen. Most codes do just that and nothing else; but 7700 is special. It is also known as the "Mayday squawk"; the international transponder code meaning "I am in distress". At this moment his trace on Northern Radar's screens at RAF Lindholme would, he knew, be changing from the single short dash of a normal transponder echo to the four-lines-in-a-row of a Mayday signal; at the same time an alarm bell would ring, to be hurriedly switched off by the controller. It was a perfectly sensible thing to do in the circumstances – it would remove any tiny possibility of his trace being confused with somebody else's at any time – but for some inexplicable reason it also momentarily appeased a streak of showmanship in him. Like a man who has always wanted to dive into a phone box and dial 999, he had long harboured a small secret desire to squawk Mayday just once.

He blew out cigarette smoke and said evenly, "Romeo-X squawking Mayday."

"Roger, Romeo X-ray, we have your squawk. Cleared now to switch to 126.85; call us back on 121.5 when you can."

Kerr said, "Roger, thanks," then reached out and changed frequency again. His headphones went dead quiet: 126.85 was an empty field, cleared for battle.

The time was twenty-four minutes past three.

He frowned briefly at his fuel gauges. The left tank – the one he'd been using, since a Cherokee fuel tap provides Left and Right selection but no Both position – read less than a quarter full, while the right one showed just over the quarter. His lips tightened, creating unaccustomed lines of worry at the corners of his mouth. He snapped the boost-pump on, leaned across the cockpit and twisted the tap to RIGHT, then switched the pump off again. After that he edged the red mixture lever a little further back towards the lean position, eyeing the Cylinder Head Temperature gauge as he did so. The needle moved up to the redline and a fraction

156

beyond: at the same time, the fuel-flow indication dropped back from eleven US gallons per hour to ten.

Still frowning, he turned his attention back to the runaway, hanging apparently motionless in the void off to his right. Now, he thought, there is no more time for feeding your confidence. Now, we must get some real work done.

He ground his cigarette into the ashtray and pressed the transmit switch.

13

1514–1534

WHEN A PERSON gets punched hard on the nose, there tends
to be a lot of blood about. Even if the gristle and bone escape
breakage, there are a great many tiny arteries and arterial
branches which are almost certain to be ruptured. The largest
of these arteries have a diameter of no more than five
thousandths of an inch, but nonetheless their capacity for
dribbling gore can be seemingly endless.

Edward Tomms's nose had been bleeding for over fifteen
minutes, and was still going strong. Also, his stomach seemed
to be on fire, the pain pulsing up every few minutes into a
red-hot dagger which stabbed right through to his backbone.

Slumped in a chair facing the Aero Club counter, he was
attempting to stem the nosebleed with a succession of Kleenex
tissues. The packet was half empty, and the desk beside him
was littered with the crumpled remnants, like discarded red
and white flowers. His face and shirt collar were smeared
with crimson, and spots of it speckled the brown lino floor.
The truth of the matter was that he felt very ill indeed: he
badly wanted to get to the lavatory a little way down the
corridor, but didn't think he could manage it by himself and
didn't want to ask for help. So he stayed where he was, waiting to feel better, hiding his agony behind a thickly-mumbled
monologue concerning Kerr's ingratitude and future unem-
ployability. He was bitterly aware that he was doing the
wrong thing, being stupidly aggressive in front of his staff,
but the knowledge only served to increase his anger and

frustration. He never had been good at getting on with people, and in his loneliness of the last few years the gulf had seemed to widen until it had become unbridgeable, leaving aggression and irritation as his normal reactions.

Most of his employees were conspicuously ignoring him.

Ian Mackenzie, the deputy chief instructor, was bent over the counter applying enormous concentration to the filling in of a student record form. The rest of the instructors were milling around hiding their grins and finding excuses to delay their next lessons. The only person taking any overt notice of him was Maggie, who kept darting scared little glances over her shoulder in between flustered attempts to deal with the goggling crowd of students at the counter.

The two policemen walked in on the scene at fifteen minutes past three.

They came through the door in silence, and paused just inside the threshold while the silence spread through the rooms. The white covers on the crowns of their caps labelled them as Traffic, and their cold formal expressions indicated that the visit was Duty. After a moment they walked over to the counter, taking their time. Tomms looked up, still holding the latest Kleenex to his nose.

"Eh, I'm glad you coom," he said thickly. " 'Oo called you?"

The younger of the two policemen said coldly, "No one called us, sir. We're looking for the owner of a Norton motor cycle parked outside, number XTM 817."

" 'Ere . . ." Tomms lowered the Kleenex, revealing his bloodstained face. "Tha's bloody Kerr's! He's bloke who 'it me."

The older policeman said, "Hit you, sir?"

"Aye, fuckin' right!" Tomms was aware of a stillness all around him. He started to stand up, winced, and plumped back into the chair, clasping his stomach with one hand and keeping the tissue to his nose with the other. He jerked his head at the Instructors Only door. "Coom in . . . coom round. I'll tell you. I been assaulted."

The policemen came round. The crowd of instructors and students began to melt away. Maggie shrank back nervously

159

as the blue uniforms filled the small space behind the counter with their presence. Only Mackenzie seemed unaffected; he stayed where he was, chewing his pen over the record form and ignoring the police completely.

The older policeman took off his black leather gloves and started unbuttoning the top pocket of his jacket.

"Do you want to tell us what happened, sir?"

"Aye, that I do!" Tomms dabbed with the Kleenex, then fumbled for his glasses among the tissues on the desk. He found them after a moment and perched them gingerly on his nose. One lens was cracked and the frame was bent, so that they hung ludicrously lop-sided on his face. He stared up at the policemen and said again, "That I do! My fuckin' chief instroocter 'it me, tha's what. Punched me in face an' the fuckin' stomach!"

The older policeman looked at Maggie and then back at Tomms. "There's a lady present, sir," he said woodenly.

"Oh. Aye." Tomms glared at Maggie for an instant and then back at the policeman, not sounding sorry. His nose dripped blood on to his overcoat as he moved his head. He pulled a fresh tissue out of the box, dabbed again, and said, "Well, what you goin' to do abowt it?"

The policeman regarded him stonily. After a moment he said, "Well sir, if you want to make a complaint..."

"Aye, I bloody do!" Tomms jabbed an angry finger at the air and then grabbed his stomach again as another wave of pain hit him. He leaned forward, massaging his abdomen, and gasped, "Bu... bloke 'it me... I'll 'ave 'im... bloody put away..."

The younger policeman said, "You all right, sir?"

"Aye..." Tomms leaned back, panting, as the pain receded. His face was very pale. "Aye... I'll be all right. Jus' give me the fu – the cramps, gettin' 'it like that. That bloody Kerr... punched me in the gut."

"Mr. Kerr is the man you say assaulted you, sir?"

"Yeh. Keith Kerr. 'E were my bloody chief instroocter. 'E's one who's got that bloody motor bike, an' all." Tomms stopped gasping long enough to blow his nose, gently and tenta-

160

tively. The Kleenex blossomed red. He mumbled, "Bloody bastard . . ."

"Is Mr. Kerr here now, sir?"

"No, he ain't." Tomms snatched another clean tissue out of the box and held it to his nose. His voice came out indistinctly. "Bugger went off in one o' my planes, wi'out my permission."

Both policemen stiffened. The younger one said sharply, "Without your permission, sir?"

Tomms hesitated, unsure if he was going too far. Then the pain came again, running like boiling oil through his stomach. He groaned and hunched forward, feeling sweat breaking out on his temples. The agony lasted for five seconds and then subsided to a dull throbbing, pushing out caution and leaving fury in its wake.

"Aye! Wi'out my fuckin' permission! He grabbed keys to one o' my planes, an' when I asked 'im what he were doin' he just punched me an' went off in it. Tha's bloody stealin' it, in't it?"

There was a shocked silence. Tomms became aware that Maggie was staring at him with an expression of horrified disbelief and that Mackenzie, who had been leaning against the counter with his back to the scene, was slowly turning round.

His reaction, typically, was belligerence. He glared up at the policeman, eyes staring and angry through the thick lenses of his crooked glasses.

"Well, tha's right, in't it? Stealin'?"

The older policeman said, "Stealing means taking something with intent to permanently deprive the owner of the use of it, sir. Are you alleging . . ."

"Eh, balls!" Tomms stabbed the air again. Blood ran down his top lip from his nose. "Don't fuckin' give me that! Bloke took that plane wi'out my permission: that's got to be stealin' or takin' an' drivin' away or *somethin'*, ain't it?"

"Rubbish!"

The word came from Mackenzie. Two shiny black cap-peaks and four cold official eyes pivoted round to look at him.

The older policeman said, "Who are you, sir?"

"Ian Mackenzie. I'm the deputy CFI. I'm not involved in this, but I ought to make a couple of things clear. The first is that Keith's the Chief Flying Instructor here. That means he doesn't need *anybody's* permission to fly – he's the one who *gives* flight authorisations, not receives them. Mr. Tomms himself would need Keith's permission if he wanted to fly. The second thing . . ."

Tomms exploded. "Eh, bugger that! Kerr took that fuckin' plane after he'd been fired an' after I'd told 'im to stop . . ."

". . . and the *second* thing," Mackenzie went on loudly, "is that Keith was going off on an emergency flight, and Mr. Tomms was obstructing him and delaying him."

Tomms shouted, "You *bastard*! You're bloody fired an' all . . ."

The younger policeman snapped, "What emergency?"

The older policeman said loudly, "All right, all right, all RIGHT!"

There was silence.

The older policeman looked at Mackenzie. "All right," he said again. "Now; what's this emergency flight?"

Mackenzie said, "There's a pilot been taken ill and passed out in an aeroplane flying down from Newcastle. He's left a woman on board who doesn't know how to fly. Keith's gone up to formate on her and talk her down if the guy doesn't come round."

The policeman studied him for a moment, then turned his impassive face to Tomms.

"Does that information conflict with anything you know, sir?"

Tomms snorted blood into his Kleenex. "Eh . . . well . . ."

"*Does* it, sir? What I mean is, do you dispute what Mr. Kerr is doing? Do you agree that he's engaged on an emergency flight?"

Tomms weaved his head about, like a bull looking for someone to charge. Flecks of blood landed on the floor. After a moment he said, "Aye. I know he's on soom sort of urgent flight. But that in't th' point. The thing is, he . . ."

"All *right*, sir." The policeman's voice was flat, commanding. Everyone looked at him. He went on staring levelly at Tomms's face and said, "I just want to get this straight, sir. Would I be right in thinking that this assault took place during an argument between you and Mr. Kerr, about Mr Kerr's going on this emergency flight?"

Tomms felt the pain coming again, and gripped his stomach. After a moment he gasped, "Aye . . . but I didn't know it were an emergency flight, not then. He didn't . . . tell me, see? Just – " he wiped at the sweat on his pallid face, suddenly sounding almost pathetic, "just bloody 'it me. Just like that."

The policeman watched him impassively. After eleven years on the Force he'd had enough experience of assault cases not to want to get involved in this one. If an out-and-out villain hammers an innocent person that's one thing; but when it's merely a question of two ordinary people coming to blows in the course of an argument, then the British police generally do not want to know: a constable gets no thanks from his superiors for taking on a complex and time-consuming investigation which will achieve nothing but a bound-over-to-keep-the-peace at the end of it. So the unwritten rule on punch-ups is simple: if there are no villains involved, you try to talk the complainant out of making a police issue of it. In this particular business, furthermore, the question of the "theft" of the aeroplane very obviously fell into the same category. It was doubtful if there was a case at all, and even if there was, it would plainly be a question of legal hair-splitting rather than a matter of knocking off some thief who'd decided to pinch an aircraft. Besides which, he was a Traffic cop; his duty time was filled with the quickfire pressure-cooker business of motoring prosecutions, and taking on something like this could only mean overtime, which was something he didn't want at the moment. So it would be much better all round if this bloke just went away quietly and put an ice-pack on his beezer until he'd cooled off and decided to drop it ...

After a long moment he said formally, "All right then, sir. Now if you want, I can take a complaint from you on assault. I can also take a statement of your other allegations – very serious allegations – about the aircraft, and that can be looked into, too. I don't know what the outcome of either matter will be, but I think I ought to mention this: that once we've made a report I won't be able to stop any proceedings which might arise, and neither will you. You'll have to appear in open court if it comes to it, and back up what you say." He paused, his eyes looking coldly into Tomms's while he weighed his words. "So what do you want to do, sir? Make a statement now; or leave it it until you've – eh – cleaned yourself up a bit, and that?"

Tomms hesitated, panting. Rage and uncertainty marched across his face. For all his aggression, he wasn't a fool: he was well aware that he'd just been warned to cool off, think twice before starting something which might reflect very badly on him. He groaned, rubbing his ample belly. If only his stomach would stop hurting so much ...

Mackenzie said contemptuously, "You haven't got a hope, you stupid sod. You're full of crap from the neck up."

It was the wrong thing to say; very much the wrong thing. Tomms's face mottled as his temper boiled over.

"Eh, the 'ell with you!" he shouted hoarsely. "You an' bloody Kerr, you're all the same!" He rounded on the policemen, twisted spectacles sliding down his nose. "Too bloody right I want to go through wi' it – assault *an'* stealin' bloody plane! That bugger'd been fired when he took that plane: he weren't employed 'ere no more, so he didn't 'ave no authority to take any-bloody-thing! I'll see the bugger in jail!"

The older policeman looked at Mackenzie. His face as expressionless as ever, he said, "That wasn't very wise, sir."

Mackenzie flushed, looking shaken.

Maggie said, "N-no. It ... it wasn't like that."

All four men turned to look at her. The older policeman said, "What wasn't like what, miss?"

Maggie said, "Keith. Keith being fired." She looked nervously at Tomms. "It w-wasn't like that. I heard it."

"What was it like then, miss?"

"He . . . they . . . had a row, when Keith came in. Keith said he was quitting, or that Mr. Tomms could fire him on the spot and give him a month's pay. Mr. Tomms said he was fired, but that he'd have to work the month out. S-so Keith was still employed when he . . . went off."

"Eh! Fuckin' lies!" Tomms clutched his midriff and strained forward in his chair, as if he was about to leap up. His eyes were huge and distorted behind the ruined glasses. "Fuckin' lies! I fired the bugger on th' spot! You lyin' little cow . . ."

"Hey . . ." the younger policeman slapped the flat of his hand on the counter, "– that's enough of the language, now."

Maggie backed away as far as she could, looking pale but determined. "I'm *not* lying," she said. Her voice trembled. "Mr. Tomms said Keith'd have to work the month out. I heard him."

The telephone rang. Mackenzie stepped round the desk behind Tomms and answered it.

The older policeman looked steadily at Maggie for a moment, then turned back to Tomms. "Well, sir," he said heavily. "Obviously going to be quite a . . . complicated business, isn't it? If you still want to proceed we'll have to get your statement, another one from this young lady here, and also from anyone else who was in the room at the time. If you . . ."

"Excuse me, constable." Mackenzie was holding the telephone receiver away from his ear, a hand over the mouthpiece. He looked down at Tomms. "It's the *Sunday Express*. They've heard that Keith's trying to talk that woman down, and they want to know something about it." He smiled sardonically. "They seem to think he's some kind of hero."

Tomms jerked round in his chair. Blood ran from his nose as he caught the edge of the desk with his right hand to steady himself. His face was putty-white and sweaty, his breath coming in harsh agitated gasps. His mouth worked for several seconds before any sound came out, which seemed to surprise him.

"Eh . . ." he managed. "Bloody 'ell . . . ev'body . . ."

The pain smashed into him.

It had been bad before – but this time it was totally unbearable. It drove through his abdomen from front to back in an explosion of flame; chronic indigestion a thousand, a million times multiplied.

He said, "Ugh!" quite quietly, while his face took on a look of shocked disbelief. He wanted to cry out, to scream in pain and fright, but somehow the agony was too intense. He clutched his stomach with both hands and started to double up. Something went wrong and he felt himself falling, sliding down out of the chair. He tried to save himself, dimly aware of the policemen moving forward in silent slow motion at the far end of a long, shadowy tunnel.

Then he was being hit, all over. Tumbling . . . thumps and bumps he couldn't do anything about . . . and finally stillness, with a pressure on his right side. Cool smoothness against his cheek, and a hazy brown plain stretching away sideways in front of his eyes. He blinked, slowly and heavily, before it came to him that it must be the lino. He was lying on the floor. Daft, to be lying on the floor. He ought to get up. Get up in just a minute, when the terrible pain had gone . . .

The two policemen, who'd got to Tomms a split-second too late to stop his rag-doll tumble to the floor, went down on their knees beside the still figure. The owner of the flying school was lying on his side, doubled up, with his hands pressed against his stomach. His glasses, which had fallen off his nose as he fell, were crushed under his right shoulder. His eyes were open and staring, glazed with shock.

The younger policeman said, "He's bloody fainted."

The older policeman glanced at him contemptuously, then looked up at Mackenzie. "Dial 999," he snapped. "Get an ambulance here, quick."

Mackenzie smacked his hand down on the phone cradle, cutting off the *Sunday Express*, then wheeled suddenly on the girl, who was staring at Tomms in wide-eyed shock.

166

"Maggie! Get Doc Munro! He's in the lounge waiting for a lesson with me."

Maggie seemed to shudder, then ran out of the room. Mackenzie glanced down at the policemen, said briefly, "Doc Munro's a GP, learning to fly here," and then started dialling.

The girl came back ten seconds later followed by a tall, relaxed man in his early forties wearing a red crew-neck sweater. The man glanced at Mackenzie, who shifted the telephone receiver and mouthed the word "Ambulance", and then knelt quickly beside Tomms. The younger policeman stood up and backed out of the way, automatically dusting the knees of his uniform trousers.

Munro pulled back the sleeve of his sweater so he could look at his watch, felt under Tomms's left wrist without attempting to move the hand from the bulging stomach, and started checking the pulse. Keeping his eyes on the sweep second-hand he said, "What happened? What was he complaining of?"

For a moment, nobody replied. Then Maggie knelt down beside him and said hesitantly, "Keith . . . hit him. On the nose and in the stomach."

"I know that. But what about afterwards? What did he say? Complain of?"

"Well, nothing, I don't thi . . . oh, yes; he did say he had cramp about five minutes ago. He kept holding his stomach, too, as if it was hurting. And his nose was bleeding."

Munro nodded, and finished taking the pulse. It was rapid, and the speed seemed to be increasing. He glanced up at the younger policeman and said, "Pull his legs out straight and hold them. Keep him on his side."

The policeman pushed a chair out of the way and did as he was told. Tomms groaned, a low horrible sound from deep inside him as his legs came slowly straight. His mouth worked as if he was trying to say something, but nothing came except a dribble of saliva. His breath came and went in fast tearing gulps. Blood trickled from his nose and ran down his cheek to the lino.

Working quickly, Munro unbuttoned the heavy overcoat

167

and jacket and loosened the collar and tie. Tomms gave no sign of noticing; his eyes seemed to be fixed on some faraway point across the floor. Munro glanced at the waxen face, but made no comment. Pushing jacket and overcoat back out of the way, he fumbled under the sagging stomach. The small *shwipp* of Tomms's fly-zip sounded loud in the quiet.

"Help me pull his trousers down."

The older policeman stepped over Tomms's legs and knelt down, taking Maggie's place as she backed away. He tugged at the dark blue trouser-legs while Munro pushed his hands gently under the body and worked the waistband downwards. When trousers and underpants were half-down like an old man caught on the lavatory, Munro took the bottom front of Tomms's shirt in both hands and yanked it apart. Buttons popped, revealing a dead-white bulge of belly under a shaggy matt of black hair. Munro felt around below the navel with gently-probing fingers.

Tomms's panting breath seemed to catch in his throat. He made a tiny animal noise, and his legs jerked feebly against the younger policeman's grip on his ankles. Munro squatted back for a few seconds, then leaned forward again and probed under Tomms's genitals with one hand and at the base of his neck with the other. Keeping his hands in that position he spoke without looking up.

"Was he suffering from anything before this, anyone know?"

Mackenzie and Maggie looked blank. Nobody said anything.

Munro glanced quickly at the older policeman. "Go through his pockets, will you, or as many of them as you can reach. I want to know if he was carrying any medicines." Then, to Mackenzie, "Hold your watch in front of me. I'm checking the pulse again."

Mackenzie and the policeman moved awkwardly, trying not to get in each other's way. Munro ignored them, concentrating on the watch the instructor held in front of his eyes. For what seemed to be a very long time the only sounds in the room were the ragged gasping of Tomms's breathing and the distant whine of a Viscount taxiing for take-off out on the aerodrome. Finally Munro nodded, and took his hands away from the two arteries. His face was impassive.

Mackenzie said tentatively, "What is it, John ... ?"

The older policeman said, "Ah – here we are, sir," and held up a small round pill-box.

Munro took it, opened it, and shook half a dozen pills out into his hand. They were yellow and shiny, as if they were covered in cellophane. His jaw tightened as he looked at them.

Mackenzie said, "What are they?"

"Aldomet," said Munro absently. "For blood pressure."

"Has he had a heart attack, then?"

Munro shook his head slightly, made as if to say something, then changed his mind and just shook his head again. He stayed kneeling by Tomms's side.

Tomms groaned, and started mumbling.

Maggie dropped to her knees close to his head. The sight of him horrified her. His face, so harsh and firm just a short time ago, was deathly white and flaccid, as if the flesh were too heavy to support. His right cheek was flat on the lino and his eyes, half-closed, stared vacantly ahead. Spittle dribbed from the corner of his mouth and mixed with the blood from his nose as his lips worked feebly.

"Got ... got to ... tell ..." the slow whisper faded out under the uneven rasp of his breath for a moment, then came back. "Tell ... Ge ... Gwe ..."

Hesitantly, Maggie reached out and touched his forehead. His skin felt cold and clammy against her fingers. Tomms gave no sign of noticing. She turned her frightened face to Munro and said, "Can't you *do* something?"

Outside on the aerodrome, the Viscount's engines were a thin shrill scream as it lifted off the runway.

Munro shook his head.

Tomms didn't see the gesture – it was way outside his range of vision – but even if he had, it wouldn't have registered. Everything to him seemed to be fading now, without meaning, slowing like a broken-down old film. Even the searing pain in his stomach was unconnected, not his concern any more. The whole world had come down to a narrow, soundless cone of vision in which grey shapes moved sometimes and then were gone. Vaguely, distantly, he knew that something had gone terribly wrong inside him, and that in a very short time he would be dead.

It didn't matter very much. The only thing which did matter was Gwennie.

She was here.

He couldn't see her very well, but she was definitely here. Just in front of him, reaching out and touching him. It was so warm, so wonderful. There'd been a time, a bad dream, when she'd been gone. The world had been bitter for a long, long period, cold and unfriendly without her. Always bitterness, increasing through the years. Missing her. Missing her so much, and never able to say to anyone. And now she was here. She'd just got here. A great weight, a great sorrow, suddenly rolling away. He couldn't move his hands to touch her, but he ought to speak to her. Tell her he was happy, that he loved her. She always liked to hear that, and sometimes he hadn't said it very often. He must say it now. Say it so that she'd smile softly and be happy as well . . .

He mumbled, "Gwennie . . ." but the rest wouldn't come. Wouldn't come out from under the distant crashing-surf noises in his body. He tried again, tried with everything that was in him, suddenly terrified that she wouldn't know. The words formed, but were squeezed and crushed by the rolling thunder of his breathing. His eyes filled with horror, and tears rolled sideways down his face. She wouldn't know. Wouldn't . . .

Then the tunnel of vision faded quite suddenly into blackness.

His breathing stopped.

*　　　*　　　*

Maggie screamed.

Munro stood up in one swift movement, caught her right arm, and pulled her up after him. The girl resisted for a

170

moment and then staggered on to her feet, sobbing wildly, black hair tumbling round her face.

"God ... he's *died*! You've got to *do* something!"

Munro led her towards a chair. He said gently, "There's nothing I can do, I'm afraid."

Both policemen were still kneeling, staring at the body as if they hadn't yet accepted the evidence of their own eyes. The older one looked up sharply and said, "Artificial respiration ... ?"

"No." Munro's voice was quiet but definite. "No point."

"Oh ..." The policeman looked down and then back up again, at a loss. "Well, what ... ?"

Munro frowned over the top of Maggie's head, hesitating for a moment out of professional habit. Then he said briefly, "He's had a burst aortic aneurysm. That means a split in the main artery from his heart. I'm afraid there's nothing we can do."

The older policeman said, "Christ!" looking stunned. Then, incongruously, he stood up and took off his cap. The younger policeman scrambled up and did the same, obviously not knowing what else to do. For a moment they both just stood there, looking somehow faintly ridiculous with Tomms's body lying in between them, clothes pulled open obscenely to expose the bulging black-haired belly and genitals. The sound of Maggie's crying diminished a little as Munro sat her down and handed her a wodge of tissues from the Kleenex box.

After a few seconds the older policeman said awkwardly, "You *are* sure, sir ... ?"

Munro glanced at him. "In my own mind, yes. There'll have to be a post-mortem, of course, but I'm in no doubt." He looked at Mackenzie. "Have you got a blanket or something you can put over him?"

Mackenzie seemed to shake himself. He pulled his eyes away from Tomms's body, and turned to a steel filing cabinet.

Maggie blew her nose hard, then said in a strained voice, "Wh-wo's Gwen?"

Everyone looked at her blankly, still held in shock. The

171

younger policeman cleared his throat and said, "Er – Gwen, miss?"

"His Gwen." Maggie took a shuddery breath, trying to keep the tremble out of her voice. "He said about Gwen . . ."

Mackenzie paused in his rummaging and said unexpectedly, "That was his wife."

Maggie stared fixedly at her hands, twisting the crumpled Kleenex. "Someone . . . someone'll have to tell her . . ."

Mackenzie said gently, "She died about ten years ago. Cancer."

"Oh . . . " Maggie swallowed heavily. Two big tears rolled down her cheeks. "Oh . . ."

The older policeman seemed to pull himself together with a visible effort. He looked at Munro. "I don't want to press you, sir. But could you give me some idea what might've caused this aneurysm?"

Munro frowned again, glancing quickly at Maggie. He said, "Really, I don't think this is quite the time to . . ."

"Just an outline, sir." The policeman sounded stubborn. He put his cap down deliberately on the counter. "It might be important."

Munro looked at him impassively for a moment, then gave a small shrug. "Well, the aorta is the big main artery running down from the heart. An aneurysm is localised dilatation in it, rather like . . . say, a weak spot in an innertube. A dilatation like that develops over months or years and may eventually start to leak blood or even burst altogether, as this one did. Since you say he was complaining of stomach pains before he died, I should think the process started with a leak; the blood running into the abdominal cavity is a considerable irritant. Then the leak must have developed suddenly into a major split: he had quite a considerable aneurysm, as far as I could see."

"You could . . . *see*, sir?"

"Well, feel, I mean. You can feel a massive aneurysm like that with your fingers, you understand. The aorta's only just under the flesh; the weak spot's very obvious. And then when it bursts the pulse gets faster as the blood pumps out, and

172

the carotid shows a stronger pulse than the femoral. It was all there."

"The – er – carot . . ."

"The carotid artery in the neck," said Munro impatiently. He glanced at Maggie again, who was staring at him dazedly. "The pulse is stronger in the carotid than in the femoral, which is the one on the inside of the thigh. That's because the leak's very much closer to the femoral than it is to the carotid."

"I see." The policeman paused for a moment, then added in exactly the same tone of voice, "So would you think that a blow to the stomach might have any affect on an aorta bursting under these conditions, sir?"

The room went suddenly very quiet. Maggie's head jerked round, wide-eyed, and Mackenzie halted in the act of pulling an old Army blanket out of the bottom drawer of the filing cabinet.

After a moment Munro said slowly, "You must know there's no way I can answer that. That's entirely a matter for your pathologist, and even then the result may be arguable."

"I quite understand that, sir. But just for guidance, without committing yourself, would you say there was *likely* to be a connection? More likely than not?"

The small whirring tick of the electric clock was the loudest sound in the room. Everyone looked at Munro, who thrust his hands into his trouser pockets and frowned at the floor.

"Well, yes." He spoke reluctantly, obviously picking his words. "When a person has a severe aneurysm, it's pretty obvious that a blow in the stomach could precipitate a burst. Equally obviously, it won't help if the patient has high blood pressure and remains in an agitated state." He rubbed his left ear and looked up at the policeman. "You understand that *is* only a general inference, though, not a proper medical opinion on this particular case. I won't stand by it in any way."

"I appreciate that, sir." The policeman turned to Mackenzie. "You say Mr. Kerr is in the air now, sir?"

Mackenzie tore his eyes away from Munro and straightened

up slowly, with the blanket in his hands. "Yes. He's trying to talk that woman down, the last I heard."

"Would you know the registration of the aircraft and where it's going to land, sir?"

The instructor hesitated, then said, "It's G-BCRX. I don't know where he's landing."

"I see." The policeman swung round to his companion. "Get out to the car and call in, Chris. Say what's happened and make sure it goes through to CID double quick. Don't forget to give them that registration."

Maggie stared at him in dawning horror while the younger policeman walked out.

"You're not..." Her voice trembled, little more than a whisper. "You're not... *after* Keith?"

The policeman looked at her steadily. "He'll have to help us with our enquiries, miss. I'm sure you can see that."

Mackenzie said sharply, "What are you enquiring into, exactly?"

The policeman looked down at Tomms's body and then back up at Mackenzie's face. "A man has died after an alleged assault, sir," he said formally. "I can't say whether there'll be any proceedings or not, of course. But I'm afraid we have to treat that as a murder investigation."

14

IN WHISKY TANGO's cockpit, Ann Moore was trembling with
the effort of concentrating. Moving the plane's nose up and
down was both easier and more difficult than she'd imagined :
easier inasmuch as the skill required, the deftness of hand,
was less than she'd thought, but more difficult because there
seemed to be so very much to watch out for in such an
apparently simple task. She hadn't thought of that, somehow.
She'd assumed, vaguely, that when you did anything the
plane would respond immediately and then the manoeuvre
would be over and done with : that the problems would come
in a series of being told what to do and then trying to
remember it and do it.

But it wasn't like that at all.

Now she'd come to it, the big difficulty was the unexpected
one of having to sustain what you did and recognise when
it was going wrong. The *recognising* problem was incredible;
you pulled the nose up, concentrated on keeping your back-
ward pressure on the wheel – and then, in spite of all your
watching, you'd suddenly find that the top of the dashboard
had slid back down again below the far horizon. You never
felt it happening, never noticed the movement at all until the
voice over the radio prompted you. Then, maddeningly, it
would become instantly obvious so you'd pull back again,
and the cycle would repeat itself. Hold the nose up . . . concentrate . . . no apparent change . . . and then the voice saying
it had dropped down, and the belated realisation of seeing it

175

for yourself. After a while the effort seemed unreal, almost dreamlike. Sitting in a tiny droning room in the middle of nothing, arms and neck aching with the strain of holding the wheel and peering over the nose, while you tried to relate a line of imitation leather eighteen inches in front of your face to the huge vastness of earth and sky so many miles ahead. It was ridiculous, alien, all out of scale . . .

The voice was speaking again, a metallic clatter against the steady background snore of the plane.

"That last try wasn't bad at all, love. You've still got a bit of a tendency to lose track of your nose position after a while, but you're doing very well indeed. So this time we'll lower the nose again, about three or four inches below the horizon, and I'll prompt you as you go. Tedious to have me whittering on all the time, I know, but I've got to earn my fee somehow. So let's see how we go: lower that nose now, and concentrate on what I say."

Lower the nose.

Biting her lip, Ann pressed forward on the wheel. Gently but firmly. The floor and seat tilted downwards under her, and the hazy horizon slid up the windscreen. She bit her lip and made herself hold it there. Hold it. Ignore the frosty patchwork fields all that way below, and just hold it. Forget the trembling, the pain in your stomach . . .

The voice said calmly, "You've got the nose coming up a bit there, Ann. Make a careful note of where it is on the centre windscreen pillar and *hold* it there."

The windscreen pillar. The horizon about *that* far up it, above the top of the dashboard. Watch it; keep it there. Press forward. Easier to see with the nose down than up . . .

"Letting the nose come up a bit, love. Watch that horizon. Keep it where it is."

Keep it there. Must have moved a bit and you didn't notice it. Yes – the strip of ground over the dashboard's got smaller. Still getting smaller. God, how easy it is to lose it. Keep it *there*. Watch it; don't forget where *there* is . . .

"That's better. Now just hold it; keep your eyes on that horizon."

Ann became aware that the noise-level in the cockpit was changing, the droning hum she'd grown used to rising as the Arrow accelerated in its gentle dive. She breathed shallowly and forced herself to concentrate on the horizon, ignoring the sinking pit of coldness in her stomach. Just watch the nose position, shut out everything else . . .

"That's much better, Ann. You're holding that nicely. Now, we want to come back to level flight. So just relax your pressure on the wheel a little, so that the nose comes back up to its original position, and then hold it there. Do that now."

Relax. Let the nose come up. Arm muscles trembling, feeling watery. The nose rising. Reaching the horizon. Stop it there and hold it, top of the panel just under the green line. Concentrate on holding it there, holding it for an endless time . . .

"Okay Ann, that's very good. We're back in level flight now, and I guess we've earned a bit of a rest, 'cos you're doing very well. So you can let go now, and just sit back and relax. Let go of the wheel, and sit back and relax."

Let go.

It took a long moment for the command to register. Then slowly, almost disbelievingly, she released her grip on the half-wheel. Her hands were sticky with sweat and her back and arms aching with tension.

The Arrow droned on, undisturbed, the top of the panel rock-steady just below the distant horizon.

She sank back in her seat and closed her eyes tightly, momentarily shutting out the vast cold reaches of the sky. A huge shudder ran through her body from head to foot, making her teeth chatter.

*   *   *

Two hundred yards away, Keith Kerr also made a deliberate attempt to relax. His muscles were cramped, tense with the subconscious effort of trying to reach out across the void and place his own hands and feet on the runaway's controls. It was the age-old instructor's syndrome; hands hovering but

177

not touching, trying to *will* a movement of stick or rudder to make a correction of some elementary error. At the same time gritting your teeth and keeping you mouth shut; normally to give a student every chance of seeing the mistake for himself and correcting it unprompted, but this time because of the overwhelming need to keep the chat down to a bare minimum. There were a thousand and one things he could have said – like use the rivet-lines on the centre windscreen pillar to judge the horizon-position; sit back in your seat without craning your neck so that your perspective's always the same – but none of them were as important as the vital requirement not to overload the girl with too much talk. If he missed out telling her something it might be dangerous: but if he swamped her and lost her attention it would certainly be lethal.

He sat back in his seat, stretched his club-like arms one at a time, and then fumbled for another cigarette. Except for a fleeting sweep across the instruments, his eyes never left the other Arrow. Squinting across the gap, he fancied that he could just see a dot of straw-coloured hair in the toy-like cockpit. He wished he could see her properly: you never realised how much feedback you got from looking at a student until you couldn't do it.

The cigarette lighter on the panel popped out. He lit his Gold Leaf, blew a streamer of smoke out of the corner of his mouth, and then fingered his scar for the fiftieth time.

He thought about stability.

The Piper Cherokee Arrow, in common with the vast majority of modern light aeroplanes, is "positively stable" in pitch. That is to say that once trimmed out in level flight it will naturally tend to stay that way, so long as it is not allowed to bank. If you upset things by pushing or pulling the wheel and then letting go, the nose will hunt up and down in a diminishing series of oscillations (called phugoid oscillations) and finally settle back to its original position. This inherent stability – which is so pronounced throughout the Cherokee range that Piper's themselves consider a positive altitude-hold unnecessary as part of their autopilot equipment – had so far

178

been both a major life-saving factor and a nuisance. A nuisance inasmuch as it had turned the girl's every attempt to maintain a change of pitch-attitude into a brief demonstration of phugoid flight, and a life-saver because by the same token it was that stability alone which had kept Whisky Tango droning along at a more or less steady 4,000 feet for the past hour.

Unfortunately, however, positive level flight stability is neither magical nor everlasting. It is basically the result of the four major forces acting on an aeroplane – lift from the wings, weight, thrust from the engine, and aerodynamic drag – maintaining a state of equilibrium. If any one of these forces should be altered at source – if, for example, the pilot should change the power setting – then the equation will cease to balance in the same way. In the case of a power change the nose will tend to rise if you open the throttle and drop if you close it: if the aircraft is then left to its own devices it will no longer come back to level flight, but will re-stabilise itself in a climb or descent.

Kerr's feet were beginning to stew inside his heavy boots. He wriggled his toes, feeling the subtle pulse of the Arrow's life through the rudder pedals in spite of his thick soles. After a moment he leaned forward slightly and moved the Cabin Heat lever to the fully Off position. Then he relaxed again and went back to frowning at the runaway.

It was a pity, he reflected, that the girl's next step had to be throttle control.

*　　　*　　　*

"Okay, love: we'd better pack in the tea-break now. How're you doing, there?"

Ann stirred in her seat and turned her head. The other plane was still there, a red and white dolphin-shape suspended in the bright alien void of the sky. She blinked at it, eyes dilated, shivering in the warmth of the sun. After a moment she cleared her throat, picked up the microphone, and said, mechanically, "I'm all right. Fine."

179

"Good. Have you got any particular problems you can think of, about raising and lowering the nose?"

She blinked again. Then she pressed the mike button and said, "No."

"Okay, fine. In that case then, we'll carry on and take a look at controlling the engine power, since we obviously need to reduce power to go down and increase it to go up. Okay?"

Ann said, "Yes."

"Right." The metallic voice paused for a second, then went on. "So don't touch anything until I say, and we'll just start off by talking about it. The first thing we need to do is identify the throttle lever, which is what you move; and then the manifold pressure gauge, which tells you – ah – how much you've moved it. So let's take the throttle lever first. That's situated on the quadrant which sticks out of the inst – the dashboard, in between the two control wheels. There are three levers on it altogether; one blue, one black, and one red. So have a look round, tell me when you've got those levers located, but don't touch any of them yet."

Ann looked vaguely at the instrument panel. The knobs and switches and dials and levers stared blandly back at her, totally confusing. The feeling of unreality came rushing back, stronger than ever. She wasn't even sure what a quadrant was ...

After a moment she looked away, breathing quickly. Outside the window, the white slab of the starboard wing crawled slowly across the miniature landscape far below. For an instant of time she felt a terrifying compulsion to open the door at her elbow and just step out into space ...

She shivered violently. Then she lifted the microphone.

"I ..." Her voice was a hoarse whisper out of her dry throat. She bent her head and coughed, then started again. "Could you ... could you explain that again, please? I'm sorry ..." She released the button.

"That's all right, love." The man's voice was unruffled, as calm as ever. "No sweat at all. Now if you look in the middle of the dashboard, near the bottom of it, just about directly in between where the two control wheel stalks come out, you'll find a sort of hump. It's about the size of . . . of a teacup, and it's got three levers sticking out of it. Have a look, and tell me when you've found it."

Ann looked, trying to shut out the sight of the staring dials. The sound of the engine seemed to drum through her bones. A hump the size of a teacup . . .

"I think I've got it."

'Good. Just to make sure, it's got one lever with a black T-handle, rather like a car automatic transmission lever, and two slightly smaller levers with round knobs on. One of the round knobs is blue, and the other one red. Yes?"

Ann blinked at the throttle, propeller pitch lever, and mixture. Black, blue and red. They looked plasticy, as if the manufacturer had sought to hide their seriousness behind bright colours and gimmicky design. Not like the knobs and levers on hospital equipment; they were all shiny, clinical, stark . . .

She shut her eyes again for a few seconds, then pressed the mike button.

"Yes. That's right."

"Good. Now the one we're going to be moving is the throttle, which is the black one with the T-handle. To increase power we push it forwards, and to reduce power we pull it back. Don't touch it yet, but tell me if that's clear."

Ann swallowed. "Forward to . . . increase power. Back to reduce it."

"Right on : fine. Now we'll leave that for the moment, then, and turn to the manifold pressure gauge. This is the only gauge you're going to need to look at, and it's basically a sort of measurement of power. We need it so I can tell you how *much* to reduce power by. So now; it's one of a pair of dials just to the left of the throttle quadrant, at the bottom of the panel. Just above Roy's knees. One of them says RPM on it, and the other one's a composi . . . the other one's got two scales on it, manifold pressure on the top and fuel flow underneath. It's the manifold pressure we're interested in, and it's got that written on the dial. So have a look for that, and tell me when you've found it."

Ann turned her head and looked at Roy. He was still propped up against the side of the cockpit and leaning forward on the diagonal shoulder strap. His rigid neck held his head nearly upright in a weirdly lifelike position, as if he was staring with closed eyes at his own feet. His face was ashen, and his shoulders under her white coat moved in small irregular jerks in time with his shallow breathing.

She shivered and looked down at the panel, where his right leg went under it. The two dials were there. The half-circular top scale of the left one was labelled MANIFOLD PRESSURE. Underneath the words was the abbreviation In. Hg., for inches of mercury. That at least was a sudden tiny oasis of familiarity; she wasn't sure what it meant in relation to an engine, but In. Hg. scales are familiar ground to anyone working in a hospital..

She lifted the microphone and said, "Yes. I've got that."

"Great. Perhaps you can tell me what it says?"

She frowned and peered. "The needle's on, um, twenty-four."

"That's fine. Now, the thing you need to remember is that when you *increase* power that gauge'll show a higher number, and when you reduce it, it'll show a lower one. Okay?"

"Yes. Okay."

"Good. So what I'd like you to do now, when I tell you, is reduce power just by a little bit. Bring the throttle back so that the power goes down to about twenty – that's not a very big throttle movement – and then, a little later on, increase it back up to twenty-four. You with me on that, all right?"

Ann bit her lip. After a moment she pressed the mike button and whispered, "Yes."

The speaker said, "Say agai . . . sorry, love, would you mind saying that again, please? You sounded as if you'd moved three paces away from the microphone, there."

She cleared her throat and said loudly, "Yes. Yes, I understand that."

182

"Ah, that's better. Nearly blew my ears off that time. Anyway, that's okay. Now, there's just one other thing, and that's this: as you reduce power, the nose will tend to drop down a bit, and I want you to hold it up, to prevent it dropping. Hold it up in the position it's in now. You follow that okay?"

Ann blinked, then repeated, "I've got to . . . hold the nose up, as I reduce the power." It came out mechanically, like a child reciting a catechism.

"That's it, love. Right on the ball. Actually, it isn't as difficult as it sounds. It mainly means keeping your eyes basically on the nose position, and just glancing in occasionally at the gauge. The, er – " the voice faltered for the first time as Kerr realised he was getting too complicated. After a moment he finished lamely, "Well – ah – have you got that all right then, love?"

Ann looked out at the endless blue sky beyond the invisible propeller. The microphone shivered against her top lip.

She said, "Yes."

"Good girl." Kerr was back on balance, talking slowly and easily. "Okay then, let's do that, in your own time. Throttle back until the gauge reads about twenty, and keep the nose up where it is now. Don't bother to reply to me from now on."

Ann put the microphone down in her lap and wiped the palms of her hands on her jeans. After a moment, stretching up and forward to get a better view of the horizon ahead, she took hold of the wheel with her right hand. Then, with her left, she reached out hesitantly and moved the throttle backwards a fraction of an inch.

The burr of the engine immediately muted a little, frightening her. After an hour in level flight the steady background drone had settled into her subconscious until she'd hardly been aware of it any more. Now, with the change it, suddenly leapt into perspective again, becoming a lowering roar. She could feel her hand shaking violently on the lever. She bit her lip and tried to shut the sound out, to concentrate on what she had to do. The engine was bound to get quieter if you reduced power. That was the whole idea of it . . .

After a long moment she remembered the manifold pressure gauge, and looked down at it. The needle was halfway between the twenty and twenty-four. She pulled the throttle back further, very slowly. The needle slid down until it touched the nought of the twenty.

The voice from the speaker said matter-of-factly, "You're letting the nose drop a little there, Ann."

She looked up. The top of the panel was six inches below the horizon-line, and still sinking. She let go of the throttle and jerked back on the wheel with both hands. The nose bucked, the floor pushing up against her feet for an instant. Her breath rushed out in a frightened gasp. Shivering from head to foot, she forced herself to concentrate on holding the line of the crash-pad just below the horizon. The diminishing sound of engine and slipstream in the middle of the empty sky was terrifying, seeming to suck the strength out of her body. Two ridiculous phrases kept going round and round in her head, repeating themselves idiotically like a damaged record. *Must keep the nose up . . . must keep concentrating . . .*

"Okay Ann, you're doing great. That's fine."

The studied casualness of the man's voice was oddly chilling; like a consultant saying to a patient, *"You're going to be all right, old chap"* when everyone else knew he was dying.

Staring dully ahead through the windscreen, she tried to pay attention as the voice clattered on.

"Now, still holding the nose up where you've got it, let's open the throttle again until the power goes back up to twenty-four. Look at the horizon mostly, and just glance in at the manifold pressure occasionally."

Power. More power.

She reached out to the throttle lever again, and edged it forwards. The engine note deepened, swelling up to its previous full-bodied snore. She went on looking forwards for half a minute, and then glanced down at the gauge. The needle was a couple of sub-divisions over the twenty-four. She hesitated, and then pulled the lever back a little way.

184

The manifold pressure obediently sank to twenty-three inches. She pushed the T-handle a tiny amount. The needle settled a fraction over twenty-four . . .

"Watch that nose position, Ann."

Her head jerked up. The horizon had disappeared. Her breath caught in her throat and she pushed sharply on the wheel. There was a horrible sinking sensation, the nose dropping away . . .

"Steady now! Slow and easy!"

She bit hard on her lip, forcing herself to hold the wheel still. The nose was below the horizon, the engine cowling pointing into distant toy fields. She waited a few seconds, breathing quickly, then gently pulled back. The division between earth and sky floated slowly down the windscreen until she stopped it just on top of the crash-pad and held it there, craning her neck.

The Arrow stabilised in level flight and snarled on smoothly through the winter afternoon.

*   *   *

Kerr made a last small power adjustment of his own to keep in station, then sagged back in the seat and puffed out his cheeks in a huge sigh of relief.

She'd done it.

She'd followed his instructions slowly and sloppily – but she had followed them. While the power had been reduced her life had been in her own hands for the first time, and she'd come through it.

He said aloud, "Bloody hallelujah!" the words sounding flat in the muffled rumble of the cockpit.

Then he thought about what to do next.

After a moment he ran his hand through his hair, pushing the headset down round his neck like a collar. What he wanted to work up to was practice descents and mock-landings in the air – the "landings" more to get her used to making rapid changes of power and nose-position than anything else, since you cannot seriously learn about landing

185

flare-outs up in the wide blue sky – but before that could be begun, there was the problem of the aircraft's speed to be considered. Practising landings from high speed cruising flight would be dangerously misleading: akin to trying to teach a learner driver to park a car without ever going below thirty m.p.h. So the first thing was to get the runaway slowed down in level flight to somewhere near its normal approach speed . . .

Except that slowing an aircraft in flight is a fairly complex operation. Perhaps too complex for her to manage at this stage.

Kerr chewed the inside of his cheek, frowning out at the model aeroplane crawling across the distant landscape beyond his right wing. Behind it the winter sun was lowering into the south-west, already taking on the beginning of an orange tinge against the endless washy blue of the sky. He wished again that he had some idea of what the girl was like. Whether she was short or tall, pretty or plain, timid or horsey-type. His mental image of a nurse was of someone quiet, self-possessed and sexy – and *that*, he thought savagely, was about as helpful as saying that all cats are black or all American women have large bottoms. The fact of the matter was that he just didn't *know* what she was like. Couldn't know. Without sitting beside her and seeing her react he was robbed of the subtle tools of his trade; left shouting into the empty sky. Her first successful power change might have encouraged her or it might equally well have pushed her to the very edge of panic, so that hitting her with a speed reduction now would reduce her to trembling confusion. And across a hundred yards of infinity he simply had no way of guessing which. He might *think* he knew, might kid himself he'd dredged sufficient reaction from her voice over the radio, but he couldn't be *sure* . . .

The clock on the panel said 1544: forty-five minutes to go before sunset. He shook his head angrily, irritated at his own time-wasting thoughts. At forty-four minutes past three o'clock the question of whether she was *ready* for a speed reduction was neither here nor there . . .

186

He scratched his scar with his thumbnail, and thought about what she would have to do.

The first item would have to be the mixture control. The girl's pilot would almost certainly have followed the standard procedure of leaning off the mixture in the cruise; reducing the volume of petrol flowing into the fuel injection system in order to match the depleted intake of air in the comparatively rarified atmosphere of 4,000 feet. That was fine so long as the Arrow stayed at 4,000; but when, later on, it started down into the denser air below, the leaned-off mixture would create an over-weak fuel/air ratio which would lead to engine over-heating and a possibility of a seizure. So now was the time to deal with it; have the girl push the mixture lever into full rich and leave it there.

Then would come the power reduction itself: have her bring the throttle back to about 20 In. Hg. The propeller pitch – which in an aeroplane with a constant-speed prop controls the r.p.m. – could stay where it was: if she got round to using full throttle at any time the engine would be over-boosted, like a car pulling away in too high a gear, but it ought to survive that for a while. Then following the power reduction, as the aircraft slowed down to 100 m.p.h. or so, the nose would have to be raised in order to increase the wing angle of attack, and hence the lift, enough to maintain level flight at the lower airspeed. Then the elevator trim would have to be adjusted to remove the need for constant back-pressure on the control yoke; and finally – if there *was* a finally – the undercarriage would have to be lowered.

Kerr blew out his cheeks again, looking doubtful. Then he glanced at his fuel gauges, pulled the headset back over his ears, and started speaking cheerfully into the microphone.

15

1546–1558

IF A PERSON meets his death after being assaulted, the British police are obliged to treat the matter as a murder investigation. This does not mean the end result will automatically be a murder *charge*, of course; it is more a question of the urgency with which the police conduct their enquiries, and the degree of precedence given to the case when it comes to the use of manpower and facilities. The eventual outcome may be almost anything: it is not, for example, uncommon for a suspect to be charged with both murder and manslaughter, and for the murder count to be dropped by the prosecution if the defendant pleads guilty to the lesser charge. Or alternatively (although more rarely) it may be that a murder charge is never raised at all; that the only case to be answered is that of possible manslaughter. It has even occurred, under very unusual circumstances indeed, that the sole allegation arising out of a lengthy murder investigation has been the comparatively trivial one of assault occasioning actual bodily harm.

None of these considerations, however, carry any weight at all with the police officers investigating any particular occurrence. Their job is not to formulate the charges, but to present the Director of Public Prosecutions with a complete and accurate report of the facts at the earliest possible moment. And in order to achieve this end, the rule book states that in all such cases the full murder investigation procedure shall be invoked and carried out.

Detective Chief Inspector Neville Lauder was determined to follow the rule book to the letter.

Seven minutes after the younger traffic policeman radioed in, Lauder was being driven rapidly through Leeds's Saturday congestion in a Police XJ6. He sat exactly upright in the front passenger seat, a tall thin man in his mid-forties with a gaunt face and still, suspicious eyes. He wore the conventional uniform of upper-echelon CID men – a dark blue pin-striped three-piece suit – and his general appearance, as usual, was neat almost to the point of being irritating. He sat with his hands quietly in his lap, staring impassively out of the windscreen while he thought about the duties already carried out and the others still to come. He even used the word to himself: *duties.*

There exists, within the police force, a certain hierarchy by reputation which is completely apart from the official hierarchy of rank. According to this informal but powerful pecking order, royalty begins with the "tough guy" units such as the Serious Crimes Squad, London's Flying Squad, and the famous Special Branch. Next in line are the specialised experts such as the Drug Squad, after them come the general run of CID men, and finally, towards the bottom of the social scale, are the Traffic departments, the ordinary beat men, and the faintly untouchables such as the Vice Squad and the Pornographic Publications Squad. Promotion involving a move from one department of the Force to a more aristo-cratic branch – such as from Traffic to CID – is a regular occurrence, of course: yet any officer making such an ascension is always acutely aware that critical eyes are watching, both from below his own rank and above it, in case the newly admitted one should prove to be still contaminated with the loutish habits of his tribal ancestry.

Lauder, who had been promoted from Traffic six weeks before, knew that he was regarded by the rest of the CID staff at Leeds's Horsforth Station as being a "Process King"; pedantic, humourless, and a stickler for regulations. In short, a typical Traffic product with his mind still firmly entrenched behind the wheel of a patrol car. He also knew that there was

189

a certain basis of truth behind this reputation; he *was* a rule book man, and always would be. He saw nothing wrong with that, and resented the thinly-veiled exasperation which it engendered in his subordinates. You were safe if you stuck to the rules; especially in an instance like this. This was his first murder investigation, and the standard procedures were a comforting bulwark against any possibility of an embarrassing error.

Watching the Kirkstall Road roll past as the XJ6 swished towards the airport, he went over his duties again in his mind to make sure he hadn't missed anything out.

On receiving the traffic constable's initial report he had set several wheels in motion. As a result of three minutes' rapid work the Leeds Police Mobile Control Room van was on its way to the airport; a police photographer was also on his way, and ought to arrive shortly after Lauder himself; two motor cycle patrol men had also been detailed to the same destination for the purpose, after Lauder had seen the body and photographs had been taken of it, of escorting an ambulance to the Leeds Infirmary; the Communications Room had been instructed to locate any one of the three Home Office Pathologists who normally did police work in the city, and have him standing by to perform an immediate post-mortem examination as soon as the body came in; and lastly, a sergeant at Horsforth had been given the task of locating the aircraft which the man Kerr was flying, finding out its destination, and then requesting the nearest police station to send out a senior officer to seize Kerr for questioning the moment he stepped out of the aeroplane.

Yes, Lauder thought, that ought to cover it. Standard rule book murder investigation procedure, and nothing left out. No loose ends, no room for awkward come-backs.

He relaxed a fraction in his seat. After a moment his left hand came up and unconsciously checked the straightness of his tie.

*　　　*　　　*

At the same moment, a hundred miles to the south of Detective Chief Inspector Lauder's car as it drove round the perimeter road outside Leeds-Bradford Airport, Ann Moore was staring dazedly at the cold blue sky over Whisky Tango's nose. Her back was aching and her throat was parched, and she was too hot to think.

Which was a pity, because the man on the radio was explaining something which sounded important.

The drone of the engine and the matter-of-fact voice coming through the speaker seemed to flow together into one meaningless rumble, making it impossible to take in what he was saying. She was trying to listen, trying as hard as she could, but her brain seemed to have lost its ability to concentrate. Her thoughts kept squirreling off down idiotic sidetracks all the time: looking at the plastic trim over the windscreen pillar and thinking it was cheap and nasty; looking at the dials, and wondering vaguely what they were for; looking out at the sky, and thinking how out of place this tiny plastic box was in the enormous blue reaches of nothing . . .

It was the heat that was doing it, she decided. The heat and the glare of the sun, so much more nakedly powerful up here than it ever was on the ground. Roy ought to have shown her how to turn down the heater, and she ought to have brought her sunglasses with her. She'd have been able to think if she'd brought her sunglasses; able to be her normal cool efficient self, apply her normal intelligence . . .

The voice was talking about something called the trim wheel.

". . . down in between the seats, I'll be telling you to roll it back by a certain amount, probably about six inches. Do you follow me on that all right, honey?"

The word "honey" snagged in her mind, running round and round under the snoring of the engine. Funny he should say that; it wasn't a word most Englishmen used. Her first serious boy friend had called her honey: a young Canadian called Russ who'd come over to go to university. He'd used to say "Hey honey, howaya" every time they met, and he'd wanted her to go back to Canada with him. She wondered, dully, if the man in the plane was anything like him. The voice didn't sound completely English . . .

"Hey, Ann: d'you understand me all right, about the trim wheel?"

The trim wheel . . .

She looked down beside her left thigh. Sticking out of the blue plastic tunnel between the the seats was the top rim of a wheel about six inches in diameter, with finger-grip serrations arounds its edge. At the back of its slot were the printed words NOSE UP, and at the front NOSE DOWN. She frowned, trying to remember what the man had said. Something about moving it . . .

After a long moment she lifted the microphone and cleared her throat.

"Could you . . . sorry . . . could you say what I've got to do with it again? Please."

"Sure." The voice clattered like someone on a telephone. "When we've reduced power and raised the nose a little I'll be telling you to wind it back, probably by about six inches. It'll take the pressure off the main control wheel; otherwise you'd have to keep pulling back all the time after we've slowed down, which'd make it impossible to fly accurately. When the time comes I'd like you to move it by feel if you can, so you can keep your eyes on the nose position. You with me okay, there?"

The man was waiting for an answer. Ann blinked, then said tonelessly, "Yes. I understand."

"Ah. Good." The voice wavered for a moment, as if it was uncertain about something, then came back slowly and clearly. "Now; there's just one other thing before we start the slowing down operation, and that's to move one little lever; the red one beside the throttle. I'd just like you to locate that, and push it gently forward if it isn't fully forward already. It won't do anything to the way the aeroplane's flying, but it does need to be fully forward. Is that clear all right, love?"

Ann looked down at the throttle quadrant. The lever with

the round red handle was about halfway along its slot. She pressed the mike button and repeated dully, "I've got to push it forwards."

"That's right. Do that now, and let me know when you've done it."

She lowered the microphone, hesitated for a moment, and then reached out and pushed the lever, careful not to touch the throttle alongside it. The engine note went slightly flat as the mixture slid into full rich. Unnoticed, the exhaust gas temperature needle backed down its scale a little way. Apart from that, nothing happened.

She pressed the microphone against her top lip and said, "Yes. I've done that."

"Fine; you're doing really great. Now, if you're ready, we can start the slowing-down bit. Okay?"

She rubbed her eyes, hearing her breath rasping in her dry throat. A small shrinking part of her wanted to scream, *No! I'm not ready! I didn't understand what you said!* – but you couldn't do that. It was like doing things you didn't want to in hospital. It was no use hanging back, trying to put them off. You just had to shut your mind, make yourself into a sort of machine, and get on with them. Be efficient, detached . . .

She looked forwards, into the vast blue emptiness beyond the windscreen. After a moment she took a shaky deep breath and said, "Yes. I'm ready."

"Right then. Now you've no need to worry 'cos it's dead easy, really. All we have to do first is hold the nose where it is and bring the power back to about twenty, just like you did before. Remember to concentrate mainly on the nose position and just glance in at the manifold pressure occasionally. Don't bother to reply to me, but go ahead with that in your own time."

Go ahead.

Ann strained upwards in her seat and took hold of the control yoke. With her neck craned and her head tipped back she could just see the top surface of the engine cowling in front of the windscreen. Unused to the low seating position of aeroplanes she felt swallowed up in the bowels of the machine, like sitting on the floor of a car and trying to peer out over the bonnet. Except that this bonnet was a broad rounded snout poking out into empty space, covering miles of the toy-sized world far below as it crawled forwards over the landscape.

She reached out to the throttle. The hollow vacuum in her stomach deepened as the engine note lowered from its steady drone. She bit her lip and went on pulling the lever back.

"That's good, honey. I can see you've throttled back a bit. Have a glance in now and check that you've got the power at twenty."

She looked down, staring blankly at the rows of dials for a moment before she located the right one. The needle was a couple of divisions below the twenty figure. She eased the lever forwards again, very slowly, steadying her hand by pressing her thumb against the quadrant. The needle moved up . . .

"Pull that nose up, Ann."

The horizon was well up the windscreen. She made a small whimpering noise and pulled back on the yoke, stopping the nose rising when the crash-pad was back on the distant green-white line. Her wrists trembled as she held it there, waiting.

With the power from the engine reduced, the equation of lift-weight/thrust-drag slid gently out of balance. On the instrument panel, unnoticed, the airspeed sagged and the needle of the climb/descent indicator drooped tiredly to 300 feet a minute Down.

The voice crackled in the cockpit.

"That's great, honey. You're doing great. Now just check your power again; make sure it's on about twenty. Keep holding the nose position, and just glance in at the gauge."

Her eyes darted down. The gauge read 20 In. Hg. She looked back up – and the nose was dropping again. Pull it up, hold it . . .

"That's it; that's good. You're in great shape, love. Just stay with it. I'm going to assume you've got the power at twenty now, so if you haven't, you tell me. If everything's okay, don't bother to reply."

For a long moment there was just the muted rumble of the engine. Ann stared forwards, her back aching with tension. Hold the nose up, concentrate . . .

The voice came again.

"Okay then, that's cool. Now, we want to raise the nose a bit; raise it by about three inches. Remember, you may have to look along the side of the panel to see the horizon. So raise the nose now, by about three inches."

Raise the nose.

She pulled back harder on the wheel. The cowling lifted up in front of her like the prow of a speedboat, blotting out the horizon ahead. Over the nose was nothing but the cold expanse of the sky, pressing in, disorientating.

Shivering, she looked to the right hand side of the panel, where the crash-pad curved down to the base of the windscreen. The horizon was there, filling the vee between the panel and door pillar. She stared at it vaguely. The line was floating upwards . . .

"Hold the nose *up*, Ann. Keep taking the pills."

Pull back. Hold the nose up. It was like being in one of those dreams where you keep on doing the same thing interminably, running away or falling, and you can't stop it because your mind's wrapped in cotton wool, refusing to think. Just keep pulling, keep the nose above the horizon . . .

The Arrow's wings, pitched upwards to a slightly steeper angle of attack, generated both more lift and more drag. The soft roar of engine and airflow diminished still further, sliding down the scale. The control yoke became heavier than ever, requiring more and more back-pressure to keep the nose up.

On the panel, the airspeed drifted back to 105 m.p.h. The climb/descent needle wavered languidly, then stabilised a fraction on the CLIMB side of the zero figure.

After an age the voice chattered out of the speaker again, loud and deliberate in the new quiet.

"That is magnificent, Ann. Perfect. You're making my job real easy. Now just hang on in there, hold the nose exactly where it is, and listen to me carefully. I want you in a moment to reach down with your left hand to the trim wheel, without

195

looking at it, and roll it back by about five inches, as near as you can judge. Do it slowly, taking care to hold the nose where it is all the time. Remember that the pressure on the main control wheel will change as you move the trim, so you'll have to concentrate hard on the nose position. So do that now. Roll the trim wheel back by about five inches."

Very slowly, Ann took her left hand off the control yoke. Her fingers were stiff, tingling-numb from gripping too tightly. Still staring forwards at the horizon, she reached down and groped between the seats. The back of her wrist brushed against Roy's thigh as her fingertips encountered the wheel. She took hold of it near the front end of its slot, hesitated for a moment, and then revolved it backwards in one movement.

Much too quickly.

Fifteen feet behind her, the trim-tab on the tailplane moved downwards by just over half an inch. The airflow, in trying to push the tab back up, applied an upward force on the elevators which cancelled out the need for human back-pressure on the control yoke.

Completely unprepared for an over-abrupt trim change, Ann was still pulling back.

Instantly, the nose reared up. Seat and floor pushed hard up underneath her, and the earth disappeared. The cowling was suddenly pointing into blue emptiness and streaky clouds, the engine starting to labour.

"Push the nose down, Ann! Down, gently!"

For frozen seconds she had to think what he'd said; grasp the meaning of the words in the slow motion of terror while the plane hung impossibly nose-high in space. The moment dragged on, never-ending . . .

Then she pressed forward on the control yoke.

The plane dropped away from under her, leaving her stomach behind like an express lift. The cowling clubbed down through the horizon and then the sky was abruptly gone, replaced by a drab patchwork of fields ahead of the nose and far below.

"Hold it *there*! Just hold it! Steady!"

She held the yoke still, gripping it desperately with both hands. The sound of the engine began to wind up in the dive, like a car accelerating ponderously.

"That's good, love." The voice was quick, urgent. "Now raise the nose up, but do it very slowly and gently. I'll tell you when to stop."

Raise the nose . . .

Trembling, not knowing whether she was pulling back or merely relaxing a forward pressure, she brought the nose up. The landscape marched downwards in front of the propeller for a moment and then suddenly there was the horizon, lowering itself into place on top of the panel. She blinked at it vaguely, somehow surprised. It was important, that horizon. She had to hold it there . . .

"Keep bringing the nose up, Ann. We need it higher than that. Where we had it a minute ago."

She raised the nose higher, moving her eyes to the side of the panel again. The dreamlike feeling was stronger than ever. She didn't even know why she was doing this: lifting the nose up didn't seem to bear any relationship to taking the plane down and landing it. The man must know what he was doing, of course, but even so, it didn't seem logical. Perhaps he'd explained it and she'd forgotten what he'd said . . .

The snore of the engine changed key subtly and then stabilised as the speed washed back to around the hundred m.p.h. mark. The control yoke felt lighter, somehow, as if it wasn't doing so much as it had been before: she didn't seem to be pulling back so hard.

"That's fine." The man's voice was back to normal, calm and metallic. "Now just hold her nice and steady, as she is now. You moved the trim a bit too quickly there, that was all. But no harm done. Just hold her steady, and don't worry about a thing."

Ann blinked again, and went on staring at the horizon. After a pause the voice carried on, speaking slowly and clearly.

"All we need to do now, then, is establish whether that trim movement you made was adequate. If it was, then right now you shouldn't be having to either push or pull on the control yoke in order to hold your nose position. The – " the voice hesitated, seeking the right words. "To put it another way, if you were to let go of the wheel, the nose ought to stay more or less where it is now. So what we need to do is to test that: let go of the yoke, just for a moment, and see if the nose goes up or down or stays where it is. So I'd like you to do that now. Let go, but be prepared to take over again immediately if the nose goes up or down. Do that when you're ready, or tell me if you don't understand it."

She hesitated for a long moment, biting her lip. Then she slowly unclenched her fists, holding her trembling hands just clear of the yoke.

Very gently, almost imperceptibly, the nose pitched up an inch or so higher against the horizon. Then it remained steady, and the Arrow hung stable in the sky.

* * *

Kerr's neck was hurting. He brought his left hand up from the throttle and briefly massaged the two big muscles at the base of his cranium, which were aching sullenly from having his head turned constantly to the right. His eyes never left the streamlined shape of the other Arrow, floating serenely alongside him.

After half a minute he pressed the transmit button on his control yoke and said clearly, "Have you done that, Ann? Let go? If you have, then tell me: otherwise, do it now."

For a long moment there was nothing but the rumble of his own engine. He brushed impatiently at the sweat on his forehead and then made a tiny power adjustment to keep the runaway exactly positioned, sitting just on top of the horizon. His flying was completely reflex, automatically following the tenets of formation instruction from years ago, now rarely used. Keep your leader's outboard flap-hinge – or in this case, since he was further out, aileron tip – in line with his cockpit . . .

His headphones made a small whistling click, and the girl's

voice spoke in his ears. It sounded flat, dulled, as if she were repeating something learned long ago.

"I've let go. I'm not touching it."

Kerr stared, astonished. After a few seconds he glanced quickly in at his instruments. The airspeed was 100-and-a-bit, and the rate of climb 150 feet a minute Up. If she was trimmed out at that, that was more than good enough ...

She'd done it! Relief flowed through his body like the warmth of a stiff drink. His face split into a sudden grin, and he let out his breath in a long slow *whoosh*. Then he thumbed the transmit button again.

"That's great, honey!" He could hear the lift in his own voice, feeding back through his headset. "Now I want to tell you that's beautiful! You've got the aeroplane slowed down, and you've done it very well indeed. That was the most difficult thing you'll have to do, and now it's all over and finished with. So sit back now and have a rest for a couple of minutes. You've done very well indeed."

There was no response.

He waited for a long moment, then pressed the button again. "Did you hear me all right, Ann? Get what I said?"

There was another pause. Then the voice said tonelessly, "Yes. All right."

The remains of Kerr's grin faded. He frowned, hesitated for a few seconds, then said gently, "How do you feel, love? Everything going okay?"

Again the time lag; again the peculiar flatness when the headphones eventually spoke.

"Yes. I'm all right."

Kerr said, "Good, fine," forcing heartiness into his voice to cover the sudden coldness in his guts.

The girl's wooden response was the first positive feedback he'd had from her – and it was a danger signal as clear as a red flare. When a student sounded like that – "glazed-over", in instructing parlance – it meant that you were pushing too hard, exceeding their ability to cope. If you kept it up, continued piling on the pressure beyond the overload point, something was going to break. In his instructing adolescence he'd once had a student actually burst into tears and refuse to fly the aircraft . . .

He became aware that his scar was itching furiously. He rubbed it hard with the knuckles of his left hand, still staring out at the runaway.

He *had* been pushing her too hard, of course. He'd swamped her with too much talk, let her carry her mistakes too far, introduced new tasks before she could cope with the old ones, taken enormous risks over the trimming of the aircraft; the list of unwritten rules he'd broken was endless.

Except that he hadn't had any choice. None at all. And with the clock on the instrument panel reading seven minutes to four, he still didn't have any.

He curled his lips inwards against his teeth, a habit when he was badly worried. Then he pressed his thumb down savagely on the transmit switch.

"Okay then, Ann." He kept the anxiety out of his voice, striving to sound relaxed. "Now while we're having our rest, I guess we might as well use the time by putting the under-carriage down. The wheels down. That doesn't mean we're going to land for a while yet – we've got plenty of fuel, so we might as well make the most of it – but if we get the wheels down good and early then it'll be out of the way, and besides that you'll be able to get used to the aeroplane in the landing configuration. You understand me okay?"

There was another long silence. Then the girl said in the same dull voice, "Yes. Okay."

Kerr frowned suddenly. He heard himself say, "Er – ah – good," and then dry up. His own last words had jogged something in his mind, some forgotten detail which clamoured for attention. Too experienced a pilot to ignore a warning from his subconscious, he stopped short and glared across the void at the other Arrow. What the hell was it; what had he said? Undercarriage? Landing configuration? Fuel . . . ? *Fuel* seemed to ring the warning bell again, but it couldn't be that: he had his own fuel state constantly in mind, and Whisky Tango had enough for two and a half hours or more.

His frown deepened and he glanced in at the instruments,

eyes flicking over the dials with the speed of long habit. Revs . . . manifold pressure . . . fuel pressure and contents . . . oil pressure and temperature . . . altitude . . . airspeed below the maximum wheels-down speed . . .

All okay – but the nagging feeling of having forgotten something persisted. He wriggled in his seat and shifted his left earphone a fraction on his head. What the hell was it, just out of reach, nudging . . . ?

His eyes passed over the clock, nestling in the extreme left corner of the panel alongside the airspeed. As he watched it the second hand completed a sweep, and it was 1556.

He said "Balls!" to himself, very loudly in the softly-drumming cockpit. Whatever it was bothering him, however important it was, there was no more time for it.

He cleared his throat, pressed the transmit button again, and started talking about the undercarriage switch.

*   *   *

". . . you pull the switch out against the spring pressure, move it downwards to its full extent, and then let go of it. Is that clear okay, honey?"

In Whisky Tango's cockpit, Ann blinked vaguely at the round green knob of the undercarriage switch, on the far side of the throttle quadrant. Bazzard also seemed to be looking at it, his closed eyes staring forward and down while his head made tiny slow nodding movements to the rise and fall of his breathing. She chewed her lip, making an enormous effort to concentrate on what should have been so simple. Just pull the lever outwards and then move it . . .

She raised the microphone and said, "Yes. I understand."

The calm, confident voice came back immediately.

"Okay, that's fine. Now, you won't need to touch the controls at all while you put the wheels down, so you can sit back and relax. The nose will drop a fraction when they're down, but that won't matter because you're in a gentle climb at the moment anyway. The only other thing is that there'll be a rumbling noise while the undercarriage is actually lowering;

it's quite normal, and I just mention it so you'll be expecting it. Okay?"

Ann pressed the button again and said, "All right."

"Good. So put the wheels down now, then."

For several seconds she went on staring at the panel. Then she reached out with her left hand, gripped the green switch-knob, and jerked it out and down.

There was an immediate subterranean rumble, like a huge door opening at the bottom of a large empty building. The Arrow hesitated, slowed fractionally, and then nodded its nose down slightly, as if a giant invisible hand had reached out and changed its flight path. Ann gasped and pressed back, gripping the side of her seat. The rumbling went on, hollow and drumming, sending tremors of vibration through the airframe. On the instrument panel, unseen, a small red light bearing the words GEAR UP went out and was replaced by an amber light alongside it saying GEAR CYCLING. After a long moment there was a final multiple *thonk* from somewhere in the depths of the machine. The amber light blinked out, and three green lights below the undercarriage switch came on.

The speaker said calmly, "That's fine, Ann. You've got all three wheels down and locked. I can see them from here. Any problems at your end?"

Ann looked out of the side window, eyes dilated. Everything seemed the same; the naked blue hugeness of the sky, the frosty landscape crawling far below like a vast rumpled map. Yet the plane felt ... different, somehow. Or maybe sounded different. A sort of hollow hiss under the noise of the engine that hadn't been there before ...

She shuddered, and hugged her stomach with her left hand. The microphone trembled against her lips as she pressed the transmit button.

"No." Her throat was dry and contracted, making her voice husk. "It's ... it's all right."

"That's fine. We're in great shape. Now you just sit back and relax and I'll tell you about what we're going to do next. That'll be a gentle descent and a mock landing, up here where there's plenty of room. You'll probably find that pretty easy after what you've been doing. So sit back, and tell me when you're ready to listen."

Tell me when you're ready ...

She leaned back again, blinking in the sun-lit cockpit, looking round at the few things that were now familiar. The undercarriage switch was in the DOWN position, and the manifold pressure gauge reading just over 19 In. Hg. After a long moment she raised her eyes back to the small vee of horizon between the side of the panel and the windscreen pillar. Then she lifted the microphone again.

"Yes. I'm ready now."

Kerr started talking, his voice flowing over the hum of the engine. Ann frowned, concentrating on listening, the instruments forgotten.

*   *   *

Directly above the manifold pressure gauge, unnoticed, one small rectangular dial looked out of place. Alone out of all the instruments on Whisky Tango's panel its needle was far over to the left, nearly covering a thin red line at the bottom of its scale.

Underneath it were the printed words FUEL LEFT TANK.

16

IN THE CID room at Horsforth Police Station, Detective
Sergeant Arthur Barnes crashed down the telephone receiver
and expressed his feelings with an explosive four-letter word.

The cause of his irritation was nine small minutes by the
clock on the wall. Nine minutes which he'd spent so far
groping through the unfamiliar territory of the Air Traffic
Control Service in an effort to locate Piper aircraft G-BCRX
– and nine minutes which a certain Detective Chief Inspector
was sure to regard as an unnecessary delay, especially if it
led to any time lost in the arrest of the man Kerr.

He'd started the search by phoning Leeds-Bradford Control
Tower. They'd told him that Arrow Romeo X-ray had taken
off from Leeds at 1501 hours on an emergency flight of unknown destination, and had been handed off to the control
of Northern Radar at RAF Lindholme at 1520. So then he'd
phoned Lindholme and been told that the aircraft had been
taken over by Waddington Radar. Waddington, in their turn,
reported that Romeo X-ray had been passed on by them to
Wyton Radar and had also suggested, rather acidly, that since
the machine was on an emergency flight, and since it was
common knowledge that all emergency flights in England
are either monitored or controlled by the Distress and Diversion Cell at the London Air Traffic Control Centre, the police
might be best advised to contact D and D direct instead of
wasting everybody's valuable time chasing the aircraft step-
by-step all the way down the country.

Barnes swore again, devoted thirty seconds to the unproductive hope that Kerr hadn't landed somewhere while he'd been talking to the various controllers, then snatched up the receiver and started dialling for the fourth time.

*   *   *

As air traffic radar consoles go, the ones in the Distress and Diversion Cell at West Drayton are not immediately impressive. There are only two of them, one for each controller, and each is no bigger than a small television screen.

They have, however, one or two unique features which are not always readily apparent.

The most important of these features is their versatility. Whilst "normal" radar screens are limited to one or perhaps two transmitters, the D and D sets are able to roam the whole of England; at the flick of a switch a D and D controller can "pipe in" a picture from any of the ten major route-surveillance radars in the country. This picture then goes through the electronic byways of the LATCC computer, so that the presentation which appears on the screen comes complete with illuminated transponder codings and, if necessary, the various special symbols triggered by any transponder squawking Mayday, Hi-jack, or Communications Failure.

Right now, Peterson was watching Kerr's Mayday squawk, which appeared as a pulsating circle-and-cross of orange light with the letters SOS beside it. The trace was creeping southwards and was presently about ten miles north-west of Luton. Within a short while it would be penetrating the complex block of controlled airspace which is the rather unfortunately named London Terminal Approach Area. Two minutes before, Peterson had taken over direct control of the flight from the Bedford Radar controller. The pilot of Romeo X-ray was, as yet, unaware of the hand-off; he hadn't spoken to anyone on the ground at all for over half an hour.

Peterson watched the Mayday squawk for a full minute, chewing a fingernail thoughtfully. At the end of that time he reached out and made a small cross on top of the light symbol with a Chinagraph pencil. The mark was the latest in a line of similar crosses, made at three-minute intervals, which plotted Kerr's passage over the ground.

By looking at the crosses, Peterson could tell quite a lot about what was going on. He could, for instance, by observing the slight steady bend in the line, deduce that the runaway aircraft was almost certainly still flying on at least the heading-mode of its autopilot; and that the directional-gyro, which controls the heading-hold, was precessing – wandering off heading – at the rate of approximately one degree every twelve minutes. He could also tell, since the last three crosses were fractionally closer together than the others, that at some time between six and nine minutes ago the target aircraft had slowed down from a groundspeed of 150-something m.p.h. to around a hundred. These things weren't vitally important, of course, but they were helpful to know. They also served to strengthen a peculiar sense of involvement in this particular emergency. If Peterson half-closed his eyes he could visualise the girl, alone and terrified in her unfamiliar cockpit. His mind's eye gave her the face of an old girl friend of his own; a girl called Carolyn, from way back before he'd got married. He hadn't thought about Carolyn in years and yet somehow he was weirdly certain that the girl in the Arrow was like her. Looked like her, talked like her . . .

He could also picture the instructor in Romeo X-ray, hard-pressed and sweating as he fought against time. And that was rather more to the point, because in many ways his job now was to act as a kind of alter-ego to that instructor: to anticipate the problems which the man in the air had no time to consider, and have the answers ready to hand.

The first of these problems was the emergency's position and track.

Northern Radar had reported that Romeo X-ray was intending to rely on ground assistance for his navigation; so at this moment the pilot probably didn't know his present location or where he was heading for within fifty miles. Peterson, however, was better placed. By mentally extending the line of crosses a few inches on his screen he could extrapolate with considerable accuracy the position of the two aeroplanes in eighteen minutes' time, assuming they made no attempt to turn.

And in eighteen minutes' time they would be more or less slap over the top of London Heathrow Airport.

Air traffic-wise, this was not a problem. Contrary to the public notion of white-faced controllers scattering jet airliners like minnows at the hint of an emergency in the vicinity of Heathrow, the actual juggling of traffic to allow passage of the runaway and its escort was already being accomplished with the minimum of fuss. The Northern Sector TMA controller had merely raised the bottom stacking level over the Bovingdon radio beacon to 8,000 feet, and his southern counterpart would shortly be doing the same thing with the Ockham stack, near Epsom. At the same time, the three London Director controllers at Heathrow Tower were calmly preparing to "knit a hole" in their constant stream of arrivals and departures so that their Control Zone would be completely free of traffic at all altitudes at the appropriate moment. The net result would be a ten or fifteen-minute hiatus in the flow of big jets, a delay which would probably make itself felt for the next hour or two before the system finally absorbed it. It would be a minor inconvenience to perhaps 10,000 passengers and airline staff, but for the controllers, it was no problem. Air traffic, in the well-regulated environs of Heathrow, was the least of Peterson's worries...

He pulled the left earpiece of his headset back from his ear and twisted round to look at Squadron Leader Lyle, who was sitting in a spare chair behind his left elbow.

"What do you think, sir? About the built-up areas?"

The Officer Commanding D and D removed his pipe from his mouth and blew a cloud of smoke. His permanently quizzical face looked more than ever as if he were about to utter some gem of sarcasm.

"I think," he said slowly, "that there's probably bugger-all we can do about it anyway. Where does he actually look like coming through?"

Peterson said, "Right over the top, sir, I reckon. The

Uxbridge, West Drayton, Sunbury sort of area." He paused for a second, then added, "I could – ah – suggest a turn to him, sir . . . ?"

Lyle nodded slowly, stroking his left hand over his bald head as if the action might provoke inspiration.

The question was a delicate one of command etiquette. On one hand it was not Distress and Diversion's job to pester the instructor in Romeo X-ray into trying to get the runaway turned if the girl wasn't ready for it – but on the other, as the chief emergency controller, Lyle also had a duty to any-one and everyone who might be endangered by the aircraft. And that duty very definitely included taking all reasonable steps to prevent the possibility of the machine going down in a heavily populated area. Such as Uxbridge, West Drayton, and Sunbury.

Lyle swung round in his chair and stared intently at the topographic map of England which was pasted up on the wall behind him. Unlike the glass map, it showed the usual hills, roads, railway lines and towns. After a moment, staying skewed round, he said indistinctly, "It could be a lot worse, John."

"Sir?"

Lyle turned back, making his chair squeak.

"I say it could be a lot worse. If he was a bit left of his present track he'd go smack over the centre of London, and if he was right he'd hit Slough or Farnborough or Guildford. If he's got to come over here at all, at least he's heading for the smallest target."

Peterson twisted and looked at the map himself, looking doubtful. Up to a point, Lyle was right. The untidy sprawl of London and its ring of commuter-towns, shown as a central splurge of yellow surrounded by apparently random blobs and splashes, *did* indicate that the districts directly to the north and south of Heathrow were not the most densely populated in the area. If the runaway went right over the top of London Airport then its track would take it just along the ragged western edge of suburbia. Not good, of course, but certainly not so bad as going over the middle of the city or across four or five large satellite towns a bit further out. Especially if you tried to forget that each eighth-of-an-inch bulge on the map contained hundreds of buildings and thousands of people . . .

After a moment Peterson said, "Ye-es," not sounding very convinced.

Lyle took his pipe out of his mouth and said firmly, "Yes. If he's got to come through the Zone at all, then that's the best place for him. When he comes on, John, you can ask him if he can make a turn, but don't make a big thing of it. If he can't make at least a ninety-degree turn and then hold his heading afterwards, I'd rather he kept going as he is. Okay?"

Peterson nodded slowly, still looking unhappy. He gave the map a last baleful stare, then went back to watching his radar screen. For the moment, there was nothing else he could do. The police, fire and ambulance services on the emergency route had already been alerted, the air traffic side was well in hand, and he had in front of him a list of runway data and surface winds for every aerodrome which the pilot of Romeo X-ray might conceivably wish to consider for the landing attempt. Now, the only thing left was to wait for the instructor to say something.

On the radar screen, the Mayday squawk crawled slowly southwards. After a minute or so it entered the London TMA at the northern boundary. Peterson crunched up another Polo, then nibbled his thumbnail and wished he hadn't given up smoking.

Kerr finally did say something at two minutes past four. Peterson had 121.5 switched through to the loudspeaker as well as his headset, so that the disembodied voice boomed suddenly loud in the small smoky room.

"Emergency controller from Mayday Golf Bravo Charlie Romeo X-ray, good afternoon."

Peterson jerked in his seat, slapped his headset squarely over his ears, and said quickly, "Romeo-X, this is Distress and Diversion Drayton Centre, go ahead."

"Roger, D and D. I'm still in formation with Whisky Tango,

and I've now got her slowed down with the gear down. We're climbing a little, about a hundred feet a minute, passing flight level six-zero. Have you got some airfield information, please?"

Peterson said clearly, "Affirmative, Romeo-X; I have that. But first, sir, be advised that your present heading will take you directly over Heathrow. Do you intend continuing on your present heading, or is there any possibility of making a turn in the next ten minutes or so?"

Kerr's metallic voice came back immediately.

"Negative, D and D: I say again, negative. I'm working on pitch control and throttle with her, and I don't want to interrupt that yet."

Peterson frowned, but said calmly, "Roger, Romeo-X. Can you confirm you'll be maintaining your present heading until south of the London Control Zone then, sir? That'll take you about twenty minutes at your present airspeed."

"Probably, D and D." Static hissed for a moment. "I'll advise if I'm thinking of any major course changes before then."

Peterson winced, then said, "Roger. Advise also if you're going above flight level seven-fife or below t'ree t'ousand."

"Okay; call you below three or above seven-five." The instructor's voice sounded impatient. "Now, have you got that airfield information?"

"Affirmative, Romeo-X. Can you confirm this will be a wheels-down landing, and you will *not* be requiring foam?"

"Jesus, yes; that's confirmed. Wheels down, no foam."

"Okay, Romeo-X. Now the longest hard runway is Greenham Common; I say again, Greenham Common. The runway is one-one/two-niner, t'ree t'ousand metres by sixty metres wide. There are no significant obstructions to the sides in the immediate vicinity. Surface wind at Greenham is 280 at fifteen knots. We could steer you for a straight-in on two-niner beginning with a right turn off your present track in about twenty minutes time."

There was a few seconds' pause. Then the voice out of the ether said, "Roger, D and D; copied. What about the grass fields?"

Peterson flipped a page in his notepad. "Romeo-X, the best I can do on grass airfields within your reach before dark is Lasham. They have a grass area to the north of runway one-zero/two-eight, which is one t'ousand eight hundred metres long. Otherwise RAF Bicester, which would give you an into-wind run of a t'ousand metres, or White Waltham, with twelve hundred metres east-west. White Waltham has a built-up area on the eastern boundary, and I believe the Lasham grass area may have obstructions on the north side. I can check that for you if you want to know."

For the space of ten seconds, the D and D room was very quiet. Then Kerr's voice rasped out of the speaker again, slower this time.

"Negative, D and D. Don't bother checking Lasham if it's no more than eighteen hundred metres. I'd hoped there was something a bit longer. I'll take Greenham Common, I think. Can you confirm they have full crash facilities there?"

Peterson said, "That's affirmative, sir. The US Air Force have just moved there from Upper Heyford. Three squadrons of F111s and all the equipment."

The metallic voice said dryly, "That ought to be enough. Confirm landing at Greenham Common, then. I'll call you around the south boundary of the London Zone for vectors for a straight-in approach to their runway two-niner. Switching back now to 126.85."

Peterson said, "Roger Romeo-X; good luck, sir," then leaned back in his chair. The small creak of the backrest sounded loud in the sudden silence.

Lyle was the first to speak. He took the cold pipe from between his teeth and said quietly, "All right, John. You speak to Greenham, and I'll talk to Latsie about the routing." He glanced around the room at the other controller and the two NCOs. "The rest of you better start using up your prayer quotas. That woman's going to need all the help she can get."

*   *   *

The call from Leeds came in two minutes later. It was taken

by Peterson's corporal assistant. He listened for a moment, said, "Stand by," and waited while Peterson finished talking to the control tower at Greenham Common. Peterson unclicked the telephone switch and looked up with raised eyebrows.

"It's the Leeds police, sir. They want to speak to the duty controller."

Peterson frowned. "Tell the silly buggers the emergency passed out of their area an hour ago."

"Well, they want to speak to you, sir. The bloke says it's urgent."

"Okay." Peterson nodded briefly, pressed a button to connect the telephone into his headset, and snapped: "Yes? Number-one controller."

"Detective Sergeant Barnes here, sir, Horsforth Police Station." The voice had a heavy Midlands accent. "Are you controllin' an aircraft registration G-BCRX at the moment, sir? It's a Piper Cherokee Arrow plane."

"Yes, I've got it. It's well out of your area, though."

"Aye, I know that, sir. But can you confirm the pilot of it's a Mr. Kerr, sir? Mr. Keith Kerr?"

Peterson blinked at the unusual question – controllers deal with aircraft callsigns, not pilots' names – then glanced down at his jotting pad. The words KERR – LEEDS were printed halfway down the page, surrounded by the swoops and circles of his preoccupied doodling.

"That's affirmative," he said into the microphone. "Why do you want to know?"

"We want Mr. Kerr to help us with some enquiries, sir. So I'd be obliged if you could tell me where the aircraft is now and where and when it'll be landing, if you can."

Peterson glanced at his radar screen and said, "Well, he's about twenty miles north of here at the moment at 6,000 feet, if that's any help to you. And he'll be landing at Greenham Common, near Newbury, some time before dark, as far as we know. What sort of enquiries do you want him for?"

The Midlands voice hesitated for a moment, then said evenly, "We want him for questionin' in connection with a murder investigation here, sir."

Peterson felt himself gaping. "A *murder* investigation! What . . . he's witnessed something, you mean . . . ?"

"Eh, well, sir, I can't really say, I'm afraid. My instructions are to find where he's landing an' arrange for his arrest there."

"*Arrest!*" For a long moment Peterson literally couldn't believe his ears. He was conscious of thinking inanely, *No, I've mis-heard that. It's a silly joke. It* can't *be right . . .*

Finally he said, "S-say that again?"

The stolid official voice repeated, "Mr. Kerr is wanted for questionin' in a murder investigation, sir. My instructions are to have him arrested when he lands."

Peterson said, "Oof!" After a full ten seconds, oblivious to the fact that he was still wearing his headset and would therefore be heard by the man at the other end of the line, he swung round in his chair and said urgently, "Sir! Can you . . . deal with something, here?"

Squadron Leader Lyle, sitting sideways-on to Peterson while he talked to the southern sector Terminal Approach Area controller, frowned warningly and waggled the fore-finger of his left hand for silence.

"It's urgent, sir . . ." Peterson gestured helplessly at his headset, obviously at a loss.

Lyle said, "Stand by, please," into his microphone, covered it with his hand, and swivelled an accusing eye on to his number-one controller.

"There's a copper on here, sir." Peterson swallowed. "A copper from Leeds. He says they want the pilot of Romeo-X in connection with . . . with a murder investigation."

There was dead silence. The other four men in the room froze for a moment in shock, and then four heads turned to stare at Peterson unbelievingly. Lyle's lower jaw sagged open in exactly the same way Peterson's had thirty seconds before.

"They . . . they . . ." Peterson gave up. "Would you speak to him, sir?"

Lyle seemed to shake himself. He said to the TMA con-troller, "I'll call you back in a minute," then tapped the buttons to connect his headset into the telephone.

"Squadron Leader Lyle here, Officer Commanding D and D. Who am I speaking to, please?"

There was silence as the headset replied. Everyone in the room watched Lyle's face. After a few seconds he said, "All right, sergeant. Now tell me what this is all about."

There was another pause. Lyle's features tightened, shocked out of their normal quizzical expression. Two little knobs of bone moved at the top of his jaws. After half a minute he said, "Well, that isn't enough for me, I'm afraid. I want to speak to the senior officer handling the case. What . . . oh, is he? Well, we'll get on to him there. Good day to you."

Lyle broke the connection, stared unseeingly at the nearest radar screen for a moment, and then rounded on Peterson.

"John. That bugger won't tell me anything about it. Phone Horsforth cop-shop double quick, get on to him again, and confirm the call actually did come from him; I want to make sure it isn't some silly bastard's idea of a joke. I'm going to get on to the Leeds Aero Club. The copper in charge of the case's supposed to be there now."

"Yes sir." Peterson sounded like a man coming out of shock. His right hand reached out for the main switchboard button and then hesitated, hovering, before it got there. Looking at Lyle he said awkwardly, "Silly question I expect, sir. But . . . do you think this actually *affects* us, as it were? Affects this emergency, I mean?"

Lyle, who was zig-zagging a finger down the scrawled page of Peterson's pad in search of the Leeds Aero Club number, paused and ran his hand over his bald head.

"I'm not sure yet," he said slowly. "If you mean can we *do* anything about it, then no, we probably can't. We could hardly pull Romeo-X down at this stage even if we wanted to." He hesitated, the knobs at the top of his jaw working. Then he added: "All the same, if we've just cleared a homicidal maniac to command an emergency flight right over the London Control Zone, then I *would* like to know about it."

Peterson winced, nodded, and pressed the button.

On the steadily scanning radar screen the illuminated Mayday symbol crept towards Bovingdon VORTAC beacon, ten miles north of London.

*   *   *

The briefing room of the Leeds Aero Club, in common with all flying club briefing rooms everywhere, seemed to exist mainly for the purpose of harbouring chalk dust. Everything in the room – floor, shelves, books, the usual collection of battered model aeroplanes and sectioned aircraft instruments – was covered in a delicate grey-white patina, while still more dust floated like fine flour in the low afternoon beams of the winter sun.

As the second traffic policeman left the room Detective Constable Ivor Jones sneezed three times. He wished the Mobile Control Room would hurry up and arrive: it might be cold and cramped, but at least it was free of chalk dust. He blew his nose mightily, and then crumpled his grubby handkerchief back into a bulging pocket. When he spoke, his Welsh accent was thickened by the stuffiness of a heavy cold.

"Going to 'ave to tread softly on this one, sir."

"Oh? Why?"

Jones looked round, surprised. Detective Chief Inspector Lauder, sitting beside him at the battered instructor's desk, was regarding him stonily. He seemed to be as impervious to the dust as he was to everything else: his pin-striped suit was crisp and unsullied, in marked contrast to the growing white patches on the sleeves of Jones's sports jacket.

"Well . . ." Jones shrugged. "I mean, this bloke Kerr, see. Seems he's a bit of a hero, up there talkin' that woman down. Been some Sunday papers on the phone about it, Roberts said."

Lauder's expression, which seemed to Jones to permanently suggest that there was a faintly undesirable smell in the vicinity, remained unchanged. He said coldly, "Yes, I heard.

215

Does that make a difference, then?"

Jones hesitated, suddenly wary. This was his first job with Lauder, and you could never tell with some of these Chiefs who came up from Traffic. Jump down your throat if you opened your bloody mouth . . .

"Well, no sir," he said. "What I mean is, it doesn't seem like the usual run of murders, tha's all. Like, we'll prob'ly end up dropping the murder charge and accepting a plea of manslaughter, won't we? An' under the circumstances I shouldn't be surprised if chummy gets off with a suspended sentence or even a discharge, look."

Lauder raised one eyebrow. "Thank you, constable," he said acidly. "So in the light of your analysis, you suggest that we – ah – *tread softly*, then?"

Jones mentally raised his eyes to Heaven. Aloud, he said, "Well, we hardly need to call cavalry out, do we?"

"So just what do you suggest then, constable?"

Jones stared at his superior woodenly, and kept his mouth shut. You couldn't change the basic formula of a murder enquiry and arrest, but what you *could* do, as Lauder knew perfectly well himself, was to tone down the procedure a bit; smooth the rough edges off here and there. It was the difference between hauling a suspect off in handcuffs or merely having a copper find him and stay with him until the investigating officer arrived; between letting the procedure grind through its usual course of custody or helping things along by not objecting to a quick bail with a relatively small surety. Just little things, but they added up to treading softly, not throwing your weight about any more than you had to. Sometimes a copper was well-advised to tread softly . . .

After the silence had dragged on for half a minute, Lauder leaned back in his chair. He said deliberately, "Listen, constable, because I want you to understand this. I carry out my investigations according to the book, and I am not in the habit of *treading softly –* " he emphasised the words " – just because a few newspapers are sniffing around. There is far too much condoning of violence these days, and we are not in a position to pre-judge the outcome of any case until we have the full facts. This investigation has already got off to a slow start because a couple of officers didn't want to get involved in an assault case, and I won't have it performed in a casual manner from now on just because you've got it into your head that you know all the answers. Is that clear?"

Jones hunched his shoulders and glared at the desk-top directly in front of him, feeling his face going red. After a long moment he took a slow, deep breath and just said, "Sir."

17

ANN PULLED THE throttle back another half an inch. The snore of the engine subsided still further, becoming a low hissing ruffle of propeller and airflow.

The quiet was terrifying.

The plane was sinking.

She could feel the sinking in the pit of her stomach, the way you do in a descending lift. The feeling went on and on, interminably. But the weird thing was that there was no other evidence of going down. The miniature frosty earth a mile below the engine cowling still looked exactly the same, not coming up to meet her at all. The conflict created a weird floating sensation; the rumbling cabin just hanging there slightly nose-down in space, sinking and yet motionless, suspended in nothing in the late afternoon sunlight. It was somehow like a nightmare she used to have where she was teetering on the parapet of a tall building. There was no apparent reason for being there, and yet no reason not to take half a step forward into emptiness and be falling, falling...

The speaker clicked and came to life again, the metallic voice part of the unreality.

"That's great stuff, Ann. You're in a nice gentle powered descent, just like you will be when you come in to land. We could do with the nose an inch or so higher, that's all."

The words were loud, filling the quiet cockpit. The only trouble was that you had to reach out for them, hold them;

squeeze them hard and then pull them apart before the sense would come out.

A small part of her mind seemed to be curiously detached from her body; sitting somewhere behind her shoulder and watching the girl at the controls as if she were a different person, a stranger. It was contemptuous in a separated, distant sort of way, because the girl was reacting very stupidly. Her body was rigid with tension, and she was all jumbled up with fear when she should have been thinking calmly and clearly. She ought to relax, this silly girl ...

"Come on now, love." The voice came out of the empty sky, clear and commanding. "You want the nose higher than that. An inch or so higher."

There! The nose had drooped down, showing a six- or seven-inch bar of distant ground over the top of the crash-pad. The stupid girl at the wheel had let the nose drop, in spite of having to pull back all the time anyway. The man had told her about that; said she'd have to keep holding the nose up because of the reduced engine power. Now she was pulling harder, knuckles white. The floor tilting gently ...

The cowling lifted soggily, compressing the bar of ground to about five inches. It was difficult to tell exactly because the horizon was becoming hazy, misting in readiness for the early winter evening.

The mutter of engine and airflow slid down a few decibels as the speed decayed from 110 m.p.h. to around 100. After a long moment the voice came back again.

"That's fine, honey. Now, we want to increase the rate of descent. So bring the throttle back a bit more. About another half an inch. Ignore the manifold pressure, and just keep holding the nose position."

What had he said?

The words had come clearly into the cabin, but the meaning hadn't registered. She saw herself, the stranger at the controls, blinking vaguely as she tried to bring the words back, write them up in her mind where she could read them slowly.

But they were gone. There was just the tiny sun-lit room high above the ground, with the man on the left and the girl on the right. The girl was biting her lip again; straining forward, with the diagonal strap of the safety belt cutting deep into her right shoulder.

"Come on, Ann!" The voice was far away, like someone speaking emphatically over a long-distance phone. "Bring the throttle *back* a bit more. Hold the nose where it is."

Bring the throttle back.

She saw the girl hesitate and then reach out her left hand, leaving a shiny smear of sweat on the control wheel. The hand fumbled for a moment, found the lever with the T-handle, and pulled it backwards a fraction further. The engine quietened still more, mumbling casually in the middle of nothing. A small rhythmic cycle of vibration started up, quivering gently through control yoke and seat. The feeling of sinking increased.

A long time. Half a minute. Then the voice again.

"Good. That's nice and steady. Now we'll pretend we're getting low, and we're going to make the landing. We'll say we're at second-storey building height. So raise the nose a bit *now*."

She watched herself shudder, and then tighten her arms. Out in front, the blue prow of the cowling lifted until the hazy horizon was only just visible over the crash-pad. The nose was heavier than ever, trying to drop down . . .

"Now raise it more. Higher. We're pretending we're landing."

She saw the girl cough once, convulsively. Heard the brief dry rasp of it in the swishing quiet 5,000 feet above the ground. She didn't ought to be doing that now . . .

"*Now*, Ann! Raise the nose *now*!"

The girl pulled back. The cowling popped up above the horizon, pointing suddenly into blue sky. Patches of watery sunshine and shadow dappled across clothing and seats as the angle changed. She saw the blonde head move, craning desperately upwards for a moment before remembering to look alongside the curve of the instrument panel. The sound lowered still further.

"*Right — now close the throttle completely. All the way*

back. Expect the horn I told you about any moment."

The girl reached out to the throttle pedestal again. Her hand seemed to be moving in slow motion. Touching the quadrant . . . finding the lever . . . hesitating for an age . . .

Pulling the T-handle back to its stop.

The engine immediately died right down to tickover; a distant feeble thrustling in the cold emptiness of the sky. Ahead of the windscreen, the propeller hazed into a nearly-visible disc. The vibration slowed and shifted in key, becoming the soft continuous shuddering of a powered aeroplane in a low-speed glide.

The girl went on pulling back, holding the nose up.

The wind-hiss backed down the scale, dying.

The detached part of her brain watched dispassionately. There was a vein throbbing in the girl's left temple and a swelling ache in her stomach. The phenomena of the power-off glide and the aerodynamic stall were completely unknown to her, but the lowering sigh and the nose-high attitude a mile above the ground *felt* wrong. The plane needed the engine roaring to keep it in the sky, and now the roaring was gone . . .

The stall-warning device chirruped suddenly like a faulty car horn, then stayed on in a solid electric bleep.

She saw the girl flinch spasmodically, letting the nose sag down a fraction. The horn hesitated and then came back again. The girl quivered from head to foot as she kept up the back pressure on the wheel. A trickle of blood started down her chin from where she was biting her lip. The cabin was balanced on an invisible knife-edge in space sinking faster . . .

The voice came again, urgent over the bleating horn.

"*Right – now we'll overshoot. As if we're going round again off a bad landing. Hold the nose where it is and give her full power. Throttle fully open.*"

The girl still had her left hand on the throttle lever. Without taking her eyes off the misty horizon she pushed it forwards. The engine noise swelled into the cabin in a sudden rushing thunder, vibrating the airframe for a few seconds and then smoothing out. The nose tried to lift up by itself; a ghastly disconnected feeling of the plane getting away. She snatched her left hand back to the control wheel. The blue cowling sank down into the distant landscape as she relaxed the back pressure. She pulled back again . . .

"Hold it steady, Ann! And FULL power!"

Hold the nose. Muscles shaking uncontrollably. The horn beeping and stopping . . .

"Ann! Give her FULL power! Throttle ALL the way forwards!"

The girl hadn't moved the lever enough; just pushed it an inch or two and then stopped. She watched her hand reach out again, in the same ridiculous slow motion as before. The T-handle was slippery with sweat as she pushed it. The thunder wound up into a deep solid roar. The plane was wriggling, not steady any more. The man's unconscious body swaying against its straps. Some unseen force jostling the controls, taking over, trying to pull the nose up . . .

"Jesus, honey – FULL power!"

Push the throttle more. More. The lever suddenly hard against the stop. The engine noise huge after the quiet, swamping out thought. The plane an uncontrollable monster, still moving, the nose still coming up.

The voice again, tinny now over the roar.

"Okay, love, good. Now, push the nose down a bit. Gently, down to level flight, like before. You're doing fine."

The nose pointing way up into the blue. Blood from the girl's lip running down into the neck of her sweater. Her teeth chattering as she pushed forward on the wheel. Gently. Gently . . .

The horizon floating up over the crash-pad. The girl holding it steady, sitting numb in the engine roar.

"That's great. Now hold the nose there, and bring the power back to twenty. Take your time: you've got it made."

Bring the power back to twenty . . .

After a long moment her left hand flexed, moving the throttle slowly backwards. For an age the engine noise stayed the same, then quite suddenly began to back down. The hand stopped and the blonde head turned, staring dully at the manifold pressure gauge. It read 22 In. Hg. The hand moved again, while her eyes alternated vaguely between the gauge and looking forward throught the windscreen. The roar of the engine slid back further, became a background drone . . .

The manifold pressure was 20 In. Hg. She took her hand away from the throttle.

Time passed. The plane crawled steadily on over the vast landscape far below, frosty and clear in the sinking glare of the sun. The separated part of her saw the girl relax a fraction, exhausted by her own nervous effort. There was a sharp ache in the small of her back, and a salt taste of blood sticky in her mouth.

Eventually the voice came again, calm and clear.

"Honey, that was very, very good. You've just been through a descent, a landing, and an overshoot, and brought yourself back to level flight. The aeroplane will fly itself again now, so you can let go and relax. Just let go, sit back, and have a rest. That was very good indeed."

For nearly a minute Ann went on sitting upright, still holding the wheel. Then, when the words sank in, she unclenched her fingers, collapsed down in the seat, and buried her face in her hands.

The small, lonely sound of her sobbing was almost lost under the monotonous snore of the aircraft.

*   *   *

Kerr found that his feet were shuddering on the rudder pedals. Every muscle in his body was knotted and aching, straining with the effort of trying to reach out across the gap, to place his own hands and feet on the controls of the other aircraft. It should be so *simple*. All he had to do was *reach*, stretch, transmit his will and his skill through the girl so that *he* flew the aeroplane, *he* fed in the small pressures and responses on control yoke and rudder . . .

He wiped a tacky hand over the sweat on his face and made himself relax, untensing his leg muscles with a conscious effort. His feet were hot and slippery as he flexed his toes. After a moment he leaned forward awkwardly and pulled down the zips of his motor cycle boots, leaving the uppers flopping loosely around his shins.

A hundred yards and a million miles away the other Arrow floated placidly, a tiny man-made toy in the invisible ocean of the sky. It was very slowly climbing, looking oddly untidy to his airman's senses with its wheels down at 5,000 feet. He had his own undercarriage down to match, so as to equalise the drag and make it easier to hold formation; and that increased the feeling of wrongness still further, rather like driving a car with the nagging knowledge that one of the doors isn't properly shut.

He breathed deeply. His left thumbnail tapped softly against his boom-mike, creating a small electric clacking sound in his earphones.

When it came down to it the girl had done as well as could be expected considering the barrage of instructing she'd been getting – but all the same, Kerr had been deliberately lying when he'd said "that was very good". The past ten minutes had in fact been a non-stop running battle, slamming his own controls around to stay in station and at the same time trying to identify the other Arrow's mistakes as it rose and fell and slowed and accelerated. The main difficulty had been the slowness of her reactions, particularly on the simulated overshoot: if that had been a genuine go-around-again off a bad landing she'd have flown into the ground half a dozen times over.

He stopped tapping the microphone and rubbed the back of his neck, wondering whether to abandon the idea of a go-around altogether: concentrate on getting her on the ground any-old-how off the first approach. Such a procedure would be a drastic reversal of everything he'd ever learned or taught, but, on the other hand, so long as the wing-leveller was still switched in, even quite a serious landing accident probably wouldn't kill her, whereas attempting an overshoot and then stalling the aircraft or flying it into a tree almost certainly would. It is one of the oldest axioms of aviation that it's preferable to have your crash sliding along the ground rather than hitting something when you're airborne.

After a moment he shook his head tiredly, pushing the question out of his mind. At this time there was no possible answer to it: it would have to be decided in a split-second during the actual landing attempt, and then lived with afterwards. He could decide now that he wouldn't have her go round again for a second try except as a very last resort, but when the time came it might well be the *only* resort, however dangerous it was. If she came in pointing straight at a hangar, or tried to land fifty feet up . . .

He lit his last but one Gold Leaf, blew new smoke into the stale-smelling atmosphere of the cockpit, and thought about his other problems.

With the passing of time, the forces arrayed against him had become ever clearer, ever more pressing. The sensation was not a new one – it is always the way in flying that the factors which you push aside, for whatever reasons, are the ones which rear up later threatening to engulf you – but his afflictions on this occasion carried the additional bitterness of being totally inevitable. His diminishing reserves of time, fuel, and daylight had been on his mind ever since he'd first turned on his back and plunged down after Whisky Tango: the only difference now was simply that bankruptcy was that much more imminent. The moment had arrived when the last pauper's choices had to be made; a final plan of action formulated and adhered to.

The clock on the instrument panel said four-twelve in the afternoon. Behind the suspended profile of Whisky Tango the vastness of the western sky was changing, becoming yellowy-gold at its base and then light blue merging into deeper blue as you looked on up. In the middle of the yellow band the sun was poised just above the horizon, the blazing disc of it faintly touched with orange through a distant miasma of evening haze. At another time and in another aeroplane Kerr would have found his own special brand of peace on such a winter afternoon, drinking the heady wine of his freezing slipstream while he rolled and tumbled the

225

huge earth and sky around his wings. But now, the beauty of the panorama represented part of a deadly equation. In a quarter of an hour the sun would have set, and fifteen or twenty minutes after that it would be full dark. That meant the landing attempt would have to be made within the next thirty minutes – and *that*, in turn, dictated that the final descent from their present altitude should commence within the next quarter of an hour.

Kerr shook his head once and said "Jesus" into the soft rumble of the engine.

Then he looked at his fuel gauges for the twentieth time in half an hour, and said it again.

When he'd first seen his fuel contents, before taking off, he'd reckoned he had enough to last until dark and then a little beyond – and so, under normal circumstances and assuming the gauges were correct, he should have had. But the circumstances had not been normal: instead of droning along steadily at economy-cruise, he'd been slamming his throttle around to stay in formation with the runaway. And that sort of treatment, even when you set the prop as coarse as you dare and lean off the mixture so that the cylinder head temperature sits permanently beyond the redline, means that your fuel consumption goes up in the same manner as a car being driven in traffic. As the flight had progressed, that fact had been increasingly brought home to him as the fuel gauges claimed his attention more and more often.

Now, the left tank read between a quarter full and empty, while the right tank showed a fraction less. It *should* still be enough for another half an hour, but . . .

He dragged in a deep lungful of smoke, then reached out and clicked his undercarriage switch to UP. There was a soft shuddering rumble, ending in a low multiple *th-thud* like three fridge doors closing. Retracting the gear would make it more difficult to hold station with an aircraft which had its own undercarriage down, but, on the other hand, the dangling wheels meant burning precious extra fuel to overcome the drag.

Staring out, he waited until the other Arrow started to float slowly backwards. Then he pulled his propeller pitch back by a very small amount. The runaway stopped its relative movement and hung steady, tiny against the brilliant blue and yellow of the heavens. He watched it for a moment longer, then glanced in at his gauges again. The revs were just under 1,900 and the manifold pressure 22 In. Hg.: the old trick of low r.p.m. and high boost, bad for an engine's health but generally acknowledged to produce a marginal saving of fuel.

His fingers drummed on the throttle quadrant for a moment, then moved to the mixture lever and edged it back still further, another half an inch. The engine note went flat and harsh, taking on a vague background unsteadiness which he could feel through his bones rather than hear. The cylinder head temperature moved up slowly to 280 degrees, twenty past the redline. Shutting his senses to the warning signs, he leaned across the cockpit and twisted the fuel tap to the left tank position, noting the time as he did it. He'd stay on this one until the needle was nearly on the zero, switch back to the right tank and run that dry, and after that assume he'd got a final ten minutes remaining on the left. It wasn't a good plan – no plan which relies on the total accuracy of a pair of aircraft fuel gauges is a *good* plan – but it was the best thing he could think of. It was far too late to get someone else up to take his place now.

So much for that. Now, how to use the remaining time . . . ?

He looked ahead. The vast sprawl of London filled fifteen, twenty miles of horizon, from in front of the red engine cowling to right round beyond the left wing tip. From 5,500 feet the metropolis looked untidy but somehow clean and fresh in the low rays of the winter sun. With a flying man's eye for the character of the cities that pass beneath his wings, Kerr had always liked London: where so many younger urban areas of the world are drably laid out in the neat little chequerboard squares or brash clumps of sky-scrapers, the capital of England is refreshing in its refusal to conform. On a sunny late afternoon with the rare blessing of good visibility, the pilot approaching London sees a huge undulating carpet of civilisation; a carpet speckled with reds and browns and green and strangely predominant whites, decorated in its distant centre with the cake-icing towers and spires of the inner city.

Kerr frowned, ignored the ten million people who would shortly be sliding under his wingspread, and concentrated on the simple arithmetic of time and distance.

He had seven or eight miles to go to the northernmost tentacles of the built-up area. When he reached them, he'd be over-flying the London Control Zone with about ten minutes to run to the southern boundary – and by the time he reached *that*, he'd damn well better be ready to start down and get the girl turned due west for Greenham Common.

So . . . ?

So he was going to have to start teaching her to turn, right now. Turns first, then more pitch and power practice later if there was time.

Keeping his eyes on the other Arrow, he blew a slow jet of smoke at the windscreen, planning the moves ahead. The first step would have to be to get her to disengage the heading-hold mode of her autopilot: with that out of the way she'd be able to make turns simply by banking the aircraft, over-riding the wing-leveller. The result would be sloppy flying – the sort of rudderless, uncoordinated manoeuvre which he spent a large part of his working life growling at student pilots for – but it *would* be a turn, since it is a basic law of aerodynamics that any bank will eventually create a turn in the same direction, providing the pilot or autopilot doesn't deliberately prevent it by holding on opposite rudder. Earlier on, he'd considered leaving the heading-hold switched in and having the girl steer by turning the autopilot control index on the gyro compass. The idea had been tempting, since the Arrow would then make its turns completely automatically, but he'd finally dismissed it firstly because it would be too complicated to explain over the radio, secondly because it would distract her from the main business of holding the control yoke and watching her nose position, and lastly because it would probably be vastly oversensitive for the delicate business of getting her lined up with the runway on final approach. The only other alternative, yawing the aircraft round using the rudder pedals alone, he'd thrown out for both similar and exactly opposite reasons: again it would mean introducing a new control, and in this case the resulting turns almost certainly wouldn't be accurate enough. The snag about *not* introducing the rudder was that without it she'd have no way of steering once she was on the ground, but with an aerodrome the size of Greenham he was prepared to accept that: running off the side of the runway after landing was the least of her dangers.

He wiped his mouth with the back of his left hand, feeling the prickle of a nine-hour stubble on his chin. The inconsequential thought occurred to him that he'd have to shave again when he got back to Leeds. He had a date tonight...

For a moment his face softened, the lines of tension dissolving. Then he shook his head briefly and settled himself back to concentrating on the floating shape of Whisky Tango. His right thumb moved on the control yoke, pressing the transmit switch.

"How're you doing there, Ann?"

For ten or fifteen seconds there was no reply. Off to his right the runaway flew on blandly, undisturbed. Then there was a metallic click, and the girl's voice spoke in his ears.

"I'm –" she coughed, causing an electronic crash which made him wince, " – I'm all right, thanks." The small hiss of carrier-wave continued for a moment, then clicked off as she released her mike button.

Kerr frowned, worried by her tone, then pressed his own switch again.

"Okay then, honey. What we're going to do now are one or two gentle turns, which I expect you'll find very straightforward. But before we can do that, we need to locate the heading-hold button of your autopilot and disengage it. That won't make any difference to the way the aeroplane flies normally, but it will mean we can make our turns without the black box trying to pull us back on to our present course all the time. You with me so far?"

229

His headphones hissed for a moment. Then the girl's voice said dully, "Yes."

Kerr's frown deepened, etching webs of wrinkles at the corners of his eyes. He paused, groping for something to say to make her relax. But there wasn't anything. After a few seconds he hunched his shoulders and carried on, speaking gently and clearly.

"Right, then. Now, the autopilot control buttons are on a small white plastic panel, about six inches long by two inches deep, on the bottom left hand side of the instrument panel proper. This little panel has two buttons, with a knob in between them, and it's labelled Autocontrol Three. So have a look for that, and then tell me when you've found it. Don't touch it yet; just get it located."

This time the silence seemed to drag on forever. Kerr rested his forehead against the side window while he waited. The contact wth the cold Perspex turned the dirge of the engine into a deep drumming inside his skull.

Eventually the voice said flatly, "I've found that."

Kerr moved his head, keeping his eyes on the other Arrow.

"Okay, honey. If you look at it, then, you should find that the right hand button has the letters H-D-G written under it. They stand for heading. So just have a look and make sure that's so, will you?"

Another pause, shorter this time. Then the headphones said, "It's got that on it. H-D-G."

"Right on, Ann. Now then, I want you to press that button once, firmly, and then release it. Don't touch the other button or the knob, because they're the wing-leveller controls; we're going to leave them as they are all the way on to the ground. So just press the heading button once, and then release it. If you understand that then do it now, and let me know when you've done it."

Nothing seemed to happen. The runaway hung immobile in space, pinned in the pale blue sky above the yellow glare of the setting sun. Kerr watched it intently, taking a last pull on his cigarette and then stubbing it out. Switching out the heading-hold *shouldn't* make any difference, of course – the

230

Arrow's natural directional stability should still make it fly more or less straight so long as the wings were held level – but on the other hand, it just might. If the girl's pilot hadn't followed the normal procedure of trimming the rudder before switching in the autopilot, or if that particular aeroplane had a tendency to hold a slightly asymmetric flight configuration . . .

For some reason the word *asymmetric* jarred in his mind, ringing the same half-subconscious warning bell he'd been aware of earlier. He changed hands on the control yoke and wiped his sweat-sticky right palm on his trouser leg, frowning out at the dolphin shape beyond his right wing tip as he tried to pin down the vague sense of danger. Asymmetric. Out of balance. What could be to do with out of balance . . . ?

Whisky Tango made a tiny weathercocking movement, left and right again, then smoothed out and flew on steadily.

Kerr shook his head irritably, waited a few seconds, and then thumbed his transmit switch.

"Have you pressed that button now, love?"

"Yes. I've done that." The girl's voice sounded more strained than ever. Kerr winced, stretching his lips back against his teeth. Every instructing instinct screamed that he was swamping her, pushing on remorselessly far beyond her capacity to take everything in. His nerves jangled in protest at his own actions, like a car driver who knows he's going much too fast for his ability. At the very least he ought to give her a good long rest, perhaps some casual chatter to help her relax as far as possible . . .

But there was no time. The sun-lit clutter of London's suburbia was already creeping under his wings, and the Control Zone south boundary was only eight or nine minutes away. There was just no time at all.

He swallowed on his dry throat, and made his voice brisk and businesslike. "Good lass. Now we'll do a turn, then. A left turn, to start with. All you have to do, when I tell you, is take hold of the control wheel and turn it a little way to the left, like a car steering wheel. It'll be rather heavy to move, because you'll be over-riding the part of the autopilot

231

which holds the wings level. But if you just put a steady pressure on it the aeroplane'll bank gently to the left, which'll make it turn. You with me so far?"

The voice started to speak, caught for an instant, then said, "Yes."

"Good. You're doing great, Ann; you really are. Now, you'll be able to see the angle of bank by the angle the top of the instrument panel makes with the horizon. The angle we want's a very shallow one, maybe about twenty degrees, but you won't have to worry about that because I'll tell you when we've got there anyway. Then, when we want to come out of the turn, all you'll have to do is relax the pressure on the wheel and the autopilot'll bring the wings level again, as they are now. Okay on that?"

"Yes." It was little more than a whisper in his ears.

Kerr said firmly, "Fine. The only other thing to mention is that you want to try not to push or pull on the wheel as you turn it: we want the nose position to stay more or less as it is, not go up and down." He paused for a moment, then added, "So try a left turn now, then. In your own time."

The runaway droned on smoothly, unmoving. Kerr waited for a minute or more, staring out across the void. Then he pressed the switch again and repeated calmly, "Just turn the wheel a little to the left now, Ann. Make a small turn to the left."

The other Arrow banked suddenly towards him, showing the top surfaces of both wings against the evening sky. Kerr muttered "Shit!" and twisted his own wheel sharply to turn inside its radius, following. His left hand yanked the throttle shut for a moment and then started feeding it open again. The horizon and sky stayed tilted for a few seconds – and then the runaway's wings abruptly flattened out. Kerr followed suit, treadling the rudder pedals and finicking with the power to stay in position. His thumb moved on the transmit switch and he started speaking quickly, before the girl had time to think.

"Well, that's the general idea all right, Ann. Not so difficult, is it? You were a little bit rough with it – I rather think you

232

just gave the wheel a twist and then let go – but you can certainly see how it all works and how the autopilot brings you out of the turn when you want. So now let's do it again; only this time be a bit more gentle, and hold it in the turn until I tell you. Go ahead and do that now."

A mile in the sky about the town of Uxbridge, Whisky Tango banked hesitantly into a shallow left turn. After about twenty seconds it rolled out on Kerr's command, with its nose pointing towards the suburbs of Southall and Brentford.

The time was seventeen minutes past four. In the yellow blaze of light to the west, the bottom rim of the sun touched the hazy line of the horizon.

*   *   *

Three miles to the north-west of Uxbridge, right on the very distinct geographical and social dividing line between the satellite dormitories of Middlesex and the beginning of the Buckinghamshire "stockbroker belt", lies the broad grass field which is Denham Aerodrome. On the north side of the field are three hangars; and on the south, the Denham Flying School, the visiting aircraft park, and the aerodrome's small public car park. On weekend days the car park – and also, more dangerously, the single narrow road leading past the aerodrome – is invariably host to carloads of sightseers, their numbers varying according to the weather and the time of year.

On this January Saturday the car park contained about forty cars, perhaps a dozen of which had people in them. The yellow Rover 3500 with its nose against the fence stood out not at all, and the couple inside it were noticeable only because they were outside the usual age group of aeroplane spotters and wistful spectators. The man was in his late fifties, with thinning brown hair and a neat brown moustache. The woman beside him was about the same age, dumpy, pleasant-faced and grey haired.

Out on the airfield, it was a busy afternoon. A steady stream of Cessna 150s came wobbling down final approach, settled on the grass with varying degrees of elegance, and then opened up and went round again for another try. The man watched each one as it came and went, his head slightly cocked to one side. At the more blatantly inept performances his lips would part and his breath held until the aircraft had completed its bouncing collision with the turf and was climbing away.

Breaking a long silence, he said abruptly, "These people are damn awful."

His wife said placidly, "Well, they're learners, aren't they, dear? I expect you did some bad landings when you were learning?"

"That's true. But these people . . ." he hesitated, watching another Cessna thump down on nosewheel and mainwheels together; then, unwittingly, he put his finger on one of the main flaws of modern flight training. ". . . these people just seem to *drive* the planes on, as if they were cars. We'd never have got away with that more than once running, in my day."

The woman made no reply. Instead, she picked up the knitting in her lap and bent her head over the needles. There were times when she didn't want to remember her husband's flying days, now long gone. The sleepless nights while the Lancasters were out over Germany, the terrible waiting for the click of the door after a raid had come back . . .

A Police Volvo nosed into the car park. It paused for a moment, then drove slowly in between the two rows of stationary cars, tyres crunching on the gravel. The man looked round and saw it; watched as it came to a halt behind the Rover. A uniformed constable got out, glanced again at the Rover's rear number plate, and then walked round to the driver's door. The man wound down his window, eyebrows raised questioningly. The stiff breeze riffled his hair.

The policeman stooped down, looking awkward. He said, "Mr. and Mrs. Bazzard . . . ?"

*   *   *

At the same moment, in the Distress and Diversion Cell at

West Drayton, Flight Lieutenant Peterson was sipping tea from a chipped mug while he watched his commanding officer losing his temper.

For the past three minutes Lyle had been talking on the phone to Detective Chief Inspector Lauder at the Leeds Aero Club, and from where Peterson sat, it was obvious that the conversation was not exactly proceeding apace. Lyle's face was tight with rare anger, the two bony knobs in his jaw working continuously as he listened to the tinny rattle from the receiver. When the voice on the other end stopped, he took a slow deep breath before replying.

"I quite appreciate your position, Chief Inspector," he said coldly. "But I rather think I must have failed to make the situation clear to you. The man you want to arrest is at present in command of an emergency flight under my control; and in order to make the correct decisions from this point onwards, decisions which may have a direct bearing on the safety of a great many people under this aircraft's flight path, I *must* be informed if there is any reason to suppose that this pilot is in a dangerous or otherwise affected mental state. I should also, perhaps, point out that if you won't cooperate with me I shall firstly be obliged to put the matter to Kerr himself, and secondly to contact the Provost Marshal's office immediately to present a formal order to your superiors. I trust I have made myself quite understood?"

The receiver rattled again, sounding angry. Lyle said remorselessly, "I most certainly *do* have the authority. And I assure you I will most certainly use it." After a few more seconds he added, "I've already told you what I want. First of all, the brief facts of the case as you understand them."

There was a pause, then a quieter tone from the receiver. Lyle made quick notes on a pad, then said, "I see. So, so far, it looks as though there was no intent to kill. Correct?"

The voice on the other end spoke for nearly a minute. Lyle raised his eyes to the ceiling in exasperation, then replied acidly, "Quite so. But can I take it that as the ... *expert* on the spot, your off-the-cuff opinion would be that this man is probably not in a state of homicidal excitement at this time?"

A break then, "*Thank* you. And you say that Kerr is, as far as you know, unaware of either the death or the fact that the police are looking for him: is that correct? Right... good... then I thank you for your willing cooperation and wish you a very good afternoon, officer." He crashed the receiver down without waiting for a reply, snarled, "You *bastard!*" to no one in particular, and then swung round to the watching Peterson.

"I think we're probably okay, John. It seems that our bloke thumped his boss in the stomach during an argument about this flight, and accidentally ruptured a weak artery. The man died half an hour later, after our chap got airborne."

Caught off balance, Peterson said, "Ah... *okay*, sir?"

"Well, Christ —" Lyle spread his hands, "— it's a bloody sight better than having some homicidal nutcase in Romeo X-ray, isn't it? It's not *okay*, of course, but at least there's nothing to suggest this bloke Kerr might do anything stupid. We don't have to think about trying to pull him off, or anything like that."

"Oh. I see. Yes, sir." Peterson puffed out his cheeks, looking doubtful, then glanced automatically at the radar screen, where Kerr's Mayday squawk had just crossed the London Control Zone northern boundary. He found himself wishing that area radar gave height information as well as position: it would somehow be comforting to know that there was still plenty of airspace under the runaway as it passed over the built-up areas. After a moment he looked back at Lyle and said, "I take it you didn't mean what you said about talking to Kerr, sir? I mean, telling him about the police or anything?"

"Good Christ, no!" Lyle looked shocked. "Of course I didn't. He needs something like that now like he needs a hole in the head. No, I just wanted to make sure we haven't got some nutcase on the job, that's all."

Peterson nodded. He went back to watching the Mayday squawk and chewing a fingernail, waiting. The trace, which had started swinging round to the left, straightened up two

236

or three miles inside the Zone, heading for the moment towards the built-up areas of West London. That meant Kerr must be starting the girl on turns . . .

One minute later the loudspeaker on the wall crashed into life with shocking suddenness.

"*Mayday Romeo X-ray! Whisky Tango has just gone into an uncontrolled dive, passing 4,000 this time. Expect a crash – she doesn't look like recovering.*"

18

1619–1623

WHEN THE POWER unit of a single engine aeroplane ceases to function in flight the machine does not, contrary to popular belief, fall out of the sky like a stone. Instead, two things happen. The first, assuming the failure is a carburation or ignition fault rather than a seizure or some other major breakage, is that the engine revs drop to somewhere near tickover speed and then stay there as the propeller windmills in the airflow. And the second, owing to the fact that nearly all aircraft are deliberately designed to pitch down when power is reduced, is that the nose tends to drop. If no action is taken to check this pitchdown and assume a normal gliding angle, the result will be a fairly steep power-off dive with a rate of descent of perhaps 2,000 feet a minute at terminal velocity.

Whisky Tango's engine failed at exactly nineteen minutes past four, at 6,000 feet over the London Borough of Ealing.

It went with practically no warning at all, just as Ann let go of the control wheel after completing her first proper turn. One moment it was snoring away evenly and the next it hesitated, picked up for a few seconds in a ragged blast of vibration, and then cut out altogether. The propeller slowed to a gently shuddering idle, leaving the only sound in the cabin the ominous hiss of the airflow.

In the silence the nose swung down, smoothly but inexorably, into a thirty-degree gliding dive.

Ann blinked in surprise.

For several seconds her mind seemed to just watch numbly, as if what was happening wasn't directly to do with her. The faltering and cutting out, the ghastly sinking feeling as the nose fell away – these things were unreal, too sudden to be accepted. She was aware of deciding, with icy clarity, that it was just one thing among the thousand things she didn't understand; that there was no need to think about it because in a moment the engine would come on again and everything would be back the way it was. It couldn't be anything *wrong*; when the engine came back on the instructor would tell her about it . . .

The radio was silent. The moan of the wind swelled in volume as the Arrow began to accelerate in the dive. Ahead of her the engine cowling steadied, pointing steeply down into a criss-cross vista of tiny streets and buildings far below.

Shock finally penetrated. She brought her fists up to the sides of her face and screamed and screamed, continuously.

*　　　*　　　*

With no reason to think in terms of an engine failure, Kerr's first reaction to the other Arrow's sudden dive was remarkably similar to Ann's. As the runaway dropped suddenly out of position, with no warning and for no apparent reason, he wasted the first few moments staring in blank disbelief. The girl *couldn't* be doing something crazy now: not now, not over London. She must have just knocked her control yoke or something: in a moment the nose would lift up again . . .

His flying sense came back in a rush.

Whisky Tango was falling away, a clean white cross sinking into the sprawling townscape a mile below. He shoved his own nose down to follow it, belatedly thumbing the transmit button.

"Hey, Ann! C'mon! Get your nose up!"

There was no response.

The runaway appeared to float up and back towards him. He started reducing power, found he was still overtaking too fast, and yanked his throttle all the way shut. The engine noise died, replaced by the empty hiss of the air.

"Ann! Come *on*! What's happened?"

No reply. Just the other Arrow bobbing and sliding ahead of him like a jiggled camera projection. Still coming back too quickly . . .

He slapped the propeller pitch into fully fine and waited a few seconds as the engine revs shuddered up the scale, like a fast-moving car slammed into a lower gear. The extra drag slowed him, but not enough; the runaway went on reversing up out of the depths, expanding as it came. He hesitated for an instant, then reached past the throttle quadrant and snatched the undercarriage switch to the Down position, trying the radio again as the wheels unfolded with a hollow rumble. His acceleration slowed still further, finally matching speed with dreamlike laziness as he drifted alongside fifty feet from Whisky Tango's port wing tip. Staring out sideways at it, the horizon-line too distant at this height to give any perspective on their rate of descent, he had the weird feeling for long drawn-out seconds that they weren't going down at all; Whisky Tango was just hanging pitched-down and motionless in the sky, the only movement the result of his own jockeying on control yoke and pitch lever as he varied the drag of his propeller disc to stay in station. They could carry on floating like this for hours; there was no suggestion at all of any headlong rush towards the ground . . .

He snatched a glance in at his instruments, and the illusion vanished instantly. The speed was 140 m.p.h. and increasing, rate of descent about 1,500 feet a minute, altitude passing 5,000. His left hand went out in a reflex action to pull the wheels up before they exceeded the maximum gear-down speed of 150 m.p.h. – and then snatched away again without touching the switch. He had to have the undercarriage down to act as a dive-brake or he'd go skating on past her: if the wind ripped the gear doors off it ripped the bloody gear-doors off.

He shouted into the radio again. Still nothing.

Fear was a hot sickness in his stomach. Thoughts tumbled through his head, desperate with urgency but seeming to move with hideous slowness under the moan of the airflow. What had *happened?* Had she fainted? Accidentally wound on a handful of forward trim? The man stirred and jammed the stick? Engine failure . . . ?

Engine failure!

It had to be. If he needed gear down and power off to stay with her, it couldn't be anything else; she'd had an engine failure, then panicked and let go of the wheel.

He yelled, "Jesus bloody *God!*" An engine failure now wasn't fair, wasn't reasonable . . .

The speed was 150. The altimeter winding through 4,500.

So okay – forget the chances against it happening, forget the shock-reaction time, and think. Think of the procedures you're always teaching. Into the glide, find a field, plan your approach, look for the cause of the failure . . .

He jammed his thumb on the transmit switch and shouted, "Ann! For Christ's sake pull back! Pull *back!*"

Nothing happened. The runaway kept pointing down, like a formation leader diving for speed before a loop. Kerr was close enough to see the rivet-lines on the airframe and the two heads in the cockpit. Neither of them moved.

155 m.p.h.; passing 4,000 feet.

She was going to crash.

The realisation turned his muscles to water. She was going to crash because plunging down at 2,000 feet a minute she was simply going to run out of time. If he'd been in her cockpit himself he'd have had all the time in the world – more than enough to establish a proper slow glide, locate a reasonable landing field even in this area, and still have minutes left to search for the cause of the failure – but across fifty yards of thin air, there was no chance at all. No way. All he could do was follow the insane thundering dive until the ground got too close and he had to pull out and leave her to carry on down alone . . .

She was really going to crash. On London.

Kerr felt sweat pouring down his face and into his roll-neck collar. He snatched his left hand up to the radio and twisted the knobs, flicking his eyes in and out to the frequency window until 121.5 came up. His own voice fed back hoarsely through his earphones as he snapped out his Mayday call. When he'd done it he didn't wait for a reply, but switched back immediately to 126.85 and tried the girl again.

Still nothing. Just the mounting roar of the air, the erratic vibration of the windmilling propeller as he juggled the pitch lever, and the plunging shark shape of the other Arrow alongside.

Passing 3,500 feet, he looked straight ahead for a moment as he pressed the transmit button again. Over the red curve of the nose was a calm solid toy-town of inner suburbia, roads and houses and factories expanding slowly up to meet him. Here and there the setting sun glinted on windows, flashing brilliant diamonds among the speckled browns and whites. He had a vivid split-second image of the bobbing model aeroplane alongside his right wing ploughing into that toy-town, smashing through real buildings and real people and finishing up in a raging ball of fire as the remainder of the fuel went up . . .

Oh, Jesus God – FUEL! That was it! He'd forgotten to have the girl change fucking fuel tanks!

The realisation hit him like a physical blow. For seconds on end he seemed to be paralysed in the shuddering cockpit, his body swamping fire-hot and ice-cold.

The oldest, most basic error in the book, and he'd been so preoccupied with his own problems, so fixed in the notion that the girl had plenty of fuel while he hadn't, that he'd walked right into it: committed the incredible, unforgivable error of forgetting to tell her to switch from one wing-tank to the other. He'd even half-thought of it – the words fuel *and* asymmetric *which had nudged in his brain – and ignored his own warnings. So she'd flown for two hours on whichever tank she'd started from Newcastle on, and now that tank had run dry. The other one might be full to the brim – almost certainly was, in fact – but unless she could be induced to find the fuel tap and switch it over, its contents might as well be on the moon. God, that he of all people hadn't thought of that . . .*

242

Passing 3,000 feet. The airspeed clawing past 160.

No time.

His thumb was slippery on the transmit switch. He swallowed on his bone-dry throat and heard his own voice high-pitched and strange in the earphones.

"Ann! Listen to me! All that's happened is we've run one fuel tank dry, so we need to switch to the other one! Do you hear me?"

The only response was the whistling howl of the dive. The altimeter unwound through 2,500. At this height the hanging-in-space illusion gone completely: now, Whisky Tango seemed to be diving into a vast brown bowl, a bowl whose edges were expanding steadily upwards to engulf them as the horizon-perspective shifted. As he stared across the void something detached itself from the underside of the runaway and was gone in an instant, whipped away backwards in the slipstream. He ducked instinctively, although it had come nowhere near him, then thought *undercarriage door* and dismissed it from his mind. In one minute's time the loss of a gear-door was going to be totally academic . . .

Eyes fixed on the other cockpit, he pressed the yoke button again and went on talking, urgently and continuously.

*   *   *

In Whisky Tango's cabin, the departure of the starboard undercarriage door sounded horrific. The operating linkage gave way under the air pressure first, allowing the door to flutter against the wing for a moment with a noise like machine-gun fire. The hellish tattoo cut off Ann's hysterical screaming and froze her stock-still, not even breathing. It went on for four or five seconds, then ceased abruptly as the door ripped off.

It was immediately replaced by the instructor's voice, crackling loud out of the speaker over the howl of the wind.

"Come *on*, Ann! Reach across to the wall behind Roy's left leg and turn the fuel tap. Just *turn* it! It doesn't matter which way."

243

The words lapped and receded in her head, without meaning. Now that her screaming had stopped she seemed to be stunned, trapped in a dull acceptance of the inevitable. Her frail command of the controls was a thing of the past, dashed away in an instant: the plane had taken over completely and was crashing, carrying them both with it, and there was nothing in the world that would stop it. The streets and houses filled the windscreen, swelling hypnotically as they rushed upwards towards her.

The thought formed in her mind, weirdly calm and clear under the roaring airflow, that these were the last few seconds of her life.

"Ann! Turn the fuel tap! Behind Roy's left knee. Then the plane'll recover!"

Recover . . . ?

This time, the words vaguely registered. *Recover* beat like a gong, penetrating the barrier of shock. She had to turn the fuel tap . . .

She didn't know where it was.

The detached part of her consciousness watched herself reacting in dreadful slow motion, wasting endless moments in confusion as the plane went on down. Her head moved from side to side and her left hand reached towards the panel and then stopped, not knowing where to go. Roy's unconscious body stirred beside her, leaning into its harness and swaying gently. The crowded dials and levers were a mass of complication, more unfamiliar than ever with the cockpit in its pitched-down attitude and the wind-noise battering her senses. Nothing even looked like a tap . . .

"Turn the fuel tap, behind Roy's left knee! Just turn it from one tank to the other!"

Behind Roy's knee . . .

She twisted sideways, reaching across the cockpit. The shoulder strap of the safety harness brought her up short. For seconds she struggled against it in treacle-slow desperation, then wriggled her right arm out from under it and grabbed across Roy's lap, scrabbling his legs towards her so she could see. There was something on the side wall of the

244

cockpit, down near the floor: a red-painted circular thing shaped like a dog's feeding bowl, with a lever in the middle of it. Straining against her lap-strap, fumbling to hold Roy's knees out of the way with one hand, she stretched down and tried to twist the lever backwards.

It wouldn't move. Solid. The airflow was an eerie rushing whistle, drowning out the urgent clattering of the radio speaker somewhere over her head. She tugged frantically, distantly feeling pain in her fingers. The lever still didn't move. She made a small animal noise of terror and tried it the other way, forwards . . .

It revolved smoothly round through ninety degrees, and came up against a stop.

The engine bellowed into life.

It came back even more suddenly than it had stopped. There was no preliminary coughing or spluttering, just an explosion of thunder running immediately up the scale to a huge roar. A giant invisible hand yanked forwards and slightly left as the Arrow yawed in the slipstream helix.

The nose started to lift, pitching slowly upwards in the normal reaction to engine thrust.

Ann pushed herself back off Roy's lap. Over the roaring she could hear a thin high screaming sound, on the edge of hysteria. It was several seconds before she realised she was making it herself. She clapped her hands over her ears.

The altimeter unwound past 1,000 feet.

Below, the streets and houses and cars were very clear, cold and long-shadowed in the last minutes of the winter sun. The blue engine cowling crawled over them, moving from street to street, rising slowly out of the dive of its own accord.

The radio yelled, *"Ann! Pull back! You're too low. Pull back on the wheel!"*

She didn't hear it. The pull-up, mild as it was, seemed to be pressing her into her seat like a huge weight on her shoulders. She was trapped in the bowels of the machine, powerless . . . .

At 600 feet, still going down and with the speed passing

180, the port undercarriage door gave way. It went instantly, a quick *snap-bang* that was almost lost under the roar of engine and slipstream. Two seconds later the engine r.p.m., which had exceeded the 2,700 redline almost immediately after the re-start because of the high airspeed, hit 2,850 on the revcounter. The figure had no special significance – aero engines are designed to operate with a considerable margin of safety, and a Lycoming 0-360 will hold together at well over 3,000 r.p.m. for a short period – except that at *that* particular combination of barometric pressure and temperature, 2,850 just so happened to be the revs at which the outermost tips of the propeller blades reached the speed of sound. The prop went supersonic in a drawn-out bandsaw scream which was heard ten miles away. Down in the streets below, a thousand tiny white pinpricks blossomed as people looked up at the sky.

Whimpering in terror, Ann pressed the palms of her hands hard against her ears and squeezed her eyes tight shut.

Whisky Tango stopped going down at 300 feet above the ground, doing 190 m.p.h. It passed gracefully through level flight and continued pitching gently nose-up into a shallow climb, dissipating its excess speed.

19

1621–1627

ON THE WALL of the Distress and Diversion Cell, above the glass-plate map of England, is an electric clock. It is a standard government-issue model, permanently set to Greenwich Mean Time, and its record of reliability is practically unblemished.

By twenty-one minutes past four, Flight Lieutenant Peterson was convinced it had slowed to a fraction of its normal pace.

Initially, Kerr's Mayday call had sparked off a burst of feverish activity. For just over a minute, everyone in the room had been engaged in talking urgently into telephones, ignoring the drama in the air which they could do nothing about and concentrating on warning the various emergency services of the new imminence of disaster. Then, quite suddenly, it had all been done. The police, fire, and ambulance services would be carrying on, flashing the information along their own lines of communication, but for the Emergency Cell, at the apex of the alert, the task was over. Silence settled in the room, deepening as the seconds ticked by. Every eye was glued to Peterson's radar screen, switched now to the Heathrow Airport scanner and cranked down to its minimum range to cover only the immediate environs of London. Kerr's Mayday squawk, pulsating like an orange-red heartbeat under the steady circular sweep of the scanner line, moved slowly across Ealing and Brentford on a track of 140 degrees magnetic. There was no trace of the runaway on the screen at all; if it was still in the air, its radar echo was being swamped by the proximity of Romeo X-ray's transponder-return.

The five watchers breathed softly, waiting for the Mayday squawk to stop flying straight and start circling. There could only be one reason for Kerr to start circling.

Peterson spat out a fragment of thumbnail, the small *pfft* sounding loud in the dim-lit quiet.

"Anyone got a cigarette?"

His corporal assistant gave him a Players Number 6. Keeping his eyes on the radar screen, Lyle scraped a match and held it out. No one reminded Peterson he was giving up smoking.

Outside in the corridor, someone clattered teacups.

The minute hand of the clock made a tiny movement to twenty-two minutes past the hour. The second hand went on crawling round the dial. Peterson sucked hard on his cigarette, exhaled slowly, and stared at the screen through the floating smoke.

Twenty-three minutes past.

Lyle muttered, "Christ, will you *do* something!" The words fell into the quietness like pebbles.

Peterson stirred and said softly, "Might just make Richmond Park." Nobody replied.

The radio speaker clacked suddenly and blared into life.

"D and D, Romeo-X. Whisky Tango has recovered from the dive. Climbing away now, passing 800 feet this time."

For a second, no one moved. Then Peterson jerked forward in his chair, slammed his palm down on the transmit button, and almost shouted into his microphone.

"*Roger*, Romeo-X! What happened?"

There was a moment's pause, then Kerr's voice came back. Even through the metallic reproduction of the speaker it sounded suddenly tired and old.

"She didn't change fuel tanks, and ran one dry. I forgot to tell her. My fault."

Peterson made a silent *ouch* with his lips, glancing at Lyle. Then he looked forward again, pressed the button, and said calmly, "Not to worry, sir; these things happen. Confirm she's changed tanks now?" He winced for a second time as he spoke, realising as the words came out that it was a stupid question. If the girl hadn't changed tanks she certainly wouldn't be climbing away.

The speaker said briefly, "Affirmative."

Peterson said, "Roger, Romeo-X. What are your intentions now?"

Another brief pause. Then the metallic voice said, "She's levelling off now at about 1,000 feet. We'll maintain that altitude, and I'll try to get her turned due west and then call you for steers to Greenham Common."

"Roger, Romeo-X. We'll be standing by for that. Will you be making a straight-in approach at Greenham?"

"Affirmative." The speaker crackled for several seconds, then cleared. ". . . ear of the runway, if you would."

Peterson pressed his left earphone hard against his head. "Say again, Romeo-X? You were breaking up on that last transmission."

"I say again, affirmative, this will be a straight-in approach. I want to intercept the Greenham centre-line as far out as possible, and Whisky Tango will be landing first time unless there's no chance at all. Also, tell Greenham to keep their crash wagons well clear of the runway. Whisky Tango will be landing without using rudder, and will almost certainly run off the side. Lastly, please advise them I may be landing behind her myself."

Peterson frowned, then said, "Understand keep the crash wagons clear, Romeo-X. And . . . you'll be landing *behind* Whisky Tango, confirm?"

"Affirmative." The voice clashed in another short burst of static, ". . . a small fuel problem myself. I'll want to land as soon as possible once Whisky Tango's down. Maybe behind her."

Peterson muttered "Jesus!" without pressing the mike button. He drew breath to speak, then hesitated as he caught sight of Lyle shaking his head furiously. He breathed out, gave a tiny nod, and said matter-of-factly into the microphone, "Okay, Romeo-X, that's understood. I'll pass it on."

"Thanks. Switching now, and call you for steers in a few minutes."

"Roger, Romeo-X."

The speaker double-clicked and went quiet. In the sudden hush Peterson sat back, pushed one headphone away from his ear, and looked at Lyle. Lyle ran a hand over his bald head and said "Phe-ew!" in a long drawn-out sigh. As an afterthought he added, "No point in following up about his fuel. Just waste time."

Peterson nodded; half nod, half helpless shrug. Then he said flatly, "Not good, though."

"Well, Christ, don't break your face seeing the bright side. I was waiting for a major disaster, there."

"There's time yet."

"Jesus, tell me something new. What's the matter with you?"

"Well . . ." Peterson frowned and shrugged again, searching for words, ". . . this bloke in Romeo-X. Kerr. First the coppers want him, then he nearly crashes the woman in the middle of bloody London, then he hasn't taught her to use the rudder, and now he says he's low on fuel himself. You know what I mean . . . ?" His voice trailed off. He pulled on his cigarette, watching Lyle's face.

Lyle leaned forward in his chair and picked up his pipe. He stared at it thoughtfully, turning it over in his fingers.

"I don't know so much, John," he said slowly. "Anyone could forget something like having her change tanks. Christ, *we* forgot it, for that matter: have you thought of that? We're sitting here fat, dumb and happy, and neither of us thought of it. And don't forget he did work it out in the end. He realised it in the middle of a very high pressure situation, *and* managed to do something about it. Now you and I call ourselves pilots – so would *you* have worked that one out, in that situation? I'm not too sure I would."

Peterson nibbled a fingernail. After a moment he said doubtfully, "Yeah . . ."

"Yeah." Lyle looked up. "I think you're wrong if you're

worrying about him, John. Forget the fuel and the other thing for a moment, and look at what's he's done. He's only had an hour or so and he's got her slowed up, climbing and descending, making turns, and got her wheels down. Think about it; whatever he might have missed out, I reckon that's bloody good going."

Peterson sucked and blew smoke, still frowning. "Maybe . . . well, yes, I guess so. But what about her not using rudder? How's she going to steer on the ground?"

Lyle shrugged. "So what if she doesn't? I haven't flown a Cherokee, but I expect it's pretty stable in a straight line anyway. It's not as if it was a tailwheel kite. No, I reckon that shows our lad's got his priorities right: he's having her turn on ailerons alone, probably over-riding the wing-leveller, so that all she'll have to think about's the control wheel and the throttle. And I think that's pretty bright of him, with the pressure he's under." He ran a hand over his bald head. "If you ask me, I reckon he's a bloody good instructor."

Peterson nodded again, drumming his fingers on the arm of his chair. After a few seconds he leaned forward suddenly, mashed his cigarette into a tin-lid ashtray, and reached for the Mediator phone. While the Greenham Common number burred in his ear he glanced at Lyle again.

"I hope you're right, sir," he said softly. "I do so hope you're right."

*   *   *

At that moment, one person who would not have agreed with Lyle about Keith Kerr was Keith Kerr.

Closing on Whisky Tango as the runaway settled back into level flight at the top of its climb, he was literally trembling from head to toe. His feet were dancing on the rudder pedals, and his stomach was tingling-hollow. For the first time in as long as he could remember, the cockpit of an aeroplane seemed an alien place. Like a man who has had a bad fright in a car, all he wanted to do was stop. Land, walk around in the cold open air of the winter afternoon, and not fly again or make any more flying decisions until he'd had a quiet time to come to terms with himself.

He could feel himself handling the Arrow jerkily; gripping the control yoke with a rigid fist like a nervous student. He squeezed his eyes shut for a moment and flexed his fingers, trying to force himself into the natural rhythm of flight. The emergency was over and there were cockpit chores to be done: he moved the undercarriage switch to Up, then pushed the mixture lever into full rich for a few seconds before pulling it slowly back again towards the lean position. His eyes flicked to the cylinder head temperature and his airman's sense registered vaguely that this was exceptional: that you don't normally lean off an engine as low as 1,000 feet anyway, and especially you don't lean it off until the CHT is twenty degrees over the max. His right hand still clutched the half-wheel tightly, knuckles white.

The other Arrow floated gently back towards him, dipping below the misting horizon and then rising slowly above it as the phugoid oscillations of the level-out diminished and the speed stabilised. As the range closed to 200 feet he could see the details of the undercarriage. The wheels seemed to be undamaged, but the bare tubes of the Oleo legs, naked without the main gear-doors, were an accusing reminder of how close the runaway had been to disaster.

His fault. His stupid, ridiculous error of omission which had nearly killed two people for certain plus an unknown number of others on the ground.

His fault.

In his own mind, the final avoidance of catastrophe had been purely a matter of luck. Luck that the modern Cherokee Arrow fuel tap has a detent trigger on the Off position, so that merely moving the lever without pressing the trigger can only switch the feed from one tank to the other and not turn it off altogether – and still more luck that the girl had reacted when she did, and not a few seconds later. From above and behind, the bottom of the runaway's pull-out had seemed to be right down among the roof tops. He had faintly heard the scream of the supersonic propeller above the howl of his own dive as he'd waited, agonised, for Whisky Tango to explode into the streets and houses below...

Shuddering, he fumbled the last Gold Leaf out of the packet on the seat beside him. The other Arrow was steady now, swimming smoothly over the tight-packed roads and buildings of London. He knew he should be talking to the girl, but the words wouldn't come. His mind seemed to be numbed, completely blank. What *could* you say when you'd nearly crashed someone under your command...?

Suddenly, he saw old Piet van den Hoyt.

It was the day – Christ, what was it? Ten years ago? – when he'd lost a customer for the first time: pushed too hard in the morning of his enthusiasm for flight, and then been astonished when the student had stalked off in a rage at the end of the lesson. And then Vandy, slumped in his cane chair in the torpid Kenyan heat. Not angry; just talking about the art of instructing in his hoarse Afrikaans accent. *"Remember you will make mistakes often, Keith. Forget to tell something or do something... press people too hard... become angry when they are slow... these things we all do. But the thing when it happens is to learn to stop yourself. Admit the mistake in your mind. Then make a deep breath, put it behind you, and start again fresh. Otherwise it will throw you; that one screw-up will fly the airplane for you the rest of the lesson and maybe the rest of the day. And that is the real danger, that carrying on when you are angry with yourself and thinking wrong. That is what kills people."*

Kerr lifted the lighter to his cigarette, aware of his hand shaking. His mouth was dry and sticky-sweet and the smoke tasted foul, rolling in his throat in the drumming of the engine. He sucked down a long, deep drag, held it for a moment, then tilted his head back and exhaled slowly towards the top of the windscreen.

Put the mistake behind you... start again fresh. Easy to say, but much more difficult to do. One of the intangible, unteachable disciplines which a professional instructor must acquire the hard way over the years...

He brought his head down, and looked round the sky.

253

Behind and to the right the blaze of sunset was losing its brilliance. The huge red orb was half-sunken below the horizon, the broad bands of gold turning orange and magenta across the cold evening sky. Beneath the moving white plank of his wing the freshness was gone from the city in sympathy, leaving a drab grey-brown sprawl slashed with curlicues of roads and the winding ribbon of the Thames. Past his aileron, about five miles away, he could make out the light-coloured smear of Heathrow Airport, the sky around it oddly empty with the big jets stilled for the passage of the emergency.

He took another drag on his cigarette and looked ahead of the wing, at Whisky Tango. The dying rays of the sun picked out its outline in sharp relief as it slid on over the city.

He rubbed his scar for a moment, thinking briefly about position and time. Greenham Common was twenty miles away or more to the west. They should have turned towards it several minutes ago, which meant that now they'd be approaching on a time-wasting dogleg in a race against the failing daylight. With full dark in twenty, twenty-five minutes it would be a tight thing. And then there was his own fuel situation . . .

He hunched his shoulders once, then reached out and twisted the radio knobs from 121.5 back to 126.85.

*   *   *

If the human brain is subjected to extreme fright for an extended period of time, it eventually reaches a saturation point. Unable to cope with the intolerable stress any longer, the conscious mind cuts out fully or partially into a state of confusion. The syndrome is well known and well understood : members of the medical profession sometimes refer to it as nature's anaesthetic.

It is more commonly called shock.

As Whisky Tango settled gradually into level flight at the top of its climb, Ann's crying ceased. She stared out of the windows, the pupils of her eyes dilated almost to pinpoints.

254

The snore of the engine, normal now the Arrow was stabilising at around 100 m.p.h., seemed to be a background which had always been there. Streets and buildings slid smoothly under the wings, 900 feet below. At this height she could see specks which were individual people, unheeding people walking on tiny pavements and crossing tiny roads. The sight of them had no effect. Existence on the ground was something in the past, like a film once seen or an old memory; the whole world now was this little burring room in space, Roy's unconscious body, and the vast empty sky all around.

The cabin smelt rather like a hospital. Faintly plastic and metal and disinfectant.

She thought about the hospital.

You see things in a casualty ward, a lot of them not pleasant. You see people brought in, mangled and broken, after a car crash or an industrial accident. And you sometimes see a doctor shake his head and then administer a dosage of sedative or morphine which he knows full well will be lethal. Euthanasia is not legal, not recognised – but it happens, every day of the week in most big hospitals. People who are too terribly injured or seriously ill to survive given a shot which cushions the pain but which their ruined systems cannot hope to absorb, so that they slip away in peace . . .

Maybe we'll be like that, she thought vacantly. After the plane crashes.

She knew it *was* going to crash; knew it quite certainly. But the odd thing was that she couldn't imagine what it was going to be like. The cockpit was too warm and solid to think of it shattering and crumpling in an instant of time. Earlier on she'd been terrified of falling, of the plane going out of control and tumbling down into the void – but now, now it was really going to happen, she couldn't imagine it at all. It was as if the horror had been used up, dulled by overexposure. *Crash* was just a word. The plane was going to crash, and that was all.

The hospital was easy to picture, though. That was familiar. The blood and mucus and dirt, the careful desperate haste, the quiet scurrying of nurses and doctors. It would be strange to see it all from the other side; watch other nurses going through the hopeless motions of trying to save your own life. Maybe that was what she was frightened of, more than the crash. Or maybe simply oblivion, ending, nothing else to come after ...

Over her head, the radio speaker said something.

Moving in a daze, without knowing why she did it, she reached for the curly black lead under the throttle pedestal and pulled the microphone up from the floor. For a moment she just stared at it in her hands. Then she lifted it and said blankly, "Yes."

The voice came back, metallically calm. "How're you doing then, love? Okay now?"

She heard herself say again, "Yes. Okay." The words came out dully, automatic, without any meaning. She swayed in her seat as the Arrow rocked for a moment, snarling through a patch of glow-level turbulence. Out of the corner of her eye she saw her coat slip down off Roy's right shoulder.

The man said something else, but she didn't bother to reply.

Time seemed to be expanding and contracting. One moment she had a hollow fluttery feeling in her stomach and the plane seemed to be racing over the ground, and the next, everything appeared to be going on in slow-motion, almost static. It was unreal; as if you were very drunk, or were trying to wake up from a bad dream ...

But then, that was a symptom of shock. Shock and nervous exhaustion. It was funny how you could sit back and recognise symptoms in yourself, as if it were somebody else. It didn't seem to help, though. You could see the symptoms, but you couldn't do anything about them. It was easier just to let go, let your mind drift ...

"Come on, Ann! Answer me!"

She raised the microphone and said "Yes" again.

"How's Roy doing, honey?" The voice had an edge of desperation to it, which she didn't notice.

Roy.

She turned her head slowly to look at him. The man she'd

been falling in love with. His mouth was open and his features slack and vacant, like an idiot. The only sign of life was his breathing, his chest moving in shallow, irregular gasps. She thought mechanically. *Pressure in the subarachnoid cavity affecting the respiratory centre in the brain.* And possibly other centres, too. When he came round – *if* he came round – he might be all right, he might be partially paralysed, or he might be nothing but a vegetable for the rest of his life. It depended on the extent of the brain damage caused by the pressure of the blood leakage inside his skull. And that there was no way of telling so long as he remained in coma and untreated. The fact that his condition had stayed unchanged for nearly two hours could be a good sign, but you could never really tell. Not with a subarachnoid. If he was in hospital they might inject a radio-opaque dye into his bloodstream, take an X-ray, and then possibly operate, drilling into the skull to relieve the pressure and tie off the burst artery. That was in hospital . . .

But he wasn't going to get to hospital, of course. The plane was going to crash.

She looked round the gently humming cockpit, almost as if she were surprised at finding herself still there. Then her thoughts wandered back to Roy again. As he'd been when he'd picked her up this morning. It seemed an age ago and in a different world. He'd been warm. Confident. Easy to be with.

Easy to fall in love with.

I could have fallen in love with him, she decided in a detached way. He's kind and he's nice. I'd probably have gone to bed with him tonight or tomorrow night, and that would have been important. And now he's dead. Quite certainly. Still breathing, but because of the crash to come, he's dead.

Without any particular emotion, she found herself remembering something he'd said just after they'd taken off "*If you really don't like it, just say. We can always go back and drive down instead.*" She'd had her chance then, and missed it; so what happened was her fault. If she'd been honest and admitted she was frightened . . .

The Arrow bumped again, growling through an invisible column of warmer air rising from a Saturday-working factory near Wandsworth. Ann blinked, starting two big new tears rolling down her cheeks. She reached out slowly, picked up Roy's limp right hand, and held it in her own.

The speaker said urgently, "Come *on*, Ann! Let's hear from you! Tell me how Roy is."

She twisted her head further, so she could see the other aeroplane through the left rear cabin window. It was floating in space close alongside and slightly behind, neat and stream-lined. Rising, falling, and weaving gently all the time, with the city sliding past below. She could even see the pilot, just. His face was turned towards her. He was the man who kept talking over the radio, wanting her to answer. Funny to have someone so close and talking to you, in the middle of the sky. Unreal . . .

The thought occurred to her that she'd never met the man. Never even seen him. Somehow, that made it more strange than ever. There he was, so near, and he was just a voice. She knew nothing about him. Not the colour of his hair, nor how tall he was, not what he was like. And now she never would see him, either. She was perfectly sure of that, beyond any question: it was just a fact, unassailable, like the forth-coming crash.

She didn't even know his name. She had a vague recol-lection that he'd said it once, but she'd forgotten it.

The radio said again, "Come *on* now, Ann! Will you please answer me!"

The voice was loud and commanding. Staring at the other cockpit she thought she could see the man's head move a little. He was still waiting, asking her to say something.

She lifted the microphone and said tonelessly, "He's . . . the same. Still the same."

The voice clattered back immediately, sharp with relief.

"Good. I'm glad to hear that. Now listen; I'm sorry about that dive just now. But it's all over now and you're okay. Nothing like that'll happen again. All right?"

"Yes. All right." Her own voice sounded odd, flat, repeating a litany into the snore of the engine.

"Good. Great girl. In fact, it actually helped us in one way, getting rid of all that excess height. Anyway, we'll forget it now and carry on. So what I want to do is make a gentle turn to the right, so that we start heading towards the place where we're going to land. So just take hold of the wheel and turn it a little. Like we were doing . . . doing before. Turn it to the right. I'll tell you when to stop."

Turn.

She let go of Roy's hand and looked to the front again, staring dazedly at the control yoke. It moved slightly as she watched it, a small rigid twist-and-back as the wing-leveller corrected for another patch of turbulence. The hollowness welled up in her stomach again. It wasn't fair, telling her to to do this now, before the crash. She wanted to close her eyes, rest for a moment. She'd do it in a minute, when she'd rested. That was it. In a minute . . .

She looked out to the right, at the townscape crawling under the leading edge of the wing. They were passing over a cold, brown-looking park, bisected by roads teeming with traffic. There was a pond, grey leafless trees, a football pitch with tired bare patches around the goalmouths. Parks in cities were dreary places during the winter . . .

"Hey, Ann!" The voice was hard again, almost angry. "Let's not stop now, for Christ's sake! It'll be dark in twenty minutes. And we've got to get Roy down. So let's have a simple turn to the right. Just gently. Go into it now."

Dark in twenty minutes . . .

The words seemed to mill around in her head, jumbled by the burr of the engine and the sight of the city gliding by beneath. For some reason the words were important. The sky ahead of the windscreen was changing with the sinking of the sun, taking on the huge electric-blue coldness of a clear winter evening. The cold seemed to reach suddenly into the cockpit, making her shiver. *It'll be dark in twenty minutes.* And when it got dark they'd be swallowed up; trapped in the night, just waiting. Sitting in the seats in droning blackness waiting for something which would leap out and smash them some moment, any moment . . .

She was aware of her own breathing, fast and ragged over the noise of the engine. After half a minute she lifted her right arm and wiped her face hard on the inside of her sleeve, feeling the wool rasping on her skin.

She had to go on. Just go on trying, for a little while longer. Just until it got dark.

She reached out and took hold of the wheel. It felt clammy in her hands. Straining upwards to see over the nose, she twisted it slowly to the right.

*   *   *

Holding formation, the two Arrows pivoted gently round over Clapham and Brixton. As they turned, the top rim of the sun sank finally below the horizon, leaving an orange glow at the base of a fading sky.

The time was twenty-seven minutes past four.

20

1627–1637

THE LEFT FUEL gauge read empty.

Kerr glanced at it for the hundredth time as the runaway rolled stiffly out of its turn ahead of him. There was no doubt about it; no possibility of any tiny error induced by the turn. The needle was sitting rock-steady, touching the E mark on the scale.

He dragged the back of his hand over the sweat on his face. He'd been running on the left tank for fifteen minutes, and with luck it might still have enough in it for another five or ten. With luck. Definitely not guaranteed. So he could run it dry and then switch to the starboard tank, or he could stick to his plan and switch over now, leaving the last few pints in the left tank as a reserve.

Stick to the plan, he decided. For one thing his airman's instinct rebelled against running any tank dry – even with fuel pick-ups raised above the tank floor there's always the possibility of sucking up dirt with the last drops – and for another there was psychological advantage in knowing that you could run out and still have something, even if only a couple of minutes, in reserve. He thumbed the boost pump switch, leaned across the cockpit and twisted the fuel tap to the RIGHT position, then clicked the pump off again. His left hand moved towards the mixture lever, then drew away again. The cylinder head temperature was already higher than he'd ever seen it before, and enough was enough . . .

261

He thought for a few seconds, then pressed the transmit switch.

"That was a good turn, Ann. We're heading just about right. Now I'm going off the air for a moment while I talk to the people on the ground. I'll be back to you right away. Okay?"

There was a pause. Off to the right, Whisky Tango hung steady against the vastness of the purpling western sky. Then the girl's voice said "Yes" in his earphones. He hesitated for a moment, then reached out and switched the radio frequency to 121.5.

"D and D, Mayday Romeo X-ray."

The reply boomed in his ears immediately. A new voice this time. An American voice.

"Ah, Romeo X-ray, this is Greenham Common Approach, sir. You been handed on to us by Distress an' Diversion for approach control."

"Roger, Greenham. Confirm you have me on radar?"

"Tha's affirmative, sir; we got you iden'ified bright an' clear. You're just coming up to the western boundary of the London Zone, an' you got maybe fifteen miles to run to Greenham, headin' two-eight-fahve. We usin' runway two-niner, wind three-zero-zero at one-fahve, altimeter one-zero-one-four."

"Roger. Could you give me your QFE, please?"

"QF . . . ? Oh, yeah. Stand by, sir, we don' usually use that. QFE is – ah – one-zero-zero-one."

"One-zero-zero-one." Kerr twisted the altimeter setting knob until 1001 millibars came up in the barometric pressure window: now the height scale would read zero on the ground at Greenham. He rubbed his scar for a moment, then pressed the transmit switch again.

"Greenham, I want to intercept your extended runway centre line about eight miles out, for a very long final approach. Can you give me a heading for that, please?"

"Rahger, sir. Headin' for that'd be – ah – 'bout two-eight-zero, sir. Two-eight-zero. Ah . . . be advised, though, that'll take you right through the Aldermaston Prohibited Area."

"The hell with that. We'll go through that. D'you have ILS?"

"Negative, sir. We have TACAN, but no civil facility."

"Understood. Request your runway lights on then, please. I want to see you as far out as possible."

" 'Kay sir, that's done." There was a tiny pause. "You got runway and approach lights on now. Confirm this'll be a straight-in approach?"

"Affirmative. Straight-in first time. And please keep your crash wagons well clear of the runway. The emergency aircraft will be coming in fast and might go anywhere once it's on the ground." Kerr pulled a face as he released the mike switch. What he should have said was *if* the emergency aircraft managed to get on the ground as anything other than a ball of scrap . . .

The American voice said, "Yes, sir. We already been told that."

Kerr swallowed and said, "Fine. Thanks for all you're doing."

"S'okay, sir. You jus' keep on truckin'."

Kerr double-clicked the transmit button, waited a few seconds, and then switched the radio back to 126.85. For a long moment he stared out sideways, watching the floating shape of the other Arrow while he forced himself to concentrate on what was ahead. Closing on Greenham at 100 m.p.h. they had ten or eleven minutes to go before touchdown. This was his last chance to get the approach plan perfectly clear in his mind; think of the hundred and one things he might have forgotten.

He mentally ran through the pre-landing checklist, trying to think himself into the girl's cockpit. *Brakes off . . . undercarriage down and locked . . . mixture full rich . . . propeller pitch to fine* – well, the hell with that, she didn't want to be mucking around with the revs at this stage; *pumps on* – and the hell with that, too – *carburettor heat,* not applicable to a fuel injection engine . . . *fuel fully on and sufficient . . . hatches and harness secure.* She ought to be all right on that lot . . .

So?

Well, the first essential was a long, straight approach; get her exactly lined up with the runway as far out as possible. That meant turning her twenty degrees left on to the course he'd just been given, 285, and thereafter switching the radio back constantly to Greenham for fresh steers until he had the aerodrome in sight. Then at the same time – or at least, within the next two or three minutes – he'd have to start her on a gentle descent. No flaps, because for one thing she didn't know how to use them and for another a flapless approach meant a flatter altitude and therefore a smaller pitch change for the landing. It also meant she'd be coming in fast of course, but with 10,000 feet of concrete to play with, at least *that* shouldn't be critical. A well-flown Arrow is capable of landing and stopping in less than 600 feet: so even if she slammed it on the ground at 100 m.p.h. and then let it roll to a standstill without using the brakes at all she still shouldn't have a distance problem.

So use of the brakes wasn't vital – although he ought to try to tell her about the handbrake lever if there was time – but getting her on to the ground good and solid was. The Cherokee range of aircraft are among the easiest machines in the world to land – but any aeroplane coming in at twenty or thirty m.p.h. over its normal approach speed is likely to start bouncing if the landing flare-out isn't exactly right. And this one *wasn't* going to be exactly right, or anywhere near it. In fact, the best bet was probably to have no flare-out at all in the usual sense; just aim to get her more or less levelled off about ten feet up, let the Arrow fly itself on to the ground, and then have her let go of the wheel at the moment of impact. The result would be a hell of a heavy landing, but a damn sight safer than trying to talk her through "holding off" just above the ground for a proper nose-high near-the-stall touchdown. Letting go of the wheel should make the nose nod down, which would keep the aircraft pinned to the runway during the ground-roll.

So. A long straight approach, a gentle descent, and then slam it on the ground and let go. Right?

Right.

Kerr shook his head and muttered "Jesus Christ" into the rumble of the engine. Ahead of his starboard wing the other Arrow droned on unconcernedly over the last straggling borders of suburbia, heading out into the cold greeny-grey countryside of Berkshire. Below, as the daylight began to fade on the ground, the first lights of evening were appearing, dim yellow pin-pricks of early street lamps and occasional car headlights. Not necessary yet, but a grim reminder of the night soon to come.

He swallowed, tasting the sourness in his mouth. After a moment he rubbed his left hand wearily across his eyes, then pressed the transmit switch. The false confidence in his own voice rang in his ears like a cracked bell as he started speaking.

"Okay, Ann. Back again, and you're doing great. Now all we need at the moment is a small turn to the left. You can do that as soon as you like, and I'll tell you when to stop. Then, after that, we'll be starting a very gentle descent towards an aerodrome called Greenham Common ..."

*   *   *

Greenham Common has one of the largest runways anywhere in the United Kingdom. The paved area is nearly two miles long and a shade under 200 feet wide. The world's biggest bombers and transports are capable of returning to earth in about half the available distance, and on more than one occasion light aircraft such as Cessna 150s have been deliberately landed *across* the runway without undue difficulty.

The only snag to Greenham Common is that it is normally closed.

Although formally described as an RAF station, the place is in fact a reserve base for the American NATO forces in Britain. Most of the time, apart from one large air show every year, the enormous aerodrome is devoid of flying machines and manned only by a skeleton staff. But just occasionally – perhaps once in two years or so – the need does arise and Greenham becomes activated for a brief period.

This winter was one of those times.

On this occasion the tenants were the 20th Tactical Fighter Wing of the US Air Force, transferred from their normal base at Upper Heyford in Oxfordshire while the Heyford main runway was being re-surfaced. The 55th, 77th and 79th Fighter Squadrons had moved in ten weeks before, bringing with them a classified number of F 111 swing-wing interceptors (generally believed to be about thirty-six), plus a seemingly endless stream of trucks, staff cars, tow-tractors, crash wagons, radar wagons, PX vehicles and ambulances. Along with the equipment came hundreds of personnel, ranging from the sergeants who appear to run the American Air Force through to engineers, cooks, controllers, firemen, clerks, drivers, and administrators.

They also brought their own Military Police.

At 1632 hours, the chain of events for the arrest of Keith Kerr had come to a halt at Greenham Common's main gate.

*　　　*　　　*

Parked alongside the guardhouse, the Ford Escort from Newbury police station looked small and out of place, dwarfed by the square Dodge trucks which rumbled past at a casual wave of the guard's hand and made shabby-looking by a bright line of American cars parked just inside the base fence. Inspector Philip Wylie stood on the guardhouse step and stared out over the roof of the Escort as if he were trying to disown it. Its insignificance was another pinprick in a ridiculous situation, swelling the irrational feeling that he was a supplicant whining for entry into some superior foreign country.

Behind him, the gate guard put down a telephone and spoke to his back.

"Ah . . . sir, I can't get either Sergeant Bowman or Lieutenant Ricker right now. They're gonna call me right back."

Wylie turned round and stared at the man coldly, aware that the constable in the driving seat of the Escort was watching him. The guard stayed where he was, one hip perched negligently on a scratched wooden table. Wylie put his hands behind his back and said firmly, "Very well. Who's your base commander? I want to speak to him immediately."

"Yes, sir. That's Lieutenant Colonel Lindstrom. I'll try'n call him." The guard looked in a book and then dialled a number, not hurrying. Wylie watched him, trying to stop his eyes straying down to the holstered revolver on the man's hip. The dark wooden butt bore the Smith & Wesson symbol, and Wylie presumed it was loaded. Probably cowboy-fashion with one empty chamber under the hammer, he thought. However many times he came to the base he could never get used to the sight of men blatantly carrying guns in the middle of the English countryside. Nor to a lot of other things, either, like the way you stepped through the gates and were instantly in a part of the United States. You got the impression that base life would be exactly the same whether the aerodrome was situated in Berkshire or Borneo: a goldfish bowl of American civilisation answering only to its own disciplines and having no connection with the surrounding world at all.

The guard said something into the phone, dropped the receiver casually back on to its cradle, and looked at Wylie again.

"Colonel's out on the field, sir. Seems they got some kinda emergency out there. But his secretary'll have him call soon as he gets in."

Wylie felt his face going red. He said, "My business is concerned with that emergency. If you can't get in touch with your commanding officer then I suggest you find somebody else, immediately, who *can* authorise my entry." He was aware of sounding pompous even as he spoke, and the realisation made him angrier than ever.

"Yes, sir." The guard remained completely indifferent, as if a British policeman wasn't even worthy of resentment. "I guess I won't reach anyone now till the emergency's over, but I'll sure try the police post again for you. If you wanna wait in your car I'll have an escort pick y'up soon as I can, okay?"

Wylie seethed. After a long moment he turned on his heel, stalked round the front of the police car, and snatched open the passenger door. He plumped himself violently into the seat and sat staring straight ahead, waiting.

In the guardhouse, the hands of the clock moved to thirty-four minutes past four as the sentry picked up the phone again.

*   *   *

Half a mile away across the aerodrome, Staff Sergeant Karl Haff wiped a gloved hand over the windscreen of the Oskosh P4 foam-and-water tender. Like two of the other three men in the large cab, he resembled a bulky silver spaceman in a one-piece asbestos suit. He shifted his body slightly, causing the fireproof material to rustle like heavy canvas, and looked across the expanse of concrete in the direction of the southern taxiway four hundred yards away on the other side of the threshhold of runway two-nine.

Two paved aprons adjoining the Greenham taxiways are used for flight-line parking during operational flying. The area to the south of the runway is known as Tango Row, and the northerly area is Romeo Row. Twenty minutes earlier there had been twelve F 111s parked on Tango Row; now there were only three left. Squat tow-tractors were pulling two more along taxiways towards the hangars, and a third tractor was hurrying back to the line. At this distance it looked like a nervous beetle scurrying among the mantis shapes of the fighters. The thought occurred to Haff that the rapid evacuation of Tango Row – although an obvious precaution in case the incoming emergency aircraft landed a long way to the side of the runway – possessed all the outward signs of the 20th Tactical Fighter Wing tucking in its tail and running for cover. The notion so pleased him that he chuckled out loud and started to say something.

He was interrupted by the radio on the dashboard. A voice speaking loudly and clearly, instantly stilling the rapid chatter of the full crash crew turn-out.

268

"Attention all crews. Attention all crews. All crews from Crash One. Attention. The two emergency airplanes have now commenced their final descent for landing. Arrival time is approximately five minutes. The pilot has just warned that the first aeroplane is now not likely to make a successful landing. Repeat, *not* likely to make a successful landing. It – ah – may also be off one side of the runway. Drivers to be ready for collision avoidance, but otherwise no vehicle to move till both airplanes are past his position. I say again, no vehicle to move till *both* planes have passed his position. Rescue Ten on to breathing apparatus in two minutes. Crash One out."

The cab of the Oskosh was suddenly quiet apart from the rhythmic idling of the engine, kept running according to regulations for the duration of the emergency. Haff, his mirth drained away as if it had never been, pushed his hands down between his thighs into the small warmth of his crutch. He looked along the vast empty plain of the runway, stretching away until the two lines of yellow lights converged into a distant vagueness in the cold grey shadows of evening. The lights were hedged at irregular intervals by blue and red winking beacons on the blocky shapes of the rest of the crash vehicles.

Over on Tango Row the last F 111 crawled away behind its tow-tractor, leaving the aerodrome still and waiting.

After half a minute Haff twisted in his seat and gazed into the fading turquoise sky over the runway threshold, where the aeroplanes would be appearing.

21

1637–1642

KERR FIRST SAW the runway lights from five miles away.
They materialised quite suddenly out of the dimming landscape ahead, two short strings of glittering yellow beads in
the tired grey haze of dusk.

Off to the right, of course. Parallel to the rounded snout
of his engine cowling, but five or ten degrees to the right.

He ran a sandpaper tongue over dry lips and muttered,
"Shit!" Then he flicked his eyes back to the other Arrow,
ahead of his right wing tip and slightly above him against
the fading sky. An S-turn right-left to get lined up was certainly something they could have done without...

Especially since the girl was going to pieces.

Even as his thumb hovered on the transmit button, Whisky
Tango's fuselage tilted abruptly downwards; the third or
fourth time it had happened since he'd started her on the
final descent three minutes before. The Arrow dropped away
ahead of him, a white cross sinking into the darkening patchwork of the countryside. He pushed his own nose savagely
down to follow, thumbing the button at the same time. He
wanted to scream at her, yell, jerk her into paying attention...

He took a fast ragged breath, holding himself in. The
time for the last resort of yelling was soon but not now. He
said, "Letting the nose drop again there, Ann," and heard
his own voice odd-sounding in his earphones, strained with
the effort of speaking easily. "Pick the nose up now to where

270

it was, and we'll be doing fine."

Nothing happened. The two Arrows carried on down in a shallow dive, the sound of the airflow slowly winding up. Kerr flexed his hands on control yoke and throttle, letting the gap widen but still holding formation. His body strained sideways, trying to reach out across the sky.

"C'mon, Ann! Get the nose up a bit. *Up*. About three inches. Where it was before . . ."

Slowly, very slowly, the runaway's nose lifted. The white silhouette seemed to swim lazily upwards; up out of the depths until it climbed above the horizon-line an hung there, floating against the huge purple aftermath of sunset.

Then it started down again.

Kerr shouted *"Oh God, woman!"* into the rumbling cockpit. It should be so *simple*. All she had to do was bloody hold it . . .

He squeezed the transmit button and said calmly, "Still letting the nose drop a bit, honey. Just lift it up again a little bit, then *hold* it."

The other Arrow wavered, pitching up, and then steadied. Fields and hedges unrolled 500 feet below.

"Right! Great. Now just concentrate on holding it. Stare at the horizon, all the time."

The Arrow droned on, sitting alongside and descending sedately. Kerr stared at it, stomach rigid; a juggler waiting to catch a fall. On his instrument panel the climb-descent indicator wavered, then settled uncertainly on 200 feet a minute Down.

The runway lights crawled nearer, maybe four miles to run. Still off to the side.

He dragged a shaking hand across his mouth and rested his head against the side window for a moment, letting the sound of the engine bore through his skull. His neck was aching viciously and his ears were sweaty-hot under the headphones. He was conscious of thinking, *She isn't going to make it: she's going to cock it up and crash* . . .

It was her erratic responses which were going to kill her. Before the engine failure she'd been doing more or less what she was told more or less when she was told it, but now,

271

now that it really mattered, she seemed to have lost what small command she'd had. When she let the nose drop and he told her to put it back, anything could happen. Sometimes she didn't react at all until the third or fourth time he prompted her and others, she snatched back immediately so that the Arrow bounced away upwards like a rubber ball. If she did either of those things while he was trying to land her...

He wiped his mouth again. The air in the cockpit was stale and cold now, but his body was crawling with sweat. The underside of his throat felt as if it were being scratched raw by the damp wool of his roll-neck sweater. Doubts jostled in the back of his mind, frightened scurrying treacheries in the thrumming of the slow descent. He should have had her re-trim for the approach in spite of the complication: he should be landing her wheels-up after all – except that an Arrow won't land wheels-up, of course, because of the automatic gear-down selection at low airspeeds. But he should have talked to her differently, handled the whole thing a different way...

Beyond his right wing tip the other aeroplane flew on, bare winter trees and fields sliding faster and faster under its wings in the twilight. Kerr knew the impression of speed was an illusion, a visual function of their diminishing height, but nonetheless for a moment he had the eerie feeling that the Arrow was accelerating, rushing headlong towards its end as the last few minutes of flight drained away. He shook his head irritably and forced the notion out of his mind, willing himself to concentrate, to keep trying. To find the right words, to get the girl turned to line up without pushing her over the final edge of panic...

The lights were expanding, no more than three miles ahead now. He could make out the runway itself in between them, a cold grey path of concrete in the dusky landscape.

He rubbed his scar for a few seconds, then pressed the transmit switch.

"Okay, love, that's fine. Lovely and steady. Now, still

holding it steady, we want a gentle right turn. Just go into a gentle right turn."

Nothing. The other Arrow hung where it was above the horizon, wings level. Beneath its wheels toy cars moved on a tiny dim road through the countryside, unheeding.

"Come along, Ann. Give me that turn, now. Just a small turn to the right."

The Arrow banked suddenly, showing its exhaust-streaked belly. At the same time its nose dropped.

"Good, but hold the nose *up!*" Kerr jerked the control yoke right and increased power, following. His knuckles showed white. "Hold the nose *up*, keep the turn going till I say."

The runaway curled away and down.

"Pick the nose *up*, Ann! Up!"

The Arrow pitched sharply up, showing its plan view as a white crucifix. It skated up above the horizon, sliding like a shark on a line, the wings twisting level as the girl forgot the turn. Kerr followed, ignoring the climb-descent indicator as the needle bounced to 300 feet a minute Up and then sagged down again. His eyes darted out to the distant runway, now off to the left of his nose. She'd rolled out of the turn early, but it would do. Two, two and a half miles to run, height passing 400 feet, and intercepting the centre-line. Ready to start bending left in a few seconds to line up . . .

Now.

"All right, love; now turn *left.*" His voice fed back clipped and urgent in his earphones. "We need a little turn left. *Go.*"

The wings wobbled, then tilted into a twenty-degree bank. The Arrow paused for a second or two, then seemed to slide sideways across the horizon in front of him, turning towards the path of concrete and lights. Kerr slapped his throttle shut and fed it open again, juggling yoke and rudder to keep station on the inside of the turn. He could hear himself talking, saying too much but unable to shut up.

"Good . . . that's great . . . just keep it going, now. We got to keep turning till we're pointed at the runway. That line of lights. Just keep going, keep it turni . . ."

The wings rolled suddenly level and the nose dropped.

Kerr released the transmit button and yelled, "SHIT!" The word was flat and echoless in the cockpit, vanishing into the rumble of the engine. He wrenched his own wings level and pushed forward to follow, his thumb slipping on the yoke-button.

"Hey! Pull the nose up, Ann! Pull the nose up and keep the turn going. Nose *up* and turn *left* ..."

Whisky Tango's nose jerked up. Too far. Kerr hauled back and pumped the throttle viciously, surging his engine to stay in position. The model aeroplane soared above the hazy horizon, steadied ...

And the wings canted left again.

"Great! Keep it going!" He snatched his hand off the throttle and slapped the boom-mike hard against his lips. "Hold that turn as you are! Hold it ... hold it ..."

The Arrow crawled round the horizon again, maintaining a shallow bank. Kerr turned with it, feet quivering on the rudder pedals. They were losing speed because the girl had her nose too high, but that would have to wait: the vital thing first was the turn, getting her lined up. He flicked his eyes between the aircraft and the light-studded ruler on the ground, judging. If she kept going as she was she ought to be just on the centre-line, just about right ...

His tilted engine cowling marched across the runway, blotting it out. He waited another two seconds, then jammed his thumb down on the switch.

"*Now* straighten out, Ann! Let the wings come level *now*."

The shark-shape flattened abruptly out of its bank, appearing to skate upwards and away as Kerr lost his formation position. He slammed on full power then trod hard right rudder and wound the yoke to the left, flying in a powered side-slip to get a better view forward and down. The other Arrow crabbed towards him as he closed the gap, engine howling. His left thumb moved the mixture lever an inch or so forward in its slot, his mind instinctively recoiling against giving an engine full throttle when it was leaned off at low level. His eyes darted between the model aeroplane and the

274

lines of lights, gauging, judging . . .

As far as he could tell, Whisky Tango was pointing directly down the runway. A mile or so to run, height 250 feet, and lined up.

He blinked in surprise. The realisation that there was a chance now was somehow shocking, like a renewed fright. Just a chance . . .

He reefed violently out of the slip and throttled back, juggling to hold his position. Without taking his eyes off the girl's cockpit he reached out and snapped his undercarriage switch to DOWN and the fuel boost pump on. Then he took a fast, shaky breath and started talking again.

* * *

Down here, the trees looked very close.

Ann watched numbly as they slid past 200 feet below; a small scrubby wood of dark brooding evergreens and the bare winter skeletons of beech and elm. The warm cabin was sinking slowly but finally down towards them. The tops looked soft and yielding and slow-moving, almost inviting. As if you could settle in them and sit there, engine still rumbling, until someone came along to stop everything and let you out.

The sense of unreality was stronger than ever. Every second seemed to be spaced out, allowing time for the most ridiculous thoughts. Part of her brain screamed at her to tense up, concentrate everything for the final effort, but another part refused to co-operate, refused to even accept what was happening. It *couldn't* be real. The little droning room was security. It *couldn't* be about to be smashed and buckled against the ground. She *couldn't* be about to try and land it . . .

The voice came again, speaking fast.

"Okay Ann, we're beautifully lined up. Great. Now, just lower the nose a touch. Let the nose come down a couple of inches from where it is."

The voice had been going on since the beginning of time, urgent and demanding. The only thing was that she seemed to have lost the power of concentrating on it, taking it in. It was just there, part of the softly-humming cockpit.

"*Lower* the nose, honey. *Lower* it, a couple of inches."

Lower the nose. She relaxed her back pressure on the wheel, holding it with both hands. The top of the instrument panel sagged down below the hazy horizon.

"Bit too much, there. Pull it up a bit, now. *Up* a bit."

The plane felt different, quite suddenly. Sinking around her like a lift, with the ruffle of wind and engine increasing. The horizon was a long way up the windscreen, much too far up ...

"Pull *back*, Ann! Life the nose up *now!*"

She pulled back, arms quivering. The plane pushed up under her, the top of the panel rising until it met the horizon and there was only the deep evening sky ahead.

"Right! Now hold it! Hold it there. Look alongside the nose, and just hold it."

She shifted her eyes, blinking. The effort of pulling back on the wheel seemed never-ending, pointless. There was a sharp pain in the small of her back from straining upwards in the seat. In the V between the panel-edge and the windscreen pillar she could see one side of the runway, floating backwards towards her. It looked enormous, stretching away for miles like a weird discarded motorway section in the middle of nowhere. There were white numbers and markings on it, and lorries waiting alongside in the winter dusk. The the lorries were fire engines and ambulances. Waiting for with urgency.

her, as the droning cockpit sank down towards them. Waiting for the end, just moments away.

The Arrow snarled on down, bumping nervously in the turbulence over the trees. Kerr's voice came again, brittle thought formed in her mind, startlingly cold and clear, that

"Getting low, now. Raise the nose a little and open the throttle about half an inch. *Now.*"

Throttle. Glance down to get the right lever. T-handle oily with perspiration ...

"You're dropping the bloody nose! Lift it UP! UP!"

276

Cockpit sinking again. Pull back. Nose bobbing and lifting. *Must* concentrate, not give in . . .

"Jesus, girl – power! POWER!"

Power. Throttle lever forwards. Hold the nose, one-handed. Engine winding up, roaring. Trees suddenly *very* close, moving much faster, greeny-grey blur just under the wings. Don't look at them, look ahead. Nose bucking, lifting up. Hold it. Row of orange lights on posts whipping by below . . .

The Arrow mushed, nose high and engine blaring urgently. It cleared the second row of approach lights by ten feet and clawed away upwards, climbing slowly.

"Okay! You're okay." The voice was loud and fast. "Now bring the throttle *back* an inch. Hold the nose steady and bring the throttle *back* an inch."

Ann stared ahead in the growling cockpit, hands locked rigidly on yoke and throttle. She'd got too low there, she thought distantly. Just like that, all of a sudden. She *must* get a grip on herself, *must* hold the plane steady . . .

Passing a hundred feet in a shallow climb, the two Arrows slid over the threshold of the runway. The snarl of their engines rolled across the cold countryside. The crash wagon at the first turnoff point moved out on to the runway behind them and started to accelerate.

Three thousand metres of concrete is 1.9 miles. At ninety-odd m.p.h. that distance takes around one and a quarter minutes to cover.

Kerr yelled, "Ann! Bring the throttle back and lower the nose! Throttle *back* a couple of inches, and *lower* the nose. *Now!*"

She jerked her left hand backwards, partially closing the throttle. The roar of the engine diminished, sending tremors of vibration down the fuselage. The manifold pressure sagged from 24 In. Hg. to just under 18.

"Lower the nose!" The voice crackled in the cabin, desperate with urgency. *"Do as I say – lower the nose!"*

Ann whimpered, and relaxed her pull on the wheel.

The nose dropped into a steep gliding attitude.

Over the blue engine cowling, the runway suddenly filled

the world. It rushed up at her, slightly angled to one side, vast and wide and endless. She could see black skid-marks on it, the numbered boards of the turnoff signs alongside.

For a split-second she just stared, petrified. Then she hauled back on the wheel with both hands.

The cowling reared up into the purple sky. The Arrow wallowed and then ballooned upwards, stall-warning horn blaring, an uncontrollable toy on an invisible aerial switchback. In the trailing Oskosh fire truck Sergeant Haff muttered, "Oh mother . . . she gonna stall in.' His huge left hand opened and closed on the operating bar of the fender-nozzle in the helpless fascination of a man watching somebody else's car crash.

Kerr bawled into his microphone: *"Get the nose down to the horizon! Now; immediately!"*

Gasping, Ann relaxed her pressure on the wheel. The plane instantly sank away again, mushing on the edge of the stall, the horn bleating solidly. The panic in her chest was strangling her, shutting off her breath. She had to pick up the microphone and tell them it was impossible. It had been impossible all along. The plane was shuddering, falling like a lift, the ground swelling up around her . . .

There wasn't time to tell them. The sinking sensation was suddenly less, and she could see the horizon over the crash-pad. The horn wavered, gave a final blip, and then stopped. The voice was yelling over the burr of the engine.

"Hold it! Hold it there!"

She held it jerkily, fingers locked on the yoke.

The two Arrows growled past the number-three turnoff point, half way along the runway. They were fifty feet up, running off to the left of the centre-line, and descending slowly. The crash crews saw the second machine close the gap slightly with a brief snarl of high power. Sergeant Haff, directly behind and below, saw its flaps come down one stage.

"Hold it steady and reduce power slowly. Hold it just like it is and bring the throttle back slowly. All the way back."

Ann stayed as she was, arms quivering, staring at the tree-line beyond the end of the runway. The aerodrome drifted by below, unreal as a film; hangars and buildings and expanses of concrete ambling lazily past in the fringes of her vision. A new trickle of blood ran down from her lip. It was a nightmare, it couldn't really be happening – but she had to hold the nose *there*. Concentrate . . .

At eighty m.p.h., engine still rumbling, the Arrow sank down through fifty feet, forty feet, twenty feet. The port wing tip passed over the number-four turnoff board, to the left of the runway. Six thousand feet out of ten thousand gone . . .

"Bring the power OFF, Ann! Throttle back all the way! Then raise the nose a little!"

The power command didn't register. Ann pulled the nose up a fraction, straining her head up to keep sight of the trees over the engine cowling. She was vaguely aware of the runway streaming past just below the right wing, but she mustn't look at that. She had to concentrate on the nose position, not jerk it, keep it steady . . .

The Arrow hit the ground.

The impact was shocking in its suddenness rather than actually very heavy. In the absence of a properly executed landing flare Whisky Tango simply flew into the ground, walloping on with a hollow *b-bonk* and a screech of tyres. It weaved and nodded lumpily on its nosewheel, and stayed down. The left mainwheel ran off the side of the concrete, clanging over grass and runway lights.

Ann heard herself scream, from somewhere a long way off. The plane was crashing, going to overturn . . .

She pulled back on the yoke.

The cockpit pitched up under her and bounced back into the air. She screamed again into the drumming of the engine and pushed forwards. From a height of ten feet the nose dropped sharply and the Arrow fell out of the sky.

This time the impact was tremendous. The nosewheel hit first with a huge metallic *BANG*, bursting its Oleo seals and bending the engine bearers. The shock threw Ann hard into her seat belt and snatched the yoke out of her hands. The nose tried to bounce up for an instant then smashed down again on to its flat suspension as the mainwheels slammed on. Something hit her on the forehead with a distant *thack* as the cockpit cannoned all around her . . .

Then the Arrow was on the ground and running. At eighty m.p.h.

The nose Oleo clanged resoundingly as it ran off the side of the runway on to the grass. The aerodrome rushed past like a speeded-up movie, jarring and unstoppable. A black board with a yellow number five on it leapt at her and then suddenly arced away high in the air, shattered by the propeller.

The engine growled on almost casually at low cruise power. The sound of it was lost under the thumping and clashing as the Arrow jounced over the grass.

The end of the runway came into sight, five hundred yards ahead.

Ann clapped her hands over her ears and waited to die.

*   *   *

Kerr yelled, "You did it! Sweet bloody Jesus, you did it!"

He was flying fifty feet up and out to the side, overtaking the other Arrow as it rocked and swayed along the ground. His own chance of landing behind her was gone, abandoned twenty seconds ago, but that didn't matter a damn. He had fuel to spare and the girl was down, she'd made it . . .

The white cross-shape disappeared under his wing. He snatched down full flap, banged throttle and propeller pitch fully forward together, and crossed his controls into a vicious slip. Romeo X-ray staggered sickeningly, engine waking up and blaring, hanging in the air nose high and right wing down. He slapped at the trim wheel with his left hand and craned his neck to stare down and back, flying by feel on the edge of the stall.

Whisky Tango was bumping along the grass behind him, to the left of the runway. Still doing at least sixty m.p.h.

The elation froze on his face. He flicked his eyes forwards, gauging speed and distance. Even without brakes she ought to be slowing down quicker than that . . .

"Ann!" His voice rasped dry in his throat. *"You've still got some power on! Close the throtle now! Pull it hard back!"*

The Arrow bounced on, jerking and bobbing. It was slowing gradually – he was drawing ahead, unable to reduce his own speed any further – but gradually wasn't enough. A few hundred feet in front was the large concrete pan of the holding-point at the end of the runway, and then the scrub and bushes of the over-run area.

"Ann, for Christ's sake! Pull the throttle back! Close it hard back . . ."

There was no sign of response, nothing at all. Whisky Tango nodded over the edge of the grass and carried on across the holding-point apron, its speed barely diminished. After a moment it slid out of sight under his tailplane and he slammed his control yoke left and then right again, feet treadling the rudder pedals. Romeo X-ray rolled tiredly into a steep left turn, held it for a few seconds with the engine clawing for badly-needed airspeed, then wound back to the right and stabilised in another powered sideslip. The other Arrow was further away now, level with his lowered wing tip, still running . . .

"Jesus, Ann! Listen! Pull the bloody throttle back! Throttle back and then go for the handbrake, sticking down under the panel! Throttle back first . . ."

It was useless, and he knew it. From a hundred yards out to the side he saw the Arrow run off the apron into the over-run area, wings rocking sharply as it bumped off the smooth concrete. It was still doing forty, fifty m.p.h. Bushes and leaves exploded, swirling round the propeller as it ploughed on. The scrub and heather seemed to be slowing it where he'd failed. The over-run area was about 500 feet long before it ended in trees. Maybe she'd slow down enough not to roll up in a ball when she hit . . .

The end came suddenly.

Whisky Tango was nearer the side of the over-run area

than Kerr could see in the dusk. The port wing tip hit a steel fence post, the Arrow spun round abruptly through ninety degrees ...

And the undercarriage collapsed.

Kerr hauled into a steep climbing right turn, staring down helplessly. With the deliberation of a slow-motion film the Arrow skated sideways on its belly for fifty yards, ploughing up a moving tangle of bushes and fencing as it went.

Then it stopped. Intact.

Holding his turn at a hundred feet, Kerr found he was thinking the word *survivable*.

Survivable. Very survivable. Just a skid and sliding to a stop. No problem ...

Survivable!

He thumped his fist on the crash-pad and bellowed, "You did it!" The words were absorbed into the urgent snarl of the engine. His right wing tip arced round the aircraft on the ground and then lifted up as he shallowed the bank, climbing again. He was pointing upwind, away from the runway, but it didn't matter because he still had his reserve of fuel in the left tank. Just take it round in a tight right hand circuit and ...

The engine noise dissolved suddenly into a loud grating. It went on for a second or two, then ended in a huge metallic *clang.*

The propeller stopped dead, one blade pointing straight up in front of him like an accusing finger.

For an instant, he just felt mildly surprised and somehow tired. He thought stupidly, *The damn thing's seized because you leaned it out too much; ran it too hot trying to save fuel.* His left hand reached out and slapped the mixture lever into full rich, instictively and uselessly.

Then he was flying for his life.

He had eighty m.p.h. and 150 feet: maybe enough to turn back and land downwind. He slammed on right yoke and rudder, then saw that the near end of the runway was cluttered with the moving shapes of the crash vehicles. The grass was the same, wagons bouncing across it, beacons flashing in the twilight. He cranked the wings level again and glided straight ahead, away from the aerodrome. Over the nose were trees, the light coloured crater of a gravel pit, and then a large ploughed field. Ought to make the field, just about . . .

He yanked the flaps up to one stage, reached out and switched the magnetos and master off, and tugged at his lap-strap. The field floated up and backwards towards him in the hush of the glide. He was going to make it, just creep in over the hedge . . .

A huge structure loomed up suddenly in the dusk; a conveyor gantry towering out of the gravel pit. For a split second he thought he'd pass over it, then realised he wouldn't and started to turn.

22

1642–1652

THE SILENCE WAS the deepest that Ann had ever known. The windscreen was splattered with mud, which somehow seemed shockingly unnatural. Over the nose, over a stationary bent propeller blade, the winter trees were cold and still in the fading daylight. There seemed to be things she ought to be doing, but she couldn't think what they were and they didn't feel very important. All that really mattered was the stillness and the silence and the frozen scrubby ground outside the windows.

A large blunt-nosed lorry slithered to a stop alongside, crushing bushes underneath itself. Eerie blue lights flashed round regularly, illuminating the white dirt-smothered wings. There were briars curling round, tangled . . .

The door at her elbow flew open.

The cold of the evening came in, along with forgotten sounds. There was a big man in a bulky silver overall crouched in the doorway. He was saying something . . .

Sergeant Haff said, "Y'all right, ma'am?"

Ann blinked at him.

The broad face grinned. A huge silver arm reached into the cockpit, round her waist, and unclipped the seat belt. Then there were other faces . . . hands at her elbows and under her armpits . . .

Suddenly she was outside the cabin, standing on the wing. Hands were supporting her, American voices talking. It seemed odd that they were American and she wanted to ask why, but the words wouldn't come. The lorry engine roared steadily in the dusk. A long blue station wagon with an AMBULANCE sign on it squamped over the rough ground and stopped a few yards away. There were more blue lights. Doors jumped open and figures leapt out.

In the distance, another crash wagon and ambulance roared around the perimeter track and stopped by a gate in the wire fence. Behind them, incongruously, was a British police Ford Escort, white with the familiar blue stripe. Silver men bounced out of the crash wagon and opened the gate, the convoy snarled through, and then they were off down the road outside the aerodrome. The *wow-wow-wow-wow* of an American siren rolled over the Berkshire countryside.

"P'raps you'd like to get on the stretcher, ma'am. Doctor'll be with you in just a moment."

Ann looked round the crowded faces. Two men in green fatigues were holding a stretcher, looking at her.

"No." Her voice seemed to come from a long way off, like another person speaking. "No." The strange voice wouldn't say what she wanted. "Sit. I'd like to . . . just sit . . ."

The heather was whipping round her ankles. Under the exhaust smell of the lorry was the cold scent of the winter woodlands. People were helping her walk, saying things to her while she tried to think . . .

They sat her in the front seat of the Dodge ambulance. Someone put a drab green blanket round her shoulders, and someone else got in behind the wheel to sit with her. A radio on the dash panel squawked and blattered with voices.

"Rescue Six ten-eight to Structural . . ."

"Ten-four Chief Two, negative the field ten-eight the quarry . . ."

"Roj, Two, use your weight there with the P4. Unca Sam'll afford it . . ."

"Rescue Six ten-ten Crash Cen're . . ."

"Ten-four One, Crash Two goin' in . . ."

The white shape of the plane looked wrong, out of place lying on its belly in the casual untidiness of the scrub. It was dirty now, speckled and streaked with mud, and there was a torn-off wheel lying twenty yards away in a long gouge of fresh earth. Rusty barbed wire lay over the right wing,

285

and there was a mass of fencing and undergrowth rucked up underneath and around the nose.

Three men were standing on the wing, by the open door. While Ann watched dazedly a fire-axe flashed up and down, hitting something near the wing root with a metallic *boing*. Relieved of its stay, the door swung right open against the engine cowling. One man in a silver overall dived into the cockpit, while another reached in after him and started pulling.

Roy.

They brought him out head first, turning him sideways so that he wouldn't choke on his tongue. They laid him on the stretcher alongside the trailing edge of the wing, and a big man in green fatigues with red crosses on his sleeves knelt down beside him.

Ann said, "Roy . . ." and fumbled for the door handle.

The man beside her said, "Hey, you don' have to go out there, ma'am. The Lieutenant's our Medical Officer an' he'll be right along . . ."

Ann barely heard him. She found the handle, pulled it, and started to clamber out. The door sill was higher than an English car and the ground seemed a long way off, disorientating. She was dimly aware of the man jumping out of the other side of the cab and running round to her, but she took no notice. Her arms and legs were weak and shaking, slow to respond. She got her feet on the frozen earth, shrugged the blanket off her shoulders, and pulled herself upright.

Suddenly, the man with the Red Cross armbands was in front of her. She sank down again, perching on the seat, and stared up at him.

"Lieutenant Troy, ma'am. I can tell you your fella's still with us, all right. He may be out for some while yet, but his breathin' an' pulse ain't bad, considerin'. Lookin' at him, I'd say he's got a pretty good chance of recovery."

Ann nodded. She heard herself say, "Yes. Thank you."

Then she put her head in her hands and wept.

*　　　*　　　*

286

If an aeroplane goes down on the far side of a wood, an observer on the ground has no easy way of knowing exactly how far away it is. The Greenham crash crews, knowing the terrain at the end of runway two-nine, tried the ploughed field first as being the most likely place, and then worked their way back.

Keith Kerr was alone in the gravel pit for five minutes before they found him.

He didn't move. He didn't feel as if he could, and he didn't try to. The Arrow had hit the gravel conveyor with its right wing, sliced round into the gantry, and brought the whole structure crashing down on to a man-made hill of shale. The aeroplane had gone with it, tangled up in the crumpling framework. It had whumped into the ground in a steep nose-down attitude, and in the final impact the engine had smashed the firewall nearly two feet backwards into the cabin.

Kerr's legs were underneath the engine.

The cockpit was familiar yet unfamiliar, buckled and smashed around him in the winter twilight. The windows and windscreen were shattered, all jagged edges of Perspex in front of his face. The January wind blew in, cold and raw and smelling of countryside after the stale fug of the last two hours.

He breathed softly, because breathing hurt, and listened to the ticking of cooling metal and the rapid drip-drip-drip-drip of his blood in the cockpit. There seemed to be a great deal of blood. It was splashed and smeared all around him and his lap was sodden with it, steaming gently in the cold air.

Something tinkled quietly on the far side of the crumpled instrument panel. He looked across and saw that it was the broken glass of the airspeed indicator, fallen out on to the seat. Alongside the airspeed the only undamaged dial on the panel was the clock, its sweep second hand still going round. It read exactly 1652.

It was getting dark. Dark and quiet. The remains of the

conveyor frame were twisted spidery lines against a black-purple sky.

The noise must have been fantastic. Funny how he didn't remember hearing anything.

Maybe you didn't, when you crashed.

He thought about Maggie, and the airline job.

Then the darkness closed in.

From somewhere in the distance came the *wow-wow-wow* of a siren.